VENGEANCE OF HOPE

P.J. BERMAN

TO
THE VERUSANTIAN →
EMPIRE

Aevestro
Island

KRIGANHEIM

Kriganheim
City

Jalinna

HAZGORATA

Chathran

River Chathranis

River
Lavaklam

THE
KINGDOM
OF
BENNVIKA

Severby

Faen Tira

Saviktastad

ASRANTICA

KEBBAN SEA

Celrun

THE
KINGDOM
OF
MEDRODOR

Attatan

HERTASALA

Tordvick

Ustaherta Forest

USTENNA

Alpich Bay

Ganust

LOMATTEVA

Zikaena

River Ganzig

Ustine
Isles

BASTALF
(Formerly The Bentani Kingdom)

VITRINNOLF

Iprarta

Branoff Bay

River
Denestra

Intei

THE
DEFRONI
KINGDOM

Rildayorda

Lithrofed

River
Racuna

Gronlakka

Nangosa

THE
KINGDOM
OF
ETROVANSIA

Masuvane
Mountains

ETERNAMIC OCEAN

TO
RILANA
↓

2

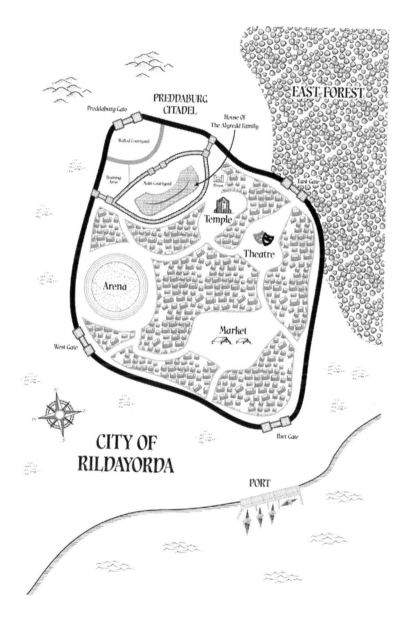

EAST FOREST

PREDDABURG CITADEL

Preddaburg Gate

House Of
The Alyredd Family

Walled Courtyard

Training
Area

Main Courtyard

Prison

East Gate

Temple

Theatre

Arena

West Gate

Market

Port Gate

CITY OF
RILDAYORDA

PORT

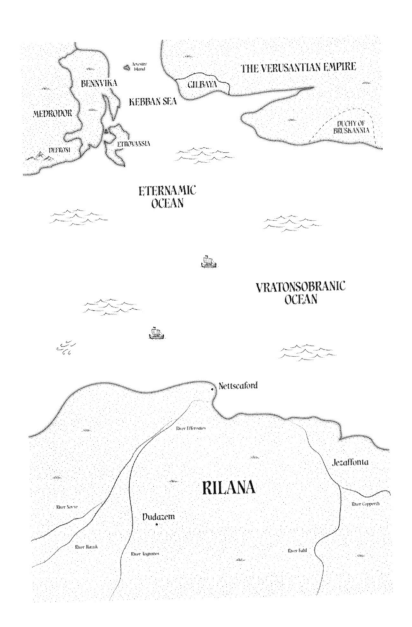

For Nikita. You are my wife, my soulmate, my best friend and quite frankly, you're awesome. I could never have achieved this without your love and support.

For Nora, our wonderful baby daughter.

Special thanks also to my parents, Anni and Mark Berman and to the Watling Street Writers Circle, the Verulam Writer's Circle, Chris Perera, Tina Ellis, Jonny Lee, Jonathan Grewcock, Andrew Houseman, Sarah Kennedy and Suzanna Hart. Your help and advice has been invaluable.

For Evie, our crazy labrador, who has probably chewed up the first copy of this novel by now!

And finally, for Bailey, our gentle cavalier. May his beautiful, kind, loving soul rest in peace.

Also by P.J. Berman

<u>Fantasy</u>

<u>The Silrith Series</u>

Vengeance of Hope – Silrith Book 1

King of the Republic – Silrith Book 2

War of Mercy – Silrith Book 3 (Due 2021)

<u>Historical Fiction</u>

Blood and Greed – Short Stories (Due 2020)

'Mother of many, Mother of none, a Queen will fall and a Warrior will come.'
An ancient prophecy of disputed origin and meaning.

First published in paperback by Amazon Kindle Direct Publishing in 2018
ISBN: 9781731387721

Cover art and maps by Oliver Bennett at More Visual Ltd.

Character List

The House of Alfwyn

Silrith – Princess of Bennvika and heir apparent after Fabrald's death.

Lissoll – King of Bennvika.

Fabrald – Silrith's deceased elder brother.

Gidrassa – Silrith's deceased mother, Queen of Bennvika.

Monissaea – Lissoll's deceased sister, wife of Yathrud Alyredd and mother of Bezekarl and Yathugarra.

Bastinian the Great – The previous King of Bennvika. He was Lissoll's father and Silrith's grandfather.

Aebrae – Bastinian's first wife, mother of Lissoll and Monissaea and grandmother to Fabrald, Silrith, Bezekarl and Yathugarra.

Tefkia – A Defroni princess who was sister to Chief Faslo, second wife of Bastinian, mother of Turiskia and grandmother of Jostan.

The House of Kazabrus

Jostan – Silrith's cousin, Lissoll's nephew and Governor of the Verusantian province of Bruskannia.

Dionius – Jostan's deceased father, the previous Governor of Bruskannia.

Turiskia – Jostan's mother and Lissoll's younger half-sister.

The House of Aethelgard

Oprion – Governor of Hazgorata. Haarksa's second husband.

Haarksa – Oprion's Medrodorian wife.

Jorikssa – Haarksa's daughter and Oprion's stepdaughter.

The House of Alyredd

Yathrud – Governor of Bastalf and Silrith's uncle.

Bezekarl – Yathrud and Monissaea's teenage son.

Yathugarra – Yathrud and Monissaea's young daughter.

Kintressa – Yathrud's second wife.

The House of Rintta

Feddilyn – Governor of Asrantica.

The House of Tanskeld

Aeoflynn – Governor of Ustenna.

The House of Haganwold

Lektik – Governor of Hertasala.

The House of Froilainn

Shappa – Prince of Etrovansia.

Kessekla – King of Etrovansia.

Ravla – Prince of Etrovansia and younger brother of Shappa.

The House of Vaaltanen

Accutina – Princess of Medrodor as daughter of King Spurvan and Queen of Bennvika as wife of King Lissoll.

Spurvan – King of Medrodor.

The House of Dronnareidius

Graggasteidus – Emperor of the Verusantian Empire.

Minor Nobles and Congressors

Zethun Maysith – A minor young nobleman from Asrantica.

Hoban Salanath – An experienced congressor from Kriganheim.

Dongrath – A congressor of Kriganheim.

Soldiers

Gasbron Wrathun – Chief Invicturion of Bastalf.

Candoc of Rildayorda – Gasbron's corpralis.

Yortha – A divisioman of Rildayorda.

Telvaen – A divisioman of Rildayorda.

Kinsaf – A divisioman of Rildayorda.

Laevon – A divisioman of Rildayorda.

Ostagantus Gormaris – Jostan's bodyguard and head of the Verusantian Lance Guardsmen in Bennvika.

Vinnitar Rhosgyth – Chief Invicturion of Asrantica.

The Hentani

Ezrina – A dancing girl.

Jezna – A dancing girl.

Hojorak – Chief of the Hentani.

Kivojo – Prince of the Hentani and brother of Hojorak.

Blavak – Hentani translator.

Jakiroc – A Hentani priest living in Rildayorda.

Askorit – Hentani Archpriest of Rildayorda.

Rilanians

Voyran Attington – A ship's captain.

Emostocran – Voyran's first mate.

Viktana – A Bennvikan translator.

Hozekeada IV – Empress of Rilana.

Janissada Attington – An experienced admiral and Voyran's mother.

Defroni

Faslo – Chief of the Defroni.

Deities

Lomatteva – Bennvikan goddess.

Vitrinnolf – Bennvikan god.

Bertakaevey – Hentani goddess.

Ursartin – Bertakaevey's companion, who takes on the shape of a bear.

Estarron – Verusantian god.

Luskaret – the King of the Underworld in the Verusantian faith.

Ibbez – Rilanian goddess.

Miscellaneous

Jithrae of Sevarby – A farmer from the province of Asrantica.

Vaezona of Sevarby – Jithrae and Mirtsana's eldest daughter.

Mirtsana – Jithrae's wife.

Kanolia – Mirtsana's sister.

Naivard – Kanolia's husband, a magistrate's clerk based in Kriganheim.

Capaea – A servant in the Bennvikan royal household.

Lyzina – Accutina's lady's maid.

Afayna – Silrith's lady's maid.

Taevuka – Silrith's junior lady's maid.

Ridenna – Servant of the House of Alyredd.

Avaresae – Servant of the House of Alyredd.

Braldor – Hoban Salanath's bodyguard.

Macciomakkia – An ancient Hingarian historian and philosopher.

Glossary

Archpriest – The head of the Hentani faith.

Chief Invicturion – An officer in charge of all ten of his or her province's divisios. The chief invicturion personally leads Divisio One. They are often referred to in the same way as the more junior invicturions.

Congressate – A council of politicians with hereditary titles who assist the sitting monarch in the governance of Bennvika.

Congressor – A member of the Congressate.

Corpralis – An officer who assists either a chief invicturion or an invicturion. The chief invicturion's corpralis is the second highest ranking soldier in the entire province.

Crossbow – A shorter range hand-held that uses a pulley system to fire the arrow.

Cuirass – Two pieces of armour, a breastplate and a backplate, fastened together.

Demokroi – A low ranking politician whose role it is to represent the common people of Bennvika.

Divisio – A unit of professional Bennvikan soldiers. Each province has ten divisios, the first of which is a heavy cavalry unit, with the others performing the role of heavy infantry.

Divisioman – A professional soldier who serves within the divisios.

Invicturion – An officer who leads a single divisio unit.

Longbow – A large bow of simple design, but with a very long range in the right hands.

Longship – A fast warship with a shallow hull and a single sail.

Militia – A group of part-time soldiers that can be raised in times of war and disbanded in times of peace.

Militiaman – A member of the militia.

Pilum – A throwing weapon similar to a javelin.

Shield Boss – A circle of metal at the centre of the shield, behind which the shield's grip is mounted.

Ship-of-the-battle-line – a large, heavy warship with multiple sails and armed with cannon.

Spangenhelm – A primitive metal helmet featuring a nasal guard.

Helmets of Divisio Ranks

Chief Invicturion – Single large white transverse horsehair crest with black stripes.

Invicturion – Single small metal crest running front to back. The invicturion also wears a white sash across their chest.

Corpralis – Single small metal crest running front to back.

Standard-bearers and Divisiomen – No crest.

About the Author

P.J. Berman grew up in Hemel Hempstead, Hertfordshire, England. Subsequently, after a brief but enjoyable spell living in Plymouth, he has now settled in Carmarthenshire, surrounded by the beautiful countryside of his adopted nation, Wales, where he lives with his wife and daughter.

Given where he has lived, he is probably one of the few people who is a fan of both Stevenage Football Club and the Scarlets. When not writing, aside from watching sport, he enjoys dog walks, travelling with his family, as well as reading.

For more information about P.J. Berman's upcoming books, check out the following web pages:

P.J. Berman Books official Facebook page - www.facebook.com/pjbermanbooks

Twitter/Instagram - @pjbermanbooks

Official website – www.pjbermanbooks.com

Chapter 1

KRIGANHEIM, KINGDOM OF BENNVIKA, 1520 YEARS AFTER UNIFICATION – SPRING

With a start, Afayna came to as icy water hit her face, swiftly followed by a stinging slap to her cheek. Sprawled on her back, she attempted to rise but realised with terror that each of her limbs were tied down with rough, coarse rope.

'Help! Gods! Where am I?'

Laughter rang out from the darkness. Only the smallest flicker of brazier fire lit the room through a window in the door, but as her eyes adjusted, she made out the shapes of two men.

'Awake again are we, Afayna my sweet? That's a good girl.'

'Why am I here? Tell me,' she pleaded. The two men smirked at her distress.

'How strange it must be for you,' one of them said, his neat blonde hair and chiselled cheekbones more visible now. 'One moment you're just another maid going about her daily business in the palace. The next, you wake up here.' Afayna scanned the room, desperately trying to control her panic. She was spread-eagled on a torture rack and now she could see that the walls had many shelves and hanging hooks that were littered with various blades of different shapes and sizes. Yet it was not the weapons that filled her with dread, but the man's calm and yet sinister tone. Every word sent paralysing fear shooting through her body once again.

Strangely, something about his confident manner and educated voice reminded her of Lord Jostan, but it wasn't him. From his dark profile, she could tell that this man lacked the foreign nobleman's exotic virility and rugged handsomeness.

'Let me go. Princess Silrith will hear about this and when she does, she'll tell the king and then you'll be sorry.'

'You honestly think you're in a position to threaten me?' The interrogator gave a nod to his accomplice and the other man, a hulking, musclebound type with short hair, moved round to the end of the rack to stand behind Afayna's head. He heaved on the roller and stretched the ropes tight, drawing an inhuman howl from the girl.

'People are always so cocky at the start. They forget who's got the power here. You see Afayna, and it surprises me that you don't already know this, the king is dying and the princess, like you, is a traitor.'

His final word turned Afayna's blood to ice, yet her fear was laced with confusion.

'What? No. It's not true.'

'Do you deny that you served the king his last meal?'

'I did, but—'

'Oh! So you knew it'd be his last meal then, eh?'

'No! I meant—'

'And is it true that you stole the Amulet of Hazgorata?'

'No! Why would I? How could I?'

Afayna bellowed in pain as the torturer heaved on the roller again, stretching her limbs while the rope tore into her skin.

'You were seen with it, Afayna. One of your fellows has testified against you. Now, I'm going to ask you once more. Did you steal the Amulet of Hazgorata?'

Afayna's reply was to spit at him in defiance, launching a good amount of sputum at least three feet in the direction of the interrogator's face, though it only hit his shoulder.

'Your passionate defence is impressive,' he laughed. 'But I'm afraid the question still stands.'

'I didn't steal it.'

'Then why were you seen with it shortly before the king was taken ill, carrying it, then twisting the lid and pouring the contents on to the king's meal?' Afayna's eyes widened in horror as she realised what she had done.

'It was given to me. I was told it contained some new flavouring that the king liked.' She realised she'd been foolishly trusting.

'Well unfortunately for you, you left some inside the Amulet and on discovery, it turned out to be poison hemlock. Deadly. What's more, you added just enough to kill him, without it being instant, giving you a chance to make your escape. If only you hadn't been seen. Looks pretty bad for you

22

now doesn't it?' He gave a disturbing smile. 'So, if it was a gift, as you claim, who gave it to you?'

'Lord Jostan,' Afayna said eventually, still breathing hard. She suddenly became aware that her body was now soaking with sweat.

'Don't play around with me. I know Lord Jostan. It's not him.' He nodded for her to be stretched again. Afayna gritted her teeth, but nonetheless, she couldn't hold back an animalistic scream.

'It's true!' she shrieked in desperation. The effort of each breath sent searing pain burning through her body.

'I was in...Princess Silrith's entourage when...when she and the others welcomed him...into the palace,' she gasped.

'So you're saying that Lord Jostan Kazabrus, our king's own nephew, sailed from his lands across the sea, marched all the way from Asrantica to the palace under escort, just so that he could plot with some inconsequential maid? Somehow I find that a little hard to believe. I doubt that if he had planned on undertaking regicide he would have chosen you as an accomplice, instead of a person of rank and consequence.'

'It was him! He noticed me...soon after he arrived last summer.'

'So you say he was an opportunist?' the interrogator asked.

'Yes. He took...an interest in me. I thought...I thought he cared for me. He said he'd marry me if I—'

'—He said he'd marry you? A maid? I don't believe this. Don't waste my time. Just because he had his way with you doesn't mean he cares about you. The king is on his death bed because of your treachery. Now, who gave you the Amulet? How about Princess Silrith? Wanted to be queen, did she?'

'No! How can you say that?' Afayna couldn't believe he was making such an implausible accusation.

A laugh escaped him once more.

'She did have the most to gain out of his death and through you she had the chance to bring it about. Anyway, you were heard by one of your fellow servants only days ago talking to her about what she'd do when she was queen.'

'She wasn't talking about that.'

'Really?'

'She wasn't. She…she was talking about the King of Gilbaya…and how he dishonours…his queen. She was talking…she was talking about what she would do if…if she was the Queen of Gilbaya!' She used all the strength she could muster and yet her words only came out in gasps as her body endured the waves of excruciating pain.

The torturer began to stretch her again. The ropes dug deeper, ripping the skin from her body, pulling at her joints so that her bones threatened to dislocate from their sockets.

'A likely story. It's interesting that you were so quick with an explanation. Anyway, you prepared the king's meal and you were the food taster. You must have known that the food was poisoned. It's hard to believe that just by chance, you tasted a bit that the poison hadn't touched.'

'But that's what happened,' Afayna whimpered.

'Sorry, I don't believe you. Now, did Princess Silrith give you the poison? Gods. You disgust me.'

An acrid stench filled the chamber. In her terror, Afayna had lost control of her bladder and part of the rack was now soaked in urine.

'No,' she said eventually, overcome with humiliation.

'Wrong answer.'

Another stretch. Afayna endured it, forcibly silencing her scream. The ropes slackened again a little and she felt her whole body heave involuntarily, causing her to cough and splutter as she was almost choked by her own vomit, before it ran down her cheek.

'Did she give it to you?'

'No.'

'You're really not getting this are you?' The interrogator gave another nod and the torturer stretched her again. This time Afayna felt pain like she'd never experienced before as her shoulders were wrenched out of their sockets. An unearthly scream escaped from her mouth and pierced the air before faltering as she slipped into unconsciousness.

She was slapped back into reality and looked straight into the eyes of her interrogator. Was death truly near?

'I didn't hear an answer. Did she give it to you?'

'No,' she spat, in one final attempt to summon up the strength of the damned.

24

He stretched her again.

And again.

And again.

Delirious with pain, barely a feeble whimper escaped her as her joints tore apart.

'Stop. Please. I confess. I confess.'

'About time. And who instructed you?'

'Silrith,' slipped from her lips. The interrogator smiled at the torturer in dark satisfaction. He walked to the door and opened it.

'That's it, boys. Home to Asrantica tomorrow. We've got our confession.'

His words were met by a merry cheer.

'Untie her and take her to her cell,' he said matter-of-factly as he re-entered the room followed by two guards. 'She dies on the morrow.'

Chapter 2

'Sire, you must name an heir.'

King Lissoll of Bennvika, third of that name, lay on his death bed, surrounded by his closest courtiers. From his right, a wizened old man in dark robes, Sankil, High Priest of Bennvika, bent over him.

'Sire, if you do not name an heir, the kingdom will descend into civil war.'

It was late evening and the large, crowded room, only sparsely decorated for a king's bedchamber, was lit with candles, although Lissoll's four-poster bed still fell into shadow.

Many of the courtiers were still dressed in their most dazzlingly extravagant finery, just as they had been for their audience with the king earlier that day. As a result, all of them were rather more colourfully attired than the priest, not least Lissoll's only surviving daughter, Princess Silrith.

By now she was a fully-grown woman of twenty-three. Her long, flowing chestnut hair, piercing dark eyes and soft skin were in stark contrast to the deep emerald velvet and shimmering gold lining of her dress. Further down, her unstructured white under-trousers protruded out from below the hem, while her feet were wrapped in fine gold sandals. Her maids had said that she looked gloriously regal, although she herself always felt awkward and overdressed in such splendour.

She'd been wearing these eastern style clothes as a political gesture of friendship towards her cousin, Lord Jostan, who had sailed across the seas some months earlier from his homeland, the Verusantian Empire, to spend the year with his Bennvikan relations. Naturally, the moment Silrith had been seen in such attire, all the ladies at court had followed suit and it was now the height of fashion across the country.

But at this particular moment Silrith had no thought for such trivial things. She was overcome with worry, yet a lifetime of being taught how to behave with dignity had helped her suppress the urge to tear through the corridors to reach her father on hearing the news of his being taken ill. Now she could only watch in silence, keeping her emotions contained within her mask-like exterior.

'Your Grace, may I speak to you in private?' Her turbulent thoughts were interrupted by the voice of a servant.

'Yes, of course.'

She followed him out of the room and the double doors were closed behind them. Instantly, she noted his worried expression.

'What has happened?'

'Well, it is hard to be sure at this point, Your Grace.'

'Go on.'

Back in the bedchamber, as it became clear that the king was in his death throws, amongst the many dignitaries present, there were a few who were only too happy to speculate on what would happen next. These included two ageing men standing towards the back of the crowded room. The first was the heavily but neatly bearded Lord Feddilyn Rintta, who wore a purple tunic and hat. He was joined by the wrinkly, wispy-haired Congressor Hoban Salanath, resplendent in his blue robes of office. Hoban was deeply concerned.

'Well doesn't this throw up a few interesting questions, my Lord Rintta?' he pondered in a hushed tone.

'Why ask questions when the answers will quickly become apparent? We can only look on as events unfold,' Feddilyn replied.

'Tell me you're not curious?'

'As a mere mortal, of course I am,' Feddilyn said. 'However, only the gods can decide the fates of men. Yet some things can be foreseen, or should have been, even. Here we see the risk of delaying the chance to remarry when you only have two surviving children. It is years now since Queen Gidrassa passed away. You and your congressor friends discouraged him from remarrying quickly and this is the result.'

'I didn't see you encouraging him,' Hoban retorted.

'My responsibilities are manifold. Those bestowed on me by the king in my role as governor by far supersede anything asked of me by anyone in the Congressate.'

'The Congressate can advise but never demand anything of a king,' said Hoban. 'This could not have been anticipated. Two surviving children are

27

enough when one of them is a strong and unchallenged heir in the late Prince Fabrald. The urgency to build a clear line of succession beyond that was not felt by the king until the prince's death. Until then, the king was more interested in finding a suitor for Princess Silrith, rather than one for himself, even though this proved more complicated than expected.'

Feddilyn sighed.

'Yet the fact remains; relying on the survival of a single son is always a risk.'

'Yes, that was a most fateful hunting trip,' Hoban conceded.

'Quite, though I'm sure you and your allies were very pleased with yourselves when you convinced the king to arrange a marriage alliance with Medrodor after Fabrald's death.'

Feddilyn gazed over at Lissoll's bed ruefully. To the left of the king sat the dainty, gently whimpering form of Accutina, Lissoll's young wife.

'Look at her,' he said. 'A mere twenty years old and now carrying the king's child. Her position is highly vulnerable. This whole marriage alliance with the Medrodorians hinged on the idea that the king would live long enough to see his son to manhood, assuming the child is even male of course.'

'Would you not agree that until today the idea that he would live that long has been recognised by all as the most likely outcome?' Hoban forced through gritted teeth, doing his best to avoid anyone around them overhearing their conversation.

'Of course, but that vision seems threatened now, doesn't it? Unless the king survives, everything hinges on the allegiances of a number of powerful people. For the sake of the future of this nation, Accutina must remarry fast and to a man of suitable status. That way he can be named as lord protector until the child comes of age.'

'I believe there are more possibilities than that, my Lord Rintta,' said Hoban. 'We cannot choose a lord protector, or even an heir if the king himself names one and he can select who he pleases. He may bestow the title on Accutina herself. Having said that, things might be simpler if he were to choose Princess Silrith as his heir. She is the next in line, after all. But even so, her position would no doubt be challenged.'

'Yes and if so, the vultures will descend very soon. That cannot be allowed to happen. It takes a man's mind and leadership to eliminate such threats. Choosing a woman to rule would be a grave mistake.'

'I disagree greatly,' Hoban said. 'Especially in the case of our princess. The people love her and there is a strength in her that few men possess. It is perfectly plausible that the king will select her as his heir.'

'I do not see it. I will not be ruled by a woman. The king must name a lord protector in anticipation of a male child. That *would* be unprecedented, but perfectly legal if the king orders it,' Feddilyn insisted.

'That could still be dangerous. He may choose his nephew, Lord Jostan. But would he be content in the role of lord protector, or would he pursue his own claim to the throne?'

'If that happens, we will all have to do what we must for the benefit of the kingdom.'

'The kingdom, or yourself, Lord Rintta? Honestly, your ambiguity never fails to amaze me and it wouldn't be the first time *your* loyalty has been called into question.'

'It's all very well standing up for honour and principles,' Feddilyn said. 'But they are little more than political obstacles. In reality, we must all choose a side. After that, we must simply pray to the gods that we chose the right one. Either way, I fear the timing could not be worse. Maybe the gods now resort to mischief, or perhaps they guide the hand of a mortal whose interests lie beyond the Royal lineage.'

Silrith re-entered the room.

'Has there been any change?' she asked Accutina, sitting down on the bed beside her, gently placing a hand on the girl's shoulder.

'Don't touch me,' Accutina spat back like a petulant child, slapping Silrith's hand away.

Silrith had given up trying to understand why Accutina had never seemed to trust her. Originally she had put it down to shyness, but it had been over a year now. Did she feel threatened?

Silrith looked at her father. He had been lying there for quite some time, but now it was clear that he was quickly weakening. He was barely breathing and his eyes were glazed and vacant. The high priest leaned over his king once again.

'Sire, you must name an heir,' he said again.

Another servant entered and this time spoke to Lord Jostan, whispering in his ear. Silrith watched, intrigued as her foreign cousin simply nodded his acknowledgement of the servant's message, then moved in behind Sankil at the bedside.

Accutina shook her head.

'It must be poison,' she said, almost in a whisper, glancing up at Jostan. 'When I discover who did this, who took him away from me-'.

She was interrupted as Lissoll grabbed Sankil by the arm with what remaining strength he could muster, trying to say something, but no sound came out. With that, his strength failed and the arm dropped, hanging limply off the side of the bed.

For a moment everyone was silent.

'Is he dead?' Somebody in the background asked.

'F-father?' Silrith whispered, her lip starting to quiver and her eyes welling up with tears. Desperately she fought to contain her emotions, but she knew it was a battle she was bound to lose. Slowly she reached to touch her father's hand; hers shaking slightly as she did. No response. She drew her arm away again, the first tears starting to fall from her eyes and run down her cheeks. She reminded herself to rally again and just about fought back the tidal wave of emotion.

Since telling them that there was nothing more he could do, the physician had stayed out of the way, not wanting to impede on Lissoll's final moments with those around him, but now the dully robed man came forward again and after a quick inspection, formally pronounced the king dead.

'Why? He was so healthy,' asked Accutina.

'It seems that your suspicions were correct, my Queen,' said the physician. 'I think there is a strong chance that he was poisoned, most likely by someone who had access to his final meal.'

'It is not for you to play prosecutor,' Silrith berated him, though in hushed tones. 'Now please leave us to grieve in peace.'

He bowed and left. Silrith was shocked by the man's lack of respect, but she was even more surprised by his diagnosis. Her father had no enemies, or at least, surely none that could reach him here. It was then that she noticed the strangest expression on Accutina's face. Her eyes were locked on to Silrith; her face tight-lipped. She appeared almost unaware of those around them, so intent was the stare with which she fixed her.

'He told me he was having stomach pains after eating. It was that maid of yours,' said Accutina.

'What?'

Silrith began to feel the hairs on the back of her neck stand on end in the eerie silence as she felt other eyes boring into her, from all around the room.

'Such a picture of innocence,' Jostan smirked.

He was thirty years old, tall, muscular, with thick raven hair and a clean-shaven chin. Jewel encrusted earrings reached almost down to his shoulders. Even in this vibrantly dressed company he stood out, with two golden sashes draped in opposite directions over a spangled sapphire tunic that reached down to his ankles. Even his boots were studded with crystals.

'I have to give it to you, Silrith, you actually nearly did it. I didn't think you would.'

Silrith glared at him, aghast, as sadness and fear temporarily gave way to anger and offence.

'Did what? Explain your impudence. My father has barely left this world and already you insult him by conducting yourself in this way?'

Jostan rolled his eyes theatrically and continued with a grim laugh.

'Honestly, your commitment to the act of the innocent daughter, the dignified and noble princess with no personal ambition is highly impressive but, alas, some of us present appear to have seen through it. It's interesting, is it not, that no other voice comes to your aid? I fear that you've given yourself away in your haste to denounce any accusations of poisoning. I'm sure your father's spirit would forgive any insult in view of what I do on his behalf now.'

Silrith's eyes narrowed, a fiery hatred burning inside her. She didn't like where this altercation appeared to be heading.

'The correct procedures will be followed and the culprit will be caught. But my father will be treated with some dignity in death,' she hissed.

31

'All of which buys you time,' Jostan said. 'I am not prepared to give you that opportunity. For the benefit of those others present and for the young princess here who seems entirely unaware of her own plot-'

'What is this?' Silrith bellowed, leaping to her feet, but she was restrained by four strong arms. She was dumbfounded to see that it was two of Jostan's Verusantian lance guardsmen in their distinctive black armour, who had sprung forward from where they had been waiting at the side of the room. Neither wore their helmets and as Silrith looked from one to the other she saw a malice-fuelled expression of warning on both their scarred faces.

'What ladylike behaviour. Gentlemen, ladies, here we see the true character of our dear sweet princess. In reality, she is fuelled only by ambition.'

'Pestiferous scum. You accept our hospitality these past few months and this is your repayment? Guards!'

Silence. Silrith looked around desperately.

'Are you wondering why they don't come running?' Jostan asked. 'Well, that would be because my own guards have taken charge and those of your soldiers that don't join their ranks will be duly punished. It's for the nation's safety, you understand. I'm saving Bennvika from being ruled by a murderer. As Queen Accutina herself testifies, it was your maid who served his last meal. That fits exactly with what the physician said, don't you think? Something you were very quick to distance yourself from by sending him away.' He fixed her with a cold stare.

'Afayna has served my father many times over the years.' Silrith countered. 'Why would she do this now?'

Jostan moved in close to her, almost close enough to kiss her lips.

'Royal promises, cousin, and royal treachery.'

'Now, as I was saying,' he went on, moving away again. 'For those who still see a princess and not a gaudily dressed murderer with royal ambitions, let me enlighten you. We all remember the noble Prince Fabrald. I still mourn him to this day, though it seems to have escaped everyone's notice that out of the whole hunting party, only the lovely Princess Silrith was within sight of him when he 'fell from his horse'. Or was he tripped, Silrith? Who can tell? I'm told that your usual sharp-shooting with the bow was

32

rather off that day. Maybe your mind was on something else, *planning* something else?'

'Even you know that is absurd,' said Silrith. She'd always known that Jostan was ambitious and ruthless, but this? So soon?

'Really? You seem very certain of that. Now, due to our beloved late king's legions of accursedly stillborn children, Fabrald's 'accident' put you next in line to the throne.' He started pacing around the room. 'That was until our new queen announced she was pregnant and suddenly that threatened everything, didn't it? You had to act quickly.'

'Liar. You mean to slander me. You mean to incriminate me and claim the crown for yourself.'

'Of course, I do not. But then, we can't give the throne to a murderer now can we?'

'You impudent fool. Is there nothing you wouldn't say to sully my name?'

'It's over, Silrith. You can stop the act now. Guards! This girl is starting to irritate me. Take her away.'

'I am Silrith Alfwyn! I am your rightful queen!' She howled as she was dragged away.

'Stop,' came a voice from the background. 'This is wrong. I will not have this.'

The guards stopped in their tracks. Silrith scanned the crowd of faces to see who had spoken. It was Hoban Salanath. Silence fell and Silrith ceased struggling.

'You would defend regicide, Congressor Salanath?' Jostan challenged him.

'Of course not. But I will not believe that the princess orchestrated it.'

'Unfortunately for you and the princess, while we have been up here, her maid has been under interrogation. Now we have a confession. One that specifically implicates the princess. Interesting. Especially given that, as everyone knows, a lady's maid knows her mistress like nobody else. Are you prepared to dispute that? People might start to ask questions why.'

Hoban was silent.

Silrith was sure Jostan must be bluffing. Surely it would be impossible to get a confession so quickly, even under torture? But then she doubted

33

these lords would believe that a maid could last long under questioning. She looked at Hoban imploringly, but something in his eyes said that there was nothing more he could do and his gaze fell.

'It would not do well for any of you to stand against me. I can tell you with the gravest certainty that if word of any divisions within this country reaches Verusantium, the emperor will not hesitate to invade,' Jostan cautioned. 'Join me and you protect Bennvika from that fate. You've all been under the princess' spell. Break it. Do not be lulled into thinking well of her. Now, guards, take her away.'

'I am the rightful queen!' Silrith called, fighting to break free. 'Jostan is the murderer. Can't you see? Can't you see?'

But it was no use. The large double doors closed behind them and Silrith heard no more from inside her father's bedchamber. She fought to free herself from the grip of the guards, but seemingly to no avail, until a slight slip. It was all she needed. Ripping her arm free from one guard, she kicked him between the legs, a weak spot despite his armour, before sinking her teeth into the hand of the other. He cursed loudly, but his grip loosened just enough and Silrith ran for her life. The guards gave chase, though of course one of them could barely run and the weight of their armour gave Silrith a crucial advantage. Silrith ran down the huge staircase into the hall at the bottom. Fortunately, they'd only been one floor up.

'Guards. Guards,' shouted Jostan, who had come out on to the upper gallery and just moments later from somewhere a trumpet blew a single note.

'Your Grace.' One of King Lissoll's royal guards ran towards Silrith, wearing full armour from neck to knee and a helmet with a black and white transverse horsehair crest, followed by two Bennvikan soldiers.

'Nalfran. Help me. Kill those men,' Silrith said desperately.

'Yes, your Grace. Now run. Run for your life.'

Unarmed as she was, she didn't argue. To the clanging sounds of blade on blade, she sprinted through the nearest doorway, almost flying down the corridor and charged through an archway into one of the palace's many lounges.

The trumpet must have been a call to more of Jostan's guards, as at least five, also in their black armour, appeared through the door at the other end of the room. Seeing her way blocked, she opened a window and was just hauling herself up on to the windowsill when a guard caught up and grabbed her leg. More men arrived and between them they overpowered her, wrestling her off the ledge despite her tenacious grip and bringing her crashing down to the floor.

Silrith kicked and flailed wildly as the men tried to hold her down until one stood above her. He took out his sword, turned it around, then raised it above his head before bringing the pommel down hard and Silrith's world went dark.

The next thing Silrith was aware of was being shaken with a strong and ungraceful grip.

'Silrith?'

She knew that voice. She opened her eyes quickly but was forced to shut them again as she felt a thwacking pain coursing through her head. She forced her eyelids open a second time. In the dim light, she saw a man's face, quite close, yet his features were still a blur.

Blinking, she saw a pale complexion, curly red hair, an unruly beard and a flamboyant yellow flat hat with a white feather.

'Silrith, are you alright?'

'Oprion. Why are you here?' She smiled as she recognised her childhood friend, who was now the Governor of Hazgorata and Bennvika's wealthiest lord. Then she looked around at the stone walls, the metal door, the small barred window and the burnt-out brazier on the wall. Lord Oprion looked most out of place here in his bright yellow tunic.

'And why am I in this cell?' she added. But after a moment it all came flooding back.

'Cell? This is rather pleasant as cells go. Count yourself lucky you've got strong walls around you and not just a few bars to separate you from the poor wretches either side.'

'It's not the time for jokes. Why are you here? Why weren't you present yesterday?'

'I was delayed on the road. But now that I'm here, I want to help you. I paid off the guard, but we still don't have that much time. I need to know what's going on. How in the name of the gods did you end up getting yourself arrested? There has to be more to it than I've been led to believe.'

'And I think I can guess what they told you,' Silrith said. 'It was such a shock. My father was taken ill. It was so sudden. Then the physician said it was poison and that evil bastard Jostan accused me of committing the crime. Me! For the death of my own father.'

'That's ridiculous. I never saw a father and daughter so close.'

Silrith awkwardly pulled herself up to stand and Oprion backed away slightly to give her some space as she did.

'I don't know what I'm going to do without him,' she said, shaking her head. She desperately wanted to grieve properly, but knew that this would only make her look weak and defeated.

'How am I going to get out of here? And what of Invicturion Nalfran?' Silrith said.

'I believe the good invicturion and his soldiers were put to the sword by Jostan's guards,' Oprion said in a wry tone, confirming Silrith's suspicions. Silrith felt a stinging pang of guilt for those who had given their lives for her in vain.

'But don't worry,' Oprion continued. 'You can still get out of this. I'll back your cause at the trial. I can pay off whoever we need to back us.'

'Oh don't be so stupid,' said Silrith, turning on him. 'I would assume that Jostan has taken the throne for himself, has he?'

'Yes. Your father didn't name a lord protector for the coming child, so Jostan was free to pursue his own claim. He's even started using the royal 'we'.'

Silrith nodded slowly. 'Well, in that case, there won't be a trial. He is a legendary orator. He exudes authority as I'm sure you've seen by now. All he has to do is make a convincing speech to the Congressate to get them to accept him as king. After that, they'll let him do what he likes to me and there will be nothing you and your money can do to stop him.'

'I doubt that.'

'Are you sure? You may be the richest man in Bennvika, but Jostan isn't from Bennvika is he? Have you seen Verusantium? Go to his residence in Bruskannia and you'll find a province rich enough to put any independent kingdom outside the Empire to shame. I appreciate the offer, but money won't work. You'll simply be outbid.'

'So what do you suggest?' Oprion asked.

Silrith began to pace around the room, trying to look in control while Oprion stood watching.

'Military action is the only option left if I am to avoid exile or execution. If you can get me out of here and over to Hazgorata, I will lead your army here to take on Jostan myself. I may not be as silver-tongued as him, but I can make up for it through leading by example. Those swordplay lessons you gave me can finally be put to good use.'

'I'm not sure you're quite ready for that yet though.'

'And I have some knowledge of navy ships. That could be useful,' she continued, ignoring him.

'Silrith, this is suicide,' Oprion implored.

'I must protect Bennvika and take revenge for my father. It was Jostan who had him poisoned. I'm certain,' she replied.

'And what proof do you have?'

'None. But what proof do I need?' Silrith was starting to become annoyed now and she clenched her fists in an effort to maintain self-control. She could feel the magnitude of her situation playing havoc with her emotions. 'Don't you think it's a bit strange that it happens while he's here, just as he's in a prime position to take advantage of my father's death?'

'I can see that and I believe you, but only because I know you so well. There are many who don't know you like I do and among them are a number of men who would rather be led by a man than by a woman. Arcane, I know, but there you have it. Anyway, what happened when you were with me in Hazgorata didn't exactly do your reputation any good, did it?'

'I did nothing that would have damaged my reputation if I'd been a man.'

'Whatever the rumours say you did, you defied your father by coming to me and learning to fight. That much is true,' Oprion pressed.

'I didn't. I simply acted without consulting him first. Why shouldn't I learn how to fight? Surely you know me well enough to know that I am my own woman, Oprion? Either way, we must not be divided. Not now. As I said, our situation dictates that our response must be military. It is the only option left. You well know of the horrific scenes I witnessed when I went with my father to Verusantium all those years ago. The emperor ordered his lords to see that everyone who refused to worship the Verusantian god was publicly executed in the most despicable of ways. Jostan's father almost took pleasure in the task and Jostan himself will be no different. Whatever he says now, he will not tolerate the worship of our gods for long. He will force our people to convert to his religion and will slaughter any who refuse.'

Oprion looked unmoved and said nothing.

'Come on, Oprion, you must have some troops that you can send to help me escape from here? There must be a rebellion and it must start now, before he can gain a foothold.'

'Silrith, I understand that you worry about what will happen to the plebeians-'

'They are not plebeians, Oprion,' said Silrith. 'They are our people and they need me to protect them and I can't do that if I am locked up in here.'

He shook his head.

'It's too risky.'

'What sort of man are you? This is our country we are talking about.' She was getting more and more animated now. 'You know, it seems strange that you were content to teach me how to fight but are now so reluctant to do it for real.'

'I cannot take up arms against the king.'

'I thought you were stronger than this,' she replied in exasperation, turning her back again. She picked up the bowl of stomach-churning slop that some guard had evidently left for her to eat.

'Silrith, I'm sorry, but-'

'Gods, are men not men anymore?' she cried, hurling the bowl at him. He only just dodged it as it flew past and smashed down on the stone floor, but some of the contents spattered on to his opulent tunic. 'There was a time when the idea that the gods were on one's side was enough to move anybody to stand up and fight, but oh no, not you. You would rather capitulate and save yourself, you coward.'

'I understand your frustration with me. But I really think I can do a deal to get you out of this.'

38

'Money won't work. I told you that. You have to help me escape.'

'I can't. I must at least make it look as if I support him, which means that I can only give my support to you in ways that are legal. I have a family to protect now, Silrith. A wife and children.'

'I seem to remember you were less interested in them before I was branded a traitor. '

'Don't unearth painful memories, Silrith. I loved you, truly I did. If only it had been reflected.'

'I did love you,' said Silrith firmly. 'All my life I loved you as a brother and if you cannot see the value in that form of love then that is a failing of yours, not mine. In any case, it matters little. I can now see from your unwillingness to help me that your love for yourself supersedes all, so you are undeserving of such affection.'

'I must protect my family.'

Silrith shook her head in dismay.

'But not your closest friend apparently. One day you'll learn that sometimes money isn't enough. Anyway, don't you realise that sooner or later he will expect all his lords to convert as well? Will you readily renounce Lomatteva and Vitrinnolf, the mother and father of this nation and instead turn to the worship of Estarron? You can be sure that under Jostan the worship of any other god will not be tolerated.'

'Of course, I will renounce them and I will order the people of my province to do the same for their own safety. Silrith, I've never been a passionate worshipper any more than you have. Forget the old gods. They have turned their backs on Bennvika, so Bennvika requires a strong new god to protect it. The people will see that in due course.'

'People should be left to worship whichever deities they will, Oprion. It should never be forced on anyone. You must see this. We are fighting for our very identities here, our culture, our way of life. Aren't you willing to commit to a side until you're certain who will win? Well, look. I'm in a cell and he's the new king. Why don't you just join his side right away? It's pretty clear to me that you've already made your choice. You have betrayed your people and betrayed your gods. It is clear to me that you care little for your sin. But your betrayal of a life-long friend? That is the part that surprises me.

Really, does everything we've been through over the years mean so little to you?'

Oprion didn't answer. Silrith nodded. Heroes and heroines were people of strength and action, not of words and after all, words were the only weapons Oprion ever used in anger. He also wasn't a man of compassion and this had always grated on Silrith. She, on the other hand, had never forgotten how lucky she had been to be born rich and was very aware of the responsibilities that came with her position.

'Well, that's it then,' she said. 'I will be exiled or worse, the nation will burn and Bennvika as we know it will be gone forever. Exactly what did you come here to achieve, Oprion?'

He looked at the floor.

'I just had to see you. I thought I could help.'

'Is that it? No witty retort? You surprise me. Another disappointment you've sent my way. You profess that you want to help me, but you're not willing to take any risks. One day you're going to have to grow up and do what is right for your people. For a moment I thought you might even have a plan. Now, get out.'

Silrith had never felt so let down in all her life. All she could do now was turn her mind to how she might be able to escape without help, but her thoughts were void of ideas.

Oprion turned to leave, but stopped just short of the door.

'Well if that is all, I shall ride home to Hazgorata. It seems there is nothing more I can do here,' he said, still with his back to her.

With that, he opened the door and in a moment, he was gone, leaving Silrith alone. Alone in her cell and alone in the world. Letting go of her emotions, she buried her head in her hands. What now? She knew she was just the first of many who would suffer under the wrath of Jostan's regime. She had seen it first-hand, but no amount of retellings over the years had made Oprion realise its true severity. It was hard to see justice in the treatment of even the pettiest of criminals in Verusantium. In a land where much of the population were forced to steal in order to eat, thieves were punished by hanging, whereas a public whipping was deemed punishment enough in Bennvika. Yet it was their attitude to religion that had shocked Silrith so deeply. Religion was important in Bennvika, but this was something

40

else entirely. Their treatment of anyone who didn't convert to the worship of the Verusantian god, Estarron, was nothing short of ethnic cleansing.

All this Silrith had witnessed first-hand as a ten-year-old when she had accompanied her father on a state visit to Bruskannia, the Verusantian province that Jostan now governed. At the time though, the area was ruled by Silrith's uncle, King Lissoll's brother-in-law Dionius. Silrith's family were visiting at the latter's invitation. Queen Gidrassa and Prince Fabrald had also come and they had stayed in the provincial capital, Gorgreb, where they were the honoured guests of Dionius, his wife Turiskia, who was also half-sister to King Lissoll, as well as Dionius and Turiskia's son, a seventeen-year-old Jostan.

The entire invitation was a propaganda exercise to try and scare her father into forcing the conversion of Bennvika to the worship of Estarron. As a convert from Bennvikanism to the Estarronic faith, Turiskia had taken the lead in this, bombarding her brother with reasons why Estarron was greater than both Vitrinnolf and Lomatteva combined. Lissoll had some good arguments of his own and the friendly debate between the four adults drifted easily between the two languages that were common to both couples. Bored by talk of religion, the young Silrith, along with Fabrald, who was twelve at that time, had gone off to explore. They had asked Jostan if he wanted to show them around, but he had sullenly refused.

Sitting in her cell and thinking back, Silrith envied the innocence of her own younger self. The debate between the adults had been of no interest to her then, yet it had also changed her life. The idea that it was nothing more than a bore was laughable now.

The next day, they had all ridden out into the city together. While viewing the many stunning buildings, Silrith had been shocked by the wretchedness of the poor compared to the rich, for in the shadow of these gold-plated spires and domes, people hurried to get away from the royal party and cowered in their shops and homes as they passed. In Kriganheim, Bennvika's capital, there would be crowds of jubilant people pushing forward to try to see them, but it was clear that these people feared their masters.

She soon saw why. When they reached the city forum they found it was teeming with people, unlike the eerie streets, yet there were no market stalls here, as there were in Kriganheim; just a crowd of people, all looking at the wooden scaffold in front of them. Even at ten, Silrith knew what a scaffold was for. As she watched, a priest with a long, grey beard and spotless white robes walked on to the stage. To his side was an executioner, dressed all in black and carrying a short sword.

'What is the meaning of this?' her father had asked.

'This is how I do my duty to almighty Estarron, by order of the divine and of the emperor,' Dionius had replied in a smug tone. 'Watch. See if their false god protects them.'

Surely that didn't mean what Silrith thought it did? People were only executed for the most heinous crimes in Bennvika, like murder, or high treason, not for practising the wrong religion. Silrith looked on in alarm as four men and a woman were manhandled on to the wooden stage by a group of soldiers. All fought to resist as they were wrestled forward and the sound of one of the men begging for mercy pierced Silrith's soul to the core. But that was as nothing compared with the horror that gripped her heart at the sight of the sixth prisoner, a girl, no more than five years old with her hair in blonde plaits. She was the only one who didn't struggle, apparently paralysed with fear.

'Here we see the most despicable of things,' said the priest in Verusantian, which Silrith's aunt Turiskia translated for her niece and nephew. The prisoners were each forced to kneel with their hands bound behind their backs. 'An entire family of apostates. They, in their folly, have renounced the Grace of our divine Lord Estarron, the one true god and instead have reverted to worshipping falsehoods and demons. This cannot go unpunished and so, with the divine blessing of Estarron, I commit them to punishment by the sword.'

As he finished, the executioner moved towards the prisoners from behind. The girl began to scream, looking over her shoulder at the executioner, while the others begged for mercy, wailing and babbling almost unintelligibly. The executioner stopped behind the first kneeling man, placed the tip blade slowly on the back of his neck, then raised it again before slicing down and snapping the man's spine, cutting off his cries. The crowd cheered as his body fell limply on to the scaffold's wooden floor, spurting blood. The screams of the girl reached a new pitch and the wails of the adults grew even more panicked as the executioner moved to the next prisoner, presumably the child's mother, and the crowd cheered again as her life was ended.

The memory of their cries, of the child's screaming and the sickening jubilation of the onlookers as the prisoners were killed was etched into Silrith's memory. They had even cheered the killing of the little girl. Silrith's family had been equally shocked. That night, Dionius again brought up the subject of religion and had even tried to convert Silrith and her family there and then. When Lissoll refused to convert the Bennvikans to the worship of Estarron, Dionius had become angry. Silrith's father had decided to cut the visit short after that and they had left the very next day. On her arrival home, Silrith had made it her life's purpose to devote herself to charity, throwing coins into the crowded streets whenever she travelled, while also intervening in public disputes as she grew older. She was never satisfied, always feeling she could do more in the fight for justice for the common people and there was always still much to do.

By the time Dionius had died five years later though, the incident in Verusantium had been forgotten by most of her family and friends. However, clearly Jostan had remembered Lissoll's refusal and had made it his life's work to convert Bennvika to the worship of Estarron. Everything Silrith had worked to build would collapse overnight. He had to be stopped.

Of course, even if she was successful in regaining the throne from Jostan and protecting Bennvika from his tyranny, that would not be the end of it. Silrith knew she bore a secret that would ensure that even if she were to be so fortunate as to win that particular victory, Bennvika's future would still hang in the balance.

There was no point dwelling on that though. First, she had to get out of here. But how? Then she remembered one man who just might still help her. He was no royalist. That much was well known, but he was as much of a philanthropist as she was. As such, he had often visited prisoners in his fight for justice. Despite his republican politics, he had been a close friend of King Lissoll, so maybe, just maybe, he would visit her. If he did, Silrith had a task for him. If he accepted, the fight for Bennvika's freedom would live on.

Jostan had no intention of giving Silrith any chance of a trial. Instead, he knew that when he presented himself to the Congressate the very next

43

day after Silrith's arrest, his skills as an orator would be enough to consolidate his claim – or if not, force was always an option.

He felt like a conqueror as he rode through the streets of Kriganheim, followed by his chief bodyguard, Ostagantus Gormaris, Head of the Verusantian Lance Guardsmen of Bruskannia, along with five other men, each in their black Verusantian armour, though protocol meant that the clamouring crowds would come later. Few of them would know who he was. After all, he wasn't yet officially king in the eyes of the Bennvikan constitution, but that was barely anything more than a formality. It mattered little. Once he had presented himself to the Congressate and been accepted as the new monarch, he would send his troops riding through the city announcing his accession. In time, every man and woman in every kingdom either side of the Kebban Sea would know of the shift in power. But for now, he was content simply to smile to himself as he looked upon the people of the city going about their daily business, each having no idea that they were laying eyes upon their new king.

His pleasure turned to disgust as he rode on and saw a large, paved clearing between the buildings. Throngs of people knelt and prayed at the feet of two enormous statues, each at least a hundred feet high. One was of a rather matriarchal looking woman and the other was of a warrior king. Both of these marble giants were depicted carrying swords that hung from their belts. Jostan supposed these idols must be Lomatteva and Vitrinnolf. The sight of the crowd of heretics worshipping their demonic gods while the priests expounded falsehoods flared Jostan's anger. But he controlled himself and he kicked his horse forward so that he no longer had to look upon them. They would soon know the folly of their polytheism. They would see that there was only one true god and they would repent for their sins or pay the price. But first, he needed the backing of the Congressate. Jostan prayed to his god that he would be blessed this day and that this would truly be the formality he hoped for.

The small column trotted quickly onward down the busy streets. Soon they were in the forum, which was full of the noises and smells of the market. Looming over it was the Congressate Hall. It was a tall building in the centre of Kriganheim and its rectangular front extended back to a circular structure, which had a domed roof with many windows in it. At the front of the building, above a number of marble steps and many grand pillars, stood a huge triangular façade, depicting the Bennvikan political hierarchy and leaving no doubt as to the Congressate's place within it. The image was split into two levels and on the lower of these were farmers, fisherman, labourers and other common people. On the higher level, fewer in number but carved larger to indicate their status, were the congressors and sitting in the middle in all his majesty, carved larger still, was the king.

Dismounting and leaving four of his armed men outside to keep away the plebeians, Jostan walked up the steps, between the great pillars and over towards the pair of large wooden doors. He stopped as his two remaining guards, one of them being Gormaris, hurried past on either side of him to open them. With that done, he strode into the first room and the guards followed him through, shutting the large doors behind them. The marble of the walls, floor and ceiling shone as the sunlight hit it through the tall windows and there was almost no sound, save for Jostan's footsteps and those of his bodyguards, along with the distant murmur of many voices on the other side of the door that led into the domed room, the hall itself. He was dressed similarly to how he had been the previous night, albeit with the blue of his attire replaced by red, though he retained the gold sashes. These two colours had been associated with Bennvikan royalty for centuries, whatever the personal colours of the ruling house at the time.

As he paced down the enormous corridor, towards the large wooden doors at the far end, he cast a smug gaze over the large portraits of the country's former monarchs. Of course, he had seen them all before while on earlier diplomatic visits, but this time he knew for sure that he too would soon be immortalised in the form of a portrait hanging in this most illustrious and noble of galleries.

When he reached the end of the corridor, he stopped again to allow his two bodyguards to move ahead of him and open the large wooden doors. Once they had been heaved open, both guards strode into the hall and each pulled out a small bugle before Gormaris declared 'Congressors, I present to you his Majesty King Jostan of Bennvika, Governor of the home province of Kriganheim and the Verusantian province of Bruskannia.' Instantly they both put their bugles to their lips and sounded the royal fanfare, at which point Jostan entered the room. Silence fell.

He looked over at the wizened old speaker, who was seated behind where Jostan now stood, opposite the Congressate members, who were ranged in front of him, dressed in their bright blue robes. In response, the man clanged his staff on the white marble floor three times and said 'The king-apparent will now address the Congressate.'

As silence fell again, for a moment the Congressate unanimously stared at Jostan expectantly, although in truth it was more of a scowl from some, but he stared right back. They numbered in their dozens and most of them were old enough to be his mother or father. Some of them were sitting at his own level, while others had needed to climb up many steps to reach the seats in the rows towards the back. Looking around, he noticed that Hoban Salanath was not in attendance.

Damn, I see the bird has flown, he thought. Finally, Jostan took a deep lungful of air and began.

'Noble leaders of the Congressate. Some of you may know why we stand before you now. Others may have heard only rumours, so let us enlighten you all. The results of recent events have led to an unexpected change in the succession to the throne of this great kingdom. Our late uncle, the beloved King Lissoll, did not meet his end as the result of a sudden illness as some would have you believe, but was murdered by his own daughter, the Princess Silrith, who personally orchestrated the audacious act using words as poisonous as the substance that ultimately brought about our good king's untimely death.

It is at times like these where deeds count far more than words. Given that we are interested only in safeguarding the peace of this nation, we have done our duty by arresting the murderer and her accomplice, her maid. Due to her royal blood, the traitorous princess will be escorted to the Ustine Isles. There she will be marooned under guard for the rest of her days, as was the fate of the terrible King Gengred, slayer of the innocents, as well as other prisoners of the Isles in centuries past. The maid, however, the one who personally added the poison to the king's final meal, will be made an example of, showing the people of this land what happens to those who plot against the king.'

As the flow of his words increased, he started to pace around the hall, as was his habit.

'Her hands, which tampered with and presented the deadly meal, will be cut off at the wrist and nailed to the Congressate Hall doors to remind the people of their place beneath us. Her head, which housed the brain that agreed to assist in this most dastardly murder, rather than report the threat, will be severed from her shoulders and placed on a spike on Kriganheim Bridge and her torso in which can be found her own traitorous heart, will be roped to a pole which will stand above the city gates. As his loving nephew, with every inch of our being, we will be the avenger of King Lissoll's noble blood!'

There was a loud cheer, but Jostan went on. Most of the congressors did not know Silrith well and he was eager to exploit this. He was starting to work himself into a frenzy now. With clenched fists, he bellowed out his words with vim and verve, such was the belief that he wanted his audience to instil in them.

'So, with Silrith duly exiled and the late King Lissoll's child as yet unborn, fate has decreed that it is we who shall now be king.' Another cheer. *This is going to be easy*, he thought. They were like putty in his hands.

'This proves, my noble lords, that the prophecy written on the famous Amulet of Hazgorata was correct. *Mother of many, Mother of none; a Queen will fall and a Warrior will come.* As the mother of many, mother of none, your goddess Lomatteva, predicted, when she was yet the mortal Queen of Hazgorata, a queen has fallen and a warrior has come. We, Jostan Kazabrus, have come.

When a man knows he is about to usher in a new chapter of history for his nation, it is important that he acknowledges the legacies, both good and bad, of his predecessors. In our first act as king, we have done away with Silrith Alfwyn, the traitor who murdered her own flesh and blood, but now we plan to consolidate and build on the achievements of the strongest Alfwyns, those who brought honour to our own mother's great house, in particular, our uncle and his father, the noble King Bastinian; conquerors both.'

Jostan calmed and lowered his voice to a more normal level as he began to outline his plans.

'There is still some resistance in the south from the Hentani tribe, but that will not last. We intend to rekindle Bennvika's alliance with the Defroni

47

tribe. As you all know, Queen Tefkia, good King Bastinian's second wife, was of that race. Soon we will march on the Hentani, among whom tumultuous voices are at this very moment calling for rebellion against us. Those barbarian rebels will bow down to Bennvika within the year or be annihilated. Meanwhile, to raise our standing on the world stage, we will use our position within the Verusantian Empire as Governor of Bruskannia to create an alliance with the emperor and to strengthen the trade agreements between our two nations. We also intend to continue our marriage alliance with Medrodor, by marrying the Dowager Queen Accutina, King Lissoll's young widow.'

There was a murmur of sympathy for Accutina over Lissoll's death, with various people voicing their agreement with Jostan's plan.

'In addition,' he continued. 'We declare the unborn child of my future wife and the late king to be our own heir, as if he were our very own son. With the military security and increased trade that these political ties will bring, Bennvika will be richer and more secure than she has ever been before.'

There was another cheer, but as it died down a congressor stood. He was a short man in his mid-fifties, with brown curly hair, flecked with grey.

'We all acknowledge your right to the throne, Your Grace-'

'You will call us 'your *Majesty*'. I am an easterner and you will use the eastern term of deference.'

'My apologies, your Majesty. But may I ask, as you are also the Governor of Bruskannia, will you not, therefore, be the Verusantian emperor's vassal? Would you have us all bow down to him?'

Jostan gave the smile he always showed to people who questioned him; delighting in the man's silent indignation.

'No, Congressor Dongrath, he is only our liege lord with regards to how we run our territories within the Empire. He holds no power over our kingdom here.' This, of course, was a complete lie. The emperor had even promised to supply Jostan with five thousand mercenaries, though when they would be setting sail for Bennvika Jostan couldn't be sure. Even so, despite his knowledge that the emperor expected Jostan to be his vassal in every way, Jostan had no intention of submitting to any master except for the Divine.

Unable to counter Jostan's statement, Dongrath sat back down. Another, rather more elderly congressor stood up stiffly.

'Your Majesty, it is widely recognised the Verusantian Empire is home to many powerful oligarchs whose ambitions threaten the peace within their nation and whose wealth gives them the means to act on it. Would you have that happen here?'

Jostan laughed patronisingly.

'Having seen the fine houses and castles that you and many of your esteemed colleagues here inhabit, Congressor Nasren and knowing our Bennvikan history, we'd say that happened here centuries ago.' Nasren looked far from satisfied with the answer, but he sat back down, evidently not daring to press the point further.

'However, we do have our connections within the Empire,' Jostan continued. 'And that will allow us to have a political presence there in the way that Bennvika has never had in the past. If Bennvika wants something from the Verusantians, then for the first time, Bennvika will get it, under our reign! Ladies, gentlemen, a new era of Bennvikan greatness has dawned. An era of honour, riches and bloody conquest.'

The entire room erupted and this soon developed into chants of 'Jostan! Jostan! Jostan!'

With a royal wave, followed by his customary smirk, Jostan turned and left.

When he returned to Kriganheim Palace, he headed straight for the women's quarters. Once there, he immediately spotted Accutina sitting at the far end of the room, engrossed in her sewing. One of her maids was seated across the room from her, playing a lute, while another sat behind her mistress, styling her tawny hair into curls. Next to the plainly dressed maids, Accutina looked even more ravishing than usual.

The dress she wore on this particular day was sapphire blue, decorated with gold patterns and lining; the low cleavage accentuating the perfect form of her small breasts, though having seen them, Jostan knew just how much help the dress was giving with regards to size. He smiled at the memory, then cleared his throat, causing all three women to look up with a start, before dropping what they were doing, standing and curtseying.

'Leave us,' Accutina instructed her maids.

'So, how was it?' she enquired once they were alone with both of the room's doors firmly shut.

'As well as could be expected, though Congressor Salanath was absent. One or two others attempted a token gesture of resistance, but they may as well not have done for all the trouble it caused. It was as if a puppet attempted a dispute with its puppeteer.'

Accutina grinned at the analogy.

'And what of our proposed marriage?' she asked.

'They accepted it. Luckily for us, they seem to feel sorry for Lissoll's poor, grief-stricken widow.'

'I must remember to be overcome with sorrow when I make my next public appearance,' Accutina laughed. 'And what of the maid?'

'She will be executed and suitably, an accident has befallen the physician. It's a pity we can't do that with anyone else. But their fates should act as a warning to others to keep their mouths shut,' Jostan assured her.

'Excellent. Now all that remains is to gain my father's approval and the alliance remains intact. That'll be a mere formality once he reads my letter's heartfelt plea.'

'Is he a doting father then?'

'No, just a pompous old fool who's easily led. A few lines about how gracious and generous it'd make him look should do the trick,' Accutina beamed. Jostan reciprocated, but in a moment his mood changed, as he suddenly recalled an awkward memory.

'Of course, we're very lucky to be in this position,' he said.

'Why? Everything went exactly to plan.' Accutina looked confused at the sudden change in tone.

'It nearly didn't. Luckily we were able to turn things to our advantage, but nevertheless, your eagerness to lay the blame on Princess Silrith almost revealed our whole plan. 'It must be poison',' he quoted her, mockingly. 'That could have waited until the physician had confirmed it and announced his diagnosis. Did it not occur to you that you are not a doctor and that someone might wonder how you, a pampered queen, might be aware of the symptoms? At that point he wasn't even dead yet.'

'I panicked.'

'Why? As you said yourself, everything was going to plan.'

'My apologies for not playing the part faultlessly after having my own husband poisoned! It's not a regular habit of mine.'

'You dare speak to us this way. We swear on the graves of our ancestors that if you were anyone else we would-'

'-But I'm not anyone else. I am Accutina Vaaltanen, Princess of Medrodor, soon again to be called Queen of Bennvika and most of all mother of *your* unborn child.'

The calming tone of her voice over those last few words seemed to have a positive effect on Jostan and Accutina took his face in her hands tenderly, her big eyes now full of love and wet with happy tears.

'The error was mine, my love,' she admitted. 'But none appeared to notice and now Bennvika is yours.' She placed his hand on her belly. He smiled, looking down at her barely perceptible bump as he felt it, then looked back into her eyes.

'Show your new subjects that they will be forced to fly *with* the wrath you will bring, because to fly in the face of it will bring about only their destruction,' she told him. 'That way you will be able to honour almighty Estarron for his blessing by converting them to his worship.'

He thought for a moment, then smiled grimly.

'Not all will convert as willingly as you did. But once we have defeated the Hentani, the people will follow me unquestioningly and will honour him. They will beg for his divine Grace or be cast out. They will be too fearful to dare to question our route to the throne, or our stance on our relationship with the Empire and our position will be safe, as will yours. Almost all of the major nobles across the land are here in Kriganheim because of the king's death. We intend to send them back to their provinces with orders to raise an army. It will be as if we were the intended heir all along. We are doing Estarron's work here, but we must be patient. First, we must prepare the army for the coming campaign. It is vital that we start by securing a quick victory and use it to set a precedent; to make a statement loud and clear. We vow that we will put every man, woman and child of the Hentani tribe to the sword. We will prove in barbarian blood that only two entities rule this kingdom now – our ambition and our will. The ambition and will of the king.'

Chapter 3

For Silrith it had seemed like there was precious little chance of many nobles standing against Jostan with any strength. They had too much to lose by doing so. Oprion's visit had reinforced this view, but she had received a subsequent visit from another politician. He had said he could do nothing more to prevent her exile, but may be able to help her in the longer term by destabilising Jostan. That could take weeks, months, or even years and all the while she would have simply to wait. She had no idea what the conditions of her exile would be. Would she live in relative comfort, or would she be left to starve? How realistic was it to suggest that she'd even survive the first week? She had no idea. But at least here was a man prepared to risk his life for her.

The same could not be said for the majority of the nobles though. They had no pity for anyone else. She was well aware that one wouldn't have had to travel far from the shining white tiles of the Congressate Hall to see that, rather than fighting for justice, the true priorities many congressors were rather different from what Silrith believed they should be. Aside from her own predicament, she had long been aware that this vying for power and wealth was greatly affecting the lives of the common people of Bennvika.

SEVARBY, ASRANTICA, BENNVIKA

By now it was early spring. Jithrae was up early that morning and with the sun still low in the sky he left his wife and four children sleeping, before eating a breakfast of bread and water, then taking his work tools outside to start the day. He was two years shy of forty, with a bushy black beard and though he dreamed daily of a comfortable, easy life, he was as poor as he had ever been, with barely any more status than the lowliest vagrant. But at least he had a roof over his head. He lived with his family on a farm on the outskirts of the little town of Sevarby, which lay over a hundred miles southeast of Kriganheim, just over the provincial border into Asrantica.

Soon it would be the time of year when most of his days would be spent planting and weeding; a relentless battle against the wild plants that would choke his crop. Now though, as it had been for the preceding month or so, it was the time where a farmer's work is largely based around ploughing and fertilising. Ploughing was in itself a job he didn't mind, but like many others, his family could not afford a plough of their own, so they shared one with a number of other families and this often caused complications. Fertilising, however, in which he was engaged at this moment, was a most laborious task, which Jithrae had hated doing when he was younger due to its sheer repetitiveness, though by now he was well used to it. To lighten the load, all the local farming families would support each other throughout the year by picking up animal manure, so that it could be used as a fertiliser the following year.

As he worked through the morning, he started to pick up the smell of the bread his wife, Mirtsana, always made for their family. Looking uphill towards his house, he took a deep breath, enjoying the rich smell as it filled his nostrils.

'You there! Are you Jithrae of Sevarby?'

Jithrae's reverie was interrupted and his heart leapt as he heard the shout from far behind him. Taken by surprise, he spun around as he got to his feet, looking to see where the voice had come from. Around two hundred metres further down the hill, he spotted a single horseman, flanked by twenty or thirty more troops on foot.

'Yes, I go by that name. Who are you?' Jithrae replied, nervously moving to where he'd left his array of crude, sharp tools.

The horseman didn't answer. He simply kicked his mount into a trot uphill towards Jithrae, motioning for the troops behind him to stay where they were. As the man approached, Jithrae could see that he was a soldier; more specifically a professional soldier from one of the province's divisios.

His fear rose as he noted the transverse black and white horsehair crest on the top of the man's highly sculpted helmet. Evidently the stranger was a man of some importance. He wore an emerald green cloak that billowed out behind him as he rode. Jithrae saw that he sported a similarly coloured knee-length tunic under his waist-length chain mail, overlaid with segmented armour to protect his shoulders. He wore steel greaves on his shins, with sandals on his feet and was heavily armed carrying a short sword, a throwing axe and a dagger in his weapons belt, though it appeared he had deemed a shield unnecessary today.

Finally, the soldier pulled up in front of Jithrae, though he did not take off his helmet.

'Vinnitar Rhosgyth, Chief Invicturion of Asrantica,' he stated in a formal and rather sinister tone. 'I hereby claim these lands in the name of Congressor Feddilyn Rintta, Governor of Asrantica. You have a right to continue living here, but on the condition that the noble governor may claim up to a quarter of your annual harvest. If you do not agree, you will leave before sunrise tomorrow. Regrettably, however, I will require your answer rather sooner than that.'

'But this is common land,' said Jithrae.

'No longer,' Vinnitar replied bluntly.

'What does your master need with this land? You mean to starve us? How are we gonna survive?'

Vinnitar chuckled smugly, before leaning down towards Jithrae.

'It's very simple. If you don't want your family to starve, make sure you have a good harvest,' he sneered. An aristocrat like him clearly had no concern for commoners. A moment later Jithrae noticed the invicturion shift his gaze over Jithrae's shoulder to something nearer the house. He turned to see that his wife and their sixteen-year-old daughter, Vaezona, had come to the door to see what was going on while keeping the younger children inside. Evidently sensing Jithrae's fear rising, Vinnitar gave a dark grin.

'Oh my, what lovely ladies. Be quick about your decision Jithrae, because I might just decide to hurry you along. Those two look to be just the kind my boys would enjoy.'

'You dare threaten my family,' Jithrae cried. He picked up a pitchfork from the collection of tools lying on the ground and wielded it wildly at the invicturion, but he stopped short of actually stabbing him with it. Vinnitar laughed and jumped to the ground, opening his arms.

'You can't do it, can you? Peasants! Come on you funny little man. Hit me. Stab me through the chest. Impale me on your mighty fork.'

Insulted, Jithrae tried to look serious, hoping his face conveyed the level of menace he felt inside him, but he was too fearful. With all his strength he thrust the fork forward at Vinnitar's chest, but the soldier simply side-stepped the attack, wrenched the fork from Jithrae's grip and whacked him over the head with the handle, knocking him to the ground.

Jithrae's ears were ringing as he tried to get back to his feet and reach the weapon, which Vinnitar had thrown down on the grass. Instead, he only found the tip of the officer's sword now hovering over his throat, stilling him.

'Will you let me speak to my family?' Jithrae asked, not knowing what else to do.

'It's a bit late for that,' Vinnitar sneered. 'It appears you need help making your decision, so I've made it for you. We're taking this land. Be gone by tomorrow or you will all be put to the sword.'

'You can't just take our land. I won't let you,' screamed a female voice from behind Jithrae.

'Vaezona, no!' he heard Mirtsana shout and Jithrae saw his daughter charge straight at Vinnitar; kitchen knife in hand, but the soldier simply laughed as he effortlessly parried the blow with his sword, knocking her weapon flying to one side. The girl's momentum carried her straight into him and with his free hand he grabbed her and turned her to face her family, bringing the sword to her neck.

'Oh dear, now look what you made me do. Stupid girl. One false move and she dies.'

Seeing this, his men had started to run towards them to assist their Invicturion, but he raised his hand to halt them, without even turning his head.

There was a momentary stand-off between Vinnitar and the family. He withdrew his sword and sheathed it, but kept his other arm around Vaezona's torso; preventing her from moving her arms. While doing this, he turned and reached with his free hand towards the kit bag that hung from the side of the horse.

'What are you doing?' asked Jithrae, getting to his feet. In a flash, the blade was back at Vaezona's throat.

'I said no false moves, Jithrae. Do you want her to die?' Vaezona looked straight at her father, tears streaming, her bottom lip quivering and mouthed 'No'. That, along with the menacing look in Vinnitar's eye, was enough to wither Jithrae. The soldier again sheathed his weapon and with one hand pulled out some rope from the kit bag. He bound Vaezona's wrists tightly behind her back, then roughly threw her on to the back of his horse. Her whimpers turned to wails, which pierced Jithrae's heart, but she clearly knew that to offer up any more resistance than that would only bring her end.

Jithrae knew the same. It was all he could do to stop himself from attacking Vinnitar with his bare hands there and then, but he knew he was more than outnumbered.

'I'll come for you, Vaezona,' he cried, not knowing what else he could do. Vinnitar simply laughed as he remounted the horse. Then with one last sneering grin, he turned and kicked, cantering back towards his men. He called out to his second in command.

'Corpralis. Mark this land down for cultivation. The inhabitants are evicted.'

'Very good, Sir.'

This act will not go without retribution, Vinnitar Rhosgyth. You stole my beloved daughter, but I will get her back, Jithrae thought. *On my life, I promise you that.*

His eyes narrowed and his blood ran hot with rage as he watched Vinnitar trotting away without a care in the world, calmly giving the orders to make it official that Jithrae's family had lost their home as easily as if he were telling a tavern owner to fetch him a mug of ale.

SAVIKTASTAD CASTLE, SAVIKTASTAD, ASRANTICA, BENNVIKA

Three days later, a large feast was taking place at Saviktastad Castle, the home of Feddilyn Rintta, Governor of Asrantica. One of the many guests was minor Asrantican noble named Zethun Maysith.

At twenty-two years of age, he had a thin face with short, brown hair and ever-serious eyes. He had recently become the head of his household following the passing of his father after a short but violent fever, though this most recent bereavement made the Maysiths a household of one. After a life poisoned out of any happiness by the loss of loved ones, he felt strangely disconnected from any feelings of grief that maybe he should have been experiencing, having gone through the process many times for someone so young. Instead, he was instinctively driven to focus solely on the progress of his burgeoning political career.

He hoped that his newfound status would bring him more influence and a place within the Congressate was a real possibility, although there were other political paths to consider too. That was the only reason that he had accepted Lord Feddilyn's invitation. Feasts like this were designed to bring opportunities to form and nurture political alliances. Meeting some of these eminent people would help him decide which path to take. To create the right impression, he wore his best white tunic and breeches; the former featuring shining, golden, flame-like patterns on the chest.

The glowing, candlelit room was square, with a relatively low roof held up by large pillars and filled with four long tables. These were arranged in a square formation around the room's centre and were piled high with a myriad of delicacies. Some guests sat at the tables, while others hovered around the edges of the room.

The walls were adorned with the Rintta family crest, a white trident on a black background, as well as various other designs in the family colours, interspersed with portraits of long-dead distinguished members of the Rintta family. Some musicians sat in the background playing lutes and an assortment of woodwind instruments and in the centre of the room, dancers performed gracefully.

Zethun had little interest in the arts and when he spotted his host, he decided to greet him, taking his chalice of wine with him. Feddilyn was dressed in a gaudy purple tunic with gold lining and by now Zethun guessed him to be in his late fifties or early sixties, as his long hair and bushy beard still held a hint of their original blond colour.

'Ah, young Zethun,' Feddilyn exclaimed, slapping him around the shoulder boisterously. 'I'm so glad you could attend. I was desolated to hear of your father's untimely death. Allow me to express my sincerest condolences, though I believe that congratulations are also in order.' A wry grin appeared on the ageing man's face. 'I have been hearing that you have plans to join the ranks of the Congressate. That would bring in some much needed young energy and ambition to compensate for the withered old fools that fill the Congressate Hall, wouldn't you say?'

'Err, well, I thank you for your kind words, Lord Rintta and I must congratulate you too on this fine feast,' said Zethun, smiling awkwardly at the governor's words, as Feddilyn himself was also a congressor and Zethun didn't know if he was being tested.

'The Congressate certainly has its appeal,' he continued evasively. 'But I've yet to make a final decision. There are other political paths to consider and I think there are a few characters within the Congressate who might find some of my ideas a little hard to swallow.'

'Nonsense. Your father was a respected man and anyhow, influencing those old codgers isn't too difficult once you're established. Having a strong presence in the Congressate isn't about what your ideas are. It's about gaining enough authority to make people listen. It all centres on politics, Zethun. Politics! Politics! Politics!'

'So, how do I gain this authority? Aside from their loyalty to the royal family, the only authority the congressors respect is that which is gained through land and money.'

Feddilyn took a gulp of wine and shrugged.

'It's simple, Zethun. Just do what your father did. All you have to do is add more land to what your family already has and make it profitable.'

'Add?' Zethun countered; his opinion of his host quickly changing as it dawned on him what Feddilyn was suggesting. He didn't like the insinuations about his father either. Moyavedd Maysith had been the son of a blacksmith who had risen to catch King Bastinian's eye through intelligence, wit and his tireless study of the law. The land and the manor house had simply come with the job.

'Yes,' said Feddilyn. 'It's only common land I grant you, but with a little work...'

'Does that not risk a revolt though if so many people are displaced?'

Feddilyn gave a light laugh.

'We give them homes, don't we? They should be grateful for that. All we ask of them is a share in their harvest.'

'As all noblemen must, clearly,' Zethun said, keeping a blank face.

'Of course,' said Feddilyn, visibly trying to read Zethun's expression.

'Zethun, you are young and full of idealism. With that passion and energy, you would be a useful ally to me in the Congressate. Think on what I have said.'

Feddilyn patted Zethun on the shoulder.

'Now if you'll excuse me. Ah, Erritwyn,' he said, getting the attention of another guest.

Zethun was still thinking about what Feddilyn had said when he exited the castle to leave later that evening. As he called for a boy to bring his horse, he heard a hurried cry from behind him.

'Zethun, wait.'

He turned and saw that an elderly congressor had followed him out. Zethun recognised the man but couldn't place him. He looked rather out of breath.

'I must speak with you,' the man said, gathering himself.

Zethun's mind raced as he tried to remember the stranger's name.

'Hoban Salanath,' the man said, smiling, as if reading his mind, while shaking Zethun's hand firmly. 'You probably don't remember me. You were but a small boy of not more than, oh, ten or twelve I should think, when we last met. Your father and I were good friends and I'm afraid the Congressate will be very much worse off for his loss.'

'Well I hope I can live up to his standard, Congressor Salanath,' Zethun replied, sensing genuine feeling in Hoban's words and glad that his failure to recall his name hadn't caused any offence.

'Only time will tell, but there are more forms of power than becoming a congressor. Do not choose that path simply because your father did. I saw that you were speaking with old Feddilyn there?'

'Yes, I was,' Zethun said, interested to see where Hoban was going with this.

'Be careful. He has already made himself a close ally of the new king. I guarantee anything you say to him will soon reach the king's ears.'

Zethun smiled. Evidently Hoban and Feddilyn were not the best of friends, but then again this was politics. He'd have to pick a side sooner or later.

'At the moment it may prove difficult to get him to come around to my politics, let alone the king himself, but with my policies I am aware that will be the case with much of the Congressate,' Zethun said.

'Interesting,' said Hoban. 'What form could such radical ideas take?'

'I believe that while this kingdom requires strong leadership, many men and women abuse the system and take far more than they need. The common people need to be led, but they must also be protected from such extravagance. Any politics that continues to take advantage of the people will surely end in revolt.'

'That is indeed a great risk,' Hoban sighed. 'But if those are your views, a position as a congressor might not be the right path for you. You will be able to fight for the rights of the common people much more if you were to become one of Kriganheim's demokroi. The city's next public assembly is very soon, so if the position appeals to you I suggest you travel there sooner rather than later. I have my contacts and I should have no trouble helping you become appointed, but while I do that you should take the time to get to know the local people. That will help you win their support.'

'I will think on it, but I would certainly be most grateful for your assistance, Congressor Salanath.'

'Oh please, call me Hoban,' the old man chuckled.

'I would be most grateful for that – Hoban,' Zethun said; slightly uncertain, wondering if he had found an ally promising genuine support after all.

'I thank you for your offer,' Zethun went on. 'But there is just one thing. Before formally accepting I must have your word that my acceptance would mean that I will be allowed to be influenced by no factor other than the will of the common people. Many of the demokroi are simply pawns for one congressor or another. I will not be one of those.'

'It warms my heart to hear you say that, Zethun,' Hoban said, putting his arm around the younger man as they slowly walked towards Zethun's horse, which a boy had just brought round. 'I can see that you do not want to compromise on your principles. An alliance between you and Feddilyn would force you to do that. Stick to what you believe. This will be a hard fight that requires the energy of a younger person such as yourself. I assure you that if I had any ulterior motives I would have already attempted to put them into practice. But as you see, now I am just an old man without the energy to fight a battle that I now realise that I should have started many, many years ago. It's not something I can do on my own, but together, Zethun, together we can win this fight.' He clasped both Zethun's hands and looked straight into his eyes as he spoke. 'Will you agree?'

Zethun still sensed that Hoban might have another reason for wanting to be back in Kriganheim, but he also saw some sincerity in his face.

'Well Hoban, you flatter me with a most appealing offer, yet I must give it some thought first. I am soon to head home to Kriganheim anyway. I've no family left now, so I plan to sell my Asrantican estate and live a frugal life in an ordinary city house. Would it be agreeable if we could meet again in Kriganheim and I could give you my answer then?'

'Of course,' Hoban smiled, looking surprised. 'I look forward to hearing your answer.'

'Then I will see you in Kriganheim, my friend,' Zethun assured him with a polite bow of his head.

Chapter 4

THE PREDDABURG CITADEL, RILDAYORDA, BASTALF, BENNVIKA

'So what answer will you give?' Yathrud heard his son Bezekarl ask. They were in one of Yathrud's private rooms in the citadel of Preddaburg, situated at the north of the coastal city of Rildayorda.

Yathrud, Governor of the southern province of Bastalf and Silrith's uncle by marriage, stood reading the letter that had been brought to him, while Bezekarl sat at the mahogany table and ate.

Not one to let his emotions show, Yathrud contained his private rage so that outwardly he maintained a veneer of control and strength. Untamed anger was never the answer.

He was a tall man of fifty-five, with long grey hair and a silver beard. He wore a dark blue tunic and black breeches. The seventeen-year-old Bezekarl was similarly attired, though his tunic was green. He too had a thick head of hair, though he lacked the flowing golden locks with which Yathrud had attracted many a female in his youth. Instead, his was black, but his lack of effort to tame it was its defining feature and as a result, it resembled an overly-used mop and his beard was a scraggly mess. Yathrud had long since given up trying to convince him to address such things.

Hanging on the walls along with various portraits was the Alyredd family standard, a vertical column of three golden dragons on a scarlet background.

As for the Preddaburg citadel itself, it had been built on a hill that overlooked the city, so the large windows on the room's south wall saw that it was well lit and it was also the perfect spot from which to survey the full view of Bennvika's newest provincial capital in all its glory.

The interior of Yathrud's quarters were no less impressive; the place was full of luxurious couches and cushions. Sitting himself down opposite Bezekarl at the large table that formed the room's centrepiece, Yathrud silently reread the letter again. Bezekarl waited patiently for an answer.

This latest development put Yathrud in a difficult position, as he was the first member of his family to be the governor of any of Bennvika's provinces. This reward and his reputation had been hard won on campaign with King Lissoll; just a prince at the time. Together they had taken this land, bringing civilisation and order to those of the Hentani tribe that lived here. In just a few years, the former Hentani town had grown to a great Bennvikan port city, Rildayorda. This name, given to it by the Bennvikans meant 'City of the Wilds,' but in truth, it was anything but that. Already, with its great temple, its theatre and with the beauty of the citadel itself, Rildayorda was fast becoming the jewel of the south; an honour of a gift to be sure.

But Lissoll's favour towards Yathrud had come at the price of great jealousy from the other nobles, especially once the prince had become king. This would not make the task he now faced any easier, but it was his sense of honour that made up Yathrud's mind. After all, Silrith was family. That had been another reward for his military successes and his closeness to Lissoll; a marriage to Lissoll's younger sister, Princess Monissaea, making him Silrith's uncle.

'There is only one response, my son and you well know what it is,' Yathrud said eventually, with a deliberate mix of calm and assertiveness.

'Err, this one,' he told a female servant who had entered and brought him two meals. He pointed to indicate his choice, a plate of beef surrounded by raisins and apple slices instead of one bearing similarly dressed lamb. He called for another servant and in moments one came forward, a young man this time, who had been waiting almost invisibly at the side of the room in case called upon.

'Burn this,' Yathrud instructed him, handing him the letter. The servant took it with a bow and headed towards the door, followed by the girl carrying the rejected lamb. Yathrud waited for them to pass through and click the door shut, leaving him alone in the room with his son. Then the old lord turned his attention back to Bezekarl.

'The slander that letter contains is an absolute outrage,' he said, grimacing as the ungainly Bezekarl tucked into a leg of chicken in a most ignoble fashion. He couldn't have been more different from his cousin Silrith. Yathrud thought of the happy memories of Silrith's childhood and teenage years. He may not generally have been one to take much notice of children,

63

but ever since her birth, Yathrud's bond with Silrith had been something to cherish. He remembered teaching her to be headstrong, of telling her stories of his battles and of giving her a sword on her sixteenth birthday. Initially, unbeknown to Yathrud at the time, she had taken the weapon with her when she had visited her friend Lord Oprion Aethelgard, who had subsequently trained her in its use, though she had told him of this in a letter. The fact that it had also been Yathrud who had accidentally given away to her father that she was learning to use the sword rather than owning it simply as an ornament, was a painful memory. Yathrud hoped he wasn't the cause of some of the evidence that Jostan was distorting to sully Silrith's reputation. When he had found out, King Lissoll had flown into a rage and Silrith, amid much scandal, had been banned from going back to Hazgorata to visit Oprion for over a year.

However, her ban had eventually been lifted and as far as Yathrud knew, the swordplay tuition had started right back up again. Yet now it seemed that her strength of character and her unwillingness to behave in a way that was usually expected of women in her position were the very personality traits that were being used against her by Jostan. The boiling rage at this was all too much for Yathrud, who was struggling to contain his anger.

'He goes too far. If only the other governors knew the princess like I do, they'd read this message and see that every word that is said here about her is a slanderous lie. I held the princess when she was but a tiny infant. I helped mould her into the woman she is. I think I have known her long enough to know her mind and her heart.'

'It will certainly come as a surprise to the Congressate,' replied Bezekarl. 'They expected Silrith to be named queen. Surely at least one or two of them know her well?'

'I do wish you'd refer to her as the princess rather than just use her name. She is of royal blood and you are only the son of a provincial governor. You'd do well to remember that.'

'Sorry, father.'

'But, that aside, you are right. It will be a surprise to the Congressate, but I can't see them having the stomach to take Jostan on in a political fight. That falls to us.' Yathrud relented.

He smiled at the incredulous look on Bezekarl's face, as his son clearly had no idea what to read into that last statement.

'Father, I know what you're thinking. But are you sure it is wise? Have you considered what might happen to us?'

'Not for a moment and I intend to keep it that way so as not to change my mind. I intend to do what is right, not simply what is safe.'

'Can you really be that sure of what the Congressate will do?'

Yathrud laughed as he chewed his food.

'There are few societies more predictable than the Congressate. Their powers on this issue are highly limited.'

Over the years Yathrud had tried his best to school his son well in the world of politics. He knew, or at least he sincerely hoped, that Bezekarl would remember that the only way the Congressate could deny Jostan his kingship would be to vote unanimously to declare him an enemy of the state and that would surely never happen. To name a person an enemy of the state was often seen as a last resort and if it concerned an individual of power, it was a risky move to orchestrate. Only when it was a unanimous vote could such a law be passed and once it did, it would be every citizen's duty to kill the person it denounced, or assist another to do so. To have this happen to a monarch though would be utterly unprecedented. The only monarchs to be deposed in Bennvikan history had been removed through military rebellion.

'The Congressate will be no obstacle at all for Jostan,' said Yathrud. 'It is full of old politicians with no stomach for a fight. He's probably brought them to heel already.'

'Yet they do have their uses, father, don't you think?' Bezekarl said, refilling his wine cup.

'What I think is that their uses may be about to become especially superficial,' said Yathrud. 'In fact, some would say that it is already the truth that in practice they are nothing more than a tool to help the king control the common people. That is why it falls to us to take matters into our own hands.'

Bezekarl still looked concerned by the prospect, but Yathrud simply smiled.

'Gasbron,' he called, 'Bring the messenger back in.'

The door behind them opened and dressed in his segmented armour, chain mail, green tunic and cape, Yathrud's battle-hardened, dark, scarred, clean-shaven chief invicturion marched the messenger back into the room. Yathrud smiled again as he stood, turning to face the messenger.

'Tell the king that we most heartily accept his demands and that we greet this news with the utmost pleasure.'

'I will do so, my Lord.' The messenger bowed and left. Once he had heard the messenger's footsteps grow distant enough, Yathrud turned to Gasbron, keeping his lined face cold and stern.

'Gasbron, I have a job for you.'

THE HALAEVIA VALLEY, ASRANTICA, BENNVIKA

Riding through the Asrantican hills, Zethun revelled in the solitude he'd been starved of for the past few days. Most nobles wouldn't have dreamt of travelling alone and would be accompanied by an entourage of bodyguards and servants, sometimes with trains of fifteen or twenty wagons. Zethun would have none of that. No, for him, some bags for his luggage, a dagger for defence and his horse for company would more than suffice.

The green of the hills and the clarity of the soft country air also gave one a chance to reflect. His interactions with Lord Feddilyn Rintta and Congressor Hoban Salanath had given him much to consider. For sure, he knew that he was much against everything that Lord Feddilyn represented. The man believed in nothing but the expectation that the poor should live at the mercy and the whims of the rich; an idea shared by much of the nobility, as Zethun had long known. The question was how to tackle this. Hoban's offer suggested one path, but Zethun still had the niggling feeling that there may be more to Hoban than first met the eye.

As he was thinking this, he began to hear many distant voices and he saw a cloud of dust rising from far below him, between the hills. Intrigued, he turned his horse in the direction of the Halaevia Valley, the main pass through Asrantica's great natural beacons. Cresting one of the tall, grassy hills, he looked down to find the valley teeming with people, carts and pack animals.

Seeing the sheer weight of humanity on the move took Zethun's breath away. This was no army, but a rabble of desperate people, marching headlong up the northern pass. Zethun guessed they must be bound for Kriganheim, displaced from their homes by Feddilyn. This was the cost of one man's greed. He knew that Feddilyn wanted to gain further riches through the export of Asrantica's natural resources and the extortion of his subjects; thus filling his pockets with gold and increasing his influence with the new king. But here was proof of the effect this was having on the province. Clearly Feddilyn didn't care that his plan left the people of his own lands with the choice of either starving or escaping.

From his lofty position cresting hilltop after hilltop, he followed the column of refugees for a time, wondering if any of them had any idea what they would actually do when they got to Kriganheim, if indeed that was where they were heading. He guessed that most of them would at least try to settle there, but he was sure that as the legions of starving people kept entering the city, the locals would become less and less welcoming. Such is the terrible hate that lies within people the world over, even those who think themselves good, he surmised sorrowfully.

All this could be avoided if it wasn't for the greed of the rich. That made up his mind for him. It may be a risk to make a political alliance with Hoban, as Zethun still had his reservations about his trustworthiness, but it was a risk he had to take. Too much was at stake for Zethun to worry about the risks to him personally or to his career.

Chapter 5

THE FOREST OF USTAHERTA, USTENNA, BENNVIKA

Downtrodden, dishonoured, vilified, helpless, shocked. Poor Silrith's brain was running out of words to describe how she was feeling about what had happened to her. It was some days now since her arrest, but still her mind was continuing inexorably around the same old circle; the same old maze. Confused, violated, scared, angry, vengeful. Alone. Totally, undeniably, alone.

There was one emotion she felt most strongly of all though and in a way it surprised her which one it was – disappointment. Specifically disappointment that many people whom she had trusted and thought would show her loyalty, had betrayed her at the first sign of a shift in power. She felt sure that there must have been people in that room who knew inside that she would never have even dreamt of harming her father, let alone murdering him. But it was apparent that the sacrifice of her life and her dignity was a price they were willing to pay to further their own advancement. Trust, it seemed, would be a luxury she would no longer be able to afford.

Oprion's refusal to risk his own neck was by far the most galling, but there were others. One such example was Sankil, the High Priest of Bennvika, who had, among others, served as her tutor when she was a child. He was the man who had taught her to read and write so that she could learn about her ancestors and worship Vitrinnolf and Lomatteva, the deified monarchs who had founded Bennvika. But he was also one of the people who had been too fearful for his own life to intervene when she needed him the most and despite his rank, he had meekly given in to Jostan without so much as breathing a word against him. In so doing he had cut her loose just like all the others did. But then again, she decided, she shouldn't be too surprised. Old Sankil was many things, but he had never been brave and he would be easily intimidated and manipulated by Jostan.

However, it seemed an unlikely hope now that anyone else would do anything different. She had more distant family elsewhere in other noble houses, but she couldn't see anything coming of that. Jostan had his stranglehold on power and surely by now everyone in the land could see the way the wind was blowing. There were still some sources of hope, some families who may decide to do the right thing and protect Bennvika from the new tyrant, but nothing could ever be guaranteed and many would be bought off easily enough.

The one thing Silrith still held on to was that, just as she thought she might, she had received a second visitor during her imprisonment, as was the man's way with political prisoners. He had thought of no way to get her out, but he had been otherwise accepting of her task. She hoped he would see it through. There always had to be hope. The future of Bennvika's people rested on that.

Also, underneath, hidden within her heart was another, darker emotion she was trying to suppress. Guilt. Though she had no intentional hand in it, she felt that her rank had brought about the death of one of her lady's maids, Afayna. With a shudder, she wondered if anything had befallen any of her other staff. But Afayna's death was all too certain.

Before she left Kriganheim Silrith's wrists had been bound together with rope that rubbed her skin raw. This had been attached to the back of a mule cart that carried some guards along with the driver as she walked behind. Clearly Jostan knew that Silrith was popular with the people, so he had ordered that they should leave the city in the dead of night, so as to avoid causing a riot, just a little over a day after her arrest. It was then that she had seen a sight that she would never forget.

The band of guardsmen were mostly militia, but two were divisiomen and as they had started to move down the first few streets, they had run into another group of guards. The two groups clearly knew each other. They stopped and began talking a while. She couldn't hear much of the conversation, but from what she could make out the other group were heading for Kriganheim Bridge.

'Sir, permission to have a look at the prisoner?' came a gruff voice.

'Of course,' came the noticeably more eloquent reply.

69

'Thank you, sir. Let's have a look-see at this little princess then, eh?' A broad, stout divisioman in scaled armour with the traditional green tunic and cape came into view, holding a blazing torch, followed by an invicturion in a transverse crested helmet. He roughly pulled her hair out of the way and held the torch so close to her face that the heat burned her skin.

'Whoa, we got ourselves a hot little slut here boys! I'm gonna have some fun with this. Let's have a go on this little whore.' More guards had gathered around her now, laughing and mocking her. The divisioman looked over to his superior for permission to continue.

'Go ahead. Don't hold back,' the invicturion said jovially. 'Take her. Give us some entertainment. Actually, why don't we place some bets, boys? I'd guess thirty seconds before he's done. Any advances on that?'

'Yeh! Twenty seconds!' someone else shouted, to raucous laughter.

'Go ahead soldier,' the officer said. 'Show us what you've got.'

With a toothy grin, the divisioman handed the torch to his superior, then lifted the front of his tunic's skirt from below his armour. He groped one of Silrith's breasts and cursed to himself as he tried to get some feeling down below. So far she had avoided any carnal attention from the guards during her short imprisonment and she was not about to let it happen now. Here was her chance.

She didn't know what possessed her to be so reckless, but instinctively she kicked her foot into the man's groin with all the force she could muster. He groaned in pain; his eyes full of shock. The other soldiers howled with laughter. Silrith met the divisioman's eyes with a defiant look. She realised how vulnerable she'd just made herself, but she didn't care. After all, she was the daughter of the warrior King Lissoll and granddaughter of Bastinian the Great. She steeled her nerve and prepared herself for whatever the soldier might do next.

The divisioman gathered himself and raised himself to full height. The laughter died down.

'Very clever. I'm gonna teach you a lesson. We've got a little present for this little whore, haven't we? Would you like to see it – *Princess*?'

Silrith didn't answer, but simply stared back resolutely.

'I think she would,' the divisioman said with certainty and the invicturion nodded his approval, clearly enjoying the spectacle. The divisioman was handed back the torch, as well as another object, but Silrith couldn't make out what it was in the darkness.

'Recognise this?' the divisioman sneered as he approached her again holding the object up to the light.

Silrith's eyes widened, her blood ran ice-cold and she just managed to stifle a shriek. By a fistful of hair, the man held Afayna's severed head. It stared back at Silrith as if in life. The expression of sheer terror may have gone from the rest of her bloodied face, but something in her eyes still retained some element of her final moments. Suddenly Silrith felt her bottom lip start to wobble uncontrollably. The divisioman laughed.

'Ha! Poor little princess. Not so brave now are we?' he jeered mockingly. 'Shall I give her a closer look?'

Handing the torch back again, he came right up to her, grabbed her by the hair and shoved the severed head in her face.

'Look! Look! Look!' he taunted her. 'Look! Look! Look!' The unseeing eyes permeated deep into hers, the stench filled her nostrils and she could even taste the dead skin as she desperately tried to move away, but the lifeless face was again and again thrust towards her.

Suddenly the divisioman withdrew a few steps as Silrith heard herself make an inhuman noise. Her insides convulsed and she vomited on the floor. Feeling that his pride was restored, the soldier exploded with laughter, as did his comrades.

'Oi! Keep walking.' A sudden pain in her back caused Silrith to snap back to the present. She had lost count of how many days had passed since the events of the night they left Kriganheim and the cart was now deep into the Forest of Ustaherta. Although they were travelling on a generally well-trodden track, the going was getting tough for Silrith, as she still had to walk behind the cart; her arms still tied to its back. The men taunted her mercilessly. One carried a whip and he would jump down from the cart and use it on her if he saw her slouching; something she was finding it harder and harder not to do.

The soles of her feet were being rubbed raw. She still wore the clothes that she had been wearing at the time of her denunciation by Jostan, or at least, the now ripped and muddied versions of the same. Her royal sandals simply weren't made to tolerate this kind of environment and as they deteriorated, the straps cut deep into her toes and ankles.

The cart was too tall and wide for her to see over or around it, so to stand any chance of knowing where they were heading, she had to strain her ears for clues she might be able to pick up by hearing snippets of the guards' conversations. The word 'Ganzig' was being mentioned more and more often, so she guessed the River Ganzig couldn't be far away. Deep into their journey, she was proven right in this.

There must have been a guard on the bridge because as they ground to a halt, she heard their driver say 'Oi, lads! Anyone got a couple of coins for the toll man?'

Having found some, the driver jumped off the cart.

It was then that Silrith was briefly aware of some movement in the trees to her right, just for a moment, but no one else seemed to notice, so she decided she must have imagined it, or maybe it had just been a bird or some other harmless animal.

Suddenly, the guards all gasped and shouted, drawing their weapons as if they'd spotted a threat up ahead. Some of them jumped off the cart and ran in the direction of the toll man, but before Silrith could gain any idea of what was happening up ahead, she heard a roar as three, no, five men in dark clothes charged out from within the tangle of trees, bellowing their challenge as they went. In their haste to aid their driver, the cart's guards had left their right flank exposed and two militiamen fell instantly, taken by surprise by their attackers. They were impaled on the ambushers' swords before they had any chance to fight back, leaving their comrades to turn to meet the new threat.

By the bridge, the astonished driver slid back off his attacker's sword and slumped on the ground. Stepping over the body, Gasbron sprinted forward to assist his men. The ambush had worked well, helped by his plain-clothed disguise, but the guards still numbered eight to their six and now the element of surprise had been lost. At least only two of the guards were soldiers of the divisios, whereas the others were lightly armed militiamen in steel kettle hats.

Gasbron wheeled his two-handed longsword above his head as a spearman ran towards him. He feigned to the left then dived to the right, causing the tip of the spear to flash past him and over his shoulder, exposing the soldier's chest. Instinctively Gasbron allowed his momentum to carry him into his opponent, the blade piercing the man's leather jerkin and impaling him. The spearman howled in pain and Gasbron held him by the shoulder as he ripped the sword out of him, pulling his guts with it and spilling them on the floor.

As he carried on running to reach his comrades, he saw another militiaman fall to his men's blades. The numbers were equal now. The two divisiomen stood firm, along with the four remaining militia. As Gasbron joined the fray, the nearest divisioman knocked one of Gasbron's men to the ground with his shield. He was about to give the killer blow, but hadn't spotted Gasbron, who slashed deeply into the side of his neck. The divisioman dropped his shield and pressed his hand to the wound as it gushed with blood, before slumping to the ground.

Gasbron ran to the back of the cart, deftly dispatching another militiaman as he did and, for the first time, Silrith's eyes met his. For a split second he was encapsulated by them; so mesmerising, dazzling, enamouring. Regaining himself, he raised his sword above his head and Silrith pulled the rope attaching her to the cart tight to achieve a quick and easy cut, wincing at the pain in her wrists as the rough rope tore deeper into her skin. Gasbron brought the sword slicing down on the rope with all his strength.

Silrith nearly stumbled backwards as the rope released its grip, but Gasbron caught her in his strong arms, sheathed his sword, took out his dagger to cut through the knot that bound her wrists. As he helped her get free of the rope, he again noticed those big dark eyes, but suddenly he saw them widen at something behind him. Dropping his dagger, he drew his sword and spun round to see a militiaman bearing down on him, but he had no chance of stopping the man piling into him and sending him sprawling. The swordsman came at him again, but as Gasbron parried the blow, his assailant was attacked from behind.

All Gasbron saw was a pair of hands holding a length of rope, which suddenly appeared from behind the man's head, followed by the surprised look on his face as it throttled him like a garrotte wire. To Gasbron's astonishment, the attacker was Silrith. She'd picked her moment perfectly. She twisted the rope tight and placed both ends of it in a strong fist. She picked up Gasbron's dagger and buried it in the man's neck, covering Gasbron in an explosion of blood. As the man put his hands over the wound he was ripped backwards, allowing Gasbron to get back to his feet.

The enemy soldier also tried to stand, but could only drop to his knees, coughing and spluttering as he bled a torrent of crimson. Silrith dropped the dagger and picked up the man's sword, standing before him. Then she spun on her heel with deadly elegance to strike him from the world with a speed that was almost merciful.

That should show these men I'm not some shrinking violet just because they saved me. Your lessons were useful after all, Oprion, Silrith thought to herself.

Silence fell around her. All of her captors were now dead and her six saviours, whoever they were, caught their breath and stared at her; wide-eyed at what they had just seen.

As she walked towards them, trying to look as though she was used to having someone else's blood on her clothes, all six men dropped to their knees and bowed low. Only one, a rugged, dark man in his thirties, evidently the group's leader, looked up to speak.

'My Queen, I bring word from your noble uncle, Lord Yathrud Alyredd. He acknowledges you as our rightful queen and offers you sanctuary in the comfort of his citadel at Preddaburg, as well as offering his army in support of your cause. Will you allow us to escort you to him?'

Silrith knew the question was virtually a formality, as she could hardly refuse, but she was impressed that the normal customs were still being observed, so she replied in the proper form.

'Why, of course,' she responded with a regal smile, while motioning for the men to stand. 'I would be most honoured to be your master's guest. I am deeply, deeply grateful for the intervention of you and your men, kind sir. What would be the names of the six brave soldiers who have come to my aid?'

'I am Gasbron Wrathun, Chief Invicturion of Bastalf, my Queen,' said the man. 'These are my men. Yortha, Telvaen, Kinsaf, Laevon and my corpralis, Candoc of Rildayorda.' With his long ginger hair and beard, Candoc's Bennvikan features didn't quite fit with his Hentani name and he could hardly have looked more different from his clean-shaven invicturion, Silrith mused.

'My Queen,' the five remaining men said harmoniously, briefly bowing their heads again. She politely bowed her head back to them in response, but then came an awkward moment where no one quite knew what to do or say next. Silrith's lessons in etiquette as a child hadn't accounted for scenarios such as these and probably none of these men had ever met a royal before. But then, given that they were assigned to serve the province of Bastalf, they had probably never expected to.

'All of you have put your lives at risk to rescue me and for that, I shall remember all your names, Gasbron, Yortha, Telvaen, Kinsaf, Laevon and Candoc,' Silrith said.

She looked at each one in turn as she said their name. Her royal training had at least taught her how to remember names and faces and how beneficial that could be. But aside from that, she decided she'd have to just make it up as she went along.

'So, shall we?' she asked cordially, indicating the cart, which had moved down the track a little, with the mules recovering from the scare of the skirmish.

'Of course, my Queen. Though please first permit us to clean the blood from our faces and weapons.'

'Certainly. I fear I too must be looking somewhat the worse for wear,' Silrith replied jovially. It was a façade of strength that she knew she had to put on. They looked suitably impressed with her bravery, but they had still saved her life and she didn't want to come across as cold.

A quick splash of water each from one of the cart's supply bottles and it was time to be on the move. As Gasbron lead her to the seat at the front of the cart, Silrith felt the searing pain in her feet and on her wrists begin to return as the adrenaline wore off, but she refrained from letting it show. As she reached to climb up, she was taken by surprise as Gasbron lifted her by the waist. Silrith was shocked. She certainly wasn't used to having so much physical contact with any man, especially one she'd just met and especially a commoner.

She said nothing though. These men had, after all, just saved her from exile and deserved her gratitude. What shocked her even more though was the fact that part of her had liked it; his strong arms around her body, his hot breath on the back of her neck, his- 'Silrith! Pull yourself together!' she heard her late mother's voice shout in her head and she swatted the thoughts from her mind. Gasbron had clambered up beside her, taking the reins and his men now sat in the back of the cart. He caught her eye momentarily as he sat down, then looked embarrassed for doing so and cracked the whip to move the cart forward towards the bridge.

Silrith bent down and slowly removed her sandals, biting down on her lip at the pain as she did. She'd have to do something to distract herself from her discomfort, she decided. She pursed her lips and tapped her fingers together subconsciously as she tried to think of an ice breaker.

'So...' she started uncertainly. 'Have you served my uncle for long?'

'Twelve years; almost since I first joined the army,' Gasbron answered monotonously, looking dead ahead.

'What's it like being a soldier? You said that you hold the reward name 'Wrathun'. You must have done something pretty brave and exciting to win that?' she asked enthusiastically. *Perhaps he'll respond better if I show an interest in him*, she thought. Anyway, she'd always been fascinated by soldiers and she had often wished that she'd been born a boy so that she could be one too. Common women could join the army and achieve the highest of ranks, but the women of the nobility and royal family generally had other expectations placed on their shoulders. Nevertheless, Silrith's nannies had always had a nightmare trying to stop her from beating up the little boys at court when she was small, but fight she did and win she did also.

'Soldiering has its good parts,' Gasbron said dismissively.

Oh sweet mercy, this is going to be a long journey, Silrith thought. Nevertheless, she waited patiently for Gasbron to continue. He must have felt her eyes on him, because he looked around at her awkwardly as he drove. She raised her eyebrows and tilted her head to indicate her further interest.

76

After travelling for what must have been at least three increments of the sundial, it was late afternoon, but being spring, it would be light for a fair while yet.

'...and so it turned out that after all that, he had no talent for falconry at all,' Silrith sniggered, as she finished a story about a young nobleman who had once tried to impress her with his falconry skill, only to find that she was much better at it than he was.

'Sounds like he was all talk and no trousers, my Queen, if you'll pardon the expression.'

After the initial awkwardness, Gasbron had lightened up a bit and while the men in the back of the cart talked amongst themselves, the two of them were getting to know each other a little.

'Quite right,' said Silrith.

As she said that she suddenly realised that Gasbron had probably never even had the opportunity to try falconry before.

'Of course, I don't mind if someone realises they lack certain skills or experience. It's when they think they're something special and then can't back up their boasts that always looks childish in my opinion,' she said.

'I couldn't agree more, my Queen. I've lost count of the number of cocky little bastards – err, sorry – recruits I've had to whip into shape over the years. Sometimes literally.'

'I can imagine. There's nothing more taxing than another person's arrogance.' Silrith gave a wry grin at her own statement, but suddenly gasped in shock as the cart lurched to the right with a crash, almost throwing its incumbents to the ground. Silrith landed in Gasbron's lap.

'My Queen, are you alright?' Gasbron instinctively asked.

'Yes, yes I'm fine, thank you,' she responded, blushing as she sat back up again, but with genuine gratitude for his concern. With that, Gasbron leapt off the cart to go and calm the mules before they caused further damage, as the other men cursed loudly in the back. That done, he returned to look at the cart.

'Everybody off,' he called. 'This cart's going no further.' Not forgetting to pick up her sandals, Silrith took Gasbron's offered hand as she stepped down on to the ground. She turned to see that a section of loose earth had given way under the cart's weight, causing the wheel to slip and the front axle had buckled after smashing down on the hard rock underneath.

Silrith turned to Gasbron, who just shook his head solemnly.

'We're going to have to walk,' he said to all those around him after a moment. 'Untie the mules. We can use them as pack animals.'

As his men set about preparing the mules for their new use, Gasbron saw that Silrith had placed her sandals back on her feet and was clumsily attempting to walk, though her pain was clear. He stepped towards her to try to help but she jutted out an arm, her palm raised and he stopped.

'I must do this myself,' she insisted breathlessly, before gritting her teeth to take another step.

Gasbron walked beside Silrith for a few paces; his eyes and those of his men, fixed on her so that when she inevitably stumbled, he caught her in his arms and sat her down on the nearest rock. It seemed Silrith had all but forgotten about the pain when she'd been sitting in the cart and when she had been running on adrenaline during the skirmish, but as soon as she had to support her full weight again and do something as apparently simple as walking, it was clear that it had come flooding back to her.

Gasbron saw how red with cuts and blisters her feet were and knelt before her, taking her left foot in his hands and looking up inquiringly. She nodded silently and he took off the sandal and then did the same with her other foot.

'Water,' he called back to the other men and one fetched a water bottle from one of the baggage packs that now adorned the mules.

He shook his head in amazement at the poor condition her feet were in, before slowly running water over each of them, then massaging them with the tenderness of a lover.

Ignoring the pain, Silrith enjoyed the attention. She may have only met him hours earlier, but she felt safe with this man.

'You must have been walking a long time. Did they make you walk the whole way from Kriganheim?' he asked.

'Yes. It's been two weeks maybe, probably closer to three,' she said quietly.

'Looking at those feet, I think I'll side with the second option, my Queen,' he said, with a wry grin. Silrith raised her eyebrows and sniffed lightly in response.

'I'm afraid that's the best I can do, for now, my Queen. Now I must insist that you ride on one of the mules. Our luggage is not so heavy that it can't be carried solely by the other animal.' Silrith nodded grudgingly. She knew the sense of it, but couldn't help feeling that she didn't want to be a burden to these men, or worse still, look weak. Sooner or later, she would make their efforts worth their while, she decided.

Chapter 6

KRIGANHEIM, BENNVIKA

After losing their home, Jithrae's family had been forced to join the hordes of desperate migrants travelling north to Kriganheim and on their arrival, they had flooded into the city. Many had been forced to find or build homes for themselves, but fortunately for Jithrae and his family, this was where his wife's sister, Kanolia and her husband, Naivard, now lived. They were richer than Jithrae and Mirtsana, as Naivard worked as a magistrate's clerk. Despite this contrast in fortunes, the two brothers-in-law had become close friends.

When the family had arrived, Naivard and Kanolia had not hesitated to invite them in and ask them to stay but, of course, the inevitable question had been asked – where was Vaezona?

Neither Jithrae nor Mirtsana or any of the three boys had found the strength to answer the question at that moment, but it was clear from their hosts' reactions that Naivard and Kanolia, who had never had children of their own, could see that something horrific had happened. Now Naivard and Jithrae sat together in a loud and dark local tavern, as Jithrae divulged the details of the day the family had been visited by Vinnitar.

'Surely what he did was illegal?' he asked hopefully when he had finished retelling the painful story. Naivard laughed grimly.

'That would involve justice, my friend.' He was some years older than Jithrae, just a little short of fifty, going thin on top and the finer quality of his clothes hinted at the difference in social status between him and his brother-in-law.

'The problem is,' Naivard continued. 'That, as you have seen, this is becoming a common story. All the congressors want to impress the new king with their wealth and power and once a congressor, especially one who is also a governor like Lord Rintta, has his eye on a piece of land, well, you've seen what happens. You've seen the vast columns of people coming into the city. I tell you, it's happening everywhere. Hazgorata has seen the worst of it, I hear.'

'What am I to do?'

'I'm not sure, Jith. The only thing I could suggest is to try to seek out this Vinnitar Rhosgyth character of yours, ideally without him knowing. If you can find him, then maybe you will be able to find some clue as to Vaezona's whereabouts.' Jithrae supped his ale as he considered this. Then Naivard's face lightened as if he'd had an idea.

'The day before you arrived it was announced that the king is raising an army for a campaign against the Hentani and that it would be the soldiers of Hazgorata that will be left to protect the north, not those of Asrantica or Kriganheim this time. I bet that's where you will be most likely to track this man down. Vaezona may even be among the camp followers. You've got to join the army. They want to have sufficient troops for them to be able to head south the day after King Lissoll's funeral.'

'Yes, if it means finding her then that's what I'll do,' Jithrae responded. 'But what if she's not there? I'll waste the next few months up to my knees in some southern bog where I'll have no hope of finding her. Anything could happen to her in that time.' He buried his face in his hands. 'Dear Gods. Even if I *do* find her, how can I possibly get her back from that bastard Rhosgyth? Who's going to back me against him, eh?'

'Calm yourself, my friend. You will gain nothing from wasting energy this way-'

'-I'll have to kill him. Yes, I'll have to kill him.'

'Oh for heaven's sake. That would be madness. Even if by some miracle you do manage to kill him without him gutting you in the process, what then? You'll surely get caught. You'll be a dead man and then what use are you to Vaezona?'

Jithrae knew Naivard was right. He shut his eyes for a moment to try to hold back the tears that threatened to burst out and bit his lip so as to stop it wobbling.

'I know. You're right of course,' he said eventually. 'I just don't understand it. Why us? What did my poor, beautiful Vaezona do to deserve this?'

'Nothing. Nothing at all. It's just one of the great injustices of the times in which we live. But as far as I can see, you joining the army is the only chance we have, Jithrae. You might still discover something. I'm unlikely to be admitted into the army at my age, but they may well still accept you and that way there is still a chance. The fact is though, technically what Vinnitar did is not illegal, as great an injustice as it is. Look, I know you well enough to know that if there is even the smallest chance of you finding her, you'd take it, correct?'

'Yes, of course, I just don't know what I'll do if I can't find her there.'

'Let's cross that bridge if and when we come to it,' Naivard reassured Jithrae, patting his friend on the shoulder. 'Anyway, as I said, even if you don't find her, you may still find some clue as to where she is.'

'Perhaps you're right.' Jithrae conceded, scolding himself internally for letting worry govern his ability to consider his options properly.

'Be careful where you go though,' Naivard cautioned. 'The king has already had Princess Silrith arrested for murdering King Lissoll. He'll still be paranoid about assassinations so make sure you don't get caught swanning around by yourself in the wrong part of the camp trying to look for Vaezona. You'll be no help to her if you're dead.'

'I know. I just want her back,' Jithrae replied.

'Then joining the army is the best way to start, but you must be careful. These are dangerous times and that's something that's only going to get worse. I'm sure of it.'

Naivard paused for a moment.

'Anyway, there's something I don't understand.' he continued, evidently trying a different tack in an attempt to distract Jithrae temporarily from his worries. 'What really perplexes me-'

'Perplexes?'

'Oh, it means 'confuse' and what confuses me is how they found out so quickly that it was the princess who murdered King Lissoll. You'd think that it'd take at least a few days to catch the culprit, especially given that they said it was poison. It looks to me like someone wanted both the old king and the princess removed.'

'What in the name of the gods are you saying?' Jithrae hissed under his breath, grabbing Naivard so hard that they were just inches apart. Just

82

then a heftily built bar girl squeezed between their table and the back of another punter's chair, carrying some empty mugs and the look on her face suggested that she'd overheard. Both men attempted to look natural, but as soon as she'd gone Jithrae rounded on Naivard again.

'What if she heard you say that? What if *anyone* heard?'

'I make no accusation, Jithrae.' Naivard stared hard into his brother-in-law's eyes. 'I simply find it all rather convenient. And don't let yourself believe that this isn't connected to what's happening to people like you, because it is.' He looked around, before continuing to whisper in a lighter voice.

'Now, in my line of work, among other things, it is my job to complete records of various cases. As I'm sure you can imagine, these contain the details of any crime that has been committed, as well as other information such as when and where it happened, who was arrested for it and when the arrest took place. It is the law that this must happen for every arrest and this case was no exception. As it turned out, I was the clerk who was tasked with drawing it up. But when I was given the details of this case I thought that it was strange that the arrest was made almost immediately after the alleged murder had taken place. Don't you think that sounds strange considering that nobody was caught in the act?'

'Well, yes I suppose. But so what?'

Naivard sighed.

'Somehow, despite nobody being caught, they were so sure of the identity of the villains that they were positively champing at the bit to arrest and exile the princess and to execute her maid. That's what the records suggest anyway. The lack of detail speaks for itself. To me, it looks too much as if they knew she was going to do it and yet for some reason didn't stop her.'

'So what are you saying?'

'I think she may be innocent. I think the king may be-'

'-What?' Jithrae hissed incredulously, though still in a hushed tone.

'I just think it should be considered-'

'-Oh my goodness,' Jithrae interrupted, burying his head in his hands again. 'You're actually going to say it, aren't you? How can you be so stupid?'

'I just think that it looks pretty suspicious that-'

'No,' Jithrae interrupted again, drawing a few looks from around the bar. 'I'll take your advice about joining the army but I'll hear no more of this nonsense. If you try this we'll all suffer for it. I'm trying to find my daughter, not get her and all of the rest of my family killed. I'd appreciate it if you did the same.'

Jithrae's worry had turned to anger now. The two attempted to outstare each other down for a moment until they were both distracted by a call from across the room.

'May I have your attention please, everyone?' Standing by the door was a young man in a brown tunic and beside him, an older, grey-haired man dressed in blue.

'My name is Zethun Maysith and this is Congressor Hoban Salanath. After many conversations with members of the Congressate, I have been appointed as the new demokroi for the district of Siggatt. But this is Kriganheim and unlike my equivalents in the country's other cities, as a demokroi here I have the power to address issues across all of Bennvika.'

'Get on with it, posh boy,' someone shouted, stirring few laughs from the audience.

The young politician continued regardless.

'It has come to my attention that many people are being forced to migrate to this city after being displaced from their lands. Lands that belong to them, not the nobility. Am I right in thinking that some of you are among those people?'

A low murmur went around the room as a few people, including Jithrae, confirmed Zethun's suggestion. He nodded approvingly.

'I thought as much. These people run our country, but they're not satisfied. Now they have taken from you your land, your livelihoods and how can we be sure that they'll be satisfied even with *that*? It would seem that they're not. While this injustice persists, there can be no freedom. If freedom for all is to prevail, injustices such as these must be stopped. Tomorrow I will be joined at the public assembly by Kriganheim's nine other demokroi and I will do my very best to address this issue, but without your votes on the day, the motion to have your lands handed back to you stands no hope of being carried forward for the king's approval. Will you join me in the city centre tomorrow?'

84

A cheer, accompanied by a few whoops and the occasional 'I'll drink to that!' was the reply and he turned and left, with a pat on the back from Congressor Salanath. Naivard turned to Jithrae.

'Well, it seems like a trip into the city centre is in order tomorrow.'

RILDAYORDA, BASTALF, BENNVIKA

As Silrith, Gasbron and their small party reached the crest of the hill, a week after the skirmish at the bridge, they finally drank in the view of the awe-inspiring citadel of Preddaburg and its beautiful surrounding fields, which basked in the midday sun, backing on to the woods to the east. It was a citadel that was designed to impress and not just from a military perspective. Its high walls, its many intricately designed turrets and its sheer breadth made for an imposing sight, yet somehow it was also rather pleasing to the eye aesthetically.

On the far side of the citadel, to the south, a huge connecting wall extended downhill to encompass Rildayorda, a large port city that had for many years been home to the once powerful but now largely defeated and pacified Hentani tribe. Beyond the city, on the horizon, Silrith saw the sparkling blue of where the Kebban Sea met the Eternamic Ocean.

As they moved along the track and approached the portcullis they attracted little attention from the peasants milling about around them, covered as they were in dirt and dripping with sweat, until the guard called out a challenge to them. Letting go of the reins of Silrith's mule, Gasbron walked up to him and stated the password.

Once the portcullis was raised and the large wooden doors behind had been opened inward, the guard led them under the enormous Preddaburg Gate. Silrith presumed that they would then be led to the Alyredd Gate, which led into the citadel's inner ward. First though, after passing through the walled courtyard into the tight streets of the outer ward, the guard directed them to a stable where they were given a horse each and he sent a messenger to Yathrud to tell him that they had arrived. After a short rest, Silrith, who felt that after her ordeal she must by now have looked like any commoner, was handed over to a pair of rather nervous looking ladies-in-waiting, who had been sent to escort her, with a guard in tow, to a specially converted room where she could wash and change.

It isn't exactly glamorous, but it will have to do, Silrith thought as she looked around inside. The room was small and fairly dark, with a curtain across the doorway and the furnace outside gave away that this would normally have been inhabited by the blacksmith. As many of the tools as possible had been moved out of the room and on the far right, where normally the end of the room would be open, another curtain had been hung to give her some privacy.

She wasn't sure why her uncle was taking this down-to-earth approach, but decided that there may be someone in the inner ward that he thought she needed to impress with a grand and regal entrance and it just wouldn't do for her to be covered in mud, sweat and blood. If that was the case, this was certainly the lesser of two evils and she was intelligent enough not to complain.

In the centre of the room was a large bucket of water and while the guard waited outside, one of the maids helped Silrith strip off her clothes and the other came in with another bucket of water, which had been on the fire just long enough for it to be mildly warm.

As she stepped into the first bucket, finding with relief that it too had been heated to a comfortable temperature, it seemed to Silrith that every single muscle in her body ached like nothing she had ever experienced before. The warm water on her skin felt exquisite as it was slowly poured over her. After she had finished bathing and drying herself, one of the girls brought her some replacement sandals and a new dress to wear; orange in colour, with white under-trousers, which they helped Silrith put on before assisting her to arrange her hair, then leading their new mistress back to her horse.

Moments later she was re-joined by Gasbron and the other men. A mounted guard led them to the open Alyredd Gate; the horses' hooves clattering against the stone floor. As those in front moved aside to form a guard-of-honour, Silrith and Gasbron lead the rest of the column into the courtyard at a canter. Having all of them come through the Alyredd Gate mounted on powerful steeds added to the ceremony. Gasbron had told her that in reality, the men had left the citadel on foot. It had been decided beforehand that having horses to tether up in the forest would add to the possibility of the ambush being spotted.

As they dismounted, Silrith looked around her approvingly. She saw that there were a fair number of people there to greet her, though many of them were the retinue of the Alyredds and their various guests. The heavily bearded Lord Yathrud stood out from all others though. He wore a tunic so yellow it was almost a shining gold, with blue patterns around the neck that matched the colour of his cloak. As she walked over to him, beaming, she could see that Yathrud's face was full of joy.

'Uncle,' she said, bowing her head slightly. But on impulse she cast all formality aside, throwing her arms around him and holding him tightly to her. He embraced her and gave an affectionate laugh.

'I cannot begin to describe my relief at seeing that you are safe, my Queen,' he said as they parted. She had thought to put on some façade of unshakable strength. Yet the mere sight of her adored uncle had undone all of that. She didn't care that this show of affection might look unseemly. Who were all these people to judge her behaviour after what had happened to her in recent days? Her father was dead, she had been arrested and her dear lady's maid executed, both accused of his murder. Then, after having to walk most of the length of the kingdom, she'd had to kill a man for the first time when Gasbron's men had saved her. Yet she knew she'd have to kill many more if she was to stand a chance of defeating Jostan, though the thought disgusted her.

To the underworld with anyone who tried to criticise her show of emotion. This was who she really was and she wanted to savour it, before the coming war turned her into someone different. Everyone in the north that she thought she could trust had either betrayed her or had been too cowardly to support her. She had courage, but what she needed now was hope. Yathrud's intervention gave her that hope and out of love for his niece, not for money or some sense of reluctant duty. Such people were hard to find. As the formality of the situation returned, Silrith gathered herself.

'My Queen,' Yathrud said with a smile. Stiffly he bent down on one knee, followed by all those surrounding them; his head still bowed so that it was almost hidden from view by his long grey hair. 'It is so wonderful to see you alive, after your predicament. If I may, I would like to take this opportunity to pledge formally and publicly my allegiance and that of my soldiers and allies, to your cause, my Queen, to fight for you and show all the world that you are the rightful Queen of Bennvika. Will you bestow this honour upon us?'

'Arise, uncle,' Silrith told him cheerfully and she deliberately continued in a voice that could be heard by all. 'It is I who should be honoured, to have such loyal and illustrious friends who would risk all to support me.'

She held out her left hand, which Yathrud took and kissed, before getting back to his feet, again followed by the others.

'And my good cousin Bezekarl,' Silrith exclaimed as she turned to the mop-haired teenager next to Yathrud.

'My Queen,' he bowed, blushing slightly.

'Oh less of that, cousin,' Silrith said, laughing lightly, taking his hands in hers and looking into his eyes. 'We're still family remember. It's been too long.'

Yathrud ushered her towards the three men next to Bezekarl.

'And may I introduce you to our guests, who have rallied to your cause. First, the Chief of the Hentani tribe, Hojorak, son of Vorad, and Blavak, his interpreter.' Hojorak was a huge man, so much so that Silrith had to take a slight step back to get a full view of him.

Broad as well as tall, he had slanted eyes and his round face was decorated with swirling blue tattoos. He had long black hair and a heavily bearded chin, while he wore a brown tunic and trousers with a similarly coloured jacket. With this, he wore a pair of boots and a large wolf-fur hat. His clothes were made of woven hemp and his boots from leather, while all were lined with goatskin for insulation – and who could fail to notice the long scimitar strapped to his belt.

Despite his imposing image, to Silrith's eye, there was little to mark him out as a man of rank at first look. She decided the quality of the sword and the goatskin must be the giveaway when compared to many of his people. Blavak, on the other hand, was much shorter and slighter in build than his master, with a somehow more expressive demeanour, Silrith sensed.

'May I express my gratitude for your support, Chief Hojorak?' Silrith began as Blavak immediately started translating. 'I only wish I could be more certain that it will be worth your while. How many warriors can you supply?'

'Two thousand, your Grace,' Blavak said proudly after conferring briefly with his master. 'One hundred and fifty of our best arrived with us, but my master says that his younger brother Prince Kivojo is marching here with the main force as we speak and is expected within two to three days.'

'It warms my heart to hear news of this kind from such a renowned warrior as yourself, Chief Hojorak.' Silrith knew that flattery of such a man couldn't do any harm in building friendships.

'And this is Prince Shappa of Etrovansia,' Yathrud said. Silrith had to catch her breath as she laid eyes on the tall, muscular prince, with his wavy hair and piercing dark eyes, wearing his shining chain mail tunic and ceremonial armour.

'Your Grace,' he said coyly, yet somehow flirtatiously, as he kissed her hand, never taking his eyes off hers.

'Noble Prince,' she replied, bowing her head slightly in greeting. They had met, but not since they were children, so in a sense, it was very much like meeting for the first time. 'What brings you here? I had heard there were some rather major events within your family back at home.'

Shappa chuckled, rolling his eyes at his own misfortune.

'Yes, I seem to have been banished. Except, no, what did they call it? I was *ordered to leave voluntarily* – yes, that was the diplomatic line. Just because my brother, wanting to take the crown for himself, convinced my father that I was plotting against him and the senile old fool believed him.'

'It seems that you and I have something in common in that regard,' Silrith said.

'And that's just the beginning of our common ground, I hope,' Shappa jested daringly, causing Silrith to raise her eyebrows. She was surprised by his familiarity, yet she couldn't deny that she appreciated it.

'Anyway,' Shappa continued. 'That explains my presence here, as well as that of my five hundred men, my ten warships and their respective crews. My father was too old and my brother too wrapped up in his own affairs at court to realise that there were some who are still loyal to me and to my late mother's family. Since many of my troops have served under me as their prince and duke for the past few years, all it took was for me to allow them to bring their families and they just seem to have 'forgotten' to turn back.'

'If only I'd had the luxury of that sort of loyalty in the north,' Silrith mused ruefully. 'But,' she said, her face lightening again. 'What I see here in the south restores my confidence in my subjects. If we can all stand together, we can show this kingdom the real truth of how Jostan claimed the throne and perhaps I may even get the chance to assist in the solving of your problem also.'

Chapter 7

KRIGANHEIM, BENNVIKA

On the day following Zethun Maysith's visit to the tavern to address the drinking customers, the streets were bustling with people. The army recruiters were out knocking on the doors of houses, surveying the quality of all the young and middle-aged men and women they could find, though in truth they would take anyone who could run while carrying a weapon. As they did, they quoted the king's call to arms and supplied crude weapons to those who weren't able to produce a better one from within their own household.

Most of the recruiters were invicturions, or were army scribes and clerks, or held one of a variety of other positions that required them to be literate. They would write down the name of each person they recruited and the man or woman would write their mark next to their name. From this point, they were honour-bound to fight, though as Jithrae soon found, the notion of the men and women themselves having any choice in this was little more than a myth.

Still, he had joined with no further hesitations after his conversation with Naivard. Naivard himself, however, as expected, was declared ineligible through a combination of his age and his position as magistrate's clerk. He would be needed to help keep order in the city. The army was not due to assemble for a few days yet, so that gave Jithrae a chance to go with Naivard to the assembly area, to witness the public assembly there.

In the middle of the city centre, there was a crudely constructed, but sturdy wooden stage topped by eleven chairs arranged in a crescent shape, facing the audience. The speaker sat in the middle chair, flanked by the ten demokroi, of whom Jithrae and Naivard could see that Zethun Maysith was seated on the far left.

As Zethun waited in his wooden chair, the speaker stood and proceeded with the formalities of welcoming the audience to the assembly, introducing the demokroi and explaining the rules for the benefit of those who hadn't attended before. The audience's voting was based on an 'aye/nay' system, the result which could be overturned either way by any individual demokroi, while any motions carried were subject to the king's approval before being put into practice.

But first, there was one further formality, which consisted of the speaker asking the demokroi if the law courts, markets, granaries and other public buildings could be opened. In reality, this was just an archaic tradition from a bygone age, as many of these places were already open at this time, but technically if any demokroi said 'no' they would have to be closed until further notice.

However, this stage passed without event and with this done, the speaker sat down as he gave permission for the demokroi to address the crowd one by one, working from left to right, thus allowing Zethun to make the first speech.

Like the nine other demokroi, he wore a brown tunic and breeches, as this was a colour commonly associated with the lower classes and therefore had become the traditional uniform of a rank designed to help them – in theory. The speaker, in stark contrast, was rather more grandly dressed in purple robes. As he stood, Zethun briefly composed himself, trying to cover his nerves and took a deep lungful of air.

'It is indeed an honour to make the opening speech in this, our first assembly under the reign of our new king, who as you all know, this very morning began putting into action his plan to raise an army to march on the Hentani. Now, this is a pre-emptive strike, designed to stop a rebellion before it starts. It is not my place to question the king's reasoning in this, but what is not being addressed is that you, the people of this kingdom, have another, greater enemy. This army is being formed to quash any chance of a full-scale rebellion from a conquered people, who have lived peacefully under Bennvikan rule for some years now. It is not the Hentani whom our families need protecting from. It is not they who steal our lands. It is not they who abduct our wives, sons and daughters.'

'No,' shouted a middle-aged man in the centre of the crowd, as others began to take up the same reply.

'No,' Zethun continued. 'Instead, it is our own nobles. Our governors and the other congressors.'

'Damned cons,' someone shouted. This was a common enough term to describe the members of the Congressate.

'A most apt description,' said Zethun. 'They try to lull you into a false sense of security by telling you that this is simply what they get in return for allowing you to live on the land that they have been appointed to govern. They tell you that you should be thankful for what you have. But how can you be thankful as you helplessly watch your own family starve, all the time knowing that some lord is growing fat on your taxes and an ever-growing share of your crops?'

Another tirade of anti-nobility shouts erupted from the crowd as the other demokroi and the speaker shifted uncomfortably in their seats, but Zethun wasn't finished yet.

'This has to stop and it has to stop now. It has always been the case in this kingdom that there is some land that belongs to no lord and is for the use by the common people, yet this fine tradition is now threatened. That is why I propose that the very first law to be put to the vote at this assembly is one that states that each nobleman must relinquish every inch of land that they have stolen from the common people and that their personal lands will be limited to those that they gained through appointment, or inherited by birthright, but not what they subsequently stole. Furthermore, I move that this new law should state that the amount of your crops to be taken by your local lord should be dropped back to the original regulation of one-tenth of what is grown, so that it may give your families a fairer chance of survival.'

A loud cheer went up and Zethun turned and bowed his head slightly to the speaker, before sitting back down. The speaker stood.

'The notion has been proposed. Now let it be put to the test,' he stated grandly.

'All those against say nay,'

Silence. Everyone in the crowd looked around nervously. This was unprecedented, but it was true, there had been no nay. For tradition's sake, the speaker completed the vote in the proper form.

'All those in favour say aye,'

'Aye!'

Hundreds of voices erupted in unison.

The speaker then turned to the ten demokroi, stating the same quotation. Zethun couldn't believe his luck when nobody vetoed to reverse the outcome. In fact, their sheer readiness to comply with Zethun's proposal suggested that perhaps they had been intimidated by the partisan quality of the day's audience. Now they simply awaited the king's approval.

A few days later, the royal army had been fully assembled. Knowing the importance of setting off in style and making a statement of strength, Jostan had his troops arranged in a guard-of-honour formation. They reached from the forum outside the Congressate Hall, where Jostan now stood, through the thronging streets of Kriganheim, to the city gate, where the Kriganheim divisios awaited him with their gleaming armour, their colourful rectangular shields and their lightweight, javelin-like spears. This was with the exception of the heavy cavalry, who were acting as his mounted escort.

He wore a red tunic today; a conscious reference to the Bennvikan style. In politics, image was everything, even if it was designed to mislead. Even a fleeting tip of the hat to local customs could be enough for him to pave the way for a longer-term Verusantian infiltration of the Bennvikan culture he ultimately hoped to supplant. It would be Verusantian robes for the campaign itself. For now though, along with the Bennvikan tunic, he wore breeches and a cape. These were the same shade of scarlet as the rest of his attire and the cape was decorated with a golden lining, as was his red flat hat with white feathers on one side. His attire made it clear that he was there to command and not to fight, though of course he still carried an ornate gold-hilted sword on the side of his belt. He looked forward to the time after his coronation when he could perfect the image by replacing the hat with his crown.

His appearance was in stark contrast to the soldiers around him; the Bennvikan flag adorning the centre section of the divisiomen's shields and the fabric that covered their mounts' flanks. Against a blood red background, it depicted a golden six-armed king, each hand holding a star which

94

represented a province, symbolising the idea that the king is the force that holds the six provinces together in one kingdom. When emblazoned on their shields, this was sandwiched between two horizontal green stripes, the colour of the divisios. Their emerald capes just added to their dramatic appearance.

These troops were joined in the forum by four hundred and fifty of Jostan's own spear-carrying Verusantian lance guardsmen, who had formed up in the forum's centre in their striking jet-black armour and their full-faced helmets and whose leader, Ostagantus Gormaris, continued to stand guarding Jostan's back, as he always did.

For a moment Jostan stood next to his horse, which itself was grandly dressed in cloth showing the Bennvikan flag, like the mounted divisiomen. He began to walk over to the large group of congressors who had gathered on the steps of the Congressate Hall, still wearing their dark blue robes. As he did, a large and comfortable looking litter, decorated in the blue and gold of the House of Vaaltanen, drew alongside him. Accutina pushed the curtains aside to look up at him.

'Tell me again, your Majesty,' she grumbled resentfully, quietly enough for those around not to hear. 'Why must I join you on this campaign? The physician advised against it.'

Jostan laughed, causing a further grimace from Accutina.

'My dear, this is a large and slow-moving army. It will take us at least a month to reach the Hentani's territory. If we leave you here, then once we have reached our foes, defeated any remaining pockets of resistance and returned north, you will more than likely have given birth. When our son enters this world it must be to the grandest of receptions, as befits a future King of Bennvika. Think how ecstatic this city will be when it celebrates the birth of our son, then celebrates our triumph, our marriage to you, our coronation and yours, all within a matter of weeks of each other. Nothing wins over the common people like grandeur and a royal birth. I trust that you have made arrangements with regards to the Amulet too?'

Accutina's answer was to give him a sneering look and quiet 'humpf' that was audible only to Jostan, she closed the curtain again. Silly girl. What could she do? He was the king and she was not yet even his wife. He turned his attention to the congressors standing a short distance away by the steps of the Congressate Hall and he moved to address more pressing matters.

'What are the final figures then, Dongrath?' he said briskly to the congressor who had heckled him so ineffectually in his opening speech.

'Along with your own lance guardsmen, your Majesty, our recruiters have managed to raise eight thousand men from Kriganheim alone, comprising of all forms of unit. Swordsmen, spearmen, heavy cavalry, light cavalry, lancers, longbowmen, crossbowmen – they're all at your disposal, as are the ten thousand divisiomen who are stationed here, your Majesty,' Dongrath replied, looking very pleased with himself, remembering to refer to Jostan using the eastern term to deference, as Jostan preferred.

'Good. Very good. And what of the other provinces?'

'Asrantica, Hertasala and Ustenna have each more than surpassed your required quota of raising two thousand militia. From the divisios of those three provinces, four thousand troops from each will join the army, leaving a further thousand in each province to man the garrisons there. Lord Oprion Aethelgard will stay in the north with all five thousand of his divisiomen, as you ordered and will garrison Hazgorata and Kriganheim. Lord Aethelgard has also raised a militia to assist with the garrisoning of his own city and fifty of your lance guardsmen have been detailed to assist the Hazgoratan divisios here. In total that takes the army to approaching forty thousand troops, which will surely rise to somewhere near fifty thousand once our Defroni allies are added into the equation. However, there is one concern...'

Jostan nodded.

'Go on.'

Dongrath looked uncomfortable, clearly choosing his words carefully.

'We have yet to receive any figures from Lord Yathrud Alyredd. I'm sure the messenger has just been delayed somewhere. It is a long road to Bastalf,' he chuckled awkwardly.

Jostan was unimpressed.

'Perhaps,' he said coldly, not sure whether or not to believe him or not. 'But if the messenger from the Defroni arrives with their official figures before the one from Bastalf does, then old Lord Yathrud will have some explaining to do.'

'We have had no such issues elsewhere though, your Majesty,' Dongrath put in, clearly eager to move things back to a more positive note. 'The army of Asrantica under Lord Feddilyn Rintta will be ready to meet with you at Faen Tira and the armies of Hertasala and Ustenna, under Lord Lektik Haganwold and Lord Aeoflynn Tanskeld, will rendezvous with your forces just north of Celrun.'

'Good. Now, what's that?' Jostan indicated the baggage of parchment and a wooden board held by one of the nearby servants. Congressor Hoban Salanath stepped forward from the crowd and addressed the king.

'These are the new law suggestions put forward after the public assembly earlier this week.'

Jostan beckoned for the parchment to be shown to him and the servant handed them to Hoban, before quickly bending down on one knee with his right side facing Jostan, his head bowed and his back straightened as much as possible. He then put the wooden board on his back. The board featured short lengths of rope at each end, one attaching the top right corner to the bottom right and the same on the left. He put his arms through these to steady the board for writing.

Hoban handed the first piece of parchment to Jostan, giving a brief introduction, before Jostan signed it, feeling little interest. Most of these turned out to be fairly trivial and Jostan had signed his name many times before, finally, he reached the parchment that, judging by the title Hoban verbalised, outlined suggested land reforms.

Hoban again began to summarise the contents of the document. The moment he mentioned the phrase 'common land to be returned to the common people' Jostan snatched the parchment out of his hand and read the rest of it himself, his eyes almost bulging out of his skull and teeth gritted so tightly he felt like he might crush them under the pressure of his own jaws.

'This insolent pig dares to question his betters?'

'Your Majesty,' Hoban began, attempting diplomacy. 'My sources tell me that the vote in favour of this law was unanimous. You need the support of the people-'

'-Do not presume to tell us what we should and shouldn't do, Congressor Salanath. We don't take kindly to instructions. We require the support of the lords. The common people must then follow their example and accept us as their anointed king. To do otherwise would be insubordination in the extreme and simply to accept that would weaken the position of the nobility in every area. If we give them what they want, they'll get a taste for it and will want more and more and more.'

Dongrath and the other congressors, with the exception of Hoban, had subconsciously taken a step back under this unexpected onslaught from Jostan.

'What is the name of the person who put this forward?'

'It was Zethun Maysith, your Majesty, the new demokroi for the district of Siggatt.'

'Well then, this is what we think of Zethun Maysith's proposals.'

Jostan held the parchment above his head and deftly ripped it in two, letting the two halves drop to the floor. He strode away quickly as he had no intention of spending any more time around people too cowardly to join the campaign or to stand up to the common people and keep the natural order.

And with the ripping of a single piece of parchment, I fear the king's relationship with his people may be permanently broken also, Hoban thought as he angrily watched Jostan march away. With one slick movement, Jostan was astride his horse and the drummer boys that were dotted along the busy streets with the king's soldiers began to strike out a march as the royal party moved forward.

Chapter 8

BASTALF, BENNVIKA

A few miles to the southwest of Rildayorda, the main column of Hentani warriors under Prince Kivojo was approaching its destination. Following the two thousand strong military force was the baggage train, populated by what must have been at least a further thousand camp followers. Some walked, while others rode in the back of carts. Many were slaves, but some were soothsayers, cooks, or men and women selling their bodies, while others were the husbands, wives and children of the warriors themselves. Some had travelled all the way from Intei, while others had joined the column closer to Lithrofed.

In the back of one open-topped yet highly claustrophobic cart crammed full of slaves and peasants from the latter of those two cities, were two young women, Ezrina and Jezna. They were dancers by profession and both wore light brown, figure-hugging dresses, decorated with birds' feathers in various shades of red, white and grey. More feathers dangled from around their bracelets, necklaces and anklets. The thin dresses extended down to a knee-length skirt and their bare arms and legs were decorated with patterns of red ochre.

At twenty-one years of age, Ezrina was the older of the two, with dark hair, tanned skin, a rounded face, big eyes and the buxom figure that was typical of the women of her race.

Jezna was three years Ezrina's junior and was similar in hair colour and complexion but had small eyes with high cheekbones and also had the slimmer figure of the two, giving her a different kind of beauty. More significantly, it gave her the look of a Bennvikan; her costume aside. Her parentage had often been questioned, though her mother had always refused to speak of it. After all, she had been born during the years of King Lissoll's conquest of the Hentani Kingdom, when he finished what his evil father had started.

'I wonder what it's going to be like in Rildayorda?' Jezna speculated.

'I think what you should be wondering is what the *people* will be like, sister,' Ezrina replied, making sure to use the word *sister*. It was something she'd long been used to saying by now.

'Yes, I'm sure they will give us a great welcome,' said Jezna with a vacant expression and letting her imagination run wild. 'Think of all the delicious food we can buy there and all the great buildings we'll see. We'll finally get to go to the Great Temple of Bertakaevey.'

Ezrina's face contorted with disgust.

'Jezna, I've told you time and again, the 'Great Temple of Bertakaevey' is a farce. Building that was all part of their plan to pacify us and make us doubt our own religious beliefs.'

'I know. You've told me before. But how do you know what they're telling us is wrong?' Jezna asked, fiddling with her necklace.

'Because it is written in the scriptures. *The righteous shall not call on me by any name but one, Bertakaevey, for all those who use another are sinners, fools and imposters.* Anyway, you mustn't trust the Bennvikans, rebellion or no rebellion. They're our oppressors and it wasn't long ago that they were rampaging through our land, burning our villages, killing and raping our people and taking them as slaves, led by the very man who now offers us friendship. The only reason I agreed to come is that deposing their new king is the best chance for our people to regain their independence. You know this. If it wasn't for them, your mother would still be alive and we'd still have your family's farm to live on.'

'Yes,' Jezna conceded dispassionately. Then she turned to Ezrina, as if suddenly thinking of something.

'But also if it wasn't for them I'd never have been born at all and I don't see how they oppress you and me any more than our own people do,' she said, dropping her voice to a whisper, looking Ezrina in the eye and taking her hand, causing Ezrina to look around the cart nervously.

'Even they oppress us just for being who we are,' whispered Jezna.

'Sssh,' said Ezrina quietly. 'Not here.'

'But it's true. Anyway, the Bennvikans haven't attacked our villages since I was a baby and those ones were fighting for their king. These Bennvikans have risen up *against* their king.'

'And what difference does that make?' Ezrina sneered. 'Don't you ever listen to yourself?'

'What?' Jezna asked, visibly hurt. Ezrina relented.

'I'm sorry,' she sighed. 'But I just don't think you should believe that the Bennvikans we will be joining will be any different from the others. They're all heretics and they will tell you that Lomatteva and Bertakaevey are the same goddess. But they may be temporarily grateful for our people's help if they win and we have to take advantage of that. That's why we are here, doing Bertakaevey's work for the benefit of our kin.'

'I know. You don't have to tell me again.'

'It's true. We are Bertakaevey's chosen people and one day her chosen daughter will rise from the ashes of our civilisation to smite down our enemies.'

'Well, maybe if you pray hard enough we'll get there and find that they've all converted to our religion already.'

Ezrina knew that wasn't a joke. It was the sort of thing Jezna would say just to end a conversation she had grown bored with. Ezrina simply looked at her in disbelief. Jezna just couldn't see that not a single Bennvikan should be trusted. She was far too naïve. Sometimes she was envious of Jezna's highly simplified view of the world. Ignorance could be bliss, she mused silently, but it was something that was bound to get Jezna into trouble sooner or later, as it already had in the past. That was the price of having a good heart in this harsh world, but then it was her implicit goodness that had made Ezrina fall in love with Jezna in the first place. It pained her so intensely that they still had to pretend to be sisters when around others. Ezrina looked at Jezna and felt a pang of guilt at the way she'd spoken. She ached to kiss her, but knew she could not. Not publicly anyway.

'Sorry,' was all she could say. Jezna smiled at her warmly; her eyes filled with the endless powers of forgiveness she always seemed to find within her heart and she put an arm around Ezrina's shoulders.

Yet it was with much regret that Ezrina knew the truth of her own statements. She could see that this was just one group of Bennvikans against another and the Hentani leaders had simply backed the side they thought would give them the most favourable outcome if they were victorious.

Hojorak, the Chief of the Hentani had sent word to all the tribal villages that Lord Yathrud had promised the tribe independence from Bennvika if he defeated King Jostan, and the discontent that had spread among the people of the Hentani in recent months had only helped with this. Ezrina found Lord Yathrud's promises hard to believe, given that he had been one of the figureheads of the Bennvikan invasion, but now all those around her were dewy-eyed with ideas of regaining their liberty as they flocked to Yathrud's banner and so she'd gone too. As far as she could see, it was the only way she could fight for the rights of those who had stayed at home to tend the farms and bring up their families. But then again, if it all went wrong, King Jostan surely would not forget it and that could spell doom for the entire tribe.

KRIGANHEIM, BENNVIKA

With Jostan's army having left Kriganheim, Zethun was to attend a public conference at which the results of the proposed laws would be announced. These were commonplace enough and usually went on without much controversy. Yet Zethun was so incensed by the response he had received from the king that he vowed to himself that this would not be the case today.

The day had already started intriguingly. Earlier that morning he had gone to meet Hoban who, strangely, had arranged to meet him at the local magistrate's clerk's office. He soon saw why. Hoban had wanted to introduce Zethun to two of his associates. The first was a man named Naivard. The office was his and it became apparent that he and Hoban had harboured a friendship for some years. It seemed he had often served Hoban to give him legal advice in certain matters. What was also noticeable was the lack of surprise shown by Naivard when Zethun told him what Jostan's response had been. Clearly this man was not the king's most passionate supporter. This had been proven when Naivard said that the oppression of the poor that was now publicly sanctioned by Jostan had resulted in some members of his extended family losing their home and, worst of all, his teenage niece being kidnapped.

The other man whom Hoban had introduced Zethun to had been someone quite different altogether. From the moment he laid eyes on him, Zethun knew that Braldor was the muscle behind the politics. Tall and well-built with a bald head but a long bushy beard, he was Hoban's bodyguard and for the foreseeable future, he would be the same to Zethun, especially on days like this.

Now standing on the stage at the public assembly, Zethun could see Hoban and Naivard in the crowd. Braldor stood with the militia guardsmen of Kriganheim's overstretched garrison, who were there in just about sufficient numbers to control the mob. Hoban and Naivard stood further back. With the speaker and the nine other demokroi waiting patiently for him to begin, Zethun opened his address. It was unusual to ask to speak before the daily business was finished, but his wish had been granted.

'Good people of Kriganheim,' he began in a low, firm tone, breaking the deathly silence. 'It is with great shame and astonishment that I reveal to you news of a deliberate and dastardly attack on the rights of the common people of this nation. When presented with the proposed land reforms designed to give the common land back to the common people, our new king rejected them.'

'No,' came the response from many members of the crowd.

'Furthermore,' Zethun continued, adding extra strength and passion to his voice. 'I have it on good authority that not only did he reject the proposal, but he personally took the parchment on which it was written and ripped it in half.'

'No,' the audience cried, much louder this time, bellowing their anger.

He raised a hand to quieten the crowd again, though this took a few moments.

'Rest assured, good people, that this is far from over and I will do everything in my power to continue this fight on your behalf.'

With that, Zethun turned to sit down; the crowd still incandescent with rage at the announcement. The guards were having to work hard to keep the heaving throng at bay and as Zethun watched, Braldor took the opportunity to slip in among them. Despite it all, the speaker stood up to start the announcements regarding the daily business. By tradition, the demokroi all had to give their approval for the city's various businesses and services to open.

'Members of the demokroi, do you give your approval for the opening of the markets and banks?'

'Objection,' Zethun stated firmly as he briefly stood. He knew that opening the markets would only attract the taxmen, who would try to do people further out of the fruits of their labours. The speaker looked stunned but, uncertain about how to react, he carried straight on.

'Members of the demokroi, do you give your approval for the opening of the baths and all other public buildings?'

'Objection,' Zethun shouted, standing up and quickly sitting down again.

'Members of the demokroi, do you give your approval for the opening of the law courts?'

'Objection,' said Zethun, getting to his feet again.

'This is madness,' the speaker exclaimed. He looked like he was about to remonstrate with Zethun, but a huge lump of what must have been human excrement flew through the air from somewhere within the pulsating rabble and hit him square in the face, knocking him to the stage's wooden floor and leaving him dazed.

It was all the distraction the crowd needed. Inevitably there had been one or two guards who had momentarily lost their footing while confused by the sight of the faecal missile and the front members of the crowd burst through the fragile line. Seeing that his plan had worked better than he could have ever imagined, Zethun had already alighted the stage and jumped on to his horse, vacating the area with all speed. He galloped in the direction of Naivard's office as people charged up the steps and on to the stage, wrecking and smashing everything in sight, so great was their anger at the rich.

Zethun knew that the violence would spread to other parts of the city, but it was a necessary evil if they were to be listened to. He would have to congratulate Braldor on an excellent shot, he thought as he rode. He worried for Hoban. Knowing the plan, the old congressor had deliberately worn plain clothes for this day, but he couldn't move very fast and spoke with a voice that gave away his nobility. He hoped that they were being escorted by Braldor, as he doubted Naivard would be much use in a fight if they needed protection.

THE PREDDABURG CITADEL, RILDAYORDA, BASTALF, BENNVIKA

The splendour of the feast was matched only by that of the room itself, Silrith decided. All around her she saw a vast array of dragons carved into the mahogany that seemed to cover every inch of the room's interior, minus the large window at the far end. There were similar depictions on the two display cabinets that sat in one corner of the room, each of which was filled with trinkets, weapons and other treasures that Yathrud had acquired on his extensive travels. Some images of the beautiful creatures had been inlaid into the wood of the chairs on which Silrith, Yathrud, Shappa and Bezekarl now sat, as well as on the table itself and even on the braziers. She had never taken much notice of them before, but now she found the sight of them inspiring. They reminded her of the many legends she had heard as a child, in which brave warriors fought these terrible animals to save the one they love. All had expected to be easy prey for the mighty beasts, but every time it was the demonic creature that had been slain. It was much the same for Silrith now, except that this time the dragons would fly on Yathrud's scarlet and gold battle standards, standing alongside the green and white of her own emblem, the prancing, snarling stallion of the Alfwyn family. More than that, in this fight, against the beast that was Jostan's army, she had to save not just one person, but an entire nation.

The room in which they sat eating was the Alyredd family's personal feasting room; the smaller one that was rarely used for hosting guests' meals. Yathrud had apparently used this room for a number of private political meetings over the years, but today, it would be used for both. Meeting in this locked and guarded room was the best way to limit the threat of listening ears of spies and, most dangerous of all, the gossiping of Yathrud's new wife. It had not been a love-match, to be sure. If Yathrud's first wife, Silrith's aunt Monissaea, had yet lived, she would almost certainly have been in attendance.

'So, cousin Bezekarl, I hear that my uncle has been educating you in the political machinations of the Congressate?' Silrith enquired, taking a sip of wine after enjoying a meal of pork, parsnips, carrots and green peas. It felt so good to be eating well again after a week of barely anything to fill her stomach.

'Err, yes, I learn as much as I can,' Bezekarl replied, looking a little abashed.

Silrith was amused by his discomfort.

'Try not to look so awkward, cousin,' she said. 'I'm not going to test you. Anyway, the political situation here is rather more straightforward.'

'Help the ones you support and stab the ones you don't. Yes, I suppose the rules of the battlefield are rather less complex than those of the Congressate,' Shappa mused.

'Actually, once you consider the number of stabbings, in some ways the battlefield and the Congressate couldn't be more alike if they tried,' Silrith quipped, causing the others to laugh.

'We will not be able to eat like this for much longer,' she continued, raising herself to stand and starting to pace a little. The room's main window overlooked the courtyard, which was full of Hentani soldiers and camp followers apparently exploring their new surroundings. She could also see many Bennvikan soldiers who were there to greet the Hentani and to see them to their posts. Expressing no interest in attending the meeting, Chief Hojorak had gone down there to meet his brother when the main army arrived. The citadel was full of soldiers, as the city too soon would be, but were there enough of them? Surely, Jostan would be able to muster five times what she and Yathrud could?

'The day will come soon when we will have to order all the farmers bring in their livestock and other goods and keep them within the city walls,' she continued. 'It won't be long before Jostan realises I'm here and marches on us, so the moment our scouts in Ustenna report that the enemy has been sighted, the farmers and their animals must be brought inside. If they are fast enough in getting word to us of the enemy's approach, we should have a few days for the farmers to salvage what they can of their crops for our use and burn what they can't save. We don't want Jostan's army feasting on our own

106

farmer's produce while we squat in here starving to death.' The others nodded gravely as they listened.

'That said,' she went on. 'We need to ensure that morale is high, so I propose that, while we still can, we hold a night of celebrations for all the soldiers. We can hold it in the inner ward. Tell them…,' she put her hand to her chin and thought for a moment. 'Tell them it's to welcome our Etrovansian and Hentani comrades. That should suffice. Earlier today I was inspecting some of the new arrivals and I met some young Hentani dancers and musicians. I'm sure they can bring some entertainment. Tomorrow we'll hold a night of feasting, dancing and general merry-making, but-' That caught her audience off guard. 'But' she said again holding out a finger, 'from the very next morning, rationing starts, as does an intense period of training for all our troops.'

'Excellent, my Queen,' Yathrud stated appreciatively. 'I can have Gasbron devise a suitable regime. He's even managed to turn young Bezekarl here into a half decent fighter,' he added, slapping Bezekarl on the back, causing his son to almost choke. Silrith wanted to laugh. Surely in truth Bezekarl's fighting skills would be as awkward as his social skills. As a nobleman, he'd had to learn the basics of how to be a cavalryman and he was physically fit, but that was about all he'd mastered as far as she'd seen.

'I should like to be involved in Gasbron's planning process,' Shappa put in. 'I'm sure some of what we do in Etrovansia will be compatible with what is done here.'

'Of course,' Silrith nodded. 'Uncle, please make the necessary arrangements for the feast.'

'It would be an honour, my Queen.'

'Good. Now all of you, leave me and see that my instructions are implemented,' said Silrith.

All three men bowed to leave, then headed for the door.

'Uncle?' Silrith called. 'Will you stay with me a moment before you go? I must speak with you.'

'Of course, my Queen.'

He walked back over to her and waited for the others to leave before speaking.

'What do you require of me, my Queen?'

107

'I want to thank you for your loyalty. Just as I thought everyone in my life had left me for dead, you saved me. There are no words for my gratitude.'

He smiled affectionately.

'It was my duty, as an uncle and as a loyal subject of the crown. I would never have thought of doing anything else.'

'Nevertheless, such dependability is rare. I am indebted to you and if we are victorious, Bennvika will be too. What we are doing here is more than just a rebellion. It is a fight against tyranny. Throughout history, the common people have had to be content simply to fight to replace one monarch with another in times of civil war. They must know that this fight is for them, not me. You saved my life. I have been given a second chance and I want to make that worth something.'

'Of course and I will do all that I can to make sure the soldiers know that,' said Yathrud.

'As will I.'

'Of that I have no doubt, but I can see that something troubles you,' he said.

Silrith sighed.

'We will be vastly outnumbered, Uncle. I do not fear for my own life. I shall embrace martyrdom if that is my fate. But I do fear for the people of Rildayorda and the rest of Bennvika. You know of the terrible things I saw in Verusantium. If they are not happening in Kriganheim at this very moment, then they will soon and it will be even worse here if Jostan takes the city. We are all that stands between Jostan and the annihilation of Bennvika as we know it. The people must know that I fight for them and not the other way around.'

'So you must inspire them. I know your strength and conviction. You must show the army that Bennvika has hope yet.'

'Of course. But I've never led troops in battle before and there is no room for error. I will need guidance. How will I reach the point where the army follows me because they want to, rather than because they feel they have to? They need to truly believe that I fight for them and that things are not the other way around. How do I win their respect?'

108

'Lead them by example. I believe in you and when you have a decision to make, you must trust your instincts; they're good. However, if you need further assistance, you have me here to guide you and it may surprise you that I will start by presenting you with a gift.'

He moved away, reached into one of the cabinets in the corner of the room and produced a small, dusty old book.

'This book has been in my family for generations. It was of great use to your father and me when we were leading the campaign to conquer this land.'

Silrith looked at the leather cover and gasped.

'Macciomakkia.'

'Yes. *'The Art of Leadership'*, her finest work.'

'I did not believe that any copies still existed.'

'I do believe this may be the last. It's a remarkable book. It's strange how the words of a scholar dead for over five centuries can still ring true in the present day.'

'Yes, I have often heard it said that the Verusantians might not have been so successful in their invasion of Hingaria, if only the defenders had read the teachings of their country's own most famous daughter. I do not intend to make the same mistake when dealing with Jostan.' She embraced Yathrud.

'Thank you, Uncle.'

At its height, the Republic of Hingaria had been the jewel of both the ancient world and the modern; a bulwark of democratic thinking. For many centuries it had fought off would-be conquerors, keeping their people safe from oppression. Yet, a quarter of a century ago, as Verusantium's armies had advanced ever westward, Hingaria's democracy had been crushed forever and the once great nation had succumbed to imperial rule.

However, Hingaria's legacy had been harder to destroy. Even after all these years, merchants still spoke of what they had seen in that country before its fall; the great feats of architecture, literature, science and technology that had been achieved through the acceptance of new ideas and how all of that had been destroyed when the republic fell and was replaced by the totalitarianism of their fanatically religious new masters. Silrith had often wondered if democracy would ever live again.

With the insight that her private reading of this book would provide, Silrith finally felt genuine confidence that she could do what would be required of her to turn the tables on Jostan. As she pulled away, she wanted to tell Yathrud everything and let him know what he was really committing to by fighting for her, but alas, she could not. He knew well that by fighting for her he was avenging the murder of her father and also fighting to save Bennvika, but could even the affable old Yathrud's loyalties be swayed if he knew her secret? Certainly, it was a secret that could leave Bennvika's future uncertain for decades. Silrith didn't like to consider the implications of that and she forced the thought from her mind.

'Now,' she said thoughtfully, 'I must speak with Gasbron.'

'Of course. I shall have him brought to you,' Yathrud replied.

'No, it's alright. I shall find him. Where is he likely to be at this time?'

'Inspecting the wall guard most likely. Or if he's finished that, he will probably be with his troops in the training area.'

'Thank you, Uncle,' said Silrith, opening the door.

After asking a sentry on Preddaburg's north wall, Silrith found that Gasbron had indeed finished his rounds there and had gone to meet the new Hentani warriors. Silrith thanked the sentry and headed purposefully towards the training area. On the way she spotted Ezrina and Jezna, the two dancers she had met earlier that day and gave them a light smile as she passed.

Such friendly gestures cost nothing and would be very important for making the common people feel valued, as she well knew. She hoped the girls could give an entertaining performance the next day that would go some way to at least providing some shared enjoyment for all her soldiers. This, in turn, would hopefully help them to create bonds so that they could work together effectively when it came to training and fighting. She had noticed though that while Jezna had returned the gesture in kind, waving happily, Ezrina's smile had been rather more forced and she was perturbed by this. She let it go for now though as she hurried on, making sure to retain a certain grace as she did so.

When she found Gasbron, he and the other soldiers were in the training area, which was a large square with a stone floor. He and a group of divisiomen were demonstrating some of the Bennvikan fighting styles and troop manoeuvres to the Hentani warriors. The new arrivals would have to work around the divisios in the coming battle and it would help if they knew exactly how to use the Bennvikan, Etrovansian and Hentani military strengths in tandem in the most cohesive way possible. At this point, wearing full armour and his chief invicturion's transverse crested helmet with its black and white horsehair stripes, Gasbron was addressing his audience while the divisiomen were demonstrating the 'tortoise' formation, before showing how quickly they could switch to a 'bow' formation. As Gasbron spoke, Blavak translated his words into Hentani.

'As you can see, just as the name suggests, this formation is shaped like the upper and lower limbs of a bow and arrow. It is designed so that as the front troops slowly gave ground to the enemy, their opponents would be engulfed as the soldiers on the flanks of the formation advance.'

As he said this, the front divisiomen, who were in the middle, began to slowly pace backwards, while their comrades on the flanks moved forwards at the same speed, until they had moved into a crescent formation.

'The beauty of the divisioman's fighting style,' he went on. 'Is their sheer versatility. Most of the men and women of the divisios perform the role of heavy infantry, but the elite are selected to serve as heavy cavalry. Up in Kriganheim, they choose a thousand of their best to perform that role, while every other province such as this one has to make do with half that, but a Bastalf divisioman is worth at least two from Kriganheim anyway.' An impromptu cheer rose up from the divisiomen around Gasbron at the compliment, drawing a wry grin from their commander.

'In battle, all divisio infantry carry a pilum, as do the cavalry when it is deemed necessary,' Gasbron said.

He indicated the tall, thin weapon that was handed to him by the nearest soldier. It looked like a lightweight spear.

'This is the divisioman's first line of defence. A wave of these thrown at any enemy is enough to knock them right back, at least for a few seconds. That gives him or her time to get back behind their shield.' He handed the pilum back to the divisioman, then paced on.

'As you can see, the divisioman's shield is quite large. We have round wooden ones for the cavalry and rectangular ones for the infantry, though the cavalry have also been known to ride with a rectangular shield on their back so that they can perform infantry duties if they need to. Every unit's province of origin is identifiable through the crest depicted on the shield, which will be that of their governor, or the Bennvikan national flag in Kriganheim's case. Learn the designs so that you may tell friend from foe.'

He indicated his own shield which, like his comrades, featured a green horizontal strip on the upper and lower thirds, with the Alyredd coat of arms, the three golden dragons on a scarlet background, emblazoned across the middle.

'Chief Invicturion Wrathun,' Silrith called from the edge of the square. Gasbron looked round. Silrith hadn't interrupted him, but he looked surprised by her presence anyway.

'Yes, my Queen?' He said with a bow as she approached. The divisiomen had disengaged from their formation and knelt before their queen. She felt a little out of place on a military training ground in her scarlet dress and white under trousers, but she noticed Gasbron regarding her with an appreciative eye.

'Wrathun,' she said again. 'I find myself in need of some help and I believe my requirements could be met in kind by your talents and experience.'

One of the divisiomen sniggered, catching the attention of Gasbron and Silrith alike. Silrith caught the eye of the guilty divisioman, a woman in her thirties, who dropped her gaze but continued smiling.

'Have I said something funny?' she asked with a withering glare. Anger flared within her, but quickly she swatted the thought from her mind. There were more important things to deal with.

'Come,' she said to Gasbron as she turned to leave.

'Corpralis Candoc, you take the demonstration from here,' Gasbron said to his subordinate, before following Silrith.

'What do you require of me, my Queen?' Gasbron enquired as they walked through the claustrophobic streets of the inner ward.

'I need you to train me to fight with a sword, shield and spear,' she said without dropping her pace. 'I am able enough when it comes to the use of a bow and arrow, but that is hardly the weapon of a leader. I have had some training in the techniques of swordplay, as you yourself have seen, but given the situation, I feel that what I can currently achieve needs some refining.'

Gasbron looked taken aback, apparently unsure whether to take her seriously or not.

'My Queen, won't your uncle, the Lord Yathrud, be leading the army?'

Silrith stopped in her tracks and rounded on Gasbron.

'I will lead my own troops. Of course, I will use my uncle's experience and advice to my advantage, but how can I expect my troops to fight and die for my cause if I do not? You think I'd be a better leader if I cowered in my rooms like a frightened child, instead of taking control of my own destiny? Is that the kind of ruler you'd rather serve?'

She fixed her eyes on his, tight-lipped, almost daring him to answer, but evidently he wasn't that stupid.

'Now, that is where I find myself in requirement of you,' she continued in a lighter tone, pleased that her words appeared to have hit home. Gasbron pursed his lips awkwardly as he thought about his response.

'My Queen, I'm afraid it's not as simple as-'

'-So you're not up to it then?' Silrith interrupted, angry that she hadn't already made her point as clearly as she thought she had. 'I thought turning novices into professional soldiers was your bread and butter when not on campaign. What I am asking of you is less than that. Now I'm sure you were selected as this province's chief invicturion because of your particular talent in that area, or was that a mistake? Is this attitude that you show me now just a lack of commitment? This wouldn't be a time to be on a charge for insubordination now would it?'

'I saved your life,' Gasbron exclaimed.

'You were instructed to,' Silrith countered. 'Do not think that I believe that you have any feeling towards me. Now, you will do as I command.'

Gasbron sighed.

'I will obey your orders, my Queen,' he said.

'Good. Now take me to the armoury. We start immediately.' She turned and they started walking again. She would share in any hardships endured by her troops. She would show her love for her people by leading by example. She cared less for whether or not she was loved. She simply needed them to see that her purpose in life was to protect the helpless. In any case, she would need their loyalty when her secret came out, which it had to eventually. There was no way around it. People would find out one way or another, but if this happened at the wrong time, many people would die and the thought of that sickened Silrith.

'Of course, my Queen,' Gasbron said. 'I'm sure I can find you some appropriate weapons, though a suit of armour will not be possible. You see, they are made to fit the wearer and they take some weeks to make.'

'I've already thought of that,' Silrith said, the smile returning to her face. 'Earlier today I had a servant find me some padded armour, chain mail and boots that fit well. Now I just need some form of supplementary armour and of course some weapons.'

For some reason, Gasbron had a slightly awkward and rather embarrassed expression on his face. Silrith looked at him, confused.

'Speak,' she said.

'Well, wouldn't trying the armour for size be a problem, my Queen?' He asked carefully, looking again at what she was wearing.

'Why?' Silrith rolled her eyes and grinned wryly as she caught his meaning. 'I *have* set aside somewhere where I can change discreetly, Gasbron. You will just have to wait outside while I do so,' she said, trying to keep the exasperation out of her tone.

THE FIELDS OUTSIDE FAEN TIRA, ASRANTICA, BENNVIKA

The camp of Jostan's army sprawled across the lush green fields to the south of the city of Faen Tira. The daffodils were out, birds sang and the morale of the troops was sky high as they basked in the sunshine under which they had met with the reinforcements supplied by Lord Feddilyn Rintta. Tomorrow they would march again and in the coming days, they would meet with the further reinforcements led by Lord Lektik Haganwold and Lord Aeoflynn Tanskeld.

Jithrae, however, was feeling no such confidence. After all, he had joined the army specifically so that he could attempt to find Vaezona. There had been little chance of that so far. He knew that wherever Vinnitar was, there was a chance that Vaezona might be there also, but as he was not a professional soldier, Jithrae had to join the militia, where he served as a spearman.

This meant that his tent would have to be far away from those of the divisiomen. To be caught snooping around the officers' quarters in the gloom of the night was to risk being cut down by an over-exuberant guard who took you for an enemy. Equally, it was impossible simply to drop out of line while on the march to look for her among the camp followers, because aimlessly searching the baggage train for a familiar face would be like looking for a needle in a haystack. Anyway, he decided, some uncouth mercenary would probably spot him straight away and whip him back into line before he'd dropped back ten paces.

This day of rest, however, presented him with an opportunity. Because of the number of refugees who had been coming into Kriganheim and because it was already a great trading city full of people who originally hailed from elsewhere, it had been possible to sign up for units from any part of the kingdom. Being an Asrantican, Jithrae had joined a unit assigned to his home province, whom he had joined up with when Feddilyn's army had met and merged with the main force.

Joining an Asrantican unit meant that it would be easier to find Vinnitar and, hopefully, Vaezona too. As he approached the cordoned off camp, whose flags depicted the black and white trident, the standard of the Rintta family, he headed straight for the nearest sentry, carrying his spear in his right hand and his large round shield in his left.

'Alright, son,' he said casually to the sentry, before realising it was most certainly a mathematical possibility when he saw the boyish face that looked back at him. 'It's midday. End of your patrol, mate. Go get some rest.'

'Cheers, mate,' the sentry replied gratefully as he relinquished his position to Jithrae and sauntered off.

That was easy, Jithrae thought to himself as he attempted to look casual yet vigilant in the way that good sentries always seem to manage. There was a fair amount of activity in the cordoned off area. Many soldiers were present, but also others such as clerks, cooks, horse groomers and, most significantly, servants. Every so often Jithrae would spot a dark-haired girl whom he hadn't seen previously and his heart would leap, only for him to realise it wasn't Vaezona. After what had seemed like an age he was starting to give up.

That was when he spotted a group of divisiomen who had gathered around a table outside one of the larger tents. They wore their armour, but their heads were bare and they tucked into huge lumps of meat, bread and cheese while laughing loudly and telling lewd jokes and stories. The sight of the food reminded Jithrae of his own hunger. Subconsciously he licked his lips. Maybe he'd get some hot stew when he got back to his comrades, but then again maybe he wouldn't. Suddenly he recognised one of the voices, causing him to focus more closely on the men for a moment. Vinnitar!

Transfixed, Jithrae didn't realise he'd stopped.

'Oi! What're you looking at?'

Shit! Jithrae silently cursed to himself.

'Want some food do you? Here, have some,' Vinnitar picked up a lump of cheese, which he deliberately threw so lightly that it landed on the grass just out of Jithrae's reach. The divisiomen howled with mocking laughter at Jithrae's longing expression. Once he realised he was doing it he hastily turned to carry on his patrol. He would have to try again at night, whatever the risk.

'Oi! I know you.'

That got Jithrae's attention. He hesitated momentarily, then started moving again in the hope that Vinnitar would lose interest and let him go.

'Hey! Don't you walk away from me.'

Jithrae halted, briefly closed his eyes, took a deep breath and turned to face Vinnitar. The chief invicturion was on his feet now, standing close to the fence, with all the humour gone from his face, though he smiled slyly.

'Yes, it is you! How're you doing, Jithrae? Are you looking for daddy's little girl?' Vinnitar exclaimed derisively, clearly taking much pleasure in Jithrae's discomfort. He turned back to the other soldiers.

'Hey boys, this is Vaezona's daddy.' He grinned like a child. 'We all enjoyed a bit of Vaezona, didn't we boys?'

Immediately the whole group of divisiomen got to their feet and made animalistic noises, thrusting their hips as if humping the air. Vinnitar turned back to Jithrae.

'Moaned like a fucking whore, she did,' he whispered in Jithrae's ear, before withdrawing to watch the anger boil up in Jithrae's face. 'You won't find her here now though. The king's taken a shine to her.' A surprisingly rueful expression flicked across his face, but then it was gone. 'A shame. She was a lot of fun,' he added with a sneer.

Jithrae felt as if he could run Vinnitar through there and then, but he knew the penalty for such an act and to leave Vaezona fatherless would be no help at all to her in her current situation. He turned to carry on his patrol, ignoring the jeers coming from behind him. He didn't know whether or not to believe Vinnitar, but the idea of the king noticing Vaezona and having her become his own servant was perfectly conceivable.

Kings had done that many times in the past when visiting nobles and anyway, Vaezona was sixteen now and had grown into an attractive young woman. Revealing that information could have been a momentary slip by Vinnitar, but on the other hand, from what he knew of the man, Jithrae was sure that Vinnitar was just the type to throw in a red herring such as this. Either way, he had to see if it was true.

Chapter 9

Jithrae had some idea of where the king's command tent was likely to be, as he had previously seen part of the royal complex, but then again it was hard to miss. As could be expected, it was right at the centre of the camp and was full of brightly coloured tents, each flying the banners of various noble houses, including the families of the governors, who also had more tents pitched closer to their respective divisios and provincial militias.

Given that the ruling monarch also held the title of Governor of Kriganheim, the divisios of the royal province were also present and as Jithrae approached, he saw that this area, cordoned off just as the other noble areas had been, was guarded by a pair of divisiomen, rather than militia. No chance of posing as a guard then.

The two before him had no shields and their helmets lacked the transverse black and white crest he had seen on Vinnitar's helm when he had come to Jithrae's home on that fateful day. They did, however, clutch spears, ready to block the path of anyone who tried to enter without permission.

Given his lack of success thus far, Jithrae decided a more direct approach might be in order. As he nervously approached the two guards who stood at the entrance, he reminded himself he had nothing to hide, so what could he be afraid of?

'Err...g-good day sirs,' he said, attempting to sound a little more educated than he was. 'There, err, there appears to have been-,'

'-What?' one of the guards grunted, attempting to intimidate Jithrae further.

'Oh, well, there appears to have been some kind of mistake. A sort of mix up, you see.'

'Really?' The divisioman's interest looked almost genuine.

'Yes, um, my daughter, she was travelling with me, you see, err, with the camp followers. She was supposed to find me when we stopped to set up camp, but she hasn't, a-and I believe she may be here.'

The guards looked at each other, then laughed.

'You think we're going to let you in here with that story? Your daughter is lost so you come straight to the royal enclosure to look for her?'

'But, but what if I left my weapons here? Go on, search me.'

'Oh yes, you can go in if we do that.'

'Really?'

'No. Sod off.'

Jithrae cursed to himself as he walked away. That was when he spotted a small hillock off to his left, topped with a few trees and these led to a larger wood that marked the edge of the camp. Crucially though, the hillock overlooked the royal enclosure. He began walking purposefully towards it. He wondered if he'd be able to spot Vaezona from there. Just then though, he caught sight of another divisioman who, as Jithrae watched, reached the crest of the hillock and continued his patrol in Jithrae's direction. Wondering what he could try next, Jithrae watched the man, who didn't seem to have noticed him, as he was still some way off.

He paused, wondering how to get in. He withdrew a little when the third guard came past, telling Jithrae to keep away, but he still hung around wondering what to do. Then he noticed a dark-haired teenage girl some meters away on the other side of the fence, standing with her back to him, hanging bed linen on a line. She wore a nicely made yellow dress of the kind that, had it not been for the activity in which she was currently engaged, would have made it hard to tell whether she was a member of a relatively rich family or the servant of the ultra-rich, as Vaezona would surely be if she were here. Below that, she wore white under-trousers that protruded from below the dress' hem. As she worked, he squinted to make out her features. She must have felt his eyes on her, as she turned to look over her shoulder.

'Father?'

Damn! That wasn't Vaezona. His blood ran cold as he realised that although her eyes were on him, she was addressing one of the guards. Divisiomen earned a good wage and lived well, with such a lifestyle allowing their families to join them in the closed-off quarters reserved for them and their noble masters. Quickly he tried to get away while looking nonchalant, but it was no use.

'What is it, Nazarae?' he heard the guard say.

'That man. Over there. He keeps looking at me.'

'Oi, You!' the guard called to Jithrae, who gave a fearful intake of breath before turning to face his aggressor. 'I thought I told you to piss off!'

'Well, I,' Jithrae had no chance to say any more. The guard marched forward and grabbed him by the collar, knocking off his helmet in the process. Jithrae reached out for it, causing him to drop his shield, much to the amusement of the second guard. In stark contrast, the girl's face was deadly serious.

'Havin' a look-see at my daughter, were ya?' said the first guard. He paused, with a thoughtful expression on his face, as if he were trying to form an intelligent idea using less than adequate reserves of brain matter. Clearly his wages as a professional soldier were not in proportion to his intellect. Even Jithrae could see that. After a moment the man gave a toothy grin, having clearly thought of a way to exact his revenge on Jithrae for his alleged leering.

'Come on soldier, let's see what the king makes of peasants who stand around trying to get into his private enclosure.'

The guard ripped the spear out of Jithrae's hand and threw it to the floor, before half dragging him through the entrance, laughing to himself in his deep, gruff voice. After what seemed like an age, they came to a large tent, decorated in the silver and blue of the House of Kazabrus. Three flags flew from the top, each depicting the silver Kazabrus eagle on a blue background. Below, there was a large section of the front that was folded outwards making it possible to see inside.

As they entered, Jithrae was thrown to the floor roughly. Trembling, he looked up to see a number of eminent people who had clearly been discussing whatever the document on the table in the middle of the tent was and whose eyes now all fell upon him. He did not know who some of these people were, but soon worked it out.

The broad, dark-haired young man dressed in white robes was clearly the new king. He wore jewels of every colour on his fingers, with sapphires hanging from his earlobes and a golden chain that hung low on his chest. Jithrae did not know the name of either of the men in armour next to the king but was struck by the jet black armour plates that one of them wore. He had a square, scarred face and short hair and the sculpted helmet under his arm had just a single horizontal slit for his eyes. The other armoured man was of the divisios and the black and white transverse crest on his open-faced helmet with its low cheek plates and nasal guard marked him out as a chief invicturion, just like Vinnitar, though it wasn't him. The only one whose identity he knew for certain was Lord Feddilyn Rintta, who was dressed in green today. He'd seen the Governor of Asrantica once riding on horseback through the streets of Faen Tira when Jithrae had visited the city. The governor must have been on his way to some banquet or another, apparently attempting a look of consummate serenity while ignoring the jeers of his people as he passed. Yet now his beady eyes looked down his long nose at the man before him.

On the far left, in the background, reclining on a couch and looking distinctly bored, was Dowager Queen Accutina, presumably. She was being fanned by a servant girl in a pretty, knee-length, dress-like tunic and under trousers; all made of silk as white as a dove. The outfit's relative simplicity emphasised the copious amounts of material that had gone into Accutina's purple garment.

Just for a moment, the servant girl raised her eyes, Vaezona's eyes. Jithrae's heart leapt with such intensity that he had to stop himself from crying out. He could see in her eyes that the feeling was reciprocal until the moment was lost as Accutina yanked Vaezona's arm forward. Simply instructing Vaezona to wave the fan slightly closer apparently never occurred to her.

'Majesty,' the guard said with a grunt, yet somehow sounding respectful. 'I found this worm hangin' about by the royal picket line havin' a look at what's goin' on. Thought ya might wanna talk to him about what's what.'

Jostan shrugged, striding out from behind the table.

'Such eloquence as always, Etralbard,' he sighed. 'Thank you, but remember your salute next time. Forget it again and we might just take it as insubordination.'

'Very sorry, your Majesty,' the guard said. 'It won't happen again'. He quickly snapped his palm up to the side of his head, then stood to attention, but he still received a soldierly glare from the chief invicturion. Clearly, he was in for some harsh words later and he knew it.

'Gormaris,' said Jostan. 'From now on I want one of your guards on duty at the gate at all times alongside the divisiomen. Teach them some respect.'

'Yes, your majesty,' said the man in raven coloured armour.

'So, Etralbard, you're sure this man wasn't on some duty or other?' Jostan asked.

'No he wasn't, your Majesty. His spear had an Asrantican pennant. He shouldn't have been anywhere near here.'

Jostan turned to Feddilyn.

'One of your elite,' he chided him ironically, causing both men to laugh dryly.

'So, is this true, soldier? Were you spying on us?' Jostan demanded accusingly, returning to his formal tone.

'N-no, your Majesty! I was just passing-'

'-So you *were* there then?'

'Yes, but-'

'Why?' Jostan asked with a mocking expression. Jithrae thought quickly. His heart was pounding so hard that he thought it might rip its way out of his chest. He didn't dare draw attention to Vaezona.

'Well,' he began, under pressure. 'I was hungry and, err, I saw this goat, you see, so, err, I followed it but then I lost it and I thought it must have got in here, Majesty.'

A tense silence fell. King Jostan, Lord Rintta, the chief invicturion, the black armoured soldier, Queen Accutina and Vaezona all stared at him. Etralbard was still standing to attention, though having to bite his lip. Suddenly Jostan's face creased into a laugh, automatically giving the others permission to do so. Vaezona's face remained etched with pain at what she was seeing. With equal speed though, Jostan's hysterical expression dropped into one of cold austerity.

'Do not mock us, soldier. Take him away.'

'Wait,' Accutina blurted out, causing everyone to turn to her. She'd spotted the desperate, silent fear in Vaezona's eyes and she surveyed the girl with a malevolent smile. 'What's your name, girl? Vezinae isn't it?' she asked.

'Vaezona, your Majesty,' Vaezona responded, failing to meet Accutina's gaze. Accutina sniggered callously.

'Do you know this man?' she said, gesturing towards Jithrae. 'You do, don't you?' She seemed excited now and she clapped her hands together with glee. 'Is he your father? He is, isn't he? Well, when he's executed, I'll ensure you get a good view.' She laughed as heartily as if she'd just been told a juicy bit of gossip.

'No,' said Jostan.

'What?' Accutina demanded incredulously.

Jostan put his hand to his chin, semi-ignoring her. Kneeling at Jostan's feet, Jithrae was completely bewildered. He had never been so terrified in all his life. His fate and that of Vaezona hung in the balance and he knew it.

'We can use this girl for better things than fanning,' Jostan mused thoughtfully. 'Lord Rintta, did you not say earlier that our lack of word from Rildayorda and, more to the point, our lack of an explanation for that, suggests that our spies there are too few?'

'Yes, your Majesty, but surely we require someone with experience to take on such a trusted position?' questioned Feddilyn, as Accutina sulked in the background and the soldiers stayed silent.

'On the contrary,' replied Jostan. 'That's the beauty of it. She's expendable and has no provable link to us. We do not trust Lord Alyredd and we must know exactly what he's up to by failing to send us any troops. We don't want a revolt while our back is turned. In addition, spies, by their very nature are treacherous bastards and the addition of another may just cause those planning to switch sides to conclude that doing so would be a fatal idea. They need to know that we are watching them as well as their targets.'

'I quite agree, your Majesty,' said Feddilyn. 'But may I suggest, would it not be prudent to notify at least one of our spies of her approach and arrange for them to work together. That way they might interpret her arrival as being a symbol of your support for them, revitalising their loyalty to you.'

Jostan paused.

'Just one. We have a spy at the citadel at Preddaburg, if the wretch still lives. As you know, we haven't had word from there for a while and we can't be sure if there has been a change of loyalties. But we cannot risk getting word to them at this moment. We don't want old Yathrud getting any tip-offs of our suspicions. We'll have to rely on my spy's initiative and intelligence."

He looked at Jithrae.

'Oh, get him out of our sight. Lock him away,' he said.

The kneeling Jithrae cried out as Jostan kicked him in the stomach, but he made no attempt to resist Etralbard as the big divisioman pulled him back to his knees and dragged him out of the tent. He knew that to do anything else would do Vaezona no favours whatsoever.

Back inside the tent, Jostan turned to address the chief invicturion.

'Chief Invicturion Aetrun, we want you to take Vaezona here into the citadel at Preddaburg. We know it's earlier than planned, but the vanguard will march out ahead of the main army this very day. You will lead it. Take whichever units you choose. Officially, your business in Rildayorda will be to find out from Lord Yathrud personally why he has not sent me any troops. While you do that, young Vaezona will slip into the background and infiltrate the citadel's staff ranks on my behalf.' He turned to Vaezona, who was standing wide-eyed and visibly shivering with fear.

'Now, are you starting to understand what you have to do for us, in order to keep your father alive?'

Vaezona nodded solemnly.

'Yes, your Majesty.'

'Good.' Reaching into a small box on a table near Accutina's couch, he picked out a small object, hiding it with his palms and put it into Vaezona's hand, placing her other hand over the object so that not even those around them could see what it was.

'Show this to nobody,' he said with certainty and with a quick look around her, Vaezona shoved the object under her clothes, so that it just nestled against her left breast, momentarily distracting Jostan's attention.

'Nobody that is, except for one person and when you see that person, you must hand this over to them at the earliest opportunity. We are sure they will seek you out. You must not be caught with this by anyone else, or it will be discovered that you are working for us. If that happens, you will be unable to complete your mission, we will find out and your father will die. Do we make ourselves absolutely, explicitly clear?' He paused for Vaezona to answer.

'Yes, your Majesty,' she said, visibly forcing the words out, shuddering, presumably at the thought of the consequences if she failed. Jostan nodded approvingly.

'Come, girl,' he said. 'Let me tell you more about where you are going.'

Chapter 10

The dense morning mist hung low over the still damp grass. Accutina had no idea how she'd ended up there. How had she become so lost? The last thing she could remember was being in Jostan's camp, but after going out for some fresh air, she had lost all sense of direction.

She was suddenly aware that she could hear the voices of men and women, presumably bustling around the camp, but they were very faint and she couldn't pinpoint which direction they were coming from. All she could see was trees and grass. She decided to try to retrace her steps, but it was no use. She soon realised she'd been walking in this new direction for far longer than she'd previously been heading the opposite way. And that river. She had no recollection of it being there before, yet there it was, having seemed simply to appear over the past few moments.

She heard a shout. She spun around, not knowing even if the shout had been from a man, woman or child. Her pulse was racing and she found herself breathless; the harshness of the sudden cold breeze making her skin crawl as if it were covered with cockroaches.

'Who's there?' she cried.

Nobody answered. She was alone and yet in her state of extreme claustrophobia she felt another presence but could not place it. She looked around desperately and started to stumble in one direction or another, though she knew not which. As if to torment her further, it started to rain.

'Jostan! Jostan!' she cried.

She sensed movement behind her. A horse whinnied. He'd found her. But as suddenly as her fear had turned to elation, her elation turned to terror as the huge white stallion galloped into view, heading straight for her. She could not see its rider's face; in fact, she could see nothing more than a silhouette with its sword arm outstretched and the long blade ready to tear through warm flesh.

Accutina was momentarily rooted to the ground, but instinct forced her to turn and run for her life. Her gown slowed her severely, while the bank of the river was muddy and it was all she could do not to slip. Surely the rider would be on her at any moment. She could hear the panting of the horse as it came inexorably closer; the sound taunting her, playing with her. With a searing burst of pain, she felt the weapon glance across her back, ripping a wide gash into it.

As she was cut down by the faceless rider, she fell helplessly into the river, which seemed to be much wider and deeper than it had been before. She gasped for breath as she choked on her own blood. She madly kicked for land but again the thick material of her long dress pulled her deeper and she could only tread water.

'Jostan! Jostan! Somebody help me! Help me please!'

Something grabbed on to her foot from under the water. She tried to resist, splashing pathetically, but the force created by the monster below was too strong for her and with a final gurgle she slipped below the surface. As the water engulfed her, her entire world turned to a bright white. She threw herself upwards. All she could hear now were her own whimpers. Once she got them under control, she listened for other sounds.

Silence. It took Accutina a while to realise where she was. She blinked and blurred shades of blue, white, red and gold formed into cushions, her bedclothes and a semi-transparent curtain that hung around her bed in a loose square. With no small amount of relief, she realised that she was in her tent, sitting up in bed. She had no idea how far through the night it was, but she was certain that dawn was still some hours away. Jostan was not next to her. He must have stayed in his own bed that night. She laid back down and tried to fall asleep.

She was still agitated at breakfast, one of the few times in the day when she could be alone with Jostan, save for the servants. As they ate at a table set up in his tent, she carefully picked her moment to broach the subject.

'Jostan?'

'Hmm?'

'I, I've had a dream,'

'Oh yes?'

'I was cut down by a man on a horse,' Accutina warned. Jostan laughed.

'And let us guess, you're going to jump out of your skin every time you see a man on a horse from now on?'

'Jostan,' Accutina spat, trying to get through to him as his face mocked her. 'It's an omen. It was the white stallion of the Alfwyns. Estarron is telling us that Silrith lives.'

'Of course, she does. For now. Then starvation and exposure will take hold and she will die, which is what needs to happen. Silrith killed Fabrald to become the next in line to the throne, didn't she?'

Accutina said nothing.

'*Didn't she?*' Jostan repeated, more firmly this time.

Accutina nodded, failing to look Jostan in the eye.

'Exactly. And once in power, she would have stopped at nothing to stay there. We had to protect the Bennvikan people from that threat, yes?'

Accutina nodded again, colouring slightly in embarrassment, yet not totally convinced by Jostan's argument.

'She deserves her fate. Now, let's hear no more of this foolish nonsense. You have been useful to us up until this point. It'd be a shame to lose that. But be aware that you have played all the cards that you have and as yet there is no marriage to bind you to us. You have connections, but so do we. You carry our son, but he is as yet unborn and we can easily have another one with someone else. Furthermore, any desire we once had for you is growing ever more fleeting. Do not forget how replaceable you are.' he said coldly. Accutina's heart filled with fear on hearing these words.

'I'm sorry, your Majesty, it will not happen again.'

'There's a good girl,' he added approvingly, taking her hand and kissing it.

KRIGANHEIM, BENNVIKA

In the aftermath of the riot, life was beginning to return to normal in Kriganheim and revellers made their way noisily through the streets outside as night fell. Naivard greeted Hoban and Zethun in the dimly lit surroundings of his office. Braldor waited outside, keeping vigil to ensure that they were not interrupted.

Inside the small room, the three men were seated around a rectangular wooden table. There were just enough candles dotted around for all of those present to read each other's faces properly, though of course they were kept far from the scrolls and parchments which covered another table on the far side of the room, as well as a number of shelves.

'I cannot get over the callousness of the king's response. It's foolish, foul and short-sighted,' Zethun bemoaned, as he put his wine cup back on the table. Naivard's office was simple, but it wasn't without its comforts. Evidently, the decor, or lack of it, was just a sign of the balding grey man's plain tastes rather than any lack of money.

'I fear that this sort of behaviour may be typical of our new ruler,' Naivard stated coolly as he refilled Zethun's cup.

'Yes. His reaction seemed a pretty instinctive one to me,' Hoban observed. 'He appears the sort of man who believes a show of strength is the answer to everything; and even, a man who believes that to beg is to show weakness and to give concessions to those who beg is to show one's self as being weaker still.'

'Well, he can't hope to gain anything from that,' Zethun sighed. 'A nation prospers when its people are happy. If a king fails to protect his people, then what purpose does he serve? It's all very well having a great warrior as our king, but that won't stop the people from starving. If he doesn't realise soon that he needs the people as much as they need him he will lose everything and the country will descend into anarchy.'

'Oh, anarchy is already here, Zethun,' Naivard replied. 'As you know, only days ago, my own brother-in-law and his family were evicted from their house in Asrantica and my niece was kidnapped by Lord Rintta's soldiers.'

'That man is a sully to the word 'nobleman',' said Zethun, feeling a new surge of anger. 'Once again I am sorry for what has happened to your family. It makes me embarrassed to be of noble blood.'

'Your family will be in my prayers, Naivard,' said Hoban, patting his friend on the shoulder. 'Do they prosper now?'

'My wife's sister and her younger children have come to live with my wife and me, here in Kriganheim. My brother-in-law has joined the king's army. It was a group of divisiomen who took Vaezona, so we thought that if

129

there was a chance of finding her, that would be it. Yet, I fear I may never see either of them again.'

'I'm sorry,' said Zethun. He was unsure what to say and was suddenly very aware of the fact that Hoban and Naivard knew each other far better than he knew either of them. 'Your family will be in my prayers also. Yet we can still stop this from happening to others and we must. The king already brings oppression and at this rate, he will soon bring famine. Bennvika has suffered this sort of tyranny before. It cannot happen again. There is only one way to stop it. A republic.'

'Those are dangerous words, Zethun,' said Hoban with a cautioned tone. 'But these are dangerous times so I suppose they are not out of place. Naivard, tell Zethun of the theory you described to me earlier today. I believe he should hear it. It may well be that King Jostan has no care for anyone's rights except his own - something not unheard of in kings.'

'Certainly,' Naivard nodded. 'You see Zethun, on top of the current situation and the rumours of religious persecution conducted by the king and his family in Verusantium, I have concerns about how the king came to power in the first place. How a monarch gains the throne seems to me to be a good indicator as to what sort of ruler they will be. Let's face it. It's well known that it wasn't the expected line of succession was it? His claim was secondary to Princess Silrith's.'

'King Lissoll was murdered by his own daughter. What evidence can you possibly have to the contrary?' Zethun scoffed.

'Well it's all bit convenient for the king, isn't it?' Naivard suggested.

'Absolutely. But it has always been thus with royals. What's unusual about this one?'

'They were very quick to find the culprit, weren't they?' Naivard pressed.

'What are you insinuating?' Zethun asked.

'Nothing,' Naivard said. 'I just think there should be an inquiry into the cause of the king's death. If the princess and her maid really were the killers, then nobody else at court should fear the repercussions, should they? Whereas if they are nervous about such an inquiry, then that alerts my suspicions. If only we could convince the king that there may have been a third person involved in the murder, or even, we convince him that we are there investigating another crime altogether. Maybe some petty theft between the servants?'

'That's it,' Hoban said as if an idea had suddenly come to him. 'We need not speak to the nobles themselves at first. We can gain plenty of information simply by speaking to the staff. I shall have my sources seek one or two out. Speaking of which, I have heard of a rather significant rumour. The Amulet of Hazgorata has been stolen.'

'Why is that important? Did the Dowager Queen not take it with her when she travelled with the king?' Zethun asked inquisitively.

'The rumour suggests not,' Hoban replied. 'It probably isn't true. Personally, if I were looking for it, I'd start by looking for Accutina. My sources say she keeps with tradition by keeping it in her quarters much of the time. Yet, clearly, an accusation has been made, suggesting theft.'

'Who made the accusation?' asked Zethun.

'I don't know the details of the rumour's source,' said Hoban. 'But the Amulet must not get into the hands of a non-Bennvikan. If it does, then the people will believe that the thief, or at least their nation, will bring about Bennvika's fall. If only to avert the threat of panic, investigating this rumour would give us a perfectly good reason to be conducting an investigation involving palace servants if anyone asks. The loss of such a jewel would be a great embarrassment to the crown, though it would be nothing less than earthly damnation for the one who stole it. kings have feared it for centuries. You know the prophecy it carries. *Mother of many, Mother of none; a Queen will fall and a Warrior will come.* I'm told the king quoted it in the Congressate Hall. Apparently, he says that when she was yet a mortal woman, the goddess Lomatteva predicted our current situation. He is using it to his own ends, to consolidate his power.'

'I have no belief in the prophecy. But the idea of the people being manipulated by it in such a way is most disturbing,' Zethun replied thoughtfully. 'Wait a minute.'

'What?' Naivard asked.

'I've heard that quote before many times,' Zethun elaborated. 'And I know that legend says that the Amulet of Hazgorata was once owned by Lomatteva, but I've never heard anyone say that she made the prediction herself. Yes, she never had earthly children, but the Amulet was supposedly given to her as a gift from Vitrinnolf on their wedding day when he was also yet mortal and they united the lands of Hazgorata and Kriganheim to bring about Bennvika's birth. Those are the only parts that are known to be true. The rest is conjecture.'

'So what's your point?' Naivard asked.

'I don't think the king's interpretation of the prophecy stands up to scrutiny,' Zethun said. 'Firstly, he is a follower of Estarron. They don't usually react that well to the idea of there being other gods. I'd be very surprised if he even believes the prophecy himself. He's just saying what he believes the people want to hear until such time as he no longer has to concern himself with that. Secondly, we all know how hard it is for many women to accept their fate if they can't have children, especially when they are required to produce an heir, even if, like Lomatteva, they are famously a mother to their people. To me, calling her the 'mother of many, mother of none' is a bit insulting. Why would Vitrinnolf give a woman a gift with that inscription on it if it referred to her in a way that she may find repellent? Would you? I wouldn't. At any rate, who's to say that the prophecy wasn't inscribed on the Amulet at some later point? She may fit the description, but I don't believe it refers to her. It sounds to me like a prophecy that refers to characters who were yet to make their mark on history, but who are destined to do so in a significant way,'

'Which, if true, makes me believe that it doesn't refer to Princess Silrith or King Jostan either. The king's entire explanation falls down,' Hoban mused. 'But that will not stop him trying to use it anyway and its theft, if indeed it has been stolen, suggests that somebody else is trying to do the same. The Hentani believe it is one of their people that it refers to. They will be encouraged by this development. Don't forget, in the south, their religious ways are tolerated. Lord Yathrud even built a temple there to Lomatteva, saying that she and the tribal goddess Bertakaevey are one and the same.'

'An intuitive way of pacifying the conquered peoples,' Naivard commented. 'Makes me proud to be a Bennvikan.'

'And a successful approach too, until now, at least,' said Zethun. 'Yet the fact remains that whilst our religions have aspects in common, they are, after all, still quite different. I believe that in some Hentani communities, the prophecy has a longer version, doesn't it? Something about the warrior

132

coming in a rain of fire, or words to that effect. Yes, that was it, *Mother of many, Mother of none, a Queen will fall and a Warrior will come in a rain of fire and from the ashes of destruction, a daughter shall rise.'*

'There will always be some who try to make things sound even more dramatic,' said Hoban. 'Their version is heresy and should not be heeded. Only the pure, unembellished prophecy is genuine. Any extensions of it, or any mentions of a 'Daughter of Ashes', as they call this messiah they are waiting for, is total fantasy.'

'Mother of many, Mother of none, a Queen will fall and a Warrior will come,' Zethun said again in a pondering tone. 'In either version, there is no clue as to the identity of the childless woman. Heresy or not, I have read that the Hentani believe that a childless woman and a warrior will rise from ash and fire to lead them to glory and in so doing the woman will become the 'mother' of her nation. They believe that the women with a sword shown on the Amulet is an image of the Daughter of Ashes, not of our goddess Lomatteva and that the man beside her is the warrior, not Vitrinnolf.'

Naivard nodded in acknowledgement, though Hoban did not.

'So Jostan believes that he is the warrior,' Zethun theorised. 'That Silrith is the fallen queen and he professes to believe that Lomatteva is the mother of many and the mother of none. Meanwhile, he may well be aware of the Hentani's beliefs and probably wants to crush them for no reason other than that. He'll want to stop them getting any ideas about Silrith being the queen in the prophecy and therefore believing that their Daughter of Ashes and their warrior are about to come to them. Yet, somehow, again, I don't believe that even the king believes his own interpretation of the prophecy.'

'He doesn't even believe in our gods, as you said,' Naivard interjected.

'Yes. He has said that Bennvikan culture and religion will be unaffected by his rule,' said Hoban. 'But I'm not sure if anyone genuinely believes that. It's always hard to tell when people are afraid to speak plainly.'

'The king will do and say whatever suits him. He sounds like he is very good at manipulating people. But he cannot be allowed to carry on his rule in the way that he has started. A king is a man, not a god. If this nation is to have a king, then we need one who remembers that. But then we come to the prophecy. Sometimes prophecies are true, but at other times people make them look true. I shudder to think of the suffering the people of Bennvika will endure if he makes them believe his reign has been prophesied by the gods. And once he tires of tolerating our religion...'

He let the statement hang.

'Gentlemen, this man brings oppression and the threat of famine,' Zethun said. 'He may also have committed regicide to gain the throne, he appears to be manipulating a prophecy to his own ends and there is the fear of forced religious conversion in the near future. The people must be spared from living under the boot of such a man. With no other clear candidates to the throne, we have but one option. The republic must live, or Bennvika will die. We must find out all we can if we are to stand any chance against this king.'

THE PREDDABURG CITADEL, RILDAYORDA, BASTALF, BENNVIKA

The following evening, high up in the citadel, Silrith sat in her quarters. As befitted its current incumbent, it was a grand room. She'd never been obsessed with having the best of everything, but she knew that she would offend if she didn't accept the hospitality she was offered. Anyway, she knew she'd be lying if she said she didn't enjoy the comforts of her lifestyle, even though she did have a much greater idea of the plight of the poor than many of her peers did. Having said that, she knew she still had much to learn in that area.

The room was rectangular in shape, with four windows across one of the longer sides that looked out over a splendid view of the sprawling city below, every inch of which was touched by lurid red, orange and pink as the sun set on the western horizon. Each window featured carved wooden dragons around the edges. Opposite the windows was the great oak door with its ornate lion head doorknob.

Everything inside the room was designed for comfort. At one end of it, furthest from the door, was a huge mahogany four-poster bed, with fluffy white pillows and a warm red quilt. It was clearly intended for two people, but even when sleeping alone Silrith had been used to such luxuries as a princess, so this sort of set up was in no way alien to her. She had spent much time here engrossed in the pages of Macciomakkia's writings, soaking up as much of the great philosopher's teachings as she could since Yathrud had gifted the book to her. The room was dotted with lit candles and also featured a number of comfortable chairs as well as wall paintings depicting various mythical subjects. There were also shelves filled with books and at the far end was a writing table, where Silrith herself could be found at this particular moment, hesitating before putting quill to parchment.

However, this was no amateurish attempt at poetry this time, as had been the case on many occasions earlier in her life. This time was different. Knowing the gravity of her situation even with the help of Yathrud and the few Hentani and Etrovansian soldiers who swelled the ranks of her supporters, she knew she needed to find more allies, or defeat seemed almost certain.

Currently, with the divisios and Hentani combined, she had somewhere in the region of seven thousand soldiers, plus whatever numbers of militia could be raised from the city's population. Even then, a total of ten or twelve thousand was surely the most they could hope for, whereas she felt sure that by the time Jostan found out that she was still a threat to him, he could outnumber her by as many as four or five to one and he would have most of the divisios on his side, whereas she would rely largely on peasant militia and tribal warriors. She had to try to get another Bennvikan governor on her side and that was when she'd had an idea. Maybe the knowledge that Yathrud had come to her aid would be enough to convince Oprion to turn against Jostan militarily as well.

It was a long shot and a massive gamble, but she knew that if she could send a message by sea all the way north and round the coast of Bennvika to the province of Hazgorata, she might be able to avoid the letter being intercepted and stand some chance of winning an important ally. On the other hand, she knew that if Jostan was still unaware of her escape and this message fell into his hands, then her cover would be blown.

The fact that Yathrud had received an order from Jostan to raise troops to support a campaign against the Hentani suggested that he didn't know yet that she had evaded him. However just as soon as that thought came into her head, another voice deep in the back of her mind told her that this might be a trick to lull her into a false sense of security and that he was already marching south to deal with her, in which case she needed more allies as soon as possible. Either way, Jostan would soon realise that Yathrud would not be sending him any troops and it would be a matter of time before he started enquiring why. If it came to it, then with luck, Rildayorda may be able to withstand a siege, but as things stood, any further campaign would be out of the question.

This was where Oprion could help, if he was willing, unlike earlier. His money could ensure that his army was loyal to the House of Aethelgard, rather than royalty. She had no choice but to give him a second chance, despite what had happened before. If he decided to take her side, he would bring with him a sizable force.

Conferring with Yathrud and Shappa had seemed to bring up more questions than answers, so she consulted her book. Macciomakkia's writings may have been over five hundred years old, but nonetheless, something in her words transcended through the centuries and spoke to Silrith and this helped her somewhat in making up her mind. After what seemed like an age of indecision, she had decided to take the risk. She began to write.

My dear friend and noble Lord Oprion,

I trust that the arrival of this letter serves as the most tangible proof possible that, contrary to what I'm sure you have been told, I am in fact alive, well and free from captivity. I am no longer held by the troops of the usurper Jostan Kazabrus and although I am currently unaware of whether or not he has learned of my escape, time is in short supply.

I understand and forgive your reasons for not supporting me earlier, but now, as you are my oldest companion, I again beseech you; let us reignite the bond

136

that we shared in more innocent times when we were but children and not let the events of the more recent past come between us. I realise the wounds that were caused still perforate severely, but I vow to salve them with the promise of a more enduring friendship and my eternal gratitude, were you to come to my aid in my time of need.

I hope with all my heart that you still think of me with enough affection that you might support me in this cause and that the troubles of our jaded past might be forever forgotten amid the shining light of a more harmonious future. This nation will thrive only if the person who sits on its throne is there by right, not through murder and slander of the most despicable and traitorous kind.

Your support will be the key to this conflict; something that will not go unrecognised, because history will judge you by your actions in response to this letter and therefore I urge you to do the right thing, not because it is easy, but because it is right.

For reasons that I'm sure you will understand, I cannot tell you my current location until my messenger returns with your answer. Such times require careful discretion.

With all the love and affection my heart can give,

Silrith

As she finished the letter, she quickly reviewed her work. Happy with what she had written, she rolled it up and melted the end of a stick of sealing wax over a candle. She then heated the seal slightly, then firmly pressed it against the wax to complete the job. She had of course deliberately chosen a plain seal, as hers was still somewhere in Kriganheim Palace and to use Yathrud's would give away her location.

She jumped slightly as there was a knock at the door. Quickly she put the letter away. It could be sent tomorrow.

'Come in,' she said, brushing a lock of hair away from her face. Shappa opened the door, smiling.

'They're ready for you, my Lady.'

Chapter 11

Shappa led Silrith into the main courtyard where she had been greeted by Yathrud on her arrival. He announced her, causing the sudden, sharp creaking of chairs as everyone stood as a mark of respect. In the dusky evening firelight, she could see many people, mostly soldiers. She was pleased to see that the Hentani and the Etrovansians were both well represented among the more numerous Bennvikans. A large banqueting table had been set up opposite a raised stage, behind which a large fire burned and there were many smaller tables dotted about. To the side of the stage was a band, sporting a variety of Hentani instruments, from clap sticks to drums made of animal skin. A sense of anticipation hung over the crowd as they waited to see what was going to happen.

Silrith and Shappa, of course, headed straight for the main table, where they were joined by Yathrud and Bezekarl, among others, such as Yathrud's new wife, Kintressa. She was a haughty woman in her mid-thirties. Her attitude grated on Silrith, as she had discovered on her previous visit, but she had also noticed that Kintressa had been behaving in a reclusive manner recently, having claimed to be ill and unable to attend when Silrith was welcomed to the city by Yathrud, but she had made an appearance for this event.

Yathrud had only married Kintressa six months earlier. Both Yathrud and King Lissoll had been distraught, as Silrith herself had been, when Monissaea had died in childbirth two years ago. Yet out of tragedy had been born a much-loved blessing, Yathugarra. It had been a most unexpected pregnancy, given that Monissaea had been over forty. It had been hailed as a miracle, even, until Monissaea's death. These days, Yathugarra was affectionately known as 'Garra' and at two, she was far too young to join in with the night's festivities, but doubtlessly was inside with her nursemaids, bouncing and rolling around in her cot as they attempted the arduous task of getting her to sleep. How Silrith loved that little girl. What a thing it would be to have a child.

'I assume those must be your Hentani dancers,' Shappa inquired, nodding towards the two girls who had left the band and were now walking on to the stage.

'Yes,' Silrith replied. 'I hope the soldiers like them. I've never seen Hentani dancing. I'm told it's quite – intense.'

Shappa scoffed.

'What?' Silrith laughed. 'I'm guessing you've seen it before then?'

'I have, and intense is one way you could describe it.'

Silrith laughed and gave him a look that said 'Tell me more.'

'You'll see,' Shappa said, reading her expression.

As he said this Yathrud left the table and mounted the stage to address all those present.

'Attention everyone, we are all here tonight at the invitation of our beloved Queen Silrith, the rightful ruler of Bennvika, with whose presence we are blessed, to welcome to this city our respected allies Chief Hojorak and Prince Kivojo of the Hentani and their many great warriors. I know that some of you here are familiar with me, but for those new arrivals who aren't, my name is Lord Yathrud Alyredd, Governor of Bastalf. Also among our main table party tonight are my son, Bezekarl,' Bezekarl stood, turned and bowed his head to the audience, then sat back down, 'and Prince Shappa of Etrovansia.' Shappa did the same.

'Remember Prince Shappa's name,' Yathrud continued. 'Because you soldiers will be cursing it tomorrow when you see the emergency training regime that he and Invicturion Wrathun have drawn up for you.'

This prompted a laugh from the crowd, including Shappa. Silrith was pleased to see that he could take a joke, though she was disappointed when she looked further down at the other end of the table to see that Gasbron evidently couldn't. His smile seemed much more forced. Silrith couldn't stand people who were too focused on their pride.

'Now,' Yathrud went on. 'As you see there are others on this stage and I'm sure you are all eager for me to hand over to them and begin the night's merrymaking, so without further ado, I present for your viewing pleasure, Ezrina and Jezna.'

A cheer went up and all now focused their gaze on Ezrina and Jezna, who were getting into position on the stage, neatly presented in new dresses provided by Silrith.

This must be the largest crowd we've ever performed for, thought Ezrina. There had to be at least five hundred people watching.

Their short brown dresses had been brought to them by some of Lord Alyredd's servants and had now been adapted so that they were now only thigh length, making them similar to the Hentani ones that she and Jezna had travelled in. The look still produced the desired effect, especially once the red and white feathers had been added to their hair, necklaces, bracelets and anklets. The fire behind them emphasised their sultry appearance, seeming to light up the red ochre patterns on their bodies.

With the stage now clear of all but Ezrina and Jezna, they stood very close to each other, face to face, before both stepping back a few paces and taking a moment to breathe; a moment of calm before the storm.

Off to the right of the stage, the music started, with a strong beat of the drums. The girls shot out their arms in time to the music, mimicking each other's movements, before moving them more gracefully in circular motions around their heads and upper bodies, coming close but never quite touching each other, as the music became more tuneful and the string instruments were brought into play.

Their movements were totally in time with each other, yet it felt so free and effortless; as if they were in a trance. As the music of the string instruments grew faster and more intense, she and Jezna moved closer to each other again, still making their circling arm movements, yet it was as if they were unaware of all but themselves.

With a sudden movement, Ezrina reached around Jezna's waist, with Jezna dipping backwards into hold; arms outstretched, both of them turning so that Jezna's upside down face could be seen by the crowd, but most of them were only looking at Ezrina's face buried between Jezna's breasts in what they must have thought was only mock passion. Her hands were all over her lover's sweaty body until she snapped her back up into an upright position, all in time with the music.

She still held Jezna's hand and Jezna allowed herself to be spun back into Ezrina's arms, her back to her lover's chest. Ezrina now forced her face between Jezna's chin and shoulder, as if to cover her neck in kisses, before Jezna spun away again as if tempting Ezrina with her body, then repeating the movement to cheers from the audience.

As the music briefly returned to its original tune, they fell back into their former positions, doing the same arm movements as before, but with the sexual tension between the two of them far higher this time and the pace far quicker. The music dropped to a single constant beat with little accompaniment, but as it built back up, the girls moved towards each other again.

Passing, then turning to face each other, they came almost kissing close; both sensually running a hand through the other's hair, still mimicking each other perfectly, before Jezna again pushed away; the music rising as she did. But the constant pulse-like beat symbolised Ezrina's persistence and she again spun Jezna back into her arms, this time with the two landing face to face; Jezna dropping her head and arms back violently, thrusting her breasts upward and clamping her leg around Ezrina's waist, as if giving herself to her, while Ezrina herself held her around her back as the music hit fever pitch, then died.

The crowd roared. Jezna whooped and clapped, jumping up and down like an excited child – a total transformation from the exotic temptress she had been only moments previously. Ezrina smiled with genuine pleasure as she caught her breath. Jezna threw her arms around her and held her tightly in celebration. Both of them were dripping with sweat from the exertion of their intimate performance, as well as the heat of the fire behind them, but Ezrina didn't care. This was something that she and Jezna shared; a way of life they faced together and she was glad beyond measure to have her dearest love with her in these unfamiliar surroundings.

Shappa turned to Silrith.
'So, what did you think, my Lady?
She looked at him for a moment before responding slowly.

'It was...an eye-opener,' she said as she burst into a fit of giggles.

That exotic performance began a long night of partying. Nobody knew when they'd be able to relax like this again. After Ezrina and Jezna's Hentani demonstration, there was dancing of the Bennvikan kind, though this was a group affair, where every woman present of whatever rank, including Silrith, Kintressa, Ezrina and Jezna, chose a man to dance with. The dance itself featured long periods where the two partners were in hold, as well as shorter, more energetic ones where they faced each other from a short distance, furiously tapping their heels and toes on the floor in time with the music, while keeping their upper body still, hands on their hips, with all their movement below the waist.

Though out of uniform, wearing a black tunic and grey breeches, Gasbron was entitled to a seat on the main table, through being the Alyredd's chief invicturion, but he had been the wrong side of Yathrud for him to stand much chance of any proper interaction with Silrith. In fact, Yathrud, Bezekarl and Kintressa were all between him and his queen and it still surprised him how sorely Shappa's easy conversation with her grated on him.

Silrith, of course, chose to dance with Shappa, much to Gasbron's annoyance, though the emotion was abated a little when he was approached by one of the Hentani girls. After the girl, Ezrina, introduced herself, Gasbron reciprocated and accepted her offer.

She took his hand and led him to the dance floor. They began a slow dance, in hold, surrounded by all the other couples.

'You speak our language well,' Gasbron observed. 'Do you come from Rildayorda?'

The city's population these days was a vibrant mix of Hentani and Bennvikans.

'No, I come from a village called Sagorno, near Lithrofed. My sister and I arrived with the army.' Gasbron's interest was piqued further. Conversely to the more numerically equal demographic of Rildayorda, almost everyone in the cities of Lithrofed and Intei were Hentani, so surely one could easily get by there without learning Bennvikan at all? That had certainly been

143

Gasbron's observation when he had been to those cities in the past. Yet this girl's command of the language was perfect.

'You surprise me. Many of your nobles and princes require translators. How did you come to learn Bennvikan?'

As they began to move, Ezrina began to rub her body against his.

That isn't normally part of the dance, Gasbron thought.

'The invasion by Bennvika is still recent enough to cast a long shadow, especially for the elder members of our society. Our royals and most of our nobility feel that for them to learn Bennvikan would be a symbolic act of submission. Our language is part of our identity. We must keep it alive, lest it be supplanted. However, many younger people such as myself accept that we are now governed by Bennvika whether we like it or not, so it also pays to know a little of your tongue, sometimes literally.'

Gasbron gave a thin smile.

'Ah, business. It's what makes the world go around.'

'Quite. If you can only manage to learn one foreign tongue, make sure it is the one that is most useful. I myself seem to have an ear for languages. It's all about using your ambition and every skill you have to get ahead in the world and to make a better life for your people.'

'And also for yourself surely?'

'Of course. Don't you have ambition, Gasbron?' Ezrina asked, deliberately grinding her pelvis against his, pushing her thigh against his groin and almost whispering straight into his ear.

'A soldier does what he is ordered to,' he replied, trying to ignore her movements, but he couldn't control his reaction down below and he was sure she knew this.

'But you must have free will?' she enquired in a conspiratorial tone. 'Isn't there something you want?'

Subconsciously at this moment, Gasbron looked over at Silrith, who was clearly having a wonderful time laughing, flirting and dancing with Shappa. This wasn't lost on the sharp-eyed Ezrina.

'Ah, I see,' she said mischievously. Gasbron kept a cold silence and stopped moving, giving away his discomfort.

'I can't say I blame you,' Ezrina went on seductively. 'She's exquisite, isn't she? Very lovely.'

'Yes,' Gasbron sighed with some resignation in his voice, before forcibly moving his eyes away from Silrith and looking back at Ezrina. Ezrina laughed again.

'Come on. Just let loose and forget about her for a while. Do that for me and we'll both have some fun tonight. I'll make you smile from ear to ear. You'll forget all about her. You'll see.'

Gasbron didn't like the way he felt unmanned by his desire for Silrith, whereas what Ezrina was implying was more carefree, more carnal, so he allowed himself to succumb to her words.

But that would be later. For now, people danced, drank and sang. There was a rather disproportionate amount of wine compared to food, so people became drunk rather quickly. During the planning, Silrith had pointed out that drinking most of the wine during this night would mean that there was less around later and therefore less chance of some sentry being drunk on patrol when the action really started.

Events such as these could be a great leveller and as the night wore on Silrith joined the others in the singing of various folk songs known to them all, sometimes joining hands or performing actions. One told of a person whose lover had gone to war and of how they would wait for them faithfully until they returned. Another told of a traveller from lands far away and of their impressions when they came to Bennvika and a third told of a self-doubting dreamer, whom the song implores to carry on fighting; thinking of better days. After a short while Silrith saw Jezna jump back on to the stage and with the backing of the band she bounced delightfully around the place singing a joyous song of freedom, before going on to perform an equally energetic number that was supposedly about love, but also spoke of being spun out of control into a crazed zest for life. Yathrud must have specifically requested this. He must have remembered that after hearing it once, a six-year-old Silrith had requested the palace musicians to perform it time and time again at subsequent balls and banquets across the intervening years. She smiled at the happy memory as she danced.

After some hours, Silrith felt herself becoming a little more drunk than she felt could be considered dignified and so she made her excuses and left to go to bed, accepting Shappa's offer when he suggested he should escort her to her room.

Once outside the door, they paused and faced each other.

'Well, I think that went rather well,' Silrith commented after a moment, slurring her words slightly and putting a hand on the doorknob to steady herself.

'It's been a wonderful evening, my Lady,' Shappa replied sincerely.

'Oh, please,' Silrith scoffed in a playful tone, 'I do insist that you call me Silrith.'

'Silrith, then,' Shappa said tenderly. Normally at this point, he would be expected to kiss her hand, but drink had dulled the sense of proper form for them both. This was why when a smiling Silrith tilted her head slightly in appreciation of Shappa's answer, she must have accidentally made herself look more receptive than she'd intended and, misreading the signals thanks to his own clouded mind, he leaned in to kiss her on the cheek, placing a hand on her waist. A shiver raced down Silrith's spine as she was caught completely off guard, but as she took a deep breath both of them were awoken from their momentary bliss as Shappa realised what he was doing and pulled away in shocked derision at his own actions.

'Goodness. I am so sorry, Silrith. I don't-'

'-Don't be sorry,' Silrith interrupted him calmingly, with a flirtatiousness that was far from her usual nature. She took his hands in hers, allowing him to feel her soft warm skin against his.

'How can I be angry at such a lovely gesture?' she said. Shappa looked relieved. He moved his head towards hers.

'But you've had enough fun for one night, I think,' Silrith added cheekily, before quickly opening the door, darting into her room laughing, then shutting it behind her and locking it. She heard Shappa laugh from the other side.

'Goodnight, Silrith,' he called.

'Goodnight, Shappa,' said Silrith, as she leaned against the large oak frame and closed her eyes, savouring the memory of the last few moments.

She continued this as her maids, the same two that she had met when she first arrived and who appeared to have been waiting for her, began to help her undress. She went through the motions as they unfastened the ties at the back of her dress. She stepped out of it and raised her arms so that they could clothe her in her nightgown; though all the time her head was on a different planet entirely. Despite the dangers that were soon to come and the harsh life that would begin the next day, at that moment she felt more content than she had in what seemed like a very long time.

'We use this room for when lords come to stay and there's not enough room in the main house for all their servants. You'll find everything you need here, ladies, or if you don't, ask one of my lot and we'll see what we can do.' Gasbron said these words to Ezrina and Jezna in a matter-of-fact tone as he opened the door to the little hut. It was a small, barely noticeable place around the back of the divisio headquarters. Its stone walls and roof linked in with those of the divisio building and into the citadel's outer walls. Only the wooden door marked it out as a room at all. Ezrina walked into the darkness, with Jezna following.

'I'll get you some light,' said Gasbron. He fetched a burning torch from outside, followed them in and lit both of the room's candles, one of which was near the door and the other at the far end. He then exited the room to put the torch back in its brazier outside, before re-entering.

In the dim light, Ezrina saw five empty beds, whose stained sheets didn't look like they'd been washed in weeks, or even months.

'This will do nicely, thank you,' she grimaced.

'I'm glad.'

'I'm sorry, Gasbron,' said Ezrina, deliberately feigning weakness and slurring her words. 'I promised you a night of fun, but I think I've had too much to drink and I'm feeling rather sick.'

She was surprised to see a look of relief come over his face. Still thinking of his queen, no doubt.

'Perhaps another time then,' he said awkwardly. 'Now, make sure you get some sleep and as I said, let me know if you need anything,' With that, he shut the door and left.

'Well, that seems to have worked. He must have enjoyed your flirting earlier. He'll do anything you ask now,' Jezna said, in a resigned tone.

'I hated having to do it,' said Ezrina, knowing that Jezna already knew this from being in a similar position herself in the past.

'Yes, but we have to do it, my love. Think of it this way, we could have been in some tent down with the soldiers,' Jezna said. 'At least here we have some privacy.'

Ezrina gave a quiet laugh, then turned and walked towards her lover.

'Oh, I do love you Jezna,' she said. 'You always manage to see the bright side in everything.'

Jezna smiled and gave Ezrina a sultry look; her eyes surveying Ezrina's body.

'I know,' she said. 'But there's another reason you love me too.' She took hold of Ezrina's hands and stepped towards her, pushing her body against Ezrina's. She kissed her lightly on the lips.

'And do you know what I love about you?' Jezna said, giving her another kiss. 'You're a fighter, but you only fight to protect those you care about. You make me feel safe and loved. Do you know what that makes me want to do?'

'What?' asked Ezrina with a wry smile.

'This.' Jezna kissed her again and pushed her towards the bed.

There are many words that could describe how Silrith felt the following morning, all of them bad. Despite thinking that she had only been a little drunk, she awoke with what seemed to be a disproportionately large hangover. Nevertheless, she was to set a precedent for herself by training with some of her troops today, specifically Gasbron's heavy cavalry. She had discussed this with him while he found her some weapons and armour, though she was sure it would come as a surprise to some of the troops.

Silrith had been woken by the lightening of the room as one of the maids opened the curtains.

'Good morning, my Queen. Did you sleep well?' she asked in a light tone.

Reluctantly Silrith extracted herself from the bed, holding her palm to her forehead.

148

'A lovely night, thank you, Ridenna,' she lied, barely opening her eyes as she spoke.

Unsurprisingly Ridenna wasn't convinced.

'Not to worry, my Queen. Your breakfast is being brought up to you right away. I'm sure you'll feel better after you've had a nice meal.'

This was different from what it had been like when Silrith had been looked after by Afayna and Taevuka. But then, although Taevuka had only arrived a few months ago, Afayna had been Silrith's lady's maid for some years, so it wasn't fair to compare her new maids to her. Anyway, Ridenna, with the help of another maid, Avaresae, who would surely soon join them, had been trying her hardest to make Silrith feel safe and at home since her arrival. She had dark hair and one of those normally plain faces that suddenly became beautiful when she smiled. Silrith guessed she was the older of the two maids by at least five years or so, making her perhaps thirty years old.

She thought about how kind Ridenna and Avaresae had been to her over the past few days. Yes, it was their job, but it had to be said that these two maids, professionally dressed in their nicely cut blue dresses and full of positivity, were the perfect pair to look after someone who has recently had a difficult experience. Ridenna's calm and collected manner could put anyone at their ease and who could fail to love the endearing blonde Avaresae, whose apparent only goal in life was to assist and please others?

Silrith had ordered for her breakfast to be brought to her room that day because there would be no time for her to dine with Yathrud and the others before joining the soldiers. Soon Avaresae appeared with a platter of fried bread, cheese, sweetmeats and a cup of water. This was partially there to distract from the less than desirable flavour of what else she had been presented with; a paste made up of bitter almonds and fried eel, specifically designed to cure hangovers.

Silrith knew that if there was one thing worse than consuming this sickening concoction, it was the thought of doing physical exercise while feeling ill. She forced herself to take a spoonful of the paste, then quickly shoved it into her mouth, pulled a disdainful face as she chewed, then swallowed, before overriding the taste with some bread and cheese.

Supposedly it would take effect over the course of the next hour or so. In the corner of her eye, she saw the two maids watching, amused.

'I don't know what you two think is so funny. Do you enjoy watching your queen suffer?' she chided them with a laugh.

'Oh no of course not, my Queen,' they exclaimed in such harmony that all three of them descended into a fit of the giggles.

The day is getting better already, Silrith thought happily.

When she had finished eating, she asked for her armour and weapons to be brought up to her. Ridenna went to fetch them.

When she returned with her cargo, she brought with her a young male servant from the armoury to help her carry it, but quickly sent him away. Unlike Ridenna, Avaresae hadn't seen what Silrith would be wearing and carrying until that moment and she could barely hide her interest. They helped Silrith get dressed into her chain mail, over which she put on a black tunic and brown padded trousers, before putting on her large black boots. Over the tunic, she added a thick brown leather weapons belt.

Avaresae looked particularly impressed by the sword. It was a single-handed one, but still fairly large, though surprisingly light in weight. This meant that it probably wasn't as durable as some blades were, but it increased agility, so the weapon would be perfect for Silrith's strong yet very slight build. It had been given a good polish in the past day or so and Avaresae admired the sheen on the metal as she held it for a moment; her reflection clear and bright.

'Oh, my Queen! It's beautiful. Did it belong to Lord Yathrud or one of his ancestors?' Avaresae said. Silrith laughed.

'My uncle doesn't even know I'm doing this yet. Make sure someone tells him not to expect me at breakfast. No, I doubt anyone important has used this sword. Look at the grip. It's nothing special,' she indicated. It was nicely covered with leather, but had no real decoration on it, whereas some included very ornate metal designs. 'You'll notice that I have customised it though. I've had the symbol of my family, the Stallion of Alfwyn, added to it. It may be the case now that nobody significant has used this sword, but with any luck, that's something we can change.' She showed Avaresae and Ridenna the engraving of a stallion on the end of the pommel.

Suddenly Avaresae gasped as something else seemed to catch her attention. There was also a dagger, as well as a large, round, wooden shield. The latter was painted green, with the white stallion of the Alfwyn family

150

depicted on it, just like the sword, in accordance with Silrith's orders. What had caught Avaresae's attention though was the gleaming metal helmet.

It featured long cheek guards and was a shining silver, save for the highly decorated golden nasal guard, the upper section of which was sculpted into two pairs of small horns to give the wearer a more menacing look; one pair just above the eyes, the other mounted higher, just above the forehead. This was attached at the back to the helmet's silver dome.

Silrith picked it up and smiled as she watched the reactions of the girls as she put it on and tightly fitted the buckle under her chin.

'How do I look?' she asked, slightly tongue-in-cheek, pretending to pose a little. 'May I have a mirror?'

Quickly Ridenna fetched her one and Silrith was pleased with the overall effect as she inspected her reflection. Meanwhile, the two maids had tightened her weapons belt so that it securely fitted her waist, with the sword safely returned to its scabbard and the dagger tucked into her belt.

'I like the flash of gold,' said Silrith. 'It gives a sense of authority without being overbearing, wouldn't you say?'

'Oh yes, my Queen. Nobody will dare question you in this,' Avaresae gushed, causing Silrith to chuckle.

She handed back the mirror, closed her eyes for a moment and took a deep breath. This was what she was now. This was what she was going to have to be. A warrior; a commander. This was the only way she could control her destiny. To fight.

Ending her private moment, she opened her eyes and took her shield in her left hand as it was passed to her. The maids had only known her since she arrived at Preddaburg but they could evidently tell by her face that her mood had turned serious now.

'Good luck, my Queen', they both said subserviently, yet with much sincerity, as they curtsied.

'Thank you both.' With that, she turned and left.

Chapter 12

After she left the Alyredd house, Silrith soon sighted Gasbron. He was instantly recognisable with his black and white transverse horsehair crest atop his invicturion's helmet. He was standing at the head of his unit in the soldiers' training area briefing his troops. There were five hundred troops here in all and they filled the square of the training area. They would be on foot for this exercise. Corpralis Candoc, with his bushy orange beard and a single, small metal crest running front to back on his helmet, stood beside Gasbron and at the front of the unit was the standard-bearer. The standard itself was of the Alyredd family, with the three golden dragons on a scarlet background and above that was the numeral for the number one, painted gold but presumably carved from the wood of the pole. The number, of course, denoted that this was the prime divisio of the province.

'Just perfect, it's starting to rain,' Silrith cursed to herself under her breath. As she had expected there were a few surprised faces amongst the soldiers as she strode into view in full fighting gear. She took off her helmet and bowed her head respectfully to her troops.

'Company! Atten-*tion*!' Gasbron bellowed when he saw her approach. Unlike the others, he was expecting her, having been told by Silrith the previous day that she would be joining them whether he liked it or not. He turned on his heel to face her. All present snapped a salute as they were joined by their new leader.

'Thank you Chief Invicturion Wrathun. At ease.'

Gasbron turned on his heel and addressed his soldiers.

'Company! At-*ease*!'

'Right,' Gasbron continued in the relaxed tone that he had been speaking in previously, as the pattering of rain began to grow harder. 'As you all can see, we have an honoured visitor joining us for today's exercise. The session our queen has decided to join us for on this fine morning is a nice little six-mile jog around the city walls and she will also be joining us for later training sessions as well.' She was sure he wouldn't admit it, but Silrith knew she was beginning to win Gasbron over a little with regards to her physical abilities. She had to show that she was as tough as any of them.

Though this was the first time she would train alongside the soldiers as a group, he had spent much of the previous morning giving her some personal tuition in sword fighting and while her technique needed some work, it was clear to Silrith that her agility, tenacity and ingenuity had impressed him greatly. She had recovered very quickly from her recent physical ordeal. She'd also made it clear to him that she was much fitter and stronger than she felt he'd previously given her credit for.

'We will be turning left out of the Preddaburg Gate,' Gasbron continued. 'Then we will head down towards the West Gate, then the Port Gate, then heading north away from the port, into the forest for a while, past the East Gate, then returning here. The queen and I will be at the front, while Corpralis Candoc will be at the back, so everyone stay in formation.'

He took a moment to let his words sink in.

'Right, let's do this,' he said.

He spun on his heel to face away from his troops, while Candoc marched to the back of the formation.

'Company! Atten-*tion*!' Gasbron barked once Candoc was in position and five hundred feet stamped down on the stone floor. Looking at them, Silrith could see why these divisiomen had to be the fittest in the army. Even cavalry units like this one had to perform as an infantry unit on occasion, as would be the case now. Jogging in full armour looked incredibly difficult, considering the combined weight of the large helmet, the metal plates covering the chest, back and shoulders, the chain mail, the weapons and of course that very heavy looking rectangular shield. Silrith could remember Gasbron saying that they would fight with round ones when on horseback, with the rectangular ones strapped to their back in case they were needed. Silrith could imagine that it was one thing to carry these shields on one's back and quite another to run with it, with nothing more than one's arm to take the weight.

She felt grateful for the relative lightness of her own circular shield and of the extra agility that her more lightweight kit gave her, although even that was heavy enough. She realised that this made it all the more important that she completed the session with apparent ease, no matter what the conditions were like and no matter how tired she felt at the end.

Replacing her helmet, she got into position alongside and slightly behind Gasbron so that she could follow his lead and in a moment they were off, through the inner ward, then jogging through the maze that filled the majority of citadel's outer ward, through the open archway into the walled courtyard by the Preddaburg Gate and then exiting under the lifted portcullis and out of the citadel into the fields beyond. It took her a moment to get used to running in the helmet. It wasn't just its weight, but the impaired vision, even though it was less enclosed than some. There was also the constant feeling of claustrophobia that she assumed is always felt by someone who is not used to wearing one. Frustratingly, it seemed to start raining even harder once they had started and Silrith had to keep blinking to try and remove the water from her eyes, as it was hard to do it by hand with the helmet on.

After the first mile or so things were becoming more difficult. The shield seemed to become heavier in Silrith's left hand, the helmet's chin strap was starting to dig into her neck and the constant rain was saturating her leather tunic, weighing her down, while the ground underfoot was becoming a complete quagmire. The result of this was that the pace was fairly slow, but the energy involved didn't reflect this.

Even so, the pressure to perform and to comfortably match the divisiomen in every way forced every last once of adrenaline through her veins, pushing her forward.

As they splashed past the West Gate, for the first time since her arrival she got a proper view of Rildayorda Port. When she had been there before, it had been home to a few merchant vessels, but now it was teeming with boats, as Yathrud had prohibited any trade ships from leaving, save for the one carrying her letter. Most noticeable were Shappa's ten longships. These ships were larger and wider than many of the other ships, sporting a singular sail and they hung low in the water with their shallow hulls, which made them fast and able to sail up rivers that other vessels of their size couldn't.

They had an imposing look about them, Silrith decided, taking one last look as they turned north again. Once they had returned, Silrith had barely a moment to catch her breath before she heard someone calling her.

154

'Your Grace.' Blavak, the Hentani chief's interpreter, appeared with a scroll of parchment in his hand, followed by Chief Hojorak himself. 'Your Grace, my master wishes to report grave news.' Blavak looked a little flustered.

'Speak then,' Silrith replied, immediately concerned.

'My master previously sent scouts and spies north before we arrived here at Rildayorda. Two of them returned today saying that near Zikaena they intercepted a rider carrying an anonymous letter heading for Kriganheim.'

'Let me read it.' Silrith took it from Blavak and read the rest herself. Whoever the writer was, they knew Yathrud had taken her in. The letter implored Jostan to ride south and take the citadel and the city by force before she starts a full-scale rebellion.

'Did they manage to question the rider?'

'No, he could not be taken alive, so the scouts say.'

Silrith cursed to herself under her breath.

'There's more,' stated Blavak, regaining her attention. 'When the scouts caught the rider, they were already heading south with news that our spies in the city of Ganust told them. Some traders from Celrun spoke of an army they had witnessed heading for the Forest of Ustaherta. Our spies tried to find out numbers but the estimates ranged hugely from a few hundred to many thousands.'

'So, it starts today then and already we have a gamble to take.' She turned to Gasbron, who had heard the conversation and come to stand alongside her.

'We already knew Jostan would be heading south for his Hentani campaign. But it's a surprise that he's moved so soon,' Gasbron pondered.

'Yes,' said Silrith. 'And it won't have gone unnoticed that my uncle has sent no troops north, but with luck, Jostan may simply send a representative here to see what's going on. He may already know of my presence, or he may be marching on your people, Chief Hojorak, as he seems to have originally planned.'

Blavak translated and Hojorak said something in Hentani. Blavak listened carefully before turning back to Silrith.

'My master says that due to the number of warriors that we have brought to Rildayorda, the number left behind would not be enough to protect our civilians if the Bennvikan city garrisons of Lithrofed and Intei defect to King Jostan and turn their swords on our people. If the king is as yet unaware of your presence and plans to pass us by he will have no difficulty in burning our towns and villages and slaughtering our people by the thousand. You cannot expect us simply to stand by and allow our families to suffer such a fate.'

'No,' Silrith sighed and shook her head. 'No, I cannot. Nor do I have any intention of doing so. We must send a small, fast-moving force north to meet him to catch him by surprise. We cannot hope to make him retreat, but maybe he can be stalled, or we can draw him on to us here, where we can mount a proper defence and stop his army from destroying your tribe. I never approved of what Bennvika has done to the Hentani in the past. I loved my father but what he let his soldiers do to your people was a disgrace, especially when he didn't have my uncle by his side to advise him. I will not let it happen again.'

Silrith was well aware that King Lissoll's later campaigns against the Hentani had been rather different from his earlier ones. The main difference was that Yathrud was no longer with him. Having assisted in the subjugation of the eastern half of the Hentani Kingdom, Yathrud stayed behind to oversee their assimilation into Bennvikan culture. In that time Yathrud had built Preddaburg, as well as the Great Temple, dedicated to both the Bennvikan goddess Lomatteva and the Hentani goddess Bertakaevey, while making regular visits into the streets of the newly renamed city of Rildayorda to try to win hearts and minds. All this played a huge part in the Hentani's territory becoming Bennvika's new province of Bastalf.

Lissoll however, without Yathrud to assist him, had become more and more brutal towards the Hentani in the west and so they resisted him more and more. When the major Hentani strongholds of Lithrofed and Intei had eventually fallen to Bennvika, it had been catastrophic for the tribesmen and the streets had run with blood. Even now, almost twenty years later, with Lithrofed and Intei rebuilt in the form of Bennvikan cities, the Hentani still licked their wounds. If she was to keep them on her side, Silrith had to make sure that they were in no doubt that Bennvika had changed.

156

Blavak translated Silrith's words to Hojorak before the chief spoke again.

'My master says that he volunteers to take his warriors north with Prince Kivojo to meet the enemy in the Forest of Ustaherta, where we can ambush them. He would consider it an honour if one of your nobles could accompany him for such a task.'

'One of my nobles? So not me then?' Silrith said.

Blavak's face creased into a confused expression.

'I think he meant a man, your Grace. Your presence would risk the whole operation.'

'What? You call me your Grace with one breath and then insult me with the next?'

'I think what he is trying to say is that you are too valuable to be risked at this early stage,' Gasbron pitched in.

'I see,' Silrith responded, curling her lip in contempt, not believing a word of it. She tried to remind herself of her previous diplomatic thoughts. 'Well,' she went on, 'I suppose all that remains is to decide who goes in my stead.'

'I'll go.'

They all turned round in surprise to see who had spoken.

'Cousin Bezekarl. I didn't see you lurking there,' Silrith exclaimed, her mood brightening again.

'I'm sorry, my Queen, err, I just couldn't help overhearing.'

'Oh no, not at all. Well, that's done then. I'd have liked to have gone myself,' she added, being careful to hold back her rueful opinion this time. 'But it is a good opportunity for you to see battle. How soon can your master march, Blavak?'

'We can have a force of five hundred men ready to advance north at first light tomorrow. If our intelligence on the enemy's current position is correct, we will meet them in a little under three days.'

'Then we will wait patiently for your return,' Silrith assured him, keeping her offence at his previous comments well hidden. 'Go now, prepare and know that all our hopes ride with you.'

157

KRIGANHEIM, BENNVIKA

The walls of Kriganheim. Always a sight to behold, thought Lord Oprion Aethelgard as he crested the hill and laid eyes on the capital. It didn't matter that he'd been there less than a month ago. The effect was still the same. He surveyed it for a moment, taking in its imposing, thick walls and the tall, thin turrets of the city's north and west gates. He could also see the rooftops of some of the city's most recognisable buildings, such as the dome of the Congressate Hall, as well as the heads and shoulders of the two giant statues of Vitrinnolf and Lomatteva.

Behind Oprion marched his army; over a thousand troops in all. Half were of the divisios and half were militia. A sizable portion of each group would be tasked with keeping the peace in Kriganheim in King Jostan's absence, while the rest would march on to Asrantica to do the same there. Jostan's orders had told Oprion how many troops to raise in total and which provinces to protect. They hadn't, however, specified how many to send to each city. With that in mind, of his whole army, Oprion had left eight soldiers in every ten to protect his own province of Hazgorata. King Spurvan of Medrodor had long had his envious eye on the place and Oprion would not have it taken from him in his absence.

In reality though, he was certain that protecting the north would be little more than a formality. These provinces were far from the conflict zone and as far as Oprion knew there was currently no tangible evidence to suggest that Medrodor was gearing up for an attack on Bennvika any time soon. With any luck, Dowager Queen Accutina's proposed marriage to the new king would ensure that the peace continued to hold.

So it was with much confidence that Oprion had accepted the task given to him by his new royal master. Indeed it was an honour to have such recognition from the incoming monarch. He regretted the circumstances under which this was happening of course. The revelations about his friend Princess Silrith had come as something of a blow, but she had been branded a traitor and that was the end of it, especially after how she had spoken to him. There was no point risking one's estate and reputation, let alone their life, over sentimentality regarding the fate of a traitor. Of course, he was also eager to consolidate his own position and to show King Jostan that he had been right to entrust him with a responsibility such as running the city as his regent.

He raised a hand to halt the column and told one of his officers to fetch his wife, a haughty Medrodorian noble named Haarksa.

Oprion turned his horse around and trotted over to a vantage point from which he could see the baggage train. Haarksa and the children had been travelling there, but she had insisted on riding into the city at his side for the sake of appearances.

He smiled to himself as he watched her climb on to her horse in the distance, then canter past the waiting soldiers, following the course of the snaking column, riding side-saddle. She was wearing a long, purple gown and was positively dripping with jewellery. If she was attempting to look any younger than she was, it was failing – whenever they met someone who wasn't familiar with her name, they always looked a little surprised when he said the word 'wife' instead of 'mother'. In any case, she looked ridiculous next to the soldiers of the divisios, let alone the motley crew that was the militia. By contrast, of course, his own choice, a white tunic and cape that mimicked the eastern styles of King Jostan's homeland, was the prime attire for exuding authority.

Haarksa reined in alongside him and scowled as she gave her husband a very unsubtle look from head to foot.

'This country has been ruled by a Verusantian for less than a month and already you are dressing like one?' she said scornfully in the harsh tones of her north Medrodorian accent. 'Where is your sense of national identity?'

'It is quite natural that certain aspects of Verusantian culture will come to Bennvika now that we have a king from those lands,' said Oprion. 'We should embrace the chances that are coming. Anyway, one's identity is personal, not national and I think you'll find my identity is in little doubt to those who look upon my army from the city walls. They say that even the goddess Lomatteva was a member of the House of Aethelgard when she was yet a mortal.' He pointed to the Aethelgard family banner above their heads as it flapped in the wind.

Its design was the most venerable of all Bennvika's noble family standards. So much so in fact, that it even adhered to an entirely different set

159

of heraldic rules. The result was two figures, a man and a woman, outlined in black, dressed for war and surrounded by flame; all of which was shown in a vibrant gold against an orange background. Of course, the woman was the goddess Lomatteva and the man was the god Vitrinnolf, as depicted on the famous Amulet of Hazgorata, the great jewel that was passed down the generations of incumbent Bennvikan queens.

'Point to your standard all you like, Oprion,' Haarksa countered. 'Many will see this and believe that the fact that you wear Verusantian clothes while riding under such an ancient Bennvikan banner serves only as a metaphor. A metaphor that says that you profess to stand for Bennvikan interests while in reality, you are doing nothing to stop Verusantian culture supplanting that of Bennvika. We cannot afford for people to think that. I still dress and behave in a way that honours my heritage and you should do the same with yours.'

'My love, I do not have time for your protestations,' Oprion said curtly.

He turned to face his troops.

'We march to the city,' he called. 'Follow.'

He kicked his horse into a gallop, head down, bolting ahead of his army; his horse panting. Within moments he was rushing towards the city gate and dropped to a trot as the guards came out to halt him. Looking back he saw that Haarksa was still far behind, trotting alongside the divisio cavalry at the front of the column.

That woman is all about class and no energy, Oprion thought.

Turning his gaze forward again, he noticed that above the gate, tied to an upright wooden pole was the bloodied torso of a woman, presumably Silrith's traitorous maid. Oprion was revolted by the sight. Couldn't Jostan just have disposed of the body quietly? He pulled his eyes away from the gruesome spectacle and addressed the guard who had come forward.

'I am Lord Oprion Aethelgard, Governor of Hazgorata. I come with my family and my soldiers to oversee proceedings in the city in the king's absence. Would you care to announce me?' He said formally.

'Very good, my Lord,' said the guard and he ordered his troops to open the gate.

Oprion turned and waited for Haarksa and the army to catch up. He said nothing as she pulled alongside him. He looked at her and she frowned back. He made a clicking noise and the horse moved forward to enter the city. A pair of trumpets were blown from the top of the city gate.

Here it was, the glamour of a noble entrance, complete with a celebratory fanfare. The uncouthness of the drab looking plebeian crowd and the occasional mangy dog only served to emphasise the class of Oprion's own self, the majesty of his white stallion and the gleaming armour of the divisio cavalry that made up his and Haarksa's personal escort at the head of the army. Yes, this was the moment.

'Make way for Lord Oprion Aethelgard,' called the officer as Oprion crossed under the gate and into the city streets.

The silence with which the proclamation had been met by the population was startling. Oprion was shocked. Usually the crowds would push and shove to catch the merest glimpse of their betters. But this time they did nothing of the sort. True, it looked like they had been waiting for him. Oprion guessed they must have got word of his army's approach when they had reached the hill. But this was no welcome. Instead, they simply glared at him with pure malice in their eyes.

'Why are they so quiet?' Haarksa asked.

'Look, he appears to have brought the army. He's scared of us,' someone called. The voice sounded aged and well spoken. Oprion raised a hand to halt the column.

'Who was that?' he demanded. Nobody spoke.

A figure walked out from within the crowd in front of Oprion, his face hidden under the hood of his cloak.

'Reveal yourself I say,' demanded Oprion.

'On the contrary, my Lord. I do believe that it is you that must reveal your true self to us,' the man pointed a wrinkled finger at Oprion. 'You, who betrayed our beloved Princess Silrith. Our princess, who would have made a kind and generous queen and who would have restored justice to this Kingdom. But instead, it was you who sealed not just her fate, but that of every soul in this nation, by welcoming in an invader, who is already crushing the poor under his boot. The nation will starve and once we are weak and desperate, the king will try to force his false god upon us and all because of you, Lord Oprion. Therefore I brand you a traitor. A traitor against the people of Bennvika. A traitor against the gods themselves.'

'Traitor, traitor, traitor,' the crowd took up the chant, punching their fists in the air. 'Traitor, traitor, traitor.'

'I will not rise to your untruths,' Oprion raged above the clamour. 'The king has appointed me to rule in his absence. His word is the law now and you will all obey. I will have my soldiers make the streets run with blood if I have to.'

The crowd gasped and jeered angrily.

'Set your troops' blades against our peaceful protest,' cried the old man. 'And you will prove me right in every regard.'

This isn't a peaceful protest, Oprion thought. *This is a lynch mob.*

Surely it fitted the old man's cause better if Oprion's troops did attack, despite the man's protestations. The man was calling his bluff. Well, Oprion wasn't about to play into his adversary's hands by making martyrs of him and his followers.

'Invicturion, arrest that man,' he ordered. 'See that these people are cleared away.'

But the attempt was in vain. With surprising speed, the old man darted into the dense crowd and immediately disappeared among the angrily chanting throng. By the time Oprion's soldiers tried to follow, he was long gone.

Oprion cursed loudly.

'After him, after him,' he ordered. 'Clear the streets.'

He kicked his horse into a gallop.

If they try to stop me, I'll just run them down, he thought. The cavalry, along with Lady Haarksa, followed suit as they thundered through the streets at a full charge, sending people running in every direction and leaving the infantry to clear the way behind. Eventually, they reached the palace gates and safety.

'You are so weak,' Haarksa spat at her husband as they passed through the palace's North Gate and started down the long, peacefully quiet gravel track that led through the trees of the palace gardens. 'You should have made your demonstration in blood. That is what the army is for.'

'I had him arrested, didn't I? My troops will catch him sooner or later. I have shown them that I have mercy, but that I am also sensible,' said Oprion, frustrated.

'You have shown them nothing of the kind. Only that they can taunt you and get away with it. You saw how the crowd blocked your soldiers as he ran. I doubt they'll ever catch him.'

That evening, Oprion and Haarksa sat in the royal banquet hall. Due to their younger years, their five daughters ate in their own quarters and the servants fussed and bustled around the palace to make sure their guests felt at home. Oprion expected nothing less, as the baggage train had been held up outside the city for some hours because of the rioting. However, he personally didn't want to see the servants working as he ate, save for those who served his food. Therefore, he and Haarksa sat in the enormous room at the end of a long mahogany table, with only five or six staff waiting on them, under the gaze of the dozens of Bennvikan monarchs whose portraits hung on the walls in the dim candlelight, mimicking the famous *Gallery of Rulers* in the Congressate Hall.

'I have spoken to the chief servant,' said Oprion. 'It seems that there has been some unrest since the very moment the king left the city. He said there was a riot at the public assembly of the demokroi recently, initiated by a speech by a man named Zethun Maysith.'

'You know this man?' asked Haarksa.

'Not personally. But his late father was a prominent member of the Congressate in his day.'

'Then you must have him brought to you,' Haarksa said in her usual condescending tune.

'Do you think I haven't thought of that? If I bring him here, then that will look as though I am accusing him of starting the riot against me today. If I do that, I risk the wrath of the entire Congressate.'

'You are risking that anyway. He'll have his contacts there through people who knew his father. He has already started one riot in your absence. Why should he not be responsible for this as well? While you sit here, he could be making his escape, or planning his next move against you. You must

163

have him brought to you. Make him our guest. Speak with him and question him, politician to politician. Meanwhile, you must send the city into lockdown so that neither he nor any of his associates can escape. It's as simple as that.'

Sometimes, as much as Oprion hated her, he had to concede that Haarksa could be frustratingly insightful.

'Fine. I'll have it seen to. Sraeto?'

'My Lord?' said Sraeto, a thin, learned-sounding man in his fifties who wore the black tunic of a chief servant.

'Get news to the garrison. The city must be sent into lockdown. Nobody gets in or out by land or by river without my permission until the king returns.'

'Very good, my Lord.' He bowed and left.

'My Lord? May I speak with you?' came a female voice.

Oprion turned in his chair to see that a young maid had entered the hall through another entrance and was standing near the door. She was wearing a blue and white dress with golden lining and was pretty enough, in her way, he decided.

'And interrupt my dinner?' said Oprion.

'My Lord, I think you will agree that what I have to tell you is of great importance.'

She was rubbing her hands together slowly in a way that betrayed fear, but of what? Oprion gave Haarksa a confused look, but she simply shrugged.

'Of course. What is it?' he said.

'May I speak to you in private, my Lord?'

'Whatever you have to say in front of my husband can also be said in front of me,' said Haarksa angrily.

'Of course, my Lady. I simply request that no other ears hear it,' the maid stammered.

'Leave us,' said Oprion in a general address to every other servant that was dotted around the hall. The maid herself walked closer to the table.

'So, what is your name and what is this urgent news you feel I should know?' Oprion asked once the three of them were alone.

'My name is Lyzina. I am Dowager Queen Accutina's head lady's maid-'

164

'-Then why are you not with her now?' Haarksa interrupted.

'She wanted me to stay to oversee the other maids. Apparently, the king said that servants from within the camp would suffice for the campaign.'

'And she agreed to that?' said Haarksa, clearly aghast.

'I doubt she had much choice, my dear,' Oprion laughed. 'I've no doubt that our beloved new king knows when someone needs him more than he needs them. It is not for us to guess at who those people may be, but clearly, the Dowager Queen knows where she stands. So, if he wants to choose her servants for her, there isn't much she can do to stop him.'

Haarksa rolled her eyes.

'My Lord,' whaled another maid as she burst into the room. She was even younger than the first maid, barely more than a child and her face was wild and panic-stricken.

'What is it?' Oprion asked. 'What makes you think you can intrude on me in such a fashion?'

'My Lord, my Lady, you must come quickly. It's the Lady Jorikssa. She's been taken very ill.'

Haarksa's face went white with dread. She moved to follow the servant, but then paused when she noticed that Oprion hadn't moved.

'Are you coming?' she asked Oprion.

Oprion gave her a surprised look.

'Why? She's your late husband's daughter, not mine,' he said.

Haarksa gave a sigh as she turned to leave.

'If you were half the man her father was-'

'-I'd probably be dead, like him,' Oprion interrupted. 'Enough. Now go and see to your brat.'

Haarksa glared at him a moment longer, before angrily stalking out. The second maid, still overcome with panic, followed and closed the door behind her as they left. Haarksa wasn't fooling anyone. Even Oprion could see that Jorikssa had no love for her and he knew the feeling was mutual, yet the ridiculous woman insisted on carrying on the charade of playing the loving mother.

'So, girl,' said Oprion, turning back to the first maid. 'Now that we've established who you are, why are you here?' His patience was beginning to wear thin after all the commotion.

'My Lord, I must tell you that my news is based only on a rumour.'

'A rumour?'

'Yes, but an important one if it turns out to be true, especially for you. The other maids were too scared to tell you, so I thought I should do it.' Lyzina hesitated and Oprion sensed a high level of nervousness in the girl.

'Go on,' he said.

'Well, you see, it concerns Afayna, the maid who was executed for helping Princess Silrith murder her father. Apparently, sometime before the murder, she had been gossiping about a letter she had found in the princess' chambers. I never saw it, but before she was arrested, she told me the letter had gone missing.'

'What?' Oprion asked as a cold dread flowed over him.

'The letter was written by you, addressed to Princess Silrith, my Lord,' Lyzina stammered. 'Offering to leave your wife for her-'

'-Get out of my way,' Oprion said, already pushing past. He briskly marched through the corridors in the direction of Silrith's former chambers. His heart was pounding. This could not be tolerated. Somebody was plotting against him. But who? Whoever it was, any evidence had to be removed.

He was panting by the time he reached what used to be Silrith's bedchamber. He opened the door and was relieved to see no maids there. The room was dominated by an enormous four-poster bed, which was covered in green, white and gold cushions, while the elm panels were decorated with many swirling calved designs which matched the ones around the window frames. All Oprion was interested in though was the dressing table opposite the bed, with its many drawers. Surely that's where it would be.

He pulled open the first drawer and rifled through its contents. It was full of jewellery and makeup powders and paints along with various other things, but no letter. He did the same with the second and third, but to no avail.

'My Lord?'

Oprion was about to open the fourth drawer when he was interrupted by a voice behind him. He turned to see one of the palace guards, a helmetless Verusantian in black armour, standing in the doorway.

'What is it?'

166

'It's your wife, my Lord. She's been attacked.'

'Attacked?'

'Yes, my Lord. A blow to the head. One of the maids. She got away but my lot are chasing her.'

'She just got away? A maid?' Oprion raged. As he spoke he realised that Lyzina hadn't followed him.

'Find her,' Oprion commanded. 'Go!'

Lyzina just kept running. Hearing the shouting voice of the soldier chasing her, she knew that the guards on every ground exit in the palace would be alerted by now. That left only one escape route – up. As she ran, she ripped off the bottom half of her maid's dress to reveal the breeches and leather boots underneath. The letter had been seized and the household thrown into chaos. A double success, but now was the time for speed.

She sprinted up staircase after staircase, apparently pulling away from her pursuers as their voices became more distant. Finally, she got to the top floor. Had she pulled enough of a gap on the guards for her to get away? She ran from the stairs and opened the nearest door. The room was a mahogany lounge full of fine chairs and cushions, but most importantly, it had large, openable windows. She ran to the nearest one.

She flung the window open and looked down at the ground. Despite the speed of her escape, she'd navigated the building perfectly. Down below was a bush. Not a large one, but it'd do. She could hear the pounding of the soldiers' feet as they ran up the stairs.

She wondered if her friend had escaped after distracting and attacking Lady Haarksa. She lifted herself up on to the window ledge. She couldn't help but look down again. Nothing more than a bush lay between her and death. She reminded herself that if she were caught, she'd die anyway. The door burst open.

'Stop,' shouted the soldier; a Hazgorata divisioman at the head of a combined group of Bennvikans and Verusantians. Lyzina flung herself forward, closing her eyes and putting her life in the hands of the gods as she dropped through the air. With a searing pain, she crashed on to the bush's dense branches. She desperately tried to extract herself from their prickly grip. She ripped her clothes free, but she was pivoted forward by the motion and slammed down on to the hard ground. She coughed in the dust and then slowly lifted herself up to stand.

She was alive. Her nose was badly blooded and there was a terrible pain in her wrist, but she was alive. She could hear the shouting soldiers as they became more distant again, surely in an attempt to head her off elsewhere.

Taking heavy breaths, she looked around her. Against the backdrop of the vivid orange sunset, the deserted garden looked so serene. Its quietness, its beautifully crafted hedges and its brightly coloured flowers were in such contrast to what she had just experienced. She knew the guards chasing her could reappear at any moment. She checked inside her bodice to make sure the letter was still in her possession. It was.

She ran to the far end of the rectangular palace and as she rounded the corner, she saw the tall, iron railings of the palace's east gate. If she could escape from there, it would be a simple, direct run to the River Chathranis and after that, a ship to freedom. That was what the nobleman had told her to do.

She ran towards the gate, surprised to see it unmanned and slightly ajar. Beyond, as was the case on all sides of the palace walls, was a dense group of trees that parted only for the gravel track that connected this isolated place to the rest of the city that surrounded it. Still she saw no-one. Where were the guards?

As she ran through the open gates and hastily closed them behind her, she saw them. There were two of them, either side of the track, though their unseeing eyes would never spot her. The ropes and the tree branches creaked in the breeze as the men's bodies hung by their feet, their faces covered in the blood that oozed from their slit throats. In the silence, she could even hear the dripping as a pool of scarlet gathered on the ground under each body.

It was a horrific scene.

This job really does have its undesirable parts, Lyzina thought.

She took a step forward.

'You there,' shouted a gruff and aggressive male voice.

She turned to see two people standing by the wall. One was a large, muscular, bald man with a beard and brown tunic, whom Lyzina didn't recognise. The other was her young friend, dressed as a maid and who at twelve, was surely one of Bennvika's youngest spies.

'Is this her?' the man asked the younger girl.

'Yes,' the girl confirmed.

'Do you have the letter?' the man asked.

'I do,' said Lyzina.

'Good. Come with me,' said the man. 'Lord Oprion has sent the city into lockdown. I heard the order given myself. There's no escape through the city gates or by river. Follow me. I'll take you to the safe house.'

Zethun had never seen Kriganheim Palace from the inside before, so being summoned there barely a day after Lord Oprion's arrival made it explicitly clear that he'd got the wealthy governor's attention.

He and Hoban had been led into the main hall by a Verusantian guard, who in turn had sent a servant to tell Lord Oprion of their presence.

'I always did enjoy the understated feel of this place,' said Hoban in the most ironic of tones.

As Zethun looked around him, it was clear that this room was used as the king's council chamber. At each of its sides were three sets of long mahogany benches. This was where the governors, congressors and any of the king's other advisors would sit whenever a royal council was called. From the rafters hung the national flag, along with the blue and white eagle of the House of Kazabrus and around the edges of the room hung the crests of all the many great houses of Bennvika.

At the room's front was probably the most stunning piece of furniture Zethun had ever seen – the throne. Made from solid gold, it was designed solely to demonstrate the power and wealth of the crown. Each arm seemed to be resting on the back of a great beast, each of which had the head and body of a hound and the wings of an eagle. At the sides of the seat itself were a man-sized pair of rampant tigers and above it was a thick plate of gold, the top of which was sculpted into the enormous head of a roaring lion. Such a huge spectacle and made entirely of gold.

169

'Such frivolity and all the while the common people live a wretched existence,' Zethun said under his breath.

'Quite, but don't be combative with him, even if he behaves in such a way himself. Only diplomacy will be of any use. Persuasion is the key,' Hoban said.

'Oh don't worry. I'll show restraint,' said Zethun, making a show of raising his palms on mock innocence.

'Lord Oprion Aethelgard,' announced one of the palace staff and Zethun looked to see the flame-haired man himself enter the room from a door to the left of the throne.

'A thousand welcomes to you, young Zethun,' he exclaimed as he approached them, wearing an opulent sapphire tunic. Zethun disliked him already, but he reluctantly bowed his head all the same.

'And Congressor Salanath? I did not think to see you here,' Oprion added.

'Oh, Zethun and I have been doing much work together of late,' said Hoban. 'So I thought I could lend my assistance here.'

'Perfect,' said Oprion, in a happy tone but with a smile that looked less than genuine. 'Please, gentlemen, do follow me to the banqueting hall. We have much to discuss.'

They did so and Zethun found the room just as repulsively boastful of its owner's wealth as the throne room had been. Really, a room with such high ceilings was a waste of building materials and such an enormous table that could easily have seated thirty was highly unnecessary for a meeting that involved three people. Servants appeared as if from nowhere carrying every dish imaginable, but Zethun wasn't hungry.

'Now, as I'm sure you are both aware,' Oprion began, 'there has been rather a lot of unrest in the city recently. Of course, in the absence of the king, I am tasked with putting a stop to this. But I have a problem. I'm sure it is nothing for any of us to worry about, but while recent riots have been started by commoners assaulting soldiers or stealing from granaries and so on, there are two of particular note. The first of these happened at a public assembly and the second was a direct attack on my person and on my family. Now, I simply wish to draw your attention to the second incident. However, at the first, you, Congressor Salanath, were seen in the crowd and you, young

170

Zethun, were the one making the speech that got the common rabble so energised in the first place. Now, what am I supposed to read into this?'

'Oh nothing at all, my Lord,' Hoban laughed affably. 'I was there merely to oversee the proceedings.'

'Well, you didn't do a very good job, did you?'

'With respect, my Lord, I was there to see that the dignitaries themselves observed the traditions of the public assemblies in the proper form. It was up to the guards to control the mob.'

'And it was up to you as a member of the Congressate to see that they are up to the task until the time of my arrival,' Oprion snarled. 'I'd say that it is rather clear that they were not and yet you seem untroubled by this.'

'My Lord, if I may interject,' said Zethun calmly. 'Congressor Salanath is not to blame. After all, it was my speech that the people reacted to so passionately. However, the extent of the unfortunate and unforeseen rioting has been greatly exaggerated. You know how people's tongues spread rumour as if it were the plague.'

'Be that as it may. Even if starting the riot was not your intention as you claim, this was not an isolated incident,' Oprion said, relenting a little. 'As I have said, even when I arrived there was a lynch mob.'

'I have heard of this incident,' said Zethun. 'A hooded man stopped you in the street, yes? While a large crowd looked on?'

'Yes.'

'And did you not have your army at your back?'

'I did,' said Oprion.

'Then is it not clear that these people were never going to be able to kill you without bringing slaughter upon themselves?' Zethun pressed.

Oprion sighed.

'I suppose not,' he conceded.

'Then is it not clear what they were aiming to do? They feel threatened. Their new king has done nothing to stop the lords from all over the kingdom from taking land from the common people. Some of the people living out in the provinces have no option but to stay and suffer, but many are forced to leave and where do they go? Kriganheim, the city of opportunity.' Zethun said those last words with a highly ironic tone. 'They

171

think they will make their fortune here. Start their lives anew. Yet already the city is becoming overcrowded.'

'There is enough food to go around and extra people in the city means a larger workforce. I fail to see the problem with that,' said Oprion.

'The people themselves will not see it that way, especially not those who were already living here before the refugees began to arrive. Starvation doesn't have to be a genuine threat in order for people to fear it. People have been flooding through the gates for days.'

'Well there'll be no more of that,' said Oprion. 'The city gates are closed until the king returns. Any more refugees will be diverted to other provinces.'

'If the city gates are closed, how will the extra grain be transported into the city?' Hoban asked.

'If you keep them closed and rely only on the food supplies we have, then starvation becomes a real possibility,' said Zethun.

'You are trying to manipulate me and I would ask you to stop,' said Oprion curtly. 'I am not convinced by your suggestions. The man with the lynch mob was declaring that I was godless and assisting in bringing a tyrant to this land who would do away with our own gods. He mentioned nothing about the grain supply. These riots are nothing more than people being goaded by rumours and untruths and I would thank you not to obstruct me in my efforts to control the situation.'

Somehow Zethun sensed that he'd wanted to say more, but had thought better of it. Clearly something had made him fearful. Something that he wasn't letting on about.

'Now get out,' said Oprion. 'The recent events have been unfortunate and will be forgiven, but not forgotten.'

'You coward,' spat Haarksa from her bed, when Oprion went to check on her. 'You're so scared of looking weak that you won't launch an inquest to find out who those servants were working for. It'll get out eventually, even if you try to pretend it didn't happen. What sort of message does that send? There's been a security breach within days of our arrival and now any would-be attacker knows that if they escape then you don't have the stomach or ingenuity to chase them.'

Oprion knew she was right, but he had too much to lose by pursuing the girl who had attacked her and the one who had diverted Oprion after evidently stealing the letter from Silrith's chambers. If he chased the thieves, it would be very hard for him to make the letter look like a forgery if it came to light. He knew the content of the letter by heart and knew it could destroy him. The discovery of a letter in which he declared his love for Silrith, now a known traitor, could cost him his marriage and therefore his estate and fortune and possibly even his head.

Part of him pitied Haarksa as he looked at her sitting up in her bed, her temple still bearing an enormous bruise from when she'd been knocked out in the sudden attack, but the risk was too much.

'There's nothing I can do, my dear,' he said.

THE FOREST OF USTAHERTA, USTENNA, BENNVIKA

In the damp breeze of the morning, Jostan's vanguard, a group of four hundred and fifty armed soldiers and their cargo, moved nervously through the southern area of the Forest of Ustaherta. They were led by Chief Invicturion Gednab Aetrun and consisted partially of a handful of troops from the divisios. These included one hundred heavy cavalry from Kriganheim Divisio One, as well as two hundred heavy infantry from Kriganheim Divisio Two. These were joined by one hundred spear militia, fifty peasant archers and, travelling right at their centre on a small donkey, Vaezona. Their common nervousness was borne out of what they had seen before crossing the River Ganzig.

The recent rain had made the terrain very muddy and the pace was slow and tiring, so morale was already not at its highest, but their discovery had been a shock. They had been approaching a small bridge when they came upon what looked like the remains of a recent skirmish and, more disturbing still, two divisiomen were among them.

There must have been about ten bodies in all, two near the bridge, with the others further back. Among the most noticeable was one of the divisioman, whose armour had been largely stained red by a deep neck wound, though the rain had washed away most of the blood from the ground. There was even a militiaman who had apparently been both stabbed in the neck and strangled to death with a length of rope; an unusual choice of weapon under the circumstances.

Vaezona had shuddered at the sight, but what stayed with her the most was the sickeningly strong stench of the dead. She saw that it had even brought some concern to the face of that bonehead Etralbard, the divisioman who she recognised after he had reported her father to King Jostan. The sight didn't seem to bother Aetrun though and when she heard a worried sounding Etralbard comment on it, Aetrun simply responded by saying that given that they perished in such a small skirmish, the divisios were better off without such weak soldiers as them.

What a pompous fool, Vaezona thought. The man was so full of his own importance and was never willing to take advice from others it seemed; that much she had learned in the days since they had moved on ahead of the main army. It hadn't occurred to Aetrun that the bodies may have been connected with the wrecked wagon they found further down the track the very same day and even she knew that normal armed wagons didn't usually have divisiomen to guard them, especially divisiomen who were well away from their home province. Kriganheim divisiomen in Ustenna? Surely that was unusual? Whatever they had been protecting as it passed through must have been of some importance.

Satisfied with the terrain, Hojorak took up position with the main group of his force. He had taken with him one hundred horse archers, one hundred foot archers and three hundred swordsmen. They had found an area of the forest's main north-south path that was narrower than any they had found so far and according to their scouts, the enemy was now less than a day's march away.

To one side of the path there was a fairly steep gradient; enough to make a passing force potentially thin their ranks, though not enough for a horse to be fazed about charging down it. Hojorak deployed his Hentani horsemen and swordsmen at the top of the gradient, where he now sat astride his own steed, hidden within the trees, with the infantry in the centre and the cavalry on their flanks.

What made the choice of battleground perfect was that there was a particularly boggy area on the far side of the path and just beyond that was another, slightly less steep gradient and in the trees that topped that, Hojorak had hidden his foot archers. The trap was set. All they had to do now was wait.

Hojorak was joined by Blavak and Bezekarl, both of whom were also astride horses on the left flank. The right flank would be led by Kivojo. As Bezekarl watched him, Hojorak gave him a look and with a deep throaty chuckle, said something in Hentani. Blavak laughed and Bezekarl already knew they were laughing at him. He felt so isolated with these savages. He hated them. Blavak indicated Bezekarl's shaking hand.

'My master asks if you are scared, little one?' he said. 'He observes how your palm wishes to run and hide and he wonders how a great warrior such as Lord Yathrud has such a whimpering son. He says he wonders which has seen less action, your metal sword or your fleshy one.'

Bezekarl coloured and turned away in a vain attempt to hide his emotions, giving Blavak his answer. He closed his eyes and tried to shut out the barbarian's laughter. They, like the other Hentani horsemen, found it highly amusing that he had a suit of armour and a shield, while they had only thick goatskin and shields were used only by the infantry, yet he was the one that was terrified by the thought of battle. He shut it out of his mind. The crucial moment was approaching. To him, every sound seemed to be maximised beyond belief, however quiet in reality. That's when he heard it; a whinny from a horse further down the path.

Vaezona looked about her as the walkable ground thinned. She began to feel less than stable on her donkey, who was starting to find the mud difficult and she didn't like the look of the bog off to the right.

It'd be best to keep away from that, she thought.

In their new, thinned formation, Aetrun and the divisio cavalry took to the front, with Vaezona behind, flanked by the spear-carrying divisiomen on foot. The archers and spear militia followed; spearmen on the outside, archers on the inside.

The place seemed eerily silent in a way that the northern parts of the forest hadn't and the atmosphere became tense as the breeze whispered softly. All present cautiously watched the trees as they pressed on. A whinnying horse near Vaezona broke the silence and its rider leaned down to calm the nervous animal.

The next few moments seemed like hours and Vaezona was just about to breathe a sigh of relief when an arrow thwacked into the neck of a divisioman on her right. She gasped as his blood spattered on to her face and he collapsed to the ground.

'Get down!' someone shouted.

Without thinking she threw herself from her mount. She hit the ground hard but it was a reaction that saved her life, as a death-dealing volley of arrows hit the small convoy from their right flank, one of them striking the donkey in the rump. She curled into a ball to save herself from its flailing hooves, but then another arrow pierced the pathetic creature's throat and it crashed to the ground instantly, dead.

Soldiers screamed as they were dealt terrible injuries and cursed their attackers, but above the din, Vaezona could hear Aetrun shouting orders in an attempt to rally his troops.

'Stand! Stand! Divisios! Form tortoise! Spearmen! Protect archers! Archers! Fire!'

The return volley never stood a chance of being as effective as that of the attackers. The enemy archers were hard to pick out from within the trees, whereas the Bennvikans had been caught right where their opponents wanted them. Confusion reigned as they jostled for position to face the enemy and the already treacherous ground was added to by the bodies of the fallen, as more and more arrows found their mark.

Aetrun was attempting to direct proceedings by cantering up and down the back of the Bennvikan line encouraging his troops, as the remainder of his cavalry dismounted to support the infantry. The Bennvikans had already lost at least twenty or thirty soldiers and the growing mass of corpses in the confined space was forcing some of them forward into the bog, where they were even easier for the archers to pick off.

Suddenly, with no warning at all, the enemy fire ceased. Even Vaezona, from her coiled position, found the courage to lift herself nervously into a crouch, then to stand. A few of the enemy were seen running from their positions and over the lower ridge. Ludicrously some militia attempted to run after them, but a bellow from Aetrun stopped them in their tracks. Clearly those few had thought they'd won. But that was when, from beyond the top of the higher ridge, behind them, they heard the awful sound of a war horn.

The low note was met by a cacophony of war cries. With a clatter of hooves and the ominous sound of many feet, a howling barbarian army moved into view at the top of the higher slope behind the Bennvikans. Aetrun, who had moved back level with his divisiomen, turned to face the new threat, followed by his troops.

As Vaezona looked, her feet rooted to the ground in horror, the goatskin-clad tribesmen waved their scimitars in the air, baying for Bennvikan blood. They beat their weapons against their round shields, each of which was highly decorated with bird's feathers of all colours. They were toying with their prey.

Many of the enemy were infantry, but on the near flank, Aetrun could see cavalry.

'Traitor,' he exclaimed; his eyes widening as he noticed that one among the enemy cavalry was a knight with the three golden dragons of the Alyredd family emblazoned across his scarlet shield. Astride the horse next to that man was a huge tattooed warrior in a goatskin jacket and breeches, who raised his sword and gave a throaty roar, inducing an exultant cheer from his warriors and the whole force surged down the hill.

Bezekarl's heart pounded as he chased Hojorak into the fray, aiming straight at the enemy commander; who Bezekarl had recognised to be

Invicturion Gednab Aetrun. A volley of enemy pilums was hurled at the Hentani horde. Many fell with terrible screams, but the torrent of warriors charged onwards, heedless of the fate of their comrades. They crashed down on to their victims and in the unstable mud the Bennvikan line nearly collapsed there and then, but somehow they found their grip. Driven on by bloodlust, some Hentani were carried straight over the top of the divisiomen's tortoise formation by their fanaticism, while the momentum of others took them straight into a Bennvikan spear or sword.

Aetrun swung his blade at Hojorak as the Hentani chief charged forward, only to have his blow parried and the two men engaged in one-on-one combat. Bezekarl's mount reared as they got close to the solid wall presented by the divisiomen's shields and he turned to follow the other horsemen who, save for Hojorak, were wheeling around the Bennvikans and had taken out their bows, ready to pick off any soldier at will. They moved in an oval that took them up the lower slope slightly, away from the boggier mud that plagued their opponents further down. To add to the Bennvikan woe, the Hentani foot archers had reappeared; their position now largely unthreatened.

As he followed the other charging horsemen in their encircling arc, he saw that the Bennvikan archers did all they could to return fire, but they had barely any room to draw their weapons fully and the spearmen that protected them were slowly falling as the deadly horse archers thundered past. Order in the line turned to chaos as the militiamen were overwhelmed by the merciless onslaught. Those who had persisted in firing back at the enemy archers were eventually forced to drop their bows and take out their swords to defend against the tribal infantry, who were beginning to outflank them.

The already slippery ground became more and more treacherous as the bodies of both sides piled up further. Naturally, the divisiomen were holding out far better than the militia and for a moment a gap appeared between the two. As he galloped by, cutting down any Bennvikans who tried to run, Bezekarl was astonished to see a young girl cowering at the centre of the enemy line. He knew what he had to do. He threw his shield to the ground, raced over and hauled her on to the horse behind him. Fortunately for him, she was too dumbstruck to resist. With a quick turn, Bezekarl kicked his horse and fled the battlefield at a gallop.

Chief Hojorak was still busy contending with a determined Aetrun. Despite being longer than the swords used by the divisio infantry, Aetrun's weapon didn't quite have the same reach as the Hentani blade and it was obvious that he was having to put more effort into each attack than his opponent. Noticing that he was starting to wear the Bennvikan down, Hojorak continued to parry Aetrun's blows, ready to strike at any moment.

Carried in Aetrun's left hand, his shield was the wrong side to be any protection against his opposite number. He kept turning to try to get the chief on his left, but Hojorak simply moved his own horse with him as the two duelled. The invicturion's shield had already been hit by two wayward Hentani arrows that had come close hitting their own commander. With the impaled shafts causing the large shield to become an ineffective dead weight, Aetrun tossed it to the ground and pulled his bearded axe from his belt. His sword in one hand, his axe in the other, he attacked wildly; his eyes full of blood lust.

Hojorak parried another sword blow but his horse collapsed from under him as Aetrun's axe smashed down into the animal's head, splitting its skull. Hojorak was lucky not to have a leg caught under the dead horse as he scrambled to his feet. Aetrun attacked again, but as he slashed down Hojorak seized the older man's sword-arm in his powerful grip and with his other hand, he thrust his own blade upwards through Aetrun's exposed chin, piercing its way through his lower jaw, his mouth and up into his brain.

Hojorak ripped Aetrun off his horse, throwing him to the ground. After a moment, the Bennvikan's jerking body stilled and as the adrenaline wore off, Hojorak became aware of the final sounds of the battle around him, as his remaining warriors picked off the last few enemy troops; toying with them and extending their ordeal. Placing a boot on Aetrun's chest, he wrenched out his blade, which now glistened with the fresh blood and other fluids from inside the dead Bennvikan's skull.

Bending down, he removed his fallen foe's helmet. He took a handful of Aetrun's hair and began hacking away at his neck to decapitate the corpse.

179

Then he mounted the head back on the end of his sword. Slowly he drew in a deep breath of air and gave an enormous roar, to which his soldiers howled their war cries in exultation. Those few wounded Bennvikans left alive begged for death, but the Hentani had a score to settle for the threat to their villages, so they wouldn't receive it. Not yet, anyway. The Battle of Ustaherta Forest was over, but for the Bennvikan prisoners, the real suffering was about to begin.

Chapter 13

After the battle, Vaezona and her captor quickly regrouped with the rest of the Hentani army. To a man they had been jubilant at their crushing of the enemy, filling the air with the sound of their victory songs. But once on the move, they rode hard.

Each day they woke early and marched long into the night. On the third day, the exhausted men arrived back at the city. Vaezona wasn't sure which city this was, but beyond the city walls, she could see the sea. Wasn't Rildayorda by the sea? She hoped she was correct. If so, they were taking her right to her intended destination.

Given what had happened to her escort, Vaezona couldn't have dreamed for better luck gaining entry to the citadel. This didn't improve her mood though. Why had the knight helped her? Maybe he wanted to save her from being ravished just so that he could have her for himself later in the comfort of his own bed, where she couldn't get away.

Many times on the journey she had instinctively checked under the material covering her breast to check that the small trinket handed to her by King Jostan was still there. Remarkably it hadn't fallen out of place during the battle and even more remarkably her captor hadn't searched her – yet.

Clearly the young man with whom she silently rode was a figure of some importance, as he rode towards the front of the column. When they entered what Vaezona hoped was the Preddaburg citadel, many of the warriors behind them were ushered elsewhere, presumably to various billets dotted across the city itself. The lead group though carried on through the citadel and into the inner ward, where a welcome party awaited them.

By now their group numbered about twenty, though most of these were probably the commander's bodyguards, Vaezona decided. When all had reached the courtyard, they dismounted. She saw four men – the Bennvikan who had taken her and three Hentani – step forward to approach the welcome party, who consisted of an old lord in a dark blue tunic, a golden-haired young man in emerald attire, a young woman with flowing chestnut locks and who wore a long, modestly cut scarlet dress and finally a chief invicturion in full uniform, as well as about ten of their retinue. Strangely, all the men appeared to be behaving deferentially to the woman, despite the fact that she was clearly the youngest.

So, that must be Princess Silrith, Vaezona thought.

She couldn't hear most of what was being said, until suddenly she heard her captor call 'Girl, come,' as he turned and beckoned to her. Moving forward, she felt very underdressed in her dirty white servant's garb, compared with all others present in their expensive finery. She withered under the princess' piercing gaze.

'I see you've brought me a present, Bezekarl,' Silrith observed.

So her captor's name was Bezekarl. Wasn't he part of the Alyredd family? Yes. He was Lord Yathrud's son. Vaezona recollected her uncle Naivard explaining to her who was who out of the noble families.

'Yes, my Queen,' said the mop-haired Bezekarl.

Silrith looked Vaezona over, moving around her, inspecting her.

'And you say you found her on the battlefield, with the enemy?' the old lord asked of his son.

'Yes, father. I thought that she should serve here as punishment for standing with them.'

'Quite. But we do not know her background. What's your name, girl? Where do you come from?' Silrith enquired.

'Vaezona, my Queen, and I come from Sevarby,' Vaezona answered, speaking aloud for the first time in days. There was no point in lying. As far as she knew most of Bennvika was supporting Jostan and she had been picked up too far north for them to believe that she was from Bastalf.

'Ah, Asrantica,' Silrith nodded. 'Bezekarl, would you hold on to her for a minute please?'

Silrith moved out of earshot so that she was speaking only to Yathrud, Shappa and Gasbron.

'I don't want to rebuff Bezekarl, as she could be harmless, but I feel concerned by the fact that she's from Asrantica,' she said quietly.

'I agree,' Yathrud put in. 'That Feddilyn Rintta is a treacherous old dog who probably sees the rise of the House of Kazabrus as an opportunity to raise his own fortunes. However, he takes little time to win the support of the people of Asrantica and I don't see him putting such faith in a young girl, especially a commoner such as this one.'

Silrith nodded.

'All the same, I'm concerned. I don't want her near me.'

'I'll take her on as my personal servant,' Shappa offered. 'That way she can serve you as Bezekarl suggested, but only under my supervision and you can keep her at arm's length without offending him.'

Silrith looked at him.

It does seem like the safest option, she thought.

'Yes,' she said. 'That would be best I think.'

She walked back over to Bezekarl.

'I accept your offer, cousin. She will be of use to me by acting as Prince Shappa's personal servant.'

Bezekarl coloured slightly.

'Go on, girl,' he said with a hint of resignation. 'Go to your new master.'

'Right,' Bezekarl started. 'Now that we know that the enemy is coming our way and the Hentani civilians won't be slaughtered while so many of their menfolk are here, we must begin putting our defence plans into practice.'

Silrith wasn't comfortable discussing this in front of Vaezona.

'Yes,' she said. 'But first, let us eat. We'll discuss things there.' All the while she never looked away from Vaezona and she smiled as the girl again dropped her eyes to the floor under Silrith's gaze.

'Prince Shappa,' Silrith went on, turning to him. 'I trust you can take this opportunity to show your new charge her duties?'

'Of course, your Grace.' He answered with a bow, clearly very much aware that Silrith's permission for him to call her by name was for private situations only.

Silrith gave the slightest of nods and turned away, followed by Bezekarl and Yathrud. The group dispersed, causing their retinue to do the same, while Chief Hojorak, Kivojo and Blavak conversed with the other Hentani warriors present in the courtyard, having evidently long since lost interest in what the Bennvikans and their token Etrovansian were doing.

Shappa inspected Vaezona with an approving look. Clearly he thought she was attractive. She wondered what he planned to do with her.

'Remind me of your name, girl?'

'Vaezona, my Lord.'

'I am a prince. I am Prince Shappa of Etrovansia and in the ways of my people, which differ a little to how things are done here, you will refer to me as your Majesty.'

'I'm sorry, your Majesty.'

'And don't you forget it.'

Shappa continued talking as he began to walk, with Vaezona following.

'Of course, I realise you may have thought that 'your Majesty' was solely a Verusantian term of deference, but we Etrovansians use it too – just to be different from you Bennvikans really.'

He noticed Vaezona's blank expression.

'What am I saying? You've probably never met a royal before. I doubt you had any idea what to call us really. I expect you just said the first word that came into your head that sounded vaguely appropriate didn't you?'

'Yes, your Majesty.'

'Right, well, I suppose now would be a good time to show you where you're going to be living for the next little while and what I will be expecting of you.'

They exited the courtyard and Shappa spent the next half hour or so showing Vaezona around the Alyredd's house. She noticed that he made sure to only show her the rooms that would be relevant to her tasks. Mostly he planned to use her for carrying and fetching things and maybe for passing on messages if she proved herself to be loyal.

Her heart sank with resignation when he opened the door to the last room and she saw that these were his sleeping quarters. Yes, she thought he was very good looking, but she didn't want to be used in this way.

'This is where you will be spending much of your time. I will expect you to be at my beck and call. Every night, unless instructed otherwise, you will wait outside with the guard in case I need you. When the first guard's watch finishes and he or she is replaced, then you may go to your sleeping quarters, which I will arrange to be made ready for you, and you will be awoken if I call for anything else.'

Vaezona's heart rose again. She may still have to fulfil the duty of being his sexual partner at some point, but at least it wasn't looking like he was going to force himself on her. She had no idea what to say apart from 'Yes, your Majesty.'

There was a knock on the door. As they both turned, they saw a messenger standing there.

'Your Majesty, dinner is served. Our good queen requests your presence.'

'Ah, I must have taken more time than I thought. I shall be there presently.'

He turned back to Vaezona.

'Stay here while I am away. I will have some food sent up for you. You will need your energy for your work.'

'Thank you, your Majesty,' Vaezona replied dutifully with a bow.

Shappa shut the door behind him as he left and Vaezona suddenly felt incredibly vulnerable as she heard him turn the key. The room seemed darker now, despite the fact that it was only early evening and it was still light outside.

Vaezona was just having a further look around the room when she jumped at the sound of another a key in the door.

Finally some food, she thought, calming herself and realising how hungry she was. But when the door opened, it wasn't a servant who walked through. Her fear rose again as she saw that it was somebody wearing a long, thick, hooded black cloak, which revealed nothing of the person underneath, save for a glimpse of a white mask with a twisted grin and a hooked nose. Shocked by this new development, Vaezona drew back, unable to speak. As it was not yet officially night time, there was no guard on the door to intervene. Vaezona wanted to scream, but for some reason, she didn't dare. The demonic visitor shut the door.

'Come to me,' the hooded figure said, beckoning with a hand covered by a grubby black glove and using a voice that was so fake that Vaezona wasn't even sure whether it was male or female.

She was too petrified to refuse and so, gingerly, she walked towards the figure, who leaned strangely in order to keep the hood in place, with only the mask showing. As soon as Vaezona was close enough, the intruder shot out both hands and deftly pulled the shoulders of her loose fitting dress and let it drop down, held up only by the tighter fitting cut of its waist, exposing her breasts and causing a sharp clinking sound as a piece of jewellery, previously hidden, fell to the floor. Startled, Vaezona let out a squeal as she pathetically fumbled with the dress, trying to cover herself again.

It was only then that she realised that the intruder had no interest in her naked flesh, but was looking at the object that had fallen to the floor; the one that Vaezona had been given by Jostan, which the hooded figure had picked up and now held as if to marvel at it. Vaezona took the opportunity to quickly redress herself.

'Ah, King Lissoll's ring. I'm sure he'd be sickened to know that it is now being used against his daughter.' The masked entity laughed a low, hollow cackle. 'I suspected you might be carrying this. I thought you looked different when I saw you before. Most prisoners look either terrified or just resigned to their fate when being passed between captors. You didn't – until now that is. You're here at King Jostan's order, aren't you? You looked far too willing to be here on your arrival. It was as if you wanted to be here, which of course, I suppose you do, in a way. But you'll have to add a bit more sullenness in the future to make yourself believable.'

Vaezona understood now. Jostan had told her that the other spy would probably keep their identity hidden. The ring was handed back to her. She looked at it and still, even now, could not quite believe what was in her possession.

It was quite heavy for its size and was of course made of gold. On its face it had a carving of a warrior king, presumably the god Vitrinnolf, carrying his sword. It may have been King Lissoll's but before that, it had reputedly been passed down from one king to the next since the founding of Bennvika itself. As Vaezona had learned when she worshipped the gods at the temple growing up, this ring was part of a pair. Bennvika had originally been born out of the marriage between Lomatteva, the Queen of Hazgorata and Vitrinnolf, the King of Kriganheim, when they were yet mortals. At the wedding ceremony, they had exchanged rings. This one had supposedly been given to

Vitrinnolf by Lomatteva. Both of them had become the mightiest of gods after their deaths. Clearly Jostan had no belief in myths and simply wished to symbolically insult the Alfwyns.

The one that Lomatteva had received from her new husband showed a woman, also with a sword. There were many different opinions on what the pair symbolised and many thought the rings didn't date back as far as that anyway. In fact, Vaezona remembered her uncle Naivard telling her that the Hentani felt that, just as in the case of their claim about the Amulet of Hazgorata, the rings were actually of Hentani origin, stolen from them in one of their many wars with Bennvika and that the man and woman shown on them are not Vitrinnolf and Lomatteva, but deities of their own and that any similarities were mere coincidence.

The true Bennvikan belief, on the other hand, Naivard had told her, was that whether it be the images on the rings, or on the Amulet of Hazgorata, or on the standard of the province of Hazgorata, which had always been linked to the House of Aethelgard even at Bennvika's founding, the result was still the same. They believed that the woman was always Lomatteva and the man was always Vitrinnolf. That had been drummed into Vaezona and every other Bennvikan child from an early age.

'Hey. Are you listening?' the spy hissed, snapping Vaezona back to the present. She was amazed at how quickly she had relaxed after finding out that they were on the same side.

'Sorry. Yes, I was just wondering why it's necessary for you to hide your identity even from me.'

'Attention to detail. I will reveal my face to you only when I deem the time to be right, Vaezona.'

'How do you know my name? I never told you.'

She saw the spy tense slightly under the cloak and her fear rose again.

'Do not ask questions!'

'I'm sorry. I guess you've been watching me. But I must know who you are, otherwise, how will I know where to find you?'

'All you need to know is that you must follow my instructions to the letter and that I will be watching you.' Usually, that last phrase might fill one with warm confidence, but under the circumstances, it gave Vaezona a cold chill.

'Now,' said the spy with haste. 'We must be quick before I am missed. Here's what I need you to do.'

NETTSCAFORD, RILANA

Far beyond the Eternamic Ocean, in the great Empire of Rilana, Captain Voyran Attington lay on his bed, his mind ruled by one astounding thought. The undertaking that he and his crew were to begin that day could change the world forever, or at least, his country's future.

Since the beginning of time, it had been believed that the ocean to the north was too vast to cross. It had been assumed that it was the edge of the world and that any ship's captain foolhardy enough to sail to near it would end up falling off into an endless abyss. Small wonder then, that many had been dissuaded from testing this assumption.

But then, ten years previously, a naval vessel, captained by the now legendary Janissada Attington, Voyran's own mother, had been blown off course. As a result, they had ended up further north than any Rilanian had been for centuries. While attempting to head for home, they had stumbled upon what appeared to be a small merchant vessel. It was in distress and the crew were picked up by the Rilanian ship.

It had quickly become apparent that the sailors whom they had saved, some, but by no means all of whom were far lighter in complexion than the Rilanians, spoke a language that neither Janissada nor any of her crew recognised. It was clear too that none of the newcomers understood Rilanian either. More awkward still, there seemed to be no other language that was common to both factions.

Significantly though, many of the newcomers had sounded like they were saying the word 'Bennvika' while pointing to each other and then to the north. It had seemed that this was the name of the land from which they hailed and which lay in that direction.

Of course, lacking in manpower and with provisions running low, Janissada had been in no mood to pursue any reckless plans to explore the lands to the north straight away and she had ordered her crew to head for home, taking the 'Bennvikans' with her. That was how the crew of a merchant ship, as far as history could tell, had become the first Bennvikans to lay eyes on Nettscaford, capital city of Rilana.

The wise Janissada had seen the opportunity in this straight away. Voyran remembered the day the ship had landed. No sooner had the ship docked than sailors had been sent into the city shouting 'Come and see the natives of unknown lands north of the great ocean'.

Voyran had been sixteen at the time and his father, an esteemed politician in the Rilanian senate, had insisted that Voyran come to welcome his illustrious mother home from another voyage. He had been to many of these events over the years, but as they had ridden to the port, the sound of the sailors shouting about their discoveries piqued his interest. It had done the same for others too and when they had arrived, Voyran had found the scene rather amusing in a way.

Looking somewhat out of place in a busy port, dressed in their fur coats, flamboyant dresses, expensive silk jackets, leather shoes and powder blue, ponytailed wigs, the rich had arrived in force to inspect the dirty, plainly dressed, primitive-looking newcomers. Their physique was quite different and their complexions varied greatly. While a few were as dark as he was, others were like nothing Voyran had ever seen. His own dark skin declared his noble blood to all and in Rilana, anything less than that showed you were descended from the common peoples, yet these pale newcomers among the Bennvikans looked most strange to his eye. He would later learn that the Bennvikans who looked more like himself mostly had their roots in another kingdom, named Gilbaya.

The Rilanian nobility had shouted at the Bennvikans and spoken to them slowly as if that would make them suddenly understand their language. When they didn't respond, they just laughed at them. Voyran, on the other hand, could see the potential in this. There were lands to the north, ripe for exploration. The idea had obsessed him, as it had gone on to do for years since then.

Eventually, the Bennvikans had come to the attention of the already ageing Empress Hozekeada IV, who had presided over a largely peaceful and prosperous reign. The Bennvikans had been formally presented to her, but all that had followed was that the Bennvikans had been forced to learn Rilanian, so that information could be gained about their homeland. In fact, a full five years after their arrival, it had seemed to Voyran that there were no plans to actually find and explore Bennvika, or any of the other nations the newcomers had spoken of, like Gilbaya, Medrodor, Etrovansia and Verusantium.

He yearned to see these places. So, aged twenty-one and newly promoted to captain, a frustrated Voyran had personally beseeched the Empress to let him be the one to lead the first expedition. To his surprise, she had accepted, though it had taken a further five years for a crew to be formed that was brave enough and ambitious enough to follow him. A specially adapted ship, capable of reaching the northern lands, had also been required to be designed and built. Now it was ready and waiting in the port and the production of a fleet of others was well underway. Now though, the first ship was all that was required. Everything was ready. The day had finally arrived.

Voyran lifted his muscular frame from his bed, leaving his two female playmates to sleep off last night's hangover. They would be ushered out by his servants in his absence. As far as he was concerned, sex was all the preparation a sailor needed.

Dressing quickly he put on his blue uniform, complete with its dark blazer, blue shin-length trousers, long pull-up white socks, black shoes, and golden shoulder pads. Finally, he covered his short black hair with a wig of powdered azure and a large blue captain's hat. He left the house and made his way to the port.

Heading away from the large, old, stone public buildings and temples and the more recent tile-roofed houses, he moved through the crowds and stepped on to the long wooden pier, at the end of which lay their ship. She had been named the Ibbezron, after the Rilanian deity, Ibbez, the goddess of adventure and fortune.

She was a 104 gun 'lead-rate' class ship-of-the-battle-line. Looking striking with her black and gold horizontally striped paint on her broadsides, she featured three huge masts and was bristling with cannon; something the Bennvikans had not seen before coming to this country, Voyran's mother had said. Further in the distance, dwarfed by the Ibbezron, lay the group of four ore-propelled tugs that would tow the giant ship out of the harbour.

As soon as he had boarded the vessel, he saw his first mate, Emostocran Latlund.

'Everything's ready, Captain,' said Emostocran. The wrinkled old sailor's thin face was emotionless and his tone consummately professional.

'I hope she is too,' Voyran said, nodding towards a pale-skinned young woman in Navy uniform standing on the deck. She was looking around the place in a way that made her appear rather nervous. She was a Bennvikan and would be their interpreter and guide for the duration of the voyage. Despite that fact that she was some way older than Voyran, perhaps thirty-five years of age, he couldn't deny her beauty, with her dark hair and luscious curves. Her apparent nervousness just added to her appeal.

'She hasn't seen her homeland in ten years, sir,' Emostocran replied. 'I hope for our sake that she hasn't become too comfortable in our language. In all this time she's only been able to talk to her husband in their own.'

'Well at least it'll be good to have him out of the equation,' was all Voyran could say in reply.

Quickly he climbed the steps towards the poop deck and turned to address the crew who stood expectantly, filling the ship's upper level.

'Gather round. Gather round,' he called. 'We go to investigate, not to plunder.'

The sailors laughed at his irony. Most had served under him before and knew his habits well. Only the Bennvikan looked unamused.

'I jest, of course. Yet one thing that is not to be underestimated is the importance and magnitude of what we are to undertake this day. Today Rilana stretches its long arms north and sets out to pull the lands there into its rich and warm embrace. Today, the world changes. Today, we become world shapers. For Rilana.'

He thrust his sword in the air. In the midst of the cheers all around him, he got the voyage under way.

'All crew to their positions,' Voyran ordered.

With that cue, the experienced Emostocran took up the instructions.

'Up anchor!' he bellowed. 'Make ready. Prepare for the tow. Cast off.'

It was enough to set the pulse racing. Seeing the waving of the orange flag by a sailor on the Ibbezron's bow, the four tugs responded to the signal in unison, heaving forward to take up the strain. The ship began to move, picking up speed and gliding clear of the port on the shimmering waves.

'Ready the sail. Break the tow,' Emostocran ordered. The orange flag was waved again and each rope was released from its tug and was pulled back aboard the ship, which was now moving freely under its own momentum.

'Drop the sail,' Emostocran barked.

This was always an exhilarating part of any voyage for Voyran; feeling the wind running through his fingers as the ship powered forward under her mighty sails, cutting through the waves and striding out to sea as dolphins came alongside the ship's hull, jumping and diving as they went. But this time all that was surely as nothing compared with what was to come if the mission was successful.

After an hour or so, with the ship now at her cruising speed, he turned to take one last look at the shoreline of Rilana; one last sight of the city of Nettscaford before it disappeared over the horizon. Usually, he knew where he was going. Even though it was often somewhere he'd never been before, he often knew someone who had. Therefore the questions in his head tended to be very basic. How much money would he make? Would the wine be good? And most of all, what would the women there be like?

But this time, for once, there was a more poignant thought that distracted his mind temporarily from these things; how much would the world have changed by the time he returned?

Chapter 14

THE FOREST OF USTAHERTA, USTENNA, BENNVIKA

Haggard expressions adorned the faces of Jostan's troops as they took in the terrible sight around them. They had made good progress south in the past few days and it would not be long until they would emerge from the Forest of Ustaherta's southern reaches and swing southeast towards the Defroni's territory, where they would link up with their allies before marching to destroy the last independent Hentani villages.

But that was until they came upon the remains of a cart barely hours after passing the corpses of a handful of soldiers. Jostan, wearing black robes on this day, had immediately put two and two together and worked out that it must have been the one that had been transporting Silrith to her exile. Incensed, he was now even more interested to see what Aetrun would be able to glean from his visit to Yathrud. Privately he still held on to some hope that they had simply been attacked by common bandits and that she had been sold into slavery, but the troubling fact was that somehow the discrepancy between the position of the corpses and the wreckage of the cart didn't quite add up.

Then, the very next day, they'd made another, far more gruesome discovery. More bodies, lying where they had fallen, just like the others. Yet they were far more numerous this time, around three or four hundred in total; militiaman mostly at the near end of the dead pile that blocked the road, while there were mostly divisiomen, a few horses and even a donkey further ahead. It was obvious that this was the fate of Aetrun's vanguard. For Jostan's soldiers, a forest that had been in pacified territory for longer than anyone could remember suddenly felt like hostile surroundings. It hadn't taken long for the bodies to start decomposing and the air was filled with the buzzing of insects.

Jostan wrinkled his nose at the stench as he rode through the scene, though he felt otherwise unaffected. He turned to Feddilyn, whose reaction was similar.

'What happened here? There are no taverns for these drunkards and vagabonds to have been kicked out of. Tell the troops to wake up those soldiers and tell them they need a wash,' he jested.

Feddilyn smiled sycophantically at the callous joke.

'If only they could, your Majesty. We could send them to bathe in the Ganzig while we press on.'

Jostan surveyed the situation a moment longer.

'So, the enemy has a minor victory. The loss of these troops is lamentable, but only a minor setback. What are we experiencing here aside from their loss? The unyielding odour of dead peasants. The fragrance of battle. The enemy has but sniffed at the aroma that we shall soon inhale to euphoria when we crush them.'

He paused a moment to let his words sink to all those within earshot.

'They'll have to be cleared away,' he sighed, indicating the bodies; all joviality now gone.

'Very good, your Majesty, I'll order the troops to bury them,' said Feddilyn.

'There's no time. Clearly their attackers have already stolen a march on us as they've had a chance to bury their own dead and have withdrawn without us having so much as an inkling of their presence until now. Order the troops to clear the death piles to the side of the road. Then we'll keep moving.'

'Very good, your Majesty.'

All around there was the hushed noise of whispered curses at the mutilated bodies as the divisiomen and militiamen set about moving the carcasses to the side of the road. Crows dived in whenever they could to steal a dead soldier's eye, ear or finger, or some other part of their bloodied corpse. Somewhere in the background, there was the conspicuous sound of someone spilling their guts at the scene, before being berated by an officer.

'Your Majesty.'

Jostan dismounted as a young divisioman approached him, carrying a red and gold shield of Bennvikan design; not rectangular, like the shields of the divisios, but kite shaped, as carried by some members of the nobility.

'Sire. I've found this. It bears the three golden dragons of the Alyredds.'

Quickly Jostan snatched the shield from the divisioman's hands and the younger man saluted. It was definitely the Alyredd dragons that were depicted on it, no mistake. He dismissed the soldier and grinned ruefully.

'Lord Rintta, that dog Aetrun was successful in his mission after all,' He turned to Feddilyn, who had been joined by the army's two other most powerful noblemen. They were Aeoflynn Tanskeld, Governor of Ustenna, always noticeable with his long blonde hair, as well as the ageing warrior, Lektik Haganwold, Governor of Hertasala. Of course, Gormaris also stood in the background, never far from his master. Jostan clutched his newly found evidence.

'Aetrun may not have made it to Rildayorda, but still, we now know where Lord Yathrud's loyalties lie. This is the true allegiance of the Alyredds,' he declared, holding the shield aloft.

'Your Majesty.'

'What?' Jostan spat, angered at being interrupted a second time. He turned to face the new call and saw an invicturion hastily approaching him. 'Invicturion, to what do we owe this interruption?'

'Apologies, your Majesty. He's one of my men. I shall see him punished,' said Feddilyn.

'That won't be necessary, Lord Rintta. We do not mind being stalled if it is for a good reason,' Jostan said, regaining control of himself. He was amused by Feddilyn's expression. The man clearly couldn't work out whether Jostan's sudden switch from anger to joviality was genuine or not. Jostan was content to keep him guessing.

'What is your name, soldier?' he said.

'Vinnitar Rhosgyth, Sire, Chief Invicturion of the divisios of Asrantica.'

'And what did you want to tell us?'

'Sire, I believe there is something that you might want to see. The Hentani have left us a message,' Vinnitar replied, the epitome of polished formality.

'Lead on.'

He guided them further down the track, stepping over the dead when unavoidable, then stopped and pointed up the slope.

'It looks like some of our militia surrendered, your Majesty, not that it seems to have got the cowards far.'

Jostan looked at where Vinnitar had pointed and saw the naked bodies of six men hanging limply by their feet from ropes that reached down from the trees above. The branches creaked as the corpses swayed in the breeze, their dulled eyes gazing eerily down on their comrades.

'They got what they deserved for not standing and fighting,' Jostan snarled.

'I quite agree, your Majesty,' replied Vinnitar, the malevolence in his voice equal to that of his king. Suddenly Jostan's attention was caught by the slight movement of one of the bodies.

'That one's alive,' he exclaimed. 'Somebody bring him down. We need information while he lives.'

Quickly a group of soldiers climbed the slope to reach the dying man. They pulled down hard on his torso and there was a satisfying crack of wood as the branch gave way and the man fell into the arms of the group, who were barely out of the way before the branch came crashing down to the ground. They carried him hurriedly down the slope.

'What happened?' Vinnitar asked him curtly as he was dumped in front of them.

'They just fell on us, first with arrows, then with warriors and horses. We held out for as long as we could but they had us surrounded.' For the gasping man, every word was an effort and he shivered and spat blood as he spoke. 'They got Aetrun.'

'Is the enemy close by?' Vinnitar asked.

'Their army left days ago, but a few stayed to use us as bargaining tools if anyone came for us. As the days passed, they grew impatient and decided to leave a message for you to find. That was when they strung us up.'

'When?' Jostan pressed him, pushing in front of Vinnitar.

'A few hours past.'

'It seems they didn't want to negotiate after all,' Vinnitar said from behind his master. 'And that's not all, your Majesty. There's more that may interest you.'

Vinnitar carried on walking and Jostan followed, nonchalantly turning his back on the wretched peasant.

'Here,' Vinnitar said as they reached what he intended to show his king.

'Well, Aetrun didn't come out of this one too well did he, Chief Invicturion?'

'Apparently not, your Majesty.'

In front of them stood Aetrun's decapitated head, mounted on a wooden stake. Just below, against it rested a man's bloodied torso, presumably also Aetrun's and someone had carved letters into the flesh with a knife.

'As you can see, your Majesty, they're attempting to threaten us. Look, it's in Bennvikan.'

Jostan crouched down to look at the message and read it aloud.

'He who dices with the Hentani gambles fatally. The Daughter of Ashes will rise.'

Quickly he got back to his feet and turned on Vinnitar.

'What is this heresy? The Daughter of Ashes will rise?'

'It is a Hentani prophecy, my king,' intervened Feddilyn, causing both to turn to him. He had followed, but it seemed Lord Lektik and Lord Aeoflynn had stayed back to oversee the clearing of the bodies from the path.

'What does it mean?'

'I do not know, Sire. The Hentani share some of their beliefs with we Bennvikans, but other parts of their religion are all their own.'

Jostan thought on this for a moment.

'Their own, you say? We have pledged that Bennvika would be allowed to pursue its own religious beliefs, but now we can see the error in this. This heresy, this barbarian impudence will not go unchecked. We cannot ignore the fact that the gods of this kingdom have turned their backs on it. The signs are clear. If Bennvika is to prosper, all must bow down to almighty Estarron. All must prove their loyalty to him if Bennvika is to escape his wrath and enjoy his divine protection.'

Feddilyn looked both surprised and confused.

'But how, your Majesty? The soldiers will fear being struck down by Vitrinnolf and Lomatteva and subjected to eternal damnation.'

'And do you fear such a fate, Lord Rintta?'

'Majesty, putting religion aside-'

'Religion must never be put aside.'

197

'Of course, your Majesty. All I intended to say was that it is not simply the divine implications of your planned conversion of the people that I fear, but the immediate reaction. There will be a mutiny from within our own ranks,' Feddilyn warned.

'Mutineers will be executed,' said Jostan. He smiled as a thought came to him.

'Rhosgyth,' he said. 'Would you not agree, as a military man, that the officers that command the most respect are the ones that have the strength to lead their troops to victory?'

'Of course, your Majesty,' said Vinnitar earnestly.

'Then, by necessity, is that not the case for gods also? Does a soldier prefer the protection of a god who brings them defeat,' Jostan asked, gesturing at the devastation around them. 'Or one who brings them victory?'

'Victory, Sire,' Vinnitar smirked, though he kept his soldierly tone.

'Then if Estarron is to be our protector, we must all declare our loyalty to him,' Jostan declared fervently. 'We will go into battle bearing his sacred colour of white and his shining grace will see us to victory.'

He looked around him. Every soldier in sight now stared at him aghast at this outburst, with the exception of Vinnitar. Jostan looked directly up at the sky and raised up his arms.

'Do you hear me Lomatteva? Do you hear me Vitrinnolf?' he cried. 'Strike me down now if you deny that you have turned your back on the people of Bennvika.'

Silence.

'You see. Your gods have betrayed you and your comrades and even the entire kingdom. But now I come to show you the divine word of a new, stronger father of war and he will lead us to victory.'

Some troops cheered, although it was clear that they were a little unsure.

Any naysayers will soon see their error, Jostan thought.

Impulsively he pushed Vinnitar and Feddilyn out of his way and grabbed the whimpering naked militiaman from where he was lying in the foetal position. Roughly, he pulled the groaning man back to Aetrun's head and torso, laid him fully on his back, then dropped to his knees.

'Almighty Estarron, Spirit and Lifeblood of the World, I vow to you that before my reign is done, every man, woman, and child of the Hentani and all those who support them shall be put to the sword in your name, so that their blood may with your blessing fill the veins of the earth. Let not Luskaret, Lord of the Underworld, break free of the soil and cast his evil gaze upon our holy enterprise; his hounds of perdition snarling at the leash. Instead, let your divinity continue onward and light the fires at the gates of the Heavens, so that you may see the approach of the souls of our dead enemies and prevent their passage. And if Silrith is right now with the Alyredds, may you smite her from their protective grasp. Would that I may strike her from this world myself and in so doing assert your undying glory to all, so that all who do not worship you by praising your divinity, including the Bennvikan gods themselves, do so by presenting to you their fear. Even gods will kneel at your feet. This is my oath to you, oh Lord.'

With a sudden movement, he pulled out his dagger, raised it upwards in the grip of his two hands and plunged it down into the naked man's chest. The dagger slipped through a gap in his rib cage and pierced deep into his heart. The man's body shook violently and he tried to push Jostan away, but Jostan persisted regardless.

The man gave out one last cry of pain as, after removing the dagger, Jostan put the fingers of both hands into the wound and pushed outwards. He'd seen this luck ritual performed by the priests in Verusantium, but had never done it himself, so his method was not as slick as he'd have liked. A rib blocked his path, so he smashed it with the pommel of his dagger, before reaching in and wrenching out the bleeding heart with his bare hands.

'So, coward, you give your life for your king after all.'

The man's dying sight was of Jostan dipping two fingers into the heart and painting his own entire face red with blood.

Jostan turned back to his audience, as all around him, lords and soldiers alike stared back in stunned silence, as the ghastly sight addressed them. He flung the heart aside.

'Let it be known, as Estarron is my witness, that under my reign, this shall be the punishment for all cowards and deserters. Your fallen comrades, however, those who died fighting the enemy, must be avenged. Those who did this will pay in blood. Now get back to work! Move these bodies! By tomorrow I want every shield painted white, to mark our fervent fealty to the righteous Lord of War. We march in the name of almighty Estarron, Lifeblood of the World, to slaughter all who stand against my rule. We march on Rildayorda.'

'We are cursed,' Feddilyn said fearfully while Jostan was out of earshot. 'The king had pledged that he would tolerate the worship of our gods. Even convert to their worship himself.'

'He also pledged to lead us to victory and at no point did he say anything about forsaking his own god. I must correct you on that, my Lord,' Vinnitar replied. 'Anyway, did he actually say it, or did he simply imply it?'

'Do not question me, you insolent fool.'

'My Lord,' Vinnitar continued unabashed. 'If the gods were angered by his actions, would they not have struck him down? Yet I hear not the slightest rumble of thunder.'

'Do not presume to lecture me, Invicturion.'

'I seek only to advise, my Lord. It is a question worth asking. Could it be that this Estarron is stronger than our gods?'

'That's all very well, but the troops will only accept a new god if he brings us victory. If not, then sooner or later they will shout heresy and we will have a mutiny to deal with.'

'Then we'd better make sure our new almighty friend smiles on us, my Lord,' Vinnitar replied cordially.

Jostan waltzed back over to Feddilyn and Vinnitar, wiping the blood from his face with a handkerchief.

'Chief Invicturion, tell me your name again?'

'Rhosgyth, your Majesty,' Vinnitar said.

'Rhosgyth. You will understand the significance of Kriganheim's heavy cavalry. It stands for all that is good about the Bennvikan army. It shows that this is an army where the cream are not prevented from rising to the top. A Bennvikan army that includes this unit at full strength has the country's best troops riding with it. Its depleted numbers will be a psychological blow for the soldiers. There's not much we can do about the infantry that have been lost here, but the heavy cavalry of Divisio One Kriganheim must be replenished. There is no time to recruit and train more troops to the required elite standards, so horsemen from an existing divisio must take up the mantle. Are your soldiers up to the task?'

'Why of course, Sire,' Vinnitar replied, aghast.

'Good,' Jostan slapped him on the back boisterously. 'Tell whichever of your troops you choose that they are now divisiomen of Kriganheim. A hundred will need to be moved across from your previous unit. Asrantica will have to do without you for now. You will take over Aetrun's rank as Chief Invicturion of Kriganheim and I will leave it to you to select a new corpralis and standard-bearer.'

'Thank you, your Majesty,' Vinnitar beamed, relishing the thought of the glamour that went with leading the most respected unit in the Bennvikan army.

'Good man. You'll have to use your old battle standards for now though. The enemy seem to have taken Aetrun's. Your use of the Asrantican standards will be a symbol of my gratitude to Lord Rintta for allowing me the use of your services.'

'Majesty,' Feddilyn bowed as Jostan turned to leave. Evidently, he could see the long term profit in this. Personal advancement often meant knowing whose good graces you needed to be in at any specific time and any personal debts from others could be cashed in on, as long as both saw it that way.

'Well, that was a positive start, my Lord, was it not?' Vinnitar jested once Jostan was out of earshot.

Feddilyn looked at Vinnitar, then over at the departing Jostan and then back at Vinnitar again.

'You know, if I didn't know better, I'd say you were deliberately trying to be like him,' Feddilyn said.

'The gods themselves made man in their own image. Is it not, therefore, the case that any good servant should take any chance he has to emulate his master's best qualities?'

Feddilyn eyed him suspiciously.

Vinnitar smiled.

'You forget that in reality, it was me who forced out that maid's confession and put the king on the throne, not you. Don't worry, my Lord. I promise I won't come between you two,' Vinnitar said with a sly tone.

'You insolent bastard. One moment of attention from the king and you think the light of the world shines out of your behind.'

'Why yes, that does sound like me. But at least I'm an insolent bastard with a powerful new patron.'

Turning his back on Feddilyn, Vinnitar marched off to tell his troops what of their newly attained status.

Fate couldn't have dealt me a better hand, he thought. *Jostan can be watched very closely from here.*

Chapter 15

KRIGANHEIM, BENNVIKA

Things were quickly becoming very frustrating for Zethun. It had been easy for him to get the common people to back him. After all, it was their cause he was fighting for, but now he needed the king to listen, too. There wouldn't be much chance of that any time soon with Jostan on campaign on the other side of the country, especially after his initial proposals to give more rights to the common people were strongly rejected.

But it was not yet the time to start a full-scale revolt. That was to be avoided at all costs while there were other options. In any case, first, he needed information and fast. After all, Lord Oprion was watching them closely and his presence meant that searching the palace under the pretence of looking for the Amulet of Hazgorata was out of the question at this time.

However, in a stroke of luck, they soon found a contact at the palace who Zethun hoped might be able to give them some insight into the goings on there. Hoban had said he knew a girl named Capaea who was a maid there and had convinced her to come forward. Now she sat in Naivard's office, opposite Naivard himself, who was flanked by Zethun and Hoban.

As usual, Braldor stood guard, this time inside, watching over proceedings. Wearing a long white maid's dress with a loose, brown corset, Capaea regarded each of them coldly with an unsettling smile. She was an attractive girl of about twenty-five or thirty, with dark red hair and striking eyes and had the air of one who was young in years but with an arrogant confidence that was anything but naïve. Zethun conceded that, in that regard, he recognised something of himself in her demeanour. She had brought a friend with her; another maid. Capaea's companion, who wore the same uniform, appeared to be an entirely different proposition and was a dark-haired girl who couldn't have been more than twelve or thirteen. Trembling as she sat there, she made for an unimpressive sight.

'You need not fret, girl,' Naivard reassured the younger maid. 'We are here to help you and you need not fear Braldor either. He is here only for your protection. You'll be safe. All we need to do is ask you a few questions.'

Nervously she looked up at the big bodyguard. Somehow she didn't seem comforted by his presence – far from it.

'Firstly, what's your name?' Naivard began, still addressing the younger girl.

'Taevuka, sir,' she replied timidly.

'And what position do you hold at the palace?'

'She's a lady's maid. She looked after Princess Silrith before her arrest. I thought Congressor Salanath would have already told you that,' Capaea interjected curtly.

'And you yourself?' said Naivard, ignoring the jibe.

'I am a kitchen maid, though our roles meant that we frequently crossed paths when Princess Silrith sent Taevuka to fetch things. She relied on her and a few others to do basically everything. You know what royals are like.'

'And you two have worked together for some time?'

'I've been at the palace for about two years, but Taevuka is still new.' Again it was Capaea who answered.

'Now,' Naivard stated; his tone becoming a little more serious. 'It is imperative that you both tell me everything you know in relation to my next question. Nothing must be held back. There are some who seem to believe that the Amulet of Hazgorata has been stolen. Now, the palace has been predictably vague about whether or not there is any truth behind the rumour, but we feel it is our duty to the crown to launch an independent enquiry. Something as potentially serious as this must be investigated if only to dispel the rumour. However, if it truly is missing and the king finds out that you impeded us in our attempts to recover it, you will be punished most harshly for the embarrassment caused to the crown. Do you understand?'

'Yes,' they both answered. Capaea's face was cold as ever, though the curl of her lips suggested that she was taking some perverse enjoyment out of this, while Taevuka nodded vigorously. Hoban was silent, while running a ring through his fingers, taking it off and putting it back on again, in a way that seemed to be unsettling Taevuka further.

'Right then, Taevuka. Capaea mentioned to me earlier that you remember seeing something on the night of King Lissoll's death. What did you see?' Hoban asked.

'The Amulet,' said Taevuka.

'And how did you come to see it? Where was it?' asked Naivard.

Taevuka looked at her friend. For the first time, Capaea's face lightened.

'Tell them what you told me,' Capaea said, with a flicker of emotion darting across her smile.

Capaea's expression turned back to her cold sneer as she looked on the three men again. Visibly Taevuka took a deep breath. Slowly she began in a quiet voice.

'Well, I didn't actually see it exactly, but that night, shortly before we received news that the king was sick, I heard an argument happening between two other servants. They were whispering though. I had to get quite close, but I don't think they noticed me listening around the corner. I didn't suspect anything. I just wanted to get the gossip, you know.'

The pace of Taevuka's words increased as she became more confident.

'One of them said *'There it is. You've taken it,'* and the other said *'What?'* and the first one said *'The Amulet. You think I can't see it hanging around your neck?'.* So the second one said *'This? I didn't steal it. He gave it to me.'* She stopped imitating a conversation with herself, looking a little awkward.

'Was that all that was said?' Naivard asked.

'No, but I was called to kitchens to help, so I didn't hear anything else.'

'Do you know whose voices they were?' Naivard asked. Taevuka nodded.

'One was Lyzina, one of Queen Accutina's ladies. She often comes down to the kitchens to supervise the preparation of the food. The other sounded like Afayna. It sounded like Lyzina was accusing Afayna of stealing.'

'Afayna?' asked Naivard.

'She was another of Princess Silrith's lady's maids.'

Wasn't the maid that King Jostan had executed named Afayna? Zethun thought. He wasn't sure if memory served correctly and didn't want to ask leading questions.

Naivard turned to Capaea.

'Is all this true?'

'Oh yes,' she replied. 'All of it. Queen Accutina has very specific tastes, especially when it concerns dishes from her homeland. She says that Medrodorian food should be prepared in the Medrodorian fashion, though I doubt she has the slightest idea what that actually entails. So she insists on Lyzina overseeing the preparation of those meals. The problem was that Lyzina was an arrogant little sod and often muscled in, so we usually just let her get on with it. After all, the queen wants what the queen wants.'

Naivard quickly made some notes.

'These two girls. What was their relationship like normally?' asked Zethun, speaking for the first time, causing Naivard to look over his shoulder. Taevuka opened her mouth to answer but Capaea cut in first.

'Oh, they were always bickering. But since our new king's visit to the late king and his family last year and in the time leading up to King Lissoll's death, they'd been much worse. They were at each other's throats constantly.'

'I think they both liked him!' Taevuka blurted out, all former nervousness now gone.

'Liked him? In what way?' Naivard enquired, evidently attempting to avoid leading questions.

Taevuka shifted slightly in her seat.

'Well, they were attracted to him, I think,' she said, colouring slightly.

'Taevuka,' Capaea exclaimed. Zethun noted tension begin to reappear on Taevuka's face at this. Capaea turned back to the three interviewers. 'I'm sorry that my friend behaves with such immodesty.'

To Zethun's mind, the comment was inconsistent with Capaea's previous behaviour in a way that was more than a little intriguing.

'There is no immodesty in human feeling,' Naivard suggested. 'I find it entirely possible that Afayna and Lyzina both looked at him in the same way, as you suggest, Taevuka. A strong and handsome lord from the exotic lands across the sea comes to the palace. He's bound to turn a few female heads.'

'Yes,' Capaea conceded. She paused, curling her lips at the edges. 'And it is true that he had an eye for the ladies. Afayna was certainly very pretty. Someone said he lay with her.'

Zethun's eyes narrowed at this.

'Are you certain of that?' he asked.

'I am certain that there was a rumour,' said Capaea. 'Beyond that, who can be certain of anything these days?'

'Capaea,' Zethun said flatly. 'Anything said here has to be the truth and nothing but the truth. We want facts, not rumours, otherwise, we might be led to believe that all that you have said is untrue.'

'Fine,' said Capaea with a shrug. 'Try and disprove it if you can. But I guarantee you would be wasting your time. Every minute spent doing that is a minute not spent catching whoever might have stolen the Amulet, giving them more time to get further away from you, or even simply to-' she paused for a moment as if searching for words '-consolidate their position.'

'Consolidate their position?' Zethun asked curtly. 'And what position would that be? Are you accusing the king of orchestrating this?

'Orchestrating what?' Capaea curled her lips back into that eerie smile and an expression of complete innocence. 'You shouldn't make blind accusations, Zethun. Surely you know that.'

Zethun said nothing, holding her gaze.

'I can only wonder why you might think the king would steal his own Amulet and yet I sense that you want him to be guilty,' Capaea giggled darkly. 'I sense there is more you want to know about him, isn't there?'

'We should be careful,' Naivard said. 'This could be seen as treasonous talk.'

'You search me for all the information you like, but only you can put that information to the test and see if it is true. You don't honestly think I believe that this is all just about some rumour surrounding the Amulet of Hazgorata, do you?' Capaea said.

'Fine,' said Zethun, ignoring her goading words. 'Then tell me everything.'

'About the king or about Afayna?' said Capaea. 'Or am I still to pretend I believe that this is about the Amulet, which I'm sure is with the Dowager Queen as always?'

'Everything,' Zethun said flatly.

'Well,' said Capaea, putting her hand to her chin satirically. She seemed to have decided this was all a game. 'Where was I before you started sending me on a diversion?'

Zethun opened his mouth to object but Capaea carried on regardless.

'Oh yes, Afayna. Poor girl. Afayna was Silrith's prime lady's maid. Some ranks above me. I wouldn't say we were friends, but I knew her,' she said.

'And, knowing her as you did, do you believe it to be possible that the charges are true and that Afayna truly was involved with the murder of King Lissoll?' said Zethun daringly, causing Hoban and Naivard to look over at him with uncomfortable expressions. There was no point sticking with their cover story now.

'Well, the evidence against her is rather damning, isn't it? She prepared the meal after all,' Capaea said in a cold tone.

'And what of the speculation that she was known carnally to our new king?' Naivard said, shifting his uncertain gaze from Zethun to Capaea.

'I believe that to be true,' Capaea replied. 'And if you think about it, I'm sure you will come to the same conclusion. As you yourself pointed out, consider the attraction of an exotic foreigner of royal blood, full of passionate lust, who promises to marry a poor maid and take her with him back to his far-away lands where she could live a life of luxury. Many would do anything to climb the social ladder, especially that far. I might have been tempted myself if it had been me. I can't deny it. You have to admit that the possibility of a marriage offer like that has much more appeal than anything that involves working as a servant, even a royal one. Whatever Princess Silrith could have offered her, King Jostan could do better. Then, all of a sudden, King Lissoll is poisoned, Afayna and Princess Silrith are blamed and Lord Jostan is king. Some might say that all this sounds less like the actions of a princess and her maid and much more like the actions of an ambitious lord who has to remove the heir apparent, doesn't it?'

'And now who's talking treason?' said Zethun, almost laughing.

'Maybe I'm just telling you what you want to hear?' Capaea shrugged, though Taevuka looked at her, shocked.

'Be very careful, Capaea. This is not a game,' said Zethun.

'And yet we're having so much fun, little Taevuka and I,' she said. She put an arm round Taevuka's shoulders, yet the younger girl still looked incredibly nervous.

'And Lyzina? What of her?' Naivard pried patiently.

'I suppose she'd be another candidate. She's too stuck up and has no personal standards,' Capaea said. 'I have no doubt that given even the slightest encouragement she'd sleep with him just to upset Afayna, let alone any other incentive. She left the employ of the palace a few days ago apparently. Maybe she knew something? I suggest you find her.'

'And do you know where she may have gone?' Zethun asked in a frustrated tone.

Capaea gave a light laugh.

'I haven't the foggiest,' she said.

Zethun and Naivard looked at each other before Zethun cast his gaze over at Hoban. Hoban gave a slight nod.

'Well then,' Zethun said after a few seconds. 'I think we have gleaned all we can from this interview. Ladies, thank you for your contribution. We will be in contact if we need you again.'

Both left without a word, though Capaea gave Zethun one last darkly playful smile, then giggled chillingly. Braldor closed the door behind them. Naivard stood up from his chair and turned to Zethun and Hoban.

'Interesting progress, wouldn't you say, gentlemen?' Naivard said, turning to Zethun and Hoban.

'How so? Progress, yes,' Zethun replied. 'But I don't think we can draw too much from that. There is nothing there to be of any concern to the king.'

'Do not let your focus on finding the ultimate truth cloud your vision of what is in front of you,' Hoban countered. 'I think what Naivard is eluding to is that amongst the information we have gained regarding life in the palace kitchens, we have learned that there was more than one indirect royal presence there.'

'Accutina's maid? Wait a minute, you're not suggesting that the Dowager Queen might have been in on this as well?' Zethun exclaimed.

'Doesn't it seem strange to you that she left an esteemed position at the palace so soon after the king's death?' Naivard asked. 'That could easily mean that the maid Lyzina is out there somewhere bearing the knowledge that we need.'

'Or maybe somebody got rid of her,' said Zethun. 'The problem is, that we have no hard evidence to suggest that she was involved in the plot at all.'

'Maybe she wasn't?' said Naivard. 'Maybe Jostan just suspected that she might know something and got rid of her, or alternatively, she feared he may suspect that she did and escaped while she could. That would be the normal thing for someone who fears for their life to do, wouldn't it?'

'Yes,' Hoban agreed. 'I'll have Braldor send out his men to see if she's been seen anywhere.'

'If it is true that King Jostan orchestrated the murder of King Lissoll, the people have to be told,' Zethun said. 'Naturally, they will fear a king that murders his way to the throne, especially one who is a follower of another god. They will fear what a tyrant he will turn out to be. We have to inspire them to protect their kin from such a man.'

'Unfortunately, I fear it may come to that,' said Hoban. 'If we can prove that he orchestrated regicide as well as Princess Silrith's arrest so that he could claim the throne for himself then so much the better. But, I must tell you, it was raised in the Congressate today that a carrier pigeon arrived bearing an anonymous message from Rildayorda yesterday. It appears that somebody there is trying to make contact with the king, not realising that he is absent from Kriganheim. Whoever it is wants to make sure that he knows that Princess Silrith is alive, well and at large.'

'That changes everything. By the gods, Hoban. Why didn't you mention that before?' Zethun said, exasperated.

'Because I didn't want it to influence the interview. It is already clear that Princess Silrith has a spy in the midst of her supporters in Rildayorda. With that knowledge, we can be sure that Jostan has left some behind in Kriganheim in his absence.'

'That still doesn't explain why you've waited until now to tell us about the message.' Zethun gave Hoban a hard look. If anyone could be a spy, could he? Surely not. He swatted the thought from his mind. It was ridiculous.

'I didn't want to risk the maids hearing anything in case one of them is a spy. Some are very good actors and people do tend to choose those who are most expendable to do their bidding,' Hoban said.

That didn't satisfy Zethun, but he chose not to pursue it further.

'That is possible,' he conceded. 'Maybe it's time to change tactics. Maybe instead of acting in secret, it is time to appear in public again and to concentrate on forcing Jostan to be fair to the common people. We should even threaten a revolt of our own if he doesn't agree to our terms. There are many who believe we would be better off with no king at all, regardless of whether or not he used murder to attain his position. It will soon be common knowledge that Princess Silrith is alive. The common people are tired of risking their lives for kings and lords that do not value their sacrifice. We require a monarch that can keep the peace, else no monarch at all.'

'Yes, though for now, we must wait to see what happens,' Hoban said. 'When the time is right, I will invite you to the Congressate. Though you may attend, no demokroi is permitted to speak there, but I can speak for you and tell them anything you want me to say. But for now, we must wait. Princess Silrith was always popular with the people. If she is alive and wins back her crown, then the people will prosper.'

'Yes, though it must also be noted that if the king holds on to his position,' Zethun said. 'Then the people will have a ruler who will stop at nothing to consolidate his power. In that eventuality, we would have only one option left to us if we are to save this nation.'

The other two nodded grimly, showing that they were thinking in the same direction.

'To depose the king and to fight for a republic,' Zethun said.

RILDAYORDA, BASTALF, BENNVIKA

Sleep had been a long time coming for Silrith, after hearing news of the battle. Of course, she was highly encouraged by the victory, but she was very aware that this was just the start and that all the odds still pointed to Jostan prevailing sooner or later. But at least it appeared that for now, she'd saved the innocent and defenceless Hentani villagers from the slaughter Jostan would have hailed upon them. Yet now, instead, it was Rildayorda that was in danger. At least this city was strongly defended. She hoped she'd done the right thing. Eventually, after much tossing and turning, she drifted into a haunted slumber.

Outside, just around the corner at the end of the gloomy hallway, stood Vaezona, disguised as a militiaman. The spear was heavier than she'd expected and the helmet's chinstrap dug in as it was rather too tight.

Behind her, keeping to the shadows, was the spy, still dressed in the long, ghostly black shawl with the white, laughing mask that seemed to mock Vaezona every time she looked at it.

'I will remove the guard on the door, then we must ensure that he is disposed of. You know what is required of you after that,' the spy said quietly.

Vaezona looked at the very tall, broad, spear-carrying divisioman who was in full armour, save for his shield, standing guard barely ten metres away. She hoped that the spy's plan would work.

The spy reached inside his shawl and pulled out a sling and a small, rounded stone. Vaezona wondered what sort of man, for she was certain by now that the spy was male, would have this as his weapon of choice.

Carefully he placed the stone in the sling, before whirling the weapon over his head. The sound caught the guard's attention, but it was too late and with a venomous throw the spy sent the projectile hurtling towards him. Seeing her cue, Vaezona launched towards the man. The stone cracked him directly on the forehead. With a groan, he slumped backwards against the wall. Racing forward, Vaezona was there to grab his body before he could

212

topple over, but she couldn't quite catch his spear and she winced as it clattered horribly on the floor.

She didn't dare breathe, expecting to hear calling voices any moment, but amazingly, none came. She'd got away with it. It was all she could do to keep from dropping the guard's body. Gingerly she laid him on the floor, as the spy opened the door into the room next to the one the man had been guarding.

'Take his legs,' he said, as he pushed Vaezona aside and took hold of the man's shoulders.

She picked up her spear and leaned it against the wall, then took a foot under each arm, holding his knees.

'Now, lift,' said the spy and they hauled the man upward. It was hard to grip on to his broad limbs and Vaezona felt sure he would slip from her grasp at any moment.

'What are you doing?'

Vaezona almost dropped the man as she heard a female voice. She looked up and saw a young maid, wearing a long blue gown with a plain white headdress.

The tension in the maid's face made her look as if she wanted to ask a thousand questions. She gasped and took a step back as the spy turned around and she saw the mask.

'Do not be afraid, Avaresae,' said the spy, lightening his voice, suddenly all kindness. They placed the guard on the floor and the spy walked over to the girl. His back was turned to Vaezona, but she saw him raise his hands to lift his mask and show Avaresae his face.

The maid visibly breathed a sigh of relief at the sight of a man she evidently trusted and opened her mouth to speak, but the spy hushed her.

'This man is a spy,' he told her, indicating the guard. 'I wear this mask because he must not know who is questioning him. We must find out what he knows and then dispose of him. Help us drag him in here.'

Vaezona thought of the irony of that statement, though she didn't want to consider what would happen to her if she was caught.

'Ok,' Avaresae whispered with a nod, not looking entirely convinced, but evidently too fearful to do anything else. Vaezona felt sorry for Avaresae.

Just like her, in a matter of moments, the maid had been haplessly drawn into the plans of those who thought themselves her betters.

Avaresae walked towards the guard's body. Vaezona saw her hesitate as she looked at the wound to the man's head, before picking up a leg. Vaezona took the other one, while the spy replaced his mask and hood, then held the guard under the shoulders. They heaved the man's huge bulk towards the door and into the adjacent room.

Once through the door, they lay the body on the floor as quietly as they could. Vaezona went back out to fetch her spear, then returned and put the weapon on the ground. As she got back up, she looked around the room in the darkness. There was a large window at the far end and by the moonlight, it looked as if they were in a child's room, though the small bed was empty.

She looked at Avaresae, breathing shallowly, her pulse racing. With tension etched across her face, Avaresae made to leave, but the spy grabbed her from behind with his hand held tightly over her mouth, stifling her attempts to scream.

'Shut the door,' he told Vaezona. She didn't want to, but fear won through and she complied.

The spy laughed coldly at Avaresae's pathetic attempts to break free of his embrace. While manhandling her towards the window, he overpowered her, leaning in and kissing the struggling girl on the head through the open mouth of his mask as he unsheathed his knife.

'Apologies, Avaresae, but your part in this is over,' he said and in one swift move he pushed her against the wall and sliced the girl's throat open. Her eyes bulged for a moment as a torrent of blood burst out of her veins and down her body.

Vaezona watched in horror as Avaresae's legs seemed to buckle and the spy slowly laid her jerking body on the floor as her blood pooled around her. The girl burbled something but he simply hushed her in a tone full of mock compassion.

'Go quietly my love,' he said.

Vaezona saw Avaresae hold his gaze one more moment, then the maid's strength failed and she could hold on no more. It was the first time Vaezona had seen someone murdered. The fear was paralysing. She'd told herself before that it was no different from witnessing the death of livestock or even seeing soldiers falling in the battle in the forest, but it wasn't true.

'First time you've seen a murder?' the spy asked. 'Well, you better get used to it.'

The guard groaned.

'He's coming round,' the spy said, opening the large window. 'Help me carry him.'

Vaezona didn't move. The spy looked at her, though the mask blocked his expression.

'I said, help me carry him,' he repeated.

'What are you going to do?' asked Vaezona.

'We must drop the bodies. The window looks out on to the city, so there's a good chance that in the darkness they won't be found until morning. If we drop them together, those who find them might think it's some kind of double suicide. We must be long gone by the time they work out the truth. Now, help me lift the bodies.'

Vaezona hesitated. The spy laughed, then lurched forward, taking her by surprise. He roughly grabbed her collar and pulled her towards the window, before wrenching her upwards. Vaezona tried to fight back as he lifted her on to the window ledge, but he was too strong and she could do nothing about his iron grip on her neck. He thrust his arm forward so that her entire head and shoulders were out of the window.

'Do you defy me? You do exactly what I say. Do you hear?' he raged.

Vaezona couldn't help but look down at the streets far below, their buildings all lit up like little candles surrounded by revelling stick-men. One more push from the spy and she'd fall to her death.

'Yes,' Vaezona gasped, struggling to breathe as his fist began to suffocate her and her legs flailed in a desperate attempt to find hard ground.

'Do you?' said the spy.

'Yes,' shouted Vaezona.

He paused, looking right at her through the dead eyes of the mask. He relented and pulled her back. Vaezona was still in a state of shock as her feet felt solid ground again.

She expected him to say something, but he didn't. As she watched, the spy picked up Avaresae's bloodied corpse and placed it on top of the unconscious guard. Her head lolled backwards and the deep wound in her neck gaped open, still oozing blood, yet her eyes seemed to lock on to Vaezona's, just for a moment and then it was gone. Was that an accusing look in her eye?

Vaezona shuddered, feeling like the blood was draining from her body, just like Avaresae's. She turned away but then turned back again. How could she complete her mission and save her father if she let fear rule her like this? She must be strong, she told herself, whatever she had to do. She tried to clear her mind, telling herself that it was all to save her father. She touched the handle of the knife in her belt.

The spy took the guard's shoulders and Vaezona took the legs, with Avaresae's delicate form balanced on top. Vaezona was glad to be at Avaresae's feet, away from those ghostly eyes. They heaved the bodies towards the window.

With one final pull, the spy managed to lay the guard's upper body on the window ledge. Then he gave a hard push and the man's legs were ripped from Vaezona's grasp as the weight of his armour pulled him downward and he plummeted to his death, dragging the maid's corpse with him.

There was an ear-splitting crash as muscle, bone and steel hit the ground. Vaezona hoped that most people who had heard it assumed it was some brawl breaking out somewhere. Still, she questioned the logic of dropping the bodies into a public place. Surely that severely limited their escape time? But then, did the spy even need to get out? Avaresae's recognition of him suggested that she knew him. Maybe once the mission was complete he could simply drop the disguise and carry on in the citadel being whoever he really was? She was sure he didn't care what happened to her, but the potential implications of that didn't bear thinking about.

She wanted to lunge at him and kill him, but he had already shown that he was far stronger than her and she didn't plan on suffering the same fate as the guard and Avaresae.

'It is inevitable that the bodies will be found soon. So will the blood in here. Leave me to deal with that. You must work quickly if we are to escape notice. Go now.'

Vaezona wondered why the spy wasn't going in there himself. Maybe it was because Jostan thought she was more expendable than him? She had no choice, whatever the reason. This was the only way for her to save her father.

Heeding the spy's instructions, she picked up her spear and opened the door. She looked both ways down the empty corridor before exiting, with the spy behind her. He ushered her in the direction of the next one with a small push, then retreated back into the first room and shut the door behind him.

Vaezona approached the door into the next room along and took hold of the handle. She paused a moment, running Jostan's pledge through her mind once more. Do this for him and her father would be set free. It didn't matter now that she'd gained entry to the citadel through capture. She had the chance to save her father. There was no avoiding what she had to do now.

Quietly she turned the latch. The creak of the wooden door seemed unbelievably loud as she opened it, but no further noise followed, so she crept in. She took care to quietly lean her spear against the wall with one hand while clicking the door shut with the other.

As her eyes became accustomed to the darkness, she began to make out some of the details of the room and was immediately drawn to Princess Silrith's sleeping form in the large bed at the far end. Vaezona shuddered, unable to quite comprehend what she was about to do. She removed her leather gloves and tucked them under her belt. Barely making a sound as she placed one foot in front of the other, she drew closer to the bed.

She saw that Silrith was lying on her back and was wearing a white nightshirt, which exposed her neck. She desperately tried to think of Silrith as if she were no more than a goat or pig. She'd killed animals before, but killing a person was different. She'd just seen that. Her hands were growing clammy with sweat and the blade of her knife rasped in its sheath as she drew it.

Silrith mumbled something in her sleep, turning on to her front, disturbed but not woken by the slight noise.

Gods, Vaezona cursed internally. She didn't want to go through with this and something to make her hesitate was the last thing she needed. The sound of Silrith's voice had been an unwelcome reminder of her humanity.

217

She also had no idea which part of the back to stab to inflict a death blow. Maybe she could lean over and still open the neck from where she was? She had to do it. She would risk eternal damnation in the afterlife for murder, but maybe she would escape it given that it was an act to save her father. If only she could just find the courage to cut this girl's throat, the danger to him would be over, wouldn't it? She tried to think of how the spy did it, but she'd been so shocked and the attack so swift that she hadn't taken in exactly how he'd done it.

She wondered if the spy had managed to clear the blood away in the next room and if so how. Either way, she could imagine his next move would be to hover out of sight in the corridor somewhere, watching the door to make sure she completed her mission.

She was taking a life to save a life. She told herself that same sentence again and again, trying to summon up the courage to kill the girl. After all, Silrith was the enemy of the man who kept her father captive. The glistening cold steel of the knife hovered little more than an inch away from the girl's skin. Looking at the blade, Vaezona almost had the feeling that it was somebody else's hand holding it and not her own.

She reached out with her free hand to lightly move Silrith's dark hair out of the way, exposing again the vulnerable flesh of her neck. Her blood turned to ice as the young princess's eyelids flickered open. Silrith turned her head and instantly those piercing dark eyes locked on to her assailant. The princess flipped herself over and threw herself at Vaezona, grabbing her by the throat and pushing her against the wall. The knife dropped out of Vaezona's hand and clanged on the floor. Desperately she tried to remove Silrith's hands from her neck as the princess' thumbs pressed down on her windpipe.

As she fought to breathe and to break free, she saw the sheer anger and ferocity in Silrith's face; her teeth clenched and her eyes bulging with rage. Vaezona tried to throttle Silrith, but she had nothing of the princess' physical strength. Suddenly Silrith grabbed Vaezona's shoulders, wrenched her towards her and ripped off her helmet, before hurling her backwards. Vaezona's head crashed against one of the cabinets and she collapsed on the floor.

Dazed by the impact, she lay there sprawled on her back as blood trickled down her face. Her head throbbed as she tried to regain her senses. She heard Silrith calling for her guards. She tried to get up, but a sharp kick in the ribs from the princess had her down on the floor again, winded. She heard many running footsteps and the room lit up as the door flew open.

'My Queen, are you alright?' asked a broad man in civilian clothing, who was accompanied by a group of divisio guardsmen. Silrith placed her foot on Vaezona's chest to hold her down, while her long nightshirt and trousers ensured that she kept her modesty, at least mostly. Vaezona begrudgingly respected Silrith for retaining such a commanding presence even when dressed in such a way.

'I am well, thank you, Gasbron,' Silrith told the man. He may not have been in uniform as the others were, instead wearing a simple grey tunic and breeches, but the other men kept behind him as if he was in charge.

'I am relieved to see that, my Queen,' said Gasbron.

'Your speed is appreciated,' said Silrith briskly, pressing her foot harder into Vaezona's chest. 'Now, take her away. Have a physician see to that wound, then find out whatever you can from her. But do not torture her until tomorrow. I'd like to question her personally in the morning.'

Vaezona was surprised by Silrith's sudden turn of mercy. She wondered how long it would last. But the glimmer of hope did nothing to assuage her panic. She prayed her fear didn't show. She didn't offer up any resistance as the guards roughly picked her up and carried her away. Doing so might affect whether or not Silrith continued to show mercy later. Instead, Vaezona frantically tried to work out what to do and prayed to the gods for her father's life – and now her own as well.

Chapter 16

After another training session the following day, Silrith knew it was time to face the sorry business of questioning her prisoner. As she had ordered, there was a guard waiting for her in the inner ward upon her return, ready to show her to the dungeons. So, still wearing her leather jerkin, breeches, boots and a full weapons belt, she left Gasbron and his troops and headed deeper into the citadel. On the outside of the main building, there was an innocuous-looking wooden door. The guard opened it and led her down a deep staircase.

There was a palpable drop in temperature as Silrith descended the stone steps, following the torch-carrying guard down to the dungeons below. The screams and groans from within, which were so faint they could be missed completely when one stood at the top of the stairs, had now become so loud that they pierced into the darkest depths of Silrith's soul as she neared the bottom. She still felt incredibly shaken and vulnerable after the previous night's events, but she knew nobody could be allowed to see it, so she kept a stone-faced expression.

'What you're about to see is fairly standard procedure, my Queen,' said the guard nonchalantly.

'I hope you don't mean that what happened to me is a common occurrence,' said Silrith.

'Of course not, my Queen. But we commonly use these dungeons for dealing with anyone who has committed a major crime, especially if the victim is a noble. We do what we need to do here to find out what we need and then we take the criminal to the other dungeons in the city itself until it's decided what we're going to do with them. Fairly straight forward really.'

His manner didn't surprise Silrith, but yet it offended her that he could talk about another person's suffering in such a way. There must've been innocent people that had ended up in here in the past. She felt sure that most would admit to anything under torture, even if the result was a humiliating walk through the streets, followed by imprisonment or execution. It disgusted Silrith that she was involved in something so despicable.

Unfortunately though, she also knew that it was unavoidable, as in this case there was no doubt over the girl's guilt.

They reached the bottom of the staircase and were now in a long corridor, with many metal doors on all sides. Some hung open, while others were bolted shut; screams emanating from inside.

'From here, you can get to all the dungeons and torture chambers under the citadel. We haven't got much space though, so we try not to keep 'em here long before sending them to the city dungeons. They've got lots more room there. We're in here.' He directed her to a door on her right, where the most piercing screams were coming from.

'Apparently, her name's Vaezona and it won't surprise you to know that she was working for the king,' said the guard, opening the door.

Silrith was going to berate him for referring to Jostan as 'the king' but stopped herself as the screaming seemed to reach new heights the moment she entered the room. She saw that Vaezona, now wearing a dirty rag that could barely be called a dress, was tied down on to a rack. Beside her stood her torturer, who was an obese man with a sagging chin. He wore plain, civilian clothes and was almost laughing as he prodded her bare arm with a red hot poker.

'Stop,' Silrith commanded. The grin dropped from the torturer's face and was replaced by a confused expression.

'This girl must suffer for her actions,' Silrith said. 'That is unavoidable. But how can we have the moral high ground if we take pleasure in her suffering?'

Silrith looked at Vaezona, who had ceased screaming, but still groaned in pain and whimpered as she looked around her, utterly terrified. The skin of both of her arms, as well as her legs and her face, was already scorched all over with poker burns. Verily, it was evident that the torturer enjoyed his work. The thought sickened Silrith. The room stank of piss and, looking at Vaezona lying on the rack, she could see what had caused it, as the pungent smelling liquid pooled out from below the girl's dress.

'Now, leave us. I will question her alone.'

Obediently, the two men left, albeit with the obese torturer looking distinctly disappointed, shutting the door behind them. As soon as they were

221

alone, Silrith took her dagger from her weapons belt and cut the rope that bound Vaezona's arms and legs.

'Now don't even think about doing anything stupid. I've already shown you I can beat you in a fight and this time I'm the one that's armed.' She removed the ropes from around Vaezona's wrists and ankles.

'Sit,' said Silrith.

With some effort Vaezona lifted herself off the wooden contraption and into a seated position, wincing in pain as she did. She pushed herself over to the side of the rack and rested her feet on the floor. Silrith continued to stand.

'Now, why were you in my bedchamber last night? Who sent you?'

Silrith knew the guard had said it was Jostan, but she wanted to hear it for herself. The girl hesitated. She looked Silrith straight in the eye and all Silrith saw there was dread.

'It was the king,' she said finally. 'Oh, please have mercy on me. He said that if I did this he would free my father. All I wanted to do was save my father's life.'

'The most natural thing in the world. But you must see how that would have been to my detriment? It's hard to forgive someone who tried to kill you, wouldn't you say?'

The girl began to sob. Strangely, Silrith felt sorry for her, but she couldn't help thinking how pathetic she looked.

'Of course, I knew that it was highly likely to be Jostan, so when I asked you who sent you, I was asking for more names than just his. I don't believe for a moment that you were working alone. You could have killed my maid but never the guard. I'm not stupid. I can see the connection between their deaths and mine. Who was assisting you?'

'I can't. He'll kill me.'

'That's the least of your worries now. What is his name?'

'I don't know. He never told me.'

Silrith had feared she'd say that. She didn't look like the type to be privy to that sort of information.

'What did he look like?'

'I don't know. He wore a mask normally.'

'Normally?'

222

'Yes. The only time he took it off he was facing away from me. He showed his face to that poor maid. Anyway, I couldn't look at him. I was too scared.'

Surely she was lying. She knew more than this, Silrith decided, shutting out her thoughts of poor Avaresae. Her broken body, like the guard's, had been found at the foot of the citadel walls in the city streets, her throat slit and blood, presumed to be hers, still stained the floor next to Silrith's own room. It was most strange that no attempt had been made by the murderer to clear it up though.

The girl's face lit up as if she'd just remembered something.

'He said he was a prince,' she said.

'Don't lie,' said Silrith. 'Why would he not tell you his name, but still tell you his title?'

There were two princes in the city and Prince Kivojo didn't speak Bennvikan and always stayed with the Hentani. That left only one. Surely not Prince Shappa?

'He did.'

'I don't believe you.'

'You must,' the girl cried.

Silrith paused. This was going nowhere.

'Thank you. That is all I needed to know,' said Silrith.

She knew that Vaezona had to be executed, despite the regret Silrith felt about the situation. If she let her live, it would be seen as foolhardy and everyone knew it. The girl had to die.

'Open the door,' said Silrith. 'I will personally escort you to your cell.'

Vaezona hesitated a moment, apparently surprised, but then made for the door. As she passed, Silrith grabbed a handful of Vaezona's long dark hair, wrenched her head back and sliced open the girl's throat with her dagger.

Vaezona fell back against Silrith, as if trying to speak, but then she could only gurgle as the blood spilt from her neck. Her eyes rolled back and Silrith took the weight of Vaezona's limp, lifeless body, slowly laying it on the ground as the blood continued to spurt.

Yes, Vaezona had to die, but there was no reason for her to suffer death by the flames, or by hanging or by disembowelling. A quick death was

223

more merciful. She forced herself not to look at Vaezona's face as she stepped away from the corpse.

She wiped her blade on the cleaner sleeve of her otherwise blooded clothes, before sheathing it. She opened the wooden door and saw the guard and the torturer still waiting outside.

'Your Grace?' said the guard. Both men looked stunned at the sight of their queen dripping with blood. Silrith realised her deep breaths were making her whole body heave. She hoped that the steely expression she was putting on was enough to make them see it as anger and aggression and not her horror at what she had just been forced to do.

'Are you alright, my Queen?' the guard asked with a fearful look in his eye.

'I have found out all the information I require and given her the quick, merciful death she deserves,' said Silrith. 'Neither of you will speak a word of this, on pain of death. As far as everyone in the kingdom is concerned, she died under torture, understand?'

The two men nodded.

'Yes, my Queen.'

'Now, you, dispose of the body,' she said, pointing at the torturer. 'And you,' she said to the guard. 'Find a maid to bring me some new clothes and to wash these. Be quick about it and make sure they know what the consequences of any idle gossip about this sorry episode will be. Now go.'

After changing out of her black tunic and into a clean dress, blue this time, Silrith headed to Yathrud's meeting room where the others would be waiting for her. She felt like she was about to collapse under the weight of the terrible thing their situation had just forced her to do, but she fought back her emotions and kept her expression cold. She had to present herself in such a way that only a crown could make her look more of a queen. *A great leader impresses with the eye, as well as the word, but most of all through action* her book had advised her. Yathrud's gift was proving useful. Yet this particular action would have to remain a secret forever. Even those directly around her could only be allowed to know that the girl was dead and nothing more than that. She knew she'd had no choice. The girl had tried to murder her after all and yet she wondered if she'd ever be able to forgive herself. She felt sure she'd never have a clear conscience again.

She heard voices from the inside of the room. Unlike the others, this corridor had no guards stationed on it, save for on its far ends, so as to keep anything discussed in this room a secret. She paused a moment to compose herself, then reached out and turned the latch.

The discussion amongst the four men ceased immediately and was replaced by the creaking of chairs as they all stood. Yathrud, Bezekarl, Shappa and Gasbron turned their heads to face her. Gasbron wore his uniform and scaled armour save for his helmet, while the other three men wore fine tunics. Silrith shut the door behind her. They looked at her expectantly, apparently waiting for her to say something. She let the silence hang in the air a few moments longer.

'I have seen the girl,' she said eventually, motioning for them to sit. 'She didn't say much of note, save for one thing. Jostan has at least one other agent within our midst.' She searched the faces of all four of them. Could she even trust these men? But then, did she have any choice but to do so, despite the circumstances?

'She claimed she did not know the name of the man she was working alongside. However, I don't believe her,' Silrith went on. She noticed Shappa, in particular, raise his eyes at this. Could it really be? After all, he had been rather negligent. She resisted the temptation to make an accusation.

'She mentioned something about her accomplice that, if true, gives me some idea of who it might be. However, it may well be a lie designed to mislead us, so I will not tell you what it was,' said Silrith.

'She should have been watched far more closely,' she went on, giving Shappa a hard look. His expression turned to one of indignation and he coloured a little. He opened his mouth to speak, but Silrith raised her palm to hush him.

'I hope this breach in security will be learned from by all, as indeed it must,' Silrith concluded.

An awkward silence hung over them again. It felt like nobody was sure what to say next. Yathrud opened his mouth to speak but was interrupted by the sharp note of what sounded like a foghorn. It was the call to arms from the sentries on the ramparts. The note was repeated and in the distance could be heard the distant beating of a drum.

'They're here,' Bezekarl smiled, causing everyone to look in his direction. Silrith was a little bemused that he, of all people, was for the second time looking impatient to get at the enemy.

'Gentlemen,' Silrith said. 'An error was made last night, but now it must be learnt from and be put aside. The war has arrived.' With that, she strode over to the door, leading the others from the room. After descending the stairs and exiting another oak door into the courtyard, Silrith made sure to cut a purposeful figure, leaving the others trailing in her wake amid the organised chaos of a city and citadel preparing to defend a siege. As more troops poured through the gate from the inner ward to the outer ward and then the walled courtyard, people nonetheless respectfully made space for Silrith and her entourage.

Inside Preddaburg's walls, warning trumpets blew and officers shouted orders, while screams of the panicking civilian population could be heard from the city itself. Hastily Silrith led the group up the spiral staircase in the Preddaburg Gate and stepped on to the walls, laying eyes on the enemy for the first time.

Over the hill they came, marching in square units with hundreds of soldiers in each, with subsequent formations fanning out to march on the flanks of the lead group. It was an imposing sight. Each square saw lines of divisiomen at the centre, supported by militia and tribesmen, presumably the Defroni, marching at their sides. Silrith had guessed Jostan could raise as many as forty thousand troops and it looked like she was going to be proved right by the time his entire army had arrived. She could see no siege engines yet, but she knew well that no besieging army used their full force in the first attack. This sight was intimidating enough and was surely only the beginning. Above it all came that incessant drum, like the army's own beating heart.

Dum da-dum, dum da-dum, dum da-dum, dum da-dum

'I'm glad to see Jostan remembered to bring a few friends to the party,' Silrith beamed, attempting to show a confidence that she didn't truly feel.

'Don't worry, this'll be a party to remember, my Queen,' Gasbron added.

Dum da-dum, dum da-dum, dum da-dum, dum da-dum

'Corpralis. Your report please?' Silrith called to the officer who'd been on duty. A weathered face with features that suggested ginger hair under his helmet turned to look at her. He snapped to attention and gave a quick salute.

'At ease,' said Silrith.

'Thank you, my Queen. We raised the alarm as soon as they were spotted,' he stated in a common voice.

'I don't doubt that.'

'They're all approaching from loosely the same direction for now, my Queen, and they appear to be expanding outwards from their current position. The troops on all sides of the citadel and the city are being alerted to look for any signs of enemy reinforcements, especially from the forest.'

'Thank you, Corpralis.'

Dum da-dum, dum da-dum, dum da-dum, dum da-dum

Silrith turned back to Yathrud, Gasbron and Shappa.

I hope any chance of reinforcements is just a precaution. They must already outnumber us by at least four to one, she thought.

'How many extra troops were you able to recruit in the end, uncle?' she asked, her expression neutral, already knowing the answer but hoping in vain for some good news that maybe somehow hadn't reached her ears yet.

'About four thousand at the last count. That's eleven thousand when added to the divisios, the Hentani and Shappa's knights. Numbers aren't everything though, my Queen,' Yathrud reassured her. 'Not to mention the fact that when I oversaw the construction of this citadel, I made sure everything was done to make it defensible.'

'We'll hold out, your Majesty,' Gasbron added, smiling for once. He was in his element. 'Those who are less experienced can be trained during the siege, in the same ways as we've been doing since we arrived back here.'

'Most of them are peasants that have only used a knife to prepare their food or at best slaughter an animal. They're not soldiers,' Shappa pointed out.

On hearing this, Silrith inwardly reminded herself that, compared to the divisiomen, this was still much the case for her too. She knew the concept

227

of battle strategy well enough when it came to command, but she knew that she still required more training with a sword and shield.

'No,' Gasbron replied through gritted teeth, turning on the Etrovansian while strapping on the helmet he'd been carrying up to now. 'But we'll have to make the best of what we've got. Anyway, many of the population here are members of the Hentani tribe, either by birth or descent. They may have become accustomed to Bennvikan ways, but they still learn the skills of their own culture too. Don't worry, they can fight.' He paused. 'Oh, your Majesty,' he added in a mocking tone, looking directly at Shappa. The prince rolled his eyes.

'Relying on the defeated peoples to help you get out of a tight spot; always a wondrous idea. I know what I'm talking about, Gasbron. I did help you train them after all,' he retorted quietly.

'You sat on your arse and watched two sessions,' Gasbron grumbled.

'What's that? I didn't quite hear,' Shappa chided him.

'I said, your Majesty, that you'd be surprised how people fight when it's in defence of their homes.'

'Why are all the enemy shields painted white?' Silrith asked Yathrud, deftly distracting the two from their own personal conflict. 'I'm sure I haven't seen that before.'

'I cannot be certain, my Queen. I confess I haven't seen it before either. Maybe it's something Jostan has brought in. I can only see the standards of four of the other provincial governing houses though if you include Jostan's own crest.

'Yes,' Silrith agreed, as the enemy infantry splayed out in front of them while the cavalry halted far behind, nearer the hills, well out of arrow range and almost hidden behind the dust kicked up by the infantry.

It was strange that one provincial standard was missing, as Bennvika had six provinces if Bastalf was included.

'There's Jostan's Blue and Silver Eagle,' she said, scanning the enemy horde. 'And there's the Black and White Trident of the Rinttas, the Emerald and Gold Labyrinth of the Tanskelds and the White and Red Serpent of the Haganwolds,' she said, rattling off the full formal names of each standard.

'And there's the national flag,' she added, peering through the dust cloud the see the cavalry far behind. 'But I don't see the standard of the Aethelgards.'

Silrith's heart leapt as she noticed this. Maybe Oprion hadn't come south? They'd definitely see his flag if it was there. It featured the same design as the Amulet of Hazgorata, a man and a woman; both of them apparently on fire, wearing armour and carrying swords. They were shown in gold, against an orange background; a colour combination unheard of in any other form of heraldry, so it was very distinctive. What did the absence of the Hazgoratan troops mean? Had Oprion been ordered by Jostan to protect the north? Or had he received her letter and somehow convinced Jostan of his loyalty, whilst quietly planning how to assist her? It was a stupid idea, she decided and not one worth hanging on to. But at least it proved that Jostan didn't feel secure enough to leave the north in the hands of the Congressate and a few hundred militia.

Either way, Oprion wasn't present. Still troubled, she thought about what the significance of the white shields could be. Her blood turned to ice as she realised the likely meaning. She couldn't tell a soul unless her suspicions were confirmed, she decided. There was no point lowering her soldier's morale.

She moved away from the others and Shappa followed.

'Why didn't you reprimand Wrathun for such insubordination?' he asked angrily.

It took Silrith a moment to regain her thoughts and remember the petty argument with Gasbron that Shappa was referring to.

'You two were having your little disagreement under your breath. The junior officers and soldiers weren't likely to overhear, so I was content to let you fight it out,' she said.

Shappa bit his lip.

'I know he is an experienced soldier,' he said. 'But I believe that my insight is as useful as his or Lord Yathrud's.'

'I quite agree. But we are all in this together and if we are to lead these people we require their respect. A slight erosion of the class divide in some areas can help this along.'

'And of course I agree with that, my Lady, but-'

'-but nothing. We'll talk about this later.'

'Yes, your Grace, and I apologise for my negligence in watching the girl.'

'Apology accepted. Now go to your troops and see that they are prepared. Ah, Uncle,' she called over Shappa's shoulder, moving past him and back across busy walls towards Yathrud.

'Where's Bezekarl? I didn't notice him leave us.'

'Oh he said he was going to inspect the troops on the West gate,' said Yathrud.

Silrith nodded. Loud calls could be heard from the approaching army and now the figures of individual men and women could easily be picked out.

Dum da-dum, dum da-dum, dum da-dum, dum da-dum,

'Company, halt,' came the order from somewhere down below. Forty thousand feet hit the ground one last time as the drums gave one final note and the army came to a standstill. By now their formation must have stretched half a mile wide. Gasbron watched with Silrith now at his side again.

'Their divisiomen won't be able to do much for now,' he said. 'I expect they'll start building a battering ram and some ladders.'

'Gasbron's right,' Yathrud said. 'Siege towers are almost impossible to transport, so have to be built on arrival. It's possible that they will build some, but I expect that their initial attack will be with their militia using ladders, supported by their archers.'

Orders were being given down below. Looking left and right, Silrith could see that the militia and the tribesmen, who had marched on the flanks of each divisio unit, were now moving forward to congregate into a singular line at the front of the army. Among them, Jostan had brought with him many archers to support his infantry and she could see that their ranks included both longbowmen and crossbowmen.

Standing on the ramparts in a sapphire dress and covered in jewels while surrounded by soldiers made Silrith feel rather overdressed and, more to the point, more of a target.

It's the tunic and breeches for me for the next little while, she thought to herself. She wanted to be a soldier like the rest of them and anyway, she had no intention of giving some eagle-eyed enemy archer any help by standing out in her bright colours.

'I must go and prepare,' Silrith stated, turning on her heel. 'Knowing Jostan he'll probably want to taunt us with a parley soon.'

Chapter 17

For Jithrae, one thing was very clear. Sitting in an iron cage on top of a cart is no way to travel. As they had progressed ever southward, he felt every single bump in the road and as he was buffeted about, he'd had plenty of time for thought. When he'd joined the army, he knew his chances of finding Vaezona were small, but the fact that he'd come so close, yet so far, wrenched at his heart and tore away at every fibre of his being. He tried to force it to the back of his mind, but it was an impossible battle.

Additionally, in the dark recesses of his mind, there was something else - the knowledge that his own haplessness had put Vaezona in far more danger than she had been in before.

So disillusioned was Jithrae becoming, that rather than trying to escape, he had taken to spending much of the day sitting and watching the world go by, twiddling at his thumbs and his fingers repetitively. As the army had crested the hill approaching Rildayorda, which was fronted by the Preddaburg citadel, like many others he had been impressed by its size and its imposing beauty.

Unlike others though, he had been forced to wonder if his daughter was in there and if she was in danger. He begged the gods to let him hold her again and take her home, away from all of this. It was torture not knowing if he would ever see her again, or hear her voice.

Now though, an hour after their arrival, much of the besieged fortress was obscured by tents. As those who mattered paused to consider their next plan of attack, the camp was rife with a hubbub that was almost akin to that of a town, as soldiers bustled this way and that. In the midst of it all, opportunistic camp followers, mostly prostitutes, plied their trade. This had been the case all through their journey and one night Jithrae had even had to look away while one serviced the soldier who was guarding him. He thought of taking advantage of the distraction, but there was no weapon within reach or anything with which to pick the lock and anyway, they were doing it against the cage door.

Lost in his thoughts, Jithrae failed to notice a dark shape fall over him.

'Oi! You! Out!'

'Uh?'

'Out!'

The cage door had been swung open and a guard, the one who was addressing him, stood beside the one who'd been on duty.

'What's happening?' Jithrae asked, shocked.

'The king's changed his mind.' Jithrae's heart leapt. 'It's the front rank for you, laddie!' Jithrae's heart sank again. 'We'll take you to your unit.' Life was going from bad to worse and possibly getting shorter.

As evening started to fall, Silrith, now clad in her black tunic, which had been washed clean of blood, and also wearing her chain mail, breeches and boots, while carrying her helmet, was again standing on the battlements. Finally, she saw what she'd been waiting for; significant movement towards the back of the enemy line. Quickly she hot-footed it down the Preddaburg Gate's spiral staircase, through the walled courtyard, into the inner ward and made her way between the small buildings, through the Alyredd Gate and into the main courtyard, where she found Yathrud, Shappa and Bezekarl conversing with Hojorak and Kivojo, through Blavak, about their plans.

She felt that the relationship between herself and the Hentani leaders was strained already, though she could not put her finger on why. This troubled Silrith greatly and she vowed to address the problem at the next opportunity. Gasbron was also there, giving a last inspection of a unit of divisiomen.

'They're coming. I thought they might,' Silrith said to Yathrud, smiling and slightly breathless. 'A small party under the cover of parley. White flag raised.'

'Horses. To me,' Yathrud commanded. Their animals were brought around by a pair of stable boys moments later and each mounted their steed. Without another word, they followed her back the way she had come, only stopping for Gasbron to call for three mounted divisiomen to join them as their armed guard. As the gates opened inward and the portcullis outside began to rise, they left two by two, with Silrith and Yathrud at the head of the column, followed by Shappa and Bezekarl, with Gasbron and the divisiomen

233

bringing up the rear. Conversely, out of the ten horsemen that approached them, one was well ahead of the others. Silrith smirked.

Always first in line until the real fighting begins. I'd expect nothing less of you, cousin, you fool, she thought.

'It's like he doesn't realise that leading troops and showing off to them are different things. You have the better of him there, my Queen,' Yathrud said, clearly thinking the same thing.

Jostan reined in before them, astride a sleek black stallion. His face gave a hint of surprise at Silrith's presence. Like her, he was bareheaded, but at least her helmet was under her arm. He carried none at all. In fact, his elegant bright white robes, gold chain and gaudy jewels were in stark contrast to her more functional garb. Even Yathrud and Shappa were wearing their armour now, as they had been since shortly after the enemy army's initial approach.

'Well, you all look ready for a battle,' Jostan remarked heartily. 'Except we'd have thought your noble allies might have seen to it that *you* had some decent armour though, dear cousin. You look like you could be Lord Yathrud's squire. A quick haircut and the look would be complete.'

Silrith's eyes flared at the derogatory comment.

'Say what you like, Jostan, but a weapon, a shield and the will to personally fight my own battles will suffice,' she said.

'*And* these great walls,' Jostan interjected. 'It's very easy to be confident when you've got something to hide behind. Just remember though, the differences between confidence and arrogance are very subtle. We wouldn't want you to get the two confused now, would we? That could be fatal.'

'Oh we have reason to be confident,' Yathrud stated smoothly. 'There is a crucial difference between our cause and yours. In principle, our troops fight for our queen's right to rule, but really they know that it is their homes and families they defend; all of which you have come here to destroy.'

'You see, Jostan,' Silrith added, moving her horse in closer. 'Whatever we royals like to think, the personal values held by our soldiers drive them far more than any loyalty to authority. My troops either fight or die, taking their families with them. Yours, on the other hand, have a third choice. Can you really guarantee they won't desert you the moment the going gets tough?'

Jostan's blood boiled. Silrith could see it in his face.

'You see that white flag?' he raged. 'It's up to you as to whether or not it's replaced by a black one. A black flag carried aloft for my whole army to see. You know what that will tell them. You know what that will mean for the people of Rildayorda when the walls are breached. The time for parley should not be wasted, cousin.'

Silrith was undeterred.

'Do not think me a fool, Jostan. You didn't march all the way here for a parley. That's not in your nature.'

'Then you've decided your own fate, Silrith. We're sure you'll live to regret it, briefly, before we decide when and how to bring that time to an end.'

'Or rather, when you order it to be ended?' Silrith corrected him. 'Wasn't that what you meant to say, Jostan? Always getting other people to do your bidding for you; how brave of you. Meanwhile, I'll be using my own sword to kill your troops myself.'

'It's a pity both armies aren't led with such honour,' Yathrud added.

'Quite,' Silrith acknowledged him approvingly. 'To lead soldiers, one must become a soldier, wouldn't you say, Jostan? I don't need fancy clothes and the biggest stallion on the whole damned battlefield to boost *me,* by the gods!' She indicated Jostan's clothes and mount.

Jostan was enraged by this.

'You dare speak to us in such a way?'

He looked at Yathrud.

'Think on what this means for the people of your city, Lord Alyredd,' he said. 'We have refrained from the temptation to forcibly convert them to our religion and instead have decided to keep the peace of this nation by tolerating other religions and cultures in the interests of commerce and mutual benefit, meanwhile leading the army to protect the country from rebellious tribesmen and this is how you repay us? You take in this murdering witch and seek an alliance against us with Bennvika's enemies? Well, let us tell you both, in the name of almighty Estarron, Lifeblood of the World, not a man, woman or child will be spared his judgement and his hunger rises. As you see from the shields our soldiers carry, we are blessed by the one true lord. The city will burn. The men will be put to the sword, the women will be

235

ravaged until they moan for death, then ravaged and ravaged again, before we slit their throats and the children...' he paused for effect with a particularly malevolent smile. 'The children shall suffer no less than their parents. Before your life is over Silrith, you will see infants carried aloft, spitted on the ends of my troops' spears and all because of you.' With that, he galloped away.

It was a chilling promise.

'He's all about threats and nothing more,' Yathrud reassured Silrith unconvincingly as they trotted back through the portcullis.

'Is he?' she countered. 'I'm not so sure.'

'It's not in his interests to destroy Rildayorda. It's a prospering city and every king needs money,' Yathrud said.

Silrith pulled on her reins to stop the horse as they entered the walled courtyard, while the remainder of the party dismounted and went about their duties.

'The salt mines and whorehouses of Bennvika are ever in need of repopulation, so some will survive, I grant you that,' she said. 'But rest assured that if we fail, there will be death here on an industrial scale.'

They both dismounted before Silrith continued.

'Jostan's hubris knows no bounds. That's a grave concern, but an even greater one is his religious beliefs. He's clearly already begun converting his troops. That troubles me greatly.'

'Yes. It appears that he considers himself a servant of Estarron. Some say he claims to be the chosen one, or even the god's own son. But do you really think he will try to do away with our gods?'

'I cannot foresee anything else,' Silrith replied. 'When my aunt went to Verusantium to marry Jostan's father, it was on the condition that she converted to their religion and once she did so, she became a fanatic and would accept no other beliefs. She even tried to convert me at one point. Jostan is even worse. Believe me, for all his decadence the man is obsessive about his religion and accepts no alternative view.'

'I see. So to him, it is Estarron's way or nothing?' said Yathrud.

'Yes, that is precisely what he believes. I shudder to think where that might lead. After all, there is no one so godless as a religious fanatic. It is our duty to protect these people from such a man.' Silrith paused for a moment,

236

pondering her own words. 'It's quite a responsibility when you think about it, isn't it, uncle?'

Yathrud opened his mouth to reply, but just at that moment, some way above them, a number of voices burst into song. Shappa was now up on the wall and had got the soldiers singing on the ramparts, with those down below soon joining in; divisiomen, militiamen and Etrovansians alike and even some of the Hentani. Shappa turned around to look at those below and caught Silrith's eye.

'A fine tune, good Prince,' she called, before turning to Yathrud as her mood lifted. 'They're in high spirits, uncle. That's a good start. Come, let us take to the walls.'

She headed up to the wall on the left side of the Preddaburg Gate with Gasbron and Bezekarl, while Yathrud moved to join Shappa and his troops on the right. Silrith now stood amongst Gasbron's soldiers, consciously noting those divisiomen who had helped her escape en route to her place of exile.

They were supported by the units of militia spearmen, swordsmen and crossbowmen. The people had flocked to join in defence of their city. As she passed, every soldier turned and fallen to their knees, lowering their weapons and bowing their heads while uttering 'My Queen,' as she walked the length of the wall.

She stopped as she heard a voice that hinted at less conviction than the rest. She turned to see a young spearman. He couldn't have been more than sixteen years old, with a chin still devoid of even a shadow of stubble. The kneeling boy shuddered as he peered from under his kettle hat.

Feeling a motherly warmth take hold of her heart, Silrith bent down and looked him in the eye. She could sense his heart was racing.

'What's your name, boy?' she asked lightly, gently taking his face in her hands with a kindly expression.

'Dazyan, my Queen, Dazyan of the Southtown.'

'And do you fear, Dazyan?'

'No, my Queen.'

Silrith gave a compassionate smile.

'Nonsense,' she said, raising her voice so that all around her could hear. 'But there is nothing dishonourable about fear. We all fear. After all, what is fear really? Fear is what brings value to the things we do in spite of it and there can be no greater honour than that.' She motioned for the kneeling soldiers to stand. 'The thing about fear, is that it can always be superseded. There's always something stronger. Always.'

As she said this, she turned to look over the walls. A flag as black as night was being carried in front of Jostan's army, meaning that if the city fell, every man, woman and child inside was to be put to the sword. At the same moment, the drums started up again and trumpets sounded in the distance as ladders were brought forward and the enemy prepared for a frontal assault.

'All of you, ask yourselves,' Silrith continued. 'What is it that you fear the most – the one thing above all else? Is it this army that stands outside our gates? I think not. They are nothing. I can see some of you have felt the wrath of many blades before and lived to tell the tale – and some faces the better for it! I'll wager that any fear you feel is fear on behalf of others. Fear for those who depend on us. Your children, your elderly kin and anyone else who depends on you for their safety. But that is why you are here. You're here so that you can say one thing; that when fate decreed that you were the only thing that stood between all that is sacred to you and all that is evil, you stood firm. Take your fear and turn it to fire; a fire that burns like a flaming wall from which our enemies will melt away! Some of you served under my father. But he was not simply my late brother's father, or mine. He was as a father to all his people. Yet now he lies dead, slain by the usurper Jostan. Do you intend to let his murder go unavenged?'

'No!'

'And do you intend to stand by and watch as the self-same man burns your city and takes your families from you, as he has taken mine from me?'

'No!'

'So what shall we do to all who support such a man?'

'Kill! Kill! Kill!'

'Then may the gods be with us!'

Her soldiers exulted into their war cry and Silrith thrust her sword in the air; turning to face her destiny.

Down below, the cheer from the top of the walls was intimidating, to say the least. Near the front, holding on to a strut of one of the army's many huge wooden siege ladders, Jithrae tried to keep his face neutral, but that was more than could be said for some of his comrades. Above the drum beat, his ears picked out the sound of trickling liquid and with a sideways glance, he saw that it was coming from the trousers of the man next to him. From somewhere behind them came the repugnant sound of someone being sick and whoever it was, they weren't the first. The terrible anticipation was getting too much.

Finally, all the militia units detailed for the first assault were in position, where they were joined by a few hundred of the wild Defroni mercenaries and the drums went quiet. Through the momentary silence came the singular note of a bugle and the order was relayed by many other buglers throughout the army as if that first note had become a chorus of echoes. In a moment the eerie effect was lost as the drumbeat struck up again and each officer bellowed 'Forward!'

Back on the walls, there was a sense of the calm before the storm, as all watched the ladder-carrying militia units start to move, followed by the enemy archers, while the defending crossbowmen, in turn, waited for them to come into range, weapons at the ready as the enemy drums continued their steady beat.

Dum da-dum, dum da-dum, dum da-dum, dum da-dum

'The moment I give the order, loose the first volley. Concentrate your fire on those carrying the ladders. Do not get distracted by the enemy archers,' Silrith ordered, taking her helmet from a squire who had followed her and putting it on, before taking her shield as well.

'You,' she told the young squire. 'See that my orders are conveyed to the archers below.' In addition to the crossbowmen on the walls, lines of longbowmen waited down below them in the walled courtyard. The squire bowed and hurried away.

Dum da-dum, dum da-dum, dum da-dum, dum da-dum

Suddenly there was a low note blown on a war horn and the soldiers down below screamed their war cries as they broke into a run.

'Fire!' Silrith bellowed, thrusting her sword into the air, as dozens of shafts hurtled overhead and down towards the onrushing peasants and tribesmen. Within seconds dozens became hundreds as the archers intensified their barrage.

There was a unified cry from the soldiers below as some were hit, but the ladder bearers came right on regardless and their wooden cargo soon swung upwards as they reached the walls and the first troops began to climb.

'Shoot at the climbers! Do not let them get near the ramparts!' Silrith commanded.

But nevertheless, while many of the attackers were hit in the incessant hail of arrows, some of them falling and knocking their comrades from the ladders in a deadly game of dominoes, others remained untouched. A militiaman's head appeared over the top of the battlements right in front of Silrith. She parried his spear aside with her shield as he thrust it forward and she smashed down her own blade on to his head with a clang. The metal helmet withstood the strike, but even so, the dazed soldier lost his grip on the ladder and slumped backwards, plummeting to his undoubted death.

Instantly Silrith was faced with another opponent, who jabbed his spear up at her, but again her shield was her salvation and she buried the sword into the militiaman's exposed neck. Silrith ripped her blade back in a spray of blood and the man lurched backwards as he fell to the ground, just as his comrade had done.

Out of nowhere a bearded axe sliced upwards into Silrith's vision. She instinctively parried it with her own weapon, but it hit her sword with such force that it knocked her backwards. For a terrible moment, she was off balance, teetering near the edge of the wall. The man seized his chance and he climbed up and got a foot on to the ramparts. Regaining her balance, Silrith saw that he was a huge Defroni warrior; all muscle with dark tattoos, a shaggy black beard and long hair like a horse's tail, wearing a loincloth and thick, draped animal skins while bellowing his challenge. He swung at her again. Silrith raised her shield and the massive impact jarred her whole body as the axe smashed down on to it. Her legs almost buckled but still she didn't fall. The warrior came at her again, but in a desperate defensive move she

240

was able to block him a second time; the two metal weapons clanging together as she hung on defiantly.

The man withdrew the axe to attack a third time and raised it above his head with a roar. Seizing her chance, Silrith thrust forwards from behind her shield and cut deep into the man's abdomen, burying the sword halfway to the hilt before wrenching it free with a cascade of crimson.

The warrior roared to attack again, but the huge loss of blood had weakened him and as he staggered forward, Silrith darted around his axe, batting it aside with her shield, slicing her sword round in a sideways motion, sending the warrior's head flying from its shoulders. The headless body dropped to its knees and collapsed on to the hard stone below, its muscles going into spasm.

Silrith turned back to the nearest ladder as the seemingly endless number of militiamen and warriors kept on coming. As another opponent fell, Silrith and the two soldiers either side of her took hold of the top of the ladder and pushed it with all the strength they could muster, sending it crashing to the ground along with every soul on it.

While still unbalanced Silrith was alarmed to feel a pair of hands on her back and she was suddenly pitched forwards. For some moments the world appeared to slow down; her eyes interpreting the tiniest detail as she began to fall. She reached out in all directions, desperately grappling at the air in search of something to grab on to, then looking straight down at the scene below. Then, just as death seemed certain, she felt another pair of hands take hold of her right arm and haul her to safety. Her eyes met those of Gasbron; two studs of hazel from under his invicturion's helmet and his stubble-ridden face gaping somewhat as if in shock at seeing her almost fall from the ramparts. She nodded her gratitude, but the moment was shattered in an instant as he turned to bury his sword into the neck of an enemy.

On some parts of the wall, the defenders were starting to wane under the onslaught of the more numerous enemy and a few had made it on to the ramparts.

'Hold the line! Longbows, fire!' Silrith commanded, her voice carrying above the clamour.

At her order, from behind the walls on which the combatants fought, a huge volley of arrows from Silrith's longbowmen, who had been waiting in

241

reserve, looped up and over the top of them in an arc, before surging downwards on to the many onrushing militia who were still at the bottom of the enemy ladders, trying to reach the defenders while their comrades climbed. Men and women screamed as the deadly shafts found their mark.

Volley after volley came down, raining death on the soldiers further behind, leaving the attackers on the ladders isolated from the rest of the army. As the enemy wavered in the face of adversity, Silrith's army stood fast. Silrith found herself back alongside Gasbron and they held their ground tenaciously, both cutting, slashing and roaring as if they were possessed by demons.

Eventually, under the hail of arrows and the stout resistance on the walls, the enemy buglers sounded the retreat, but in truth it was nothing short of a rout.

Shouts and bellows erupted from Silrith's army, as they jeered at the running soldiers. Silrith punched her fists in the air, raising her bloodied sword and battered shield about her head, more in relief than celebration. She'd done it. She'd survived her first battle, or at least the first stage of it.

Yet something troubled her. At some point in the battle, she had noticed that, while Bezekarl had previously been on the ramparts close to her, now he seemed to have disappeared. She worried for his safety, scanning the area but not seeing his face.

'Victory is pleasing sight, is it not?' Gasbron said, apparently misinterpreting Silrith's body language.

'It is,' she said, forcing thoughts of her cousin to the back of her mind. 'Our soldiers have done well. Look at all those troops retreating.'

'Yes and plenty won't be,' said Gasbron, indicating the headless Defroni warrior at their feet. 'Dead bodies aren't a pretty sight, but at least they won't be bothering us again.'

Silrith looked at the decapitated corpse and then at the many other bodies about the place. In the cold that came after the heat of battle, Silrith found the musky stench intensely nauseating.

'Quite. Now, come with me,' Silrith said.

'You!' Silrith called to the nearest militiaman. 'Fetch Lord Yathrud and Prince Shappa. Tell them I wish to see them in Lord Yathrud's quarters immediately. And see if you can find my cousin Bezekarl as well. Give him the same message.'

Gasbron followed Silrith down the steps into the walled courtyard.

'So, how do you think I performed in my first fight?' she asked.

'Impressively well, my Queen, apart from one minor slip.'

'Do not jest about that, Gasbron. I felt a push.'

'A push?'

'Yes, a push.'

'Well, it was very crowded up there, my Queen. With all the pushing and shoving during the fight, somebody must have done it by accident.'

'This was no accident, Gasbron. I clearly felt two hands on my back,' Silrith said firmly, rounding on him, but inwardly she scolded herself and bit her tongue. 'But, again, you were there to save my life,' she added in a gentler tone. 'You seem to be making a habit of it. I cannot thank you enough.'

'Anything for you, my Queen.'

Silrith could see in his eyes that he wanted to say something more sentimental, but he'd stopped short of that.

'I say! My Lady?' The moment was broken by a shout from behind them. Silrith turned to face Prince Shappa.

'My Lady. I see that you got stuck into the sport then?' Shappa said, indicating her bloodstained clothes.

'I'm not quite certain that sport is the word I'd use to describe our fight to save Bennvika's freedom from tyranny, but yes, my attire bears witness to the fate of those who stood against me,' Silrith said awkwardly.

'Well, the streaks of scarlet suit you well,' Shappa jested.

'I doubt those who provided them would agree,' Silrith said.

'They brought it upon themselves,' said Shappa.

'You think we commoners have any choice in which royal we fight for?' said Gasbron angrily.

'I do not believe that that is what Prince Shappa meant,' said Silrith, placing a hand on Gasbron's forearm to calm him as he glared at the Etrovansian.

'But I agree,' she added. 'Shappa, it is clear to me that a life lived under Jostan's regime can only be one of terror. Those in Jostan's army still number among the very people we fight to liberate.'

There was silence between the three of them for a moment, as Shappa and Gasbron continued to stare each other down and all that could be heard was the bustling of those around them.

'Your Grace, may we speak alone for a moment?' Shappa asked, not taking his eyes off Gasbron.

'Of course. Chief Invicturion Wrathun, go and wait for us in Lord Yathrud's quarters. Tell him we will be there presently.'

'Yes, my Queen,' said Gasbron, still staring at Shappa angrily, before turning to leave.

'You shouldn't let him speak out of turn like that,' Shappa said once Gasbron was out of earshot.

'Isn't that what you're doing right now by giving me such advice?'

'Of course. My apologies. Look, I wanted to talk to you about how things have developed recently.'

'It's alright. I know you weren't at fault for the attempt on my life. Nobody saw Vaezona's accomplice, or who killed Avaresae and the guard. It could have been anyone. Don't be concerned. I don't place the blame at your door.'

'I thank you for being so understanding and while we are on the subject of recent events, there was something else I wanted to speak to you about as well. On the night of the feast, I kissed you on the cheek. Do you remember?'

'Yes of course,' Silrith chuckled. 'It was nice.'

'Good. I know you said something similar at the time but things have been different since then and I'd hate for there to be any, well, awkwardness, between us.'

'I don't feel any. Do you?'

'Well, no. I suppose not. I'm sorry. This must all sound a trifle absurd. Please, think of it as a declaration of my very high regard for you.'

Silrith laughed.

'Thank you, Shappa. I shall take it as such. Now, we really should hurry along and join the others.'

Chapter 18

Once inside the Alyredd meeting room, Silrith, Yathrud, Gasbron and Shappa sat around the large oak table to discuss the events of the first day of the siege. Bezekarl had also re-joined them.

'We've made a good start, but that's it. There are still a lot of things that need to go our way if we are to survive,' Gasbron put in, as ever playing the part of the perennial realist.

'That's a little defeatist, don't you think?' Shappa chided him.

Silrith rolled her eyes. It was getting obvious by now that Shappa would disagree with anything Gasbron said on principle.

'It's merely a statement of fact,' Gasbron stated firmly.

'And who are you to decide that, soldier?' Shappa spat.

'Oh in the name of the gods, stop it, both of you!' Silrith protested. 'This is stupid! Talk like this is cheap and wastes time.'

Instinctively they both turned to glare at her.

'Enough,' she said firmly. She turned to Yathrud and wished the affable old man would say something to help clear the air between the two men, but it never came. For some reason, he seemed happy to watch them fight it out and his face wore a brooding expression; the kind that suggested that he was following the goings-on around him, but that his mind was also somewhere else. Meanwhile, Bezekarl simply sat pathetically in the background, adding nothing to the conversation thus far.

'What are your thoughts on our situation, uncle?' Silrith asked. 'You know what they say. The one who says least hears most.'

'Wise words, as ever, my Queen,' said Yathrud. 'As for my thoughts, well, I believe Gasbron is right. It's all very well fighting the honourable way but, given the threats that Jostan has made, we must remember that there is more at stake here than just our honour. For the protection of the people of this city, we must be audacious. We mustn't present Jostan with a predictable opponent. He has the advantage of numbers and we are, for as long as we have enough food, safe in this citadel. So, what is the last thing he'd expect us to do?'

'Attack,' Silrith answered.

'Correct. He'll be gearing up for a long siege and he will soon be preparing his troops for the next advance. He thinks that he'll be able to dictate the way this fight is going to pan out.'

'So, we need to steal the initiative away from him,' Silrith said.

'What do you propose, your Grace?' Shappa enquired.

'A frontal attack is too great a risk,' said Silrith. 'That can only be a last resort. But what we have to remember is that the only thing holding that army together is Jostan himself. We have to kill him. Then this war will be over.'

Shappa nodded.

'We just need to find a willing assassin and a way to get them into the enemy camp,' he said. 'Do you have any ideas Bezekarl? You're very quiet over there.'

'Err, yes, sorry! No, my mind is blank of names to suggest. We must find reinforcements. I'll send messages to Intei and Lithrofed. That is the only way we can win.'

'There will be no further letters, Bezekarl. I have told you of the risks.' Yathrud gave him a hard look. 'It looks like we're going to have to make it official. As of today, any letters leaving Rildayorda are banned. Information comes in but does not go out. There's too much risk of treason. If we can stop all messages from getting out, then that will include those sent by enemy spies.'

'Certainly father, but it must also be considered that the assassin may be taken prisoner and may talk.'

'Oh Bezekarl,' Silrith laughed. 'And what would they tell him? That we want Jostan dead? I think he knows that already. He wouldn't learn anything about our defences either. I assure you his advisors will have worked out where we're strong and where we're weak long ago.'

Bezekarl's shoulders dropped and he went quiet again. Silrith didn't like speaking to him like that, but what he'd said was most unhelpful. This was no time to be timid.

Then it hit her. Maybe someone who could hide in plain sight would be the ideal person to infiltrate Jostan's camp.

'I believe I have thought of a way in,' she said. 'I am as aware as anyone that for centuries it has been the case that while on campaign, kings of Bennvika have had girls travelling with the camp followers brought to them for, well, some company, shall we say? I doubt Jostan will be any different. All we need is a girl fit for the job. Someone he will desire and yet someone who can undertake this mission?'

'Well, I know of someone who might do it if we asked her,' said Gasbron.

'I assume you mean your Hentani girl? Ezrina, isn't it? Do you think she'll do it?' asked Silrith.

'I'm certain of it. She's a savvy girl who hates Jostan as much as the rest of us. Plus there's that sister of hers, Jezna. I don't know her so much but I'm sure she's capable of keeping Jostan occupied.'

'Twice the distraction, twice the chance of success,' said Silrith. 'So that's settled then. Have them brought up to me as soon as you can. Let us not forget though that they have a choice in this. I shall not force anyone to do such a dangerous mission.'

'Yes, my Queen. If that'll be all, I shall fetch them right away.'

'Thank you, Gasbron.'

That night, in an almost hidden corner of Rildayorda, Silrith's plan was put into action as the moon reached its zenith. Ezrina was still unsure as to why she'd been hand-picked for the task, let alone Jezna. But she supposed that if it looked like she was going to be discovered it made sense to have Jezna there to buy her some time by causing some kind of distraction.

The dirty work would be Ezrina's task, but that didn't bother her. After all, she had sworn to her father on his death bed that she would always be an enemy to the King of Bennvika and now she had a chance to kill one. When it came to the method itself, the nature of the mission repulsed her with every fibre of her being, but it was all in the name of Bertakaevey. Even the sins they committed in life would be rewarded in the afterlife if they were done for the glory of the holy goddess. Ezrina kept telling herself this over and over.

She and Jezna had washed the red ochre patterns off their bodies and wore plain white serving girl's dresses, cut fairly short in a bid to tempt

247

Jostan further. They were joined by Gasbron, who had done away with his chief invicturion's uniform in favour of a militiaman's garb; his shield painted white for disguise and his spear tassel carrying the red and gold of Kriganheim, which also happened to be the colours of Bastalf.

'Huh, how the mighty have fallen. Suddenly not quite as ruggedly handsome as before,' Ezrina appraised him.

'Nice try, but don't think for a moment that I believe you were getting all excited just over the uniform,' he said.

'Maybe. Maybe not.'

'Well I think he looks very dashing, Ezrina,' Jezna gushed.

'You see! At least someone isn't blind,' said Gasbron.

'She's just being polite,' said Ezrina.

'You just have no appreciation for a real man,' said Gasbron. 'Either way, down to business. Let's go through this one last time.' They were now standing by a small door in the city wall, near Rildayorda's East Gate. Ezrina rolled her eyes. She already knew it all by heart and even Jezna would be able to handle herself so long as Ezrina was nearby.

'So, when we go through this door,' said Gasbron. 'We will follow the steps down into a tunnel which will take us under the walls and some way into the forest. Once there, we head for the camp. Do you both remember what to say?'

'Yes.'

'And Jezna, what else do you need to remember?'

'If someone stops us, let Ezrina do the talking.'

'That's it. When we get close to the camp, we need to hide until we see someone else being challenged by the nearest sentry. That way we'll be able to find out the password. If we can't do that, we'll have to improvise and find another way in. Once we're in, I won't be able to follow you any further. You two will be on your own for that part. Once you find Jostan's tent, do whatever you have to do to complete the mission. Are we all clear on that?'

'Yes.'

'Right then girls, here we go.'

Ezrina walked over to the door, carrying a flower basket. She would never have spotted the door without Gasbron pointing it out, covered as it was in moss. Not in the darkness she wouldn't have anyway. With both

248

hands, Gasbron pulled on the handle and the door groaned until it was fully open. Then he took a burning torch from a nearby brazier and stepped down on to the stone staircase, with the girls following. Jezna shut the door behind them.

Ezrina shivered as they reached the end of the staircase, which led into the cold, damp tunnel, yet she was a little warmer than she might have been and the trio's surroundings glowed a lurid orange with the light of the torch, causing rats to scurry away into the background.

'Ezrina! Hold my hand! I don't want to slip!' came Jezna's voice. Reaching behind her and taking Jezna's hand, she kept moving on, following Gasbron. This far down the floor was wet and the surface treacherous, and Jezna was making it awkward for Ezrina to walk. She stayed behind Ezrina, apparently not wanting to look at the rats.

'Come on,' Ezrina chided her. 'You're slowing us down.'

Eventually, through the light of Gasbron's torch, they began to make out a second stone staircase, which they soon reached and climbed. They stopped as Gasbron began to push at the ceiling and with a great effort he opened the hatch at the top of the stairs. He clambered through it, revealing the night sky above as he turned and reached for Ezrina's hand, pulling her upward.

Once back above ground, they found themselves deep in the woods. They took care to shut the hatch. The door had been covered by earth and thickly growing grass and so was perfectly camouflaged. Gasbron looked around them.

'Are you sure we'll be able to find our way back?' asked Ezrina quietly.

'Honestly, no,' said Gasbron. 'But we can't mark out this position in case the enemy find it. We'll just have to pray that the gods guide us back safely.'

Ezrina and Jezna looked at each other in shock, but Gasbron apparently didn't notice and began to stride away. Focusing her mind on the job in hand, Ezrina followed Gasbron and headed for Jostan's camp, with Jezna behind. At the very least, they trusted that Gasbron was heading in the right direction anyway. Soon they began to make out the camp's distant flickering fires.

All three of them strained their ears for any sound as they moved, freezing at anything that sounded anything like the crunch of a twig or the rustling of leaves. Anything could be out there and not just the enemy. Wolves, even demons or wood spirits. It didn't bear thinking about.

As they approached the camp, they began to hear the ominous sound of hammering on metal and wood. In the distance stood a sentry. They huddled behind an enormous oak tree. This close together, even in the shadows Ezrina could make out Gasbron's features and judging by his expression he was enjoying the perks of the job, with both her *and* Jezna pressed against him. She felt a hand squeeze her buttock. She held up a finger in warning, with a stern look, but he just looked confused. Then she realised whose hand it had been.

'Someone's coming,' Jezna whispered.

'Password!' the sentry called.

'Deadlock,' the second soldier called out.

'Deadlock?' Ezrina and Gasbron mouthed to each other. Despite the situation, the password seemed strangely overdramatic. Quietly, the three crawled away from the tree, just a few metres deeper into the forest, until Gasbron decided it was safe to stand. He began to walk back towards the camp, with the girls in tow.

'Password!'

'Deadlock!'

The guard allowed them to come closer.

'State your name and business,' he barked when they were nearly on him.

'Militiaman Yazdor of Kriganheim,' said Gasbron. 'I was out foraging for supplies when I found these two.'

'Really? And what were they doing here-Urgh!'

Thinking quickly, Ezrina had thrown away her flower basket and pulled down the shoulders of her dress and flashed her bare breasts. It was all the distraction they'd needed. With a swift thrust, Gasbron buried the spearhead into the guard's face. Ezrina was impressed and nodded her approval as the body dropped to the floor.

'Right. I can't follow you any further,' said Gasbron. 'I'll deal with the body. You go in while I stick our friend here behind one of those trees. I'll be

250

standing here on guard duty when you come out, but in the meantime, you're on your own. You'll just have to use your intuition to find your way to the royal enclosure.'

'Come on,' Ezrina told Jezna, taking her hand and they crossed the threshold into the jaws of the enemy.

There was an unnerving hammering coming from somewhere within the camp, but nobody stopped the girls for quite some time. In fact, it was like they were invisible; just another pair of camp followers running errands for their betters. Their only problem was finding their way to their target. They knew from their briefing that the royal enclosure would be towards the middle of the camp, set a long way back from the front line. Other than that, they had to work it out for themselves.

Unfortunately, there were no real giveaways. Time was in short supply and Ezrina knew that for their plan to work they had to make it there before the genuine concubine did and they had no way of knowing her current position.

'We're going to have to ask someone,' Ezrina said finally in resignation. 'Remember, I do the talking. Say nothing unless I tell you to speak. It looks like we're going to have to start our act early.'

'Are you sure this is a good idea?' Jezna asked.

'We've got no choice. Anyway, I doubt all the girls in the camp know where it is. They won't be surprised seeing a pair like us asking where to go.

'Excuse me, sir!'

A spearman looked around to see who had called.

'Excuse me, sir, we have been sent to do our duty to the king tonight, but we're not sure where to go. Can you direct us please?'

'You poor girls. Looks like you two are in for a long night.'

'It is our duty to obey our king. He honours us with his attention,' said Jezna. Ezrina glared at her for speaking and she dropped her head in apology.

'Well, if you say so, love.'

'So can you tell us where to go?' Ezrina asked.

'Better than that. I'm off duty. I'll take you there.'

They followed the soldier and soon came to a wooden fence that surrounded some larger tents. At the entrance stood a pair of guards, one of

251

whom wore strange black armour and a demonic helmet with just a single eye slit, while the other was a divisioman.

They thanked the soldier and approached the guards.

'What did he mean by a long night? That didn't sound good,' said Jezna.

'Shut up!'

'Sorry.'

The very idea of what they were about to do to get close to the king repulsed Ezrina. The idea that she might have to lie with a man she hated and see Jezna do the same. It was sickening. Still, it was a means to an end. She had to get to Jostan for the benefit of her people, even if Silrith had her own reasons for sending them there. She still didn't understand why Silrith had sent Jezna with her. Maybe Gasbron had told her of her affection for Jezna and sent both of them so that, in protection of each other, they'd see the mission through and not simply try to escape. Those Bennvikans must have believed that they really were sisters. They'd had to lie to everyone they came across for what seemed like a lifetime. After all, the true nature of their relationship was punishable by death under Hentani law, which was still implemented in many areas with high Hentani populations.

'We are the king's concubines for tonight,' Ezrina stated when they reached the guards. The soldiers looked at each other but pulled their spears out of the girls' way. They moved in and despite their fear, still chuckled to themselves as they heard quiet curses of 'lucky bastard' and the like from the guards. Immediately they spotted a tent that was much larger than the others, but there was no light inside, so it couldn't be that one. They walked on. There were many divisiomen milling about here and there, as well as more of the soldiers in black armour, but the girls were allowed to move freely.

This was, however, until they reached one of the few tents that was guarded; again by one man in that intimidating black armour, alongside a divisioman. It was the only tent comparable in size to the one they had seen earlier and this time there were many candles that could be seen burning inside.

Ezrina said the same to these guards as she had said to those on the gate earlier, but this time they demanded a search. As she was felt up by rough hands, Ezrina wondered if they were actually bothered about the king's safety, or if they just fancied a good grope of some young, firm female flesh. Looking over, she saw that Jezna looked petrified and she prayed that her lover wouldn't give them away. But then, there had probably been many girls who had been genuinely in this position as the king's concubine who had looked the same at this point.

Content that the girls carried no weapons, the guards allowed them to pass through. There was no-one inside. The interior glimmered with a deep orange tone and was filled with richly decorated furniture, along with lavish cushions and gleaming ornaments. At the far end was a bed, behind a semi-transparent curtain.

It was only once they had both stepped in fully though that Ezrina noticed the large square tapestry hanging at the side of the tent. Jezna went to lie on the bed, while Ezrina moved to inspect the image further.

It was suspended about three feet off the ground. It was mainly white, but woven into it was the outlined image of a man in long robes; his arms open in a welcoming pose. Yet his face didn't quite fit with the rest of the picture. The crazed expression he had was most unsettling and from his scalp sprouted a number of serpents. Across the top of the tapestry were woven the words 'Almighty Estarron, Lifeblood of the World'.

This wasn't any god that Ezrina recognised. Maybe this demon was the Verusantian god? Was this where Jostan prayed? Why was the god's name written in Bennvikan? Jostan must be planning to covert his followers to worship his god. Maybe his enemies too? It was a terrifying prospect and she made a prayer to Bertakaevey to protect her from such evil. She knew she'd rather die than turn her back on the true goddess.

Then she heard a voice outside.

'Get out of my way! I demand to see the king!' The voice was female.

'I'm sorry. We're under orders not to let you in until further notice, my lady.'

'Hide,' Ezrina whispered, motioning for Jezna to go and crouch behind the bed. Meanwhile, Ezrina got down on her hands and knees and crawled closer to the entrance, just out of sight of anyone who might be able to see inside.

253

'He's got a girl in there, hasn't he? I should have seen this coming,' the woman outside continued. 'I am his betrothed. Yet already he loses interest in me. This is a humiliation.'

The sound of a dress dragging on grass signified that the woman had given up and had turned to leave.

'Who's she trying to kid?' Ezrina heard one of the guards say in a gruffly common Bennvikan accent. He must have been the divisioman.

'What?' the other asked in thick Verusantian tones and a voice that suggested he was still less than comfortable in the language of his counterpart.

'*I'm his betrothed!* It's as if she thinks that she and the king are a secret. Everyone knows they've been goin' at it for weeks! Maybe months - ever since you lot got here. It's the worst kept secret in Bennvika. It's cos she's pregnant that he's losin' interest. Likes them slim, doesn't he? Old Accutina might still be a nice little piece for now, but before you know it she'll be so fat you could roll her all the way back to Kriganheim.'

'Yeh! Still, what I'd do for a roll with her tonight!' said the Verusantian with a laugh.

'Poor girl. She's used to lying with a king. I doubt she'd appreciate you porkin' her!'

'Do you think if I did she'd get pregnant twice?'

'I dunno. But if she pushed out two, the ugly one'd be yours. Seriously though, I bet that baby's not even king Lissoll's. I'll wager that's King Jostan's kid!'

Ezrina's interest flared at that. Accutina's presence in the camp was most curious, but with any luck, the Dowager Queen kept with Bennvikan tradition and carried the Amulet of Hazgorata wherever she travelled. The jewel would be just the symbol of divine favour the Hentani would need in order to find their strength if Jostan began forced conversions. She made a silent prayer to Bertakaevey in thanks for such an unexpected opportunity. Getting back to her feet, she walked over to the bed.

'Jezna,' she whispered. 'Get up. There's been a change of plan.'

As Jezna climbed out from her hiding place under the bed, Ezrina crouched down and began pulling at two tightly embedded pegs that held part of the tent in place.

'What are you doing? Where are you going?' Jezna asked.

'I'll be back as soon as I can.'

'But what if someone comes? Don't leave me here.'

Ezrina stopped and turned to her lover.

'Jezna, look, this army was on a course to destroy our homes and slaughter our people before it was diverted here. If we are going to have to fight to put that Bennvikan girl on the throne then we can damn well do something to benefit our own people too. If that unborn baby genuinely is King Jostan's, then even if we kill him, his line remains intact and there is a good chance that this *Accutina* might try and take power for herself so that she can be regent and her son can be king when he's born. When he grows up, the threat to our people remains. We have to destroy the whole line. Understand?'

Jezna nodded, but Ezrina was still frustrated with her for causing a delay.

'Good. I'm going now. Hopefully, she hasn't got too far.'

With that, Ezrina pulled the two pegs free and wriggled under the tent flaps, out into the open, picking herself up off the damp grass. She looked around and spotted a well-dressed young woman in the distance. Yes, that had to be her. Surely only a royal could carry herself with such arrogance if the Hentani's nobility were anything to go by. She must have paused to consider going back and remonstrating with the guards again, before deciding against it.

A fateful mistake, thought Ezrina as she stalked her prey, making sure to keep out of sight.

Eventually, she saw Accutina reach another tent; possibly blue or purple; it was hard to tell in the dark. It was smaller than the one she'd just come from but still fairly large. As her target paused at the entrance, Ezrina saw that unsurprisingly this one too was guarded, though this did at least prove the girl's identity.

How am I going to get past them? Ezrina thought to herself, looking at the two guards at the tent's entrance. As with each previous pair, there was one divisioman and one Verusantian. In her haste, she hadn't thought this far ahead and she didn't have a story ready this time to explain her presence. It was then that she realised that Accutina hadn't entered. Again

255

she appeared to be considering returning to Jostan's tent and trying again and this time she strutted back the way she came. Ezrina bowed subserviently as Accutina blustered past, barely appearing to notice her presence.

Thinking on her feet and taking a deep breath, Ezrina strode towards the empty tent, or at least she hoped it would be empty.

'I'm the Dowager Queen's new lady's maid,' she said when the guards blocked her from entering. 'The king selected me and sent me here to prepare her bed.'

Amazingly, the guards' faces lightened and they removed their spears from her path, but she still endured another grope as they searched her before allowing her in. Once inside, she noticed that the tent was similar in layout to Jostan's, save for the colour and size and like his, the bed was far from the entrance, behind a thin curtain. Looking around, she was frustrated to see that as before, there were no obvious weapons. She'd have to improvise. All she could do now was wait. Some indignant gabbling outside heralded Accutina's return.

'The new servant's inside, your Highness,' the guard reported.

'What new servant? Another girl he wants close by just in case he feels the urge?'

She didn't wait for an answer and strode inside. Ezrina turned and bowed, trying to look like she'd been busy, while Accutina appraised her with a steely-eyed look.

'Be careful,' Accutina said. 'The next time the king gives you an order, it'll probably be to mount him or to let him mount you. Now, get on and help me undress.'

I hope I haven't been gone too long, Ezrina thought as she stood behind Accutina and stripped off the young woman's clothes. She'd hoped to have done this quickly, but Jezna had been left alone for some minutes now. Within a few moments, Accutina stood only in her undergarment, a thin, white, knee-length chemise, which Ezrina slipped over the girl's shoulders and down to the floor, fully revealing her soft, curvaceous body. She was pretty, Ezrina decided. What a shame.

Once naked, Accutina raised her arms, waiting for them to be put through the sleeves of her negligee. Behind her, Ezrina raised the garment, then set it aside on a table a few feet away. She might well need that later. She took a moment to look at Accutina's bare body, wondering how this woman could be at this very moment carrying a baby. She had no idea how far along she was, but still, she was tiny. Either way, that baby could not be allowed to live. Inwardly she laughed at the girl's stupidity for leaving herself so vulnerable.

Quickly she sprang forward and grabbed Accutina by the neck, using her fingers and thumbs to block her victim's windpipe. Accutina didn't have enough air to scream and as Ezrina spun her around and they fell upon the bed; all sound of the attack was mercifully muffled. Ezrina leapt on top of the stunned Accutina, sitting on her chest, still maintaining her grip on Accutina's neck with one hand while using the other hand to cover her mouth as the girl grappled to push her away.

'Stop struggling and I will let you breathe,' Ezrina whispered forcefully. Accutina ignored her and carried on fighting; her screams still stifled by Ezrina's hand.

'If you scream I will be forced to kill you. You have to be quiet if you want to live. Can you do that?'

Accutina stilled her arms, paused, then nodded and obeyed, so Ezrina loosened her grip enough for her to breathe, though she still sat astride the girl as Accutina gasped for air. She took hold of Accutina's arms and moved each so that they were pinned down by Ezrina's legs.

'Good.' Ezrina surveyed her victim menacingly, savouring the moment. She smiled as she looked upon Accutina's small breasts. 'You may be a royal, but your tits aren't as good as mine! Still, one can't be choosey,'

'Tell me what you want!' Accutina asked defiantly.

'Hmm...what could I want?' Ezrina pondered, with a look of deadly seduction in her eye. She leaned down and brushed the hair away from Accutina's face, breathing in her scent, before lightly tracing her hand down the girl's cheek; her fingers gliding down over her neck, caressing over her shoulder and down to her left breast, grasping the warm mound of flesh in her palm, closing her eyes and breathing in deeply; all designed to further unsettle her victim.

Suddenly she opened her eyes again and looked back down at Accutina, all erotic pleasure now gone from her face, leaving just the dominance.

'Where is the Amulet of Hazgorata?' she demanded.

'It's been stolen.'

Ezrina clasped the Dowager Queen's neck again, cutting off Accutina's supply of air for a second time. 'Don't lie. I know you have it. Bennvikan queens never go anywhere without it. You know what I think? You weren't content with the subjugation Bennvika has wreaked upon my people for years. You had to destroy us completely. You'd accuse innocent Hentani towns and villages of being centres of malcontent and rebellion. You and your king thought you could come south and claim to your troops that you'd found the Amulet in our hands. You'd pin the theft on us and command them to reap terrible revenge on our people, while simultaneously giving yourselves holy protection against us and against anyone who said that your bloodthirsty tactics against us were unjustified. It doesn't take much imagination to understand and anticipate basic propaganda like that. But then this little rebellion flared up here and delayed your campaign against us. Am I right?'

Accutina gasped for air again as the hand was removed.

'And what would *you* do with it? You're just a barbarian,' she hissed once she'd got her breath back.

Ezrina smiled thinly, then leaned down so that her lips almost touched Accutina's.

'A barbarian with the power over your life and death,' Ezrina sneered.

She clamped down on the girl's neck again, this time with both hands. Accutina pulled her arms out from under Ezrina's legs and grappled at her arms and hands in an effort to remove the pressure, but only when she became desperate did Ezrina loosen her grip.

'Alright, alright,' Accutina gasped.

'Good. Is it in here?'

'Yes.'

'Then get up and show me. Quiet now. If you alert the guards I'll gouge out your eyes.'

Ezrina allowed Accutina to stand, but took hold of her wrists so that she couldn't escape. They moved over to a drawer.

'In there. Top drawer,' Accutina stated, jerking her head. Keeping a strong grip on Accutina's neck with one hand, Ezrina reached for the drawer with the other and opened it. Out of the drawer Ezrina pulled a small but heavy, shining gold pendant and chain. Depicted on the pendant were two figures; a man and a woman, both surrounded by flame, clutching their swords. These were not Vitrinnolf and Lomatteva as the Bennvikans said, but the Daughter of Ashes and her warrior accomplice. They were destined to one day deliver the Hentani from oppression.

Far from the Hentani stealing it from the Bennvikans as Jostan and Accutina had clearly hoped to lead their subjects to believe, the truth was that this holiest of pendants was of Hentani origin, stolen from them two millennia ago when the Hentani had been evicted from their homes in Hazgorata, centuries prior to its unification with the powerful city-state of Kriganheim and the birth of Bennvika.

The Amulet was hollow, and it featured a tiny screw-on lid at the top.

With her spare hand, Ezrina held the Amulet and turned it around. Yes, this was it. On the back it featured those immortal words, *'Mother of many, Mother of none, a Queen will fall and a Warrior will come.'*

'They may say it protects both the wearer and their country from any threat,' said Accutina scornfully. 'But rest assured it will do nothing for you. Given that all your warriors are here, once we've taken the city there will be no one to stand in our way when we march on your villages and burn them to the ground!'

That was all it took. Ezrina let the Amulet drop to the floor and wrenched the girl towards her, digging her fingers into her neck and again burying her thumbs into her windpipe. Accutina was trying to remove Ezrina's fists, but she wasn't strong enough; her slender hands gaining no purchase on her attacker's muscular arms. Almost laughing at her feeble opponent, Ezrina could see her trying to scream, but with no sound coming out. It felt wonderful to have this much power over a high-born noble, even as she transferred back to using just a single hand.

With the other, she picked up a heavy, metal candlestick holder, blew out the three candles and started moving Accutina back in the direction of the bed, back out of earshot of the guards outside.

'On you go. Keep moving. Quiet now. Good girl.'

All the while Accutina was still struggling to breathe and to remove the hand, even though she was otherwise doing as she was told. Her face had already gone red and was now starting to go a little blue. Once at the bed, Ezrina hooked her foot around Accutina's ankle and sent the girl toppling backwards while pushing down with her arm and leaping on top of her, raising the candlestick holder above her head.

She smashed it down hard on Accutina's skull and blood poured out of a gaping gash. She brought it up again and rained down blows on Accutina's head with all the force she could muster, with the pillows and bedclothes going a long way to muffling the sound. Again and again she hit her with it until finally she ran out of energy and she stopped, breathless, as she looked into Accutina's dull, lifeless eyes staring out from under the blood and pulp oozing from her smashed skull.

Once she'd composed herself, dripping with blood, Ezrina got up and quietly padded over to where she'd dropped the Amulet. She knew she couldn't wear it, as her cleavage was low enough for at least part of it to be completely visible if it were hung around her neck. However, it was on quite a long chain and this gave her an idea. Putting her foot through the loop, she pulled it up her leg, over her knee and as far up her thigh as it would go, hoping that the tight fit would be enough to hold it in place, at least temporarily.

The blood was a more immediate problem, but one that Ezrina hoped she'd also found an answer to. Taking off her dress, she wiped herself all over with the parts that had not already been soaked with red, removing the blood that covered her body as best she could. Once done, she slipped into Accutina's clean white negligee, which she was amazed and relieved to see had been far enough away to be unaffected. Surely nobody would notice the difference?

Then, just as she had done in Jostan's tent, she moved to the back and pulled out two pegs. Before leaving, she took one final look at Accutina's bloodied corpse. She'd have to act quickly. It was only a matter of time before the body would be found. Once outside, she headed straight back to the first tent to find Jezna.

She knew there was no way she could use the front entrance again. The guards would discover the Amulet on her and anyway, they might remember that they hadn't seen her leave and grow suspicious. Keeping to the shadows, she moved round to the back. Her heart pounded as she looked for any sign of movement inside, but there was nothing she could make out clearly enough. There was no sound coming from within though, so she guessed that must be a good thing.

Finally, she found the section where there were two pegs missing from when she'd crawled out earlier. Hadn't Jezna thought to replace them? Ezrina prayed to Bertakaevey that it hadn't been noticed. Checking to make sure nobody was watching, she squirmed under the flap and back inside.

'What took you so long?' Ezrina's heart lifted at the sound of Jezna's voice and then doubly so when she looked up to see that nothing had changed since she had left. They were alone.

'I told you what I was doing,' she said, trying to make light of the situation, while replacing the pegs, then moving to sit next to her on the bed. 'Look what I've got.'

She removed the Amulet from around her leg and presented it to Jezna, who gasped at its beauty.

'Is that...? But how?'

'I'll tell you later. For now, I'm going to hide it under the bed. We don't want anyone finding it, do we?' Ezrina said as she did so.

'No. Oh Ezrina, I was so worried waiting for you to come back. I'm just glad you're ok.'

The girls wrapped their arms around each other and hugged tightly in comfort.

'I love you.'

'I love you too,' said Ezrina, kissing Jezna hard on the mouth.

Ezrina pulled back a little, looking deep into Jezna's eyes, before hugging her again.

'Touching.'

Both looked up with a start as a male voice broke into their private moment. A tall, handsome man who could only be King Jostan had entered the tent. He strode forward and opened the curtain.

'We have heard it said that there is no friendship more intimate than that which is held between two women. But, alas, we must come between you tonight, but we're sure that will be no hardship.'

With a heavy heart, Ezrina moved away from Jezna and made a show of greeting Jostan with an enthusiastic smile, while patting the bed seductively and watching his eyes drinking in their exotic beauty.

'Come and join us, your Majesty,' Jezna said.

He sat down between them and immediately Jezna undid the clasp on his cape and began unfastening the buttons of his tunic. Once Jostan was naked to the waist, Jezna grabbed his face and kissed him aggressively. Taking this as her cue, Ezrina slipped away from the bed and quietly bent down to pull out a steel tent peg, which was more of a sharp nail in truth.

Taking the weapon in her hand, feeling a tension quite unlike anything she'd felt before with Accutina, Ezrina moved in behind Jostan.

'Your Majesty! Urgent news!' A divisioman raced into the tent, breathless. 'It's-oh gods!' He'd spotted the raised weapon in Ezrina's hand.

'What? Argh!'

Seizing her chance, Ezrina stabbed the sharp, thick bladed nail as deep as she could into the back of Jostan's shoulder and he reeled in pain. She'd aimed for the back of his neck but missed as he moved. There was no time for another attack and, unable to pull the weapon out of Jostan's back for further use, Ezrina knew they had to make their escape now, especially as the guard was now supported by the two from outside.

'Come on!' she called to Jezna, snatching up the Amulet as she went and slipping it around her neck.

'Stop them! Stop them!' cried Jostan.

They launched themselves at the first divisioman; their speed and combined force knocking him to the ground. The second thrust his spear downwards wildly but both rolled out of the way, causing him to hit his own comrade in the chest and though the wound did not look fatal as the chainmail took some of the impact, he was out of the fight. While the second man looked shocked at what he'd done, Ezrina took the first guard's sword

262

and buried it in the second's neck. He fell to the ground in an explosion of blood. That just left the third, the Verusantian.

'Stop them!' Jostan raged.

Ezrina allowed herself the briefest of looks over her shoulder to see that Jostan had now pulled the steel weapon out of his shoulder and was now turning to face them. In a last gasp bid for freedom, she threw herself at the guard's legs just as he jabbed his spear at Jezna, causing him to trip and as he did, she stabbed up into his groin, felling him. Quickly, Jezna armed herself by snatching a throwing axe from the dead divisioman and both ran for it.

'On to them! On to them!' Jostan bellowed, calling for more guards.

He chased them as far as the tent's entrance and picked up a spear dropped by one of the guards, hurling it like a javelin. Due to his wound his throw lacked range, yet still Jezna screamed in terror as the metal shaft came terrifyingly close to skewering her like a piece of meat, but they kept running.

They dodged this way and that as soldiers tried to stop them; their speed and agility proving to be much more protection than the weapons they each carried. Panting, they rushed towards the nearest gate, while the guards blocked their way. They had no choice but to attack, with Jezna following Ezrina's lead. Ezrina jinked round the tip of one guard's spear and stabbed her sword into his lower abdomen, never stopping running.

'Ezrina!'

'Jezna!' Turning around at the scream, Ezrina saw with horror that Jezna hadn't been so lucky with the timing of her axe blow and the other guard had easily blocked it with his spear shaft, knocking the blade from her grasp and he dragged the screaming, terrified girl back towards the king's tent. Ezrina started to run after them.

'No Ezrina! Run!'

Ezrina stopped, consumed by indecision as the first guard writhed in pain at her feet, clutching his gut as a river or scarlet streamed on to the ground. What could she do? How could she abandon Jezna, her lover? Yet that was exactly what Jezna was begging her to do.

'Ezrina, run,' Jezna screamed again, pleading with her as she was dragged away.

With her vision blurred by tears, Ezrina turned and ran. More soldiers appeared from between the other tents and gave chase, but she didn't care. She had the speed to evade them. All that mattered now was Jezna.

She'd been forced to abandon her one true love; forced by those damned Bennvikans. She felt like such a coward as she fled. She would have her revenge. She would save Jezna. But trying now would be pointless and would bring only certain death for them both.

'I will come back for you!' she called as she ran, although she doubted that Jezna heard.

'Where's Jezna?' Gasbron asked as she flew out of the last gate, where they had started.

'No time to explain! Run!'

Gasbron bolted after her. With luck, they could lose their pursuers in the woods.

Chapter 19

'So where is Jezna?' Silrith asked the following morning as the glimmering sun peered over the horizon. She was seated at the main table in Yathrud's meeting room, wearing her battle gear and eating an officer's breakfast ration of mutton, bread and water. Ezrina and Gasbron, still dressed as they had been for their overnight mission, stood before her to be debriefed.

'She was taken, your Grace. I tried to reach her but I couldn't.'

Silrith surveyed Ezrina carefully. There was none of the cold arrogance in her face that Silrith had observed previously; just fear and pain.

'Was she taken alive?'

'Yes.'

'Well, at least we don't have to worry about her giving away any information. The only things she'd be able to tell the enemy are things they'll already know. Is Jostan dead?'

'No.'

'No?' Silrith pressed, emphasising her frustrated tone.

'The Dowager Queen and her unborn child are dead,' Ezrina said defensively. 'Jostan is wounded. They were together. We were forced to attack them both.'

Silrith got up from her chair, scrutinizing Ezrina, with Gasbron standing by silently.

'Together, were they? And what were they doing together? No, you need not say it. I can guess,' Silrith said, raising a hand as Ezrina opened her mouth to speak.

There was a momentary pause.

'The rumour is that the child is Jostan's, not your father's,' Ezrina said slowly.

The thought of Accutina betraying her father made Silrith's blood turn to fire, but she held it back, stone-faced.

'I am aware of the rumour, but I will not discuss it with you,' Silrith said, maintaining a level tone. 'What I want to know, is why one of my assassins is now a prisoner of the enemy. How did you end up gaining access

265

to both Jostan and Accutina if they were in each other's company so late at night? I very much doubt that a pair of servant girls would be allowed into their quarters at that time unless they had been sent for. So do you know what I think? I think that you spotted an opportunity to kill them both. Despite the fact that I made it explicitly clear the Accutina was only a secondary target to be attacked once Jostan is dead, you ignored my orders and prioritised her assassination over his. You spread your efforts too thinly and jeopardised your chances of killing Jostan and completing your mission in accordance with the parameters I described to you.'

'That's not true.'

'You're lying to me, Ezrina. Am I going to have to send spies to watch over my own agents from now on? You may think me stupid, but that has been your mistake. Do not disobey me again.'

'I'm sorry, your Grace.'

'Good. Now get out.'

Ezrina bowed her head and headed for the door, but just as she opened it, she turned back momentarily.

'Your Grace. I beg for the chance to go back into the enemy camp to save my sister.'

'No. If she lives, you may be reunited with her after the siege, but the chances are she is dead because of your refusal to follow orders. Don't throw your life away stupidly. Now go.'

A thunderous expression etched itself across Ezrina's face, but she said nothing. Silrith watched her as she made a show of bowing her head. Then Ezrina turned, opened the door and left. The guard who had been waiting outside reached in and clicked the door shut, leaving Silrith and Gasbron alone in the room. Silrith took to her seat again and continued with her meal. Gasbron had turned to watch Ezrina leave but now turned back to Silrith.

'Don't say a thing,' Silrith said, pointing a figure at him, noticing the confused look he was giving her. She rolled her eyes when his expression didn't change.

'Fine, you may speak.'

'Do I have permission to speak my mind, my Queen?'

'On the condition that you stop calling me 'my Queen', in private. I would not let you speak freely if you weren't my friend, so you can dispense with the formalities. Take a seat.' She smiled at him; her mood lightening. He pulled out the chair opposite hers and made himself comfortable.

'Now, you were looking at me in a very particular way,' said Silrith. 'You don't think I was too harsh with her, do you?'

'Well...'

'Gasbron, please tell me what you really feel. I want to know.'

'Maybe you could have been a little more understanding. She's clearly very worried about her sister.'

Silrith nodded, closing her eyes briefly.

'Yes. You're probably right,' she sighed. 'I don't intend to sound cold and unfeeling, but it is hard to avoid that when you have to look strong. The people look to me for strength and I must make them feel it. Such is my task as their queen. But whilst I am their queen, I am also human and more specifically a woman who wants to protect what remains of her family, as well as her friends.'

She looked him straight in the eye as she said the last word. She put down her food, pushed back her chair and walked over to stand next to him.

'When I called you my friend just now, I meant it. I want us to be friends, Gasbron. You have saved my life more than once and that must be rewarded, so I say again, I want no formalities between us in private. I know that it breaks with convention, but to the underworld with it! I'd rather you just called me Silrith when we are alone.'

'It would be an honour to call you my friend, Silrith,' Gasbron said, looking completely blown away with pride by the sudden breakthrough in their relationship. But then, maybe he'd felt it too, but just hadn't thought that Silrith felt the same.

'Excellent! We'll be brother and sister in arms, you and I!'

He laughed. Silrith clasped her hands together with glee, then almost hugged him, but hesitated, then instantly regretted not breaking with the usual convention a little more. Now the moment had passed and it would be awkward. But then, was that desire in his eyes? Her heart fluttered at the thought, but she swatted it from her confused mind. Such things were scandal.

267

'On reflection, I think you were right,' she said, deliberately diverting both of their attentions. 'I was too harsh on Ezrina. But there was a reason for my anger. I had thought to use her services again, if she had been successful, but now I don't trust her, or at least, I am unsure of her reliability. You know her better than I. What do you think of her?'

'I think her words were influenced by her worries. She's single-minded and emotional, but also ambitious. That much I'm sure of so far.'

'Ambitious, yes, but what is her ambition? That is the question,' Silrith pondered.

'I believe her priority is to get her sister back to the citadel safely.'

'I agree that that is her main priority at this point, but I believe there's more. I suppose it's only natural that someone of her race would be more interested in the long term good of the Hentani than my right to be Queen of Bennvika, but it must be made clear to her and to all that the two are inexorably intertwined.'

'Yes,' said Gasbron. 'And I believe what you say is supported by what she was found to be carrying when we returned. I'm not surprised she didn't mention it. She seemed reluctant to let it go when I told her it should be left in your care. Guards!' As soon as Gasbron called, two armed men entered, one carrying a shining object.

'The Amulet of Hazgorata?' Silrith was surprised to see it. 'You're right. This fits precisely with my earlier thoughts. She must believe the myth that it gives protection to the nation of whoever bears it; something Ezrina clearly feels that the Hentani need at this time.'

'She claims to be bringing it back for the benefit of the whole city.'

'Yes and whether that's true or not, many will believe it to be so and therefore she can't be punished. I want you to keep up your *association* with her, so that she can be properly watched.'

'Of course, my Queen.'

'What interests me is why it's been brought this far south in the first place. Did she say anything about that?'

'She did. She said that, as we know, the enemy's original target was the Hentani, pre-empting an uprising from them, before they found out about you being here. She claims Jostan's plan had been to plant the Amulet somewhere in a Hentani village where their soldiers would find it when the place was burnt, so that they could claim that the Hentani had stolen it from Bennvika. I can't see it working myself, but apparently, it's an approach that has been feared for some time in the Hentani lands. Maybe Chief Hojorak had a spy at court when Jostan took your throne?'

'Perhaps he did. The Hentani are certainly right to fear the political power of such an approach. It wouldn't take much. Jostan could just claim to have found it there and then when addressing his troops, he could hold it up, telling them of how some special unit infiltrated the enemy village to steal it back. The thought of the theft of such a sacred jewel would get their blood up and ready them to rain untold fury on their victims. The risk is that he may now try to do that here. We must hope that, without the Amulet to hold up before them, his approach may be somewhat less powerful now. More importantly, both their troops and ours will be aware that the fact that we now hold the Amulet shows the gods' true allegiance, if you believe the myth, at least.' At that moment there was a hurried knock at the door.

'Enter,' said Silrith and another soldier entered the room.

'My Queen, the enemy is preparing for another assault.'

'Thank you. Gasbron, let us go and prepare the troops.'

By the time Silrith was standing on the crowded citadel walls, amid the clamour of battle horns calling all her troops to their positions, the enemy were ready to advance. She could now see the results of the hammering that had come from the enemy camp that night. Siege towers. Six hulking, domineering, looming siege towers. How had they built these so quickly? It mattered little. Either way, they were here and ranged against her. From her high position she watched as the enemy units began to move in unison to the beating of their drums, like the various parts of a living creature.

Dum da-dum, dum da-dum, dum da-dum, dum da-dum

This time they advanced with the divisios massed in the middle in an orderly sea of white shields and emerald capes. On the wings were the rag-tag militia and Jostan's Defroni allies.

Once they were in position, they stopped as the drumbeat ceased, out of range of any defensive arrow shots. The sound of heaving soldiers from behind the centre of the enemy line gave away an extra presence. It seemed the siege towers were not the only thing Jostan's troops had been building the previous night. From a distance it looked like little more than a large box on wheels, but the defenders knew it was altogether more menacing than that. A ram.

Silrith looked at Gasbron, who had changed into his invicturion's uniform.

'Siege engines? How? So soon?' she said.

'Maybe they started before they arrived here. Maybe they'd got all the materials they need from the forest by the time the girls and I were in there last night. With an army like that, he's got a big enough workforce to cut down as much wood as he needs and build anything he wants. Bloody tiring though.'

'Jostan clearly has no worries about exhausting his own troops,' Silrith said. 'But it'll only affect a fraction of his overall numbers though and I expect those troops will be kept in reserve, with fresh soldiers to carry out the attack.'

Suddenly she had an idea and picked out a militiaman who was close by.

'You! Take a few comrades and bring up buckets of oil, burning tar and some torches. And have others bring up fire pots. Take them to the troops on the other walls too. Quickly!'

The fire pots would be a lethal defensive weapon; hollow balls with bodies of thin iron and clay, filled with naphtha, which could be lit and would explode with terrible force when thrown at the enemy. As the man jumped to it, Silrith turned back and watched as the ram lumbered to the front of the enemy line. An enormous log was suspended inside it, tipped with a considerably hefty metal head, shaped like an arrow.

A wooden roof, Silrith thought, surprised. *What's he at?*

She had expected to see it covered in wet animal hide, which would give some protection to the divisiomen inside against incendiary weapons. But then, on Silrith's orders, all animals from the surrounding farms had been brought inside the city before the enemy's arrival. Jostan would have to use the animals in his own camp, of which he may have only had a small number. Or maybe he simply didn't want to kill too many of his animals too early in case it was a long siege, requiring a lot of food to sustain such a sizable army?

Either way, she resisted the temptation to believe that Jostan had simply made an error. She knew that she should always assume her enemy had thought of something that she hadn't.

She turned to Gasbron.

'We must be ready in case the ram penetrates our gates. I need you down in the walled courtyard. I will lead our troops here on the ramparts. I want you to go down there and form up Divisio One, dismounted, along with as many of the militia and the Hentani you can fit down there in support. I need you to be ready to defend the area if they break through. You know what we had planned in case they brought a ram. It's time to put it to the test.'

'Yes, my Queen.'

In a moment, he was gone, followed by those members of Divisio One who had been on the ramparts, leaving Silrith with a still tightly packed group of militiamen, archers, Hentani and troops from lesser divisios standing with her on the walls.

There was a low bugle note from down below and the drumbeat struck up again.

Dum da-dum, dum da-dum, dum da-dum, dum da-dum

Slowly the ram and the siege towers lumbered forward with troops crowded around them, keeping to their slow pace. The wheels squeaked rhythmically. The divisios advanced in silence, but the effect was overrun by the hordes of militia infantry, some of whom she could now see were bringing ladders forward, and the screaming and chanting of the Defroni warriors massing around the siege towers. Further back, in reserve, almost disappearing behind the dust cloud were the mounted divisios, as well as the cavalry of Jostan's militia.

Finally there was another sounding of the bugle and the majority of the army halted, while the ram continued moving forward of the other units, followed by first two, then four, then all six of the siege towers which advanced in pairs as the Defroni continued to chant, roar and jeer at Silrith's defenders, clearly waiting for the order to attack. The only units that continued to march onward with the siege engines were two large groups of Bennvikan archers, presumably there to give cover to the ram and the towers once the defenders started to fire.

271

At the same time, some of Silrith's own militiamen returned to the walls with flaming torches and buckets; some filled with oil, others filled with tar. Each one was placed by the wall just in front of the archers so that they could dip their arrows in the liquid. The torches were handed out among the other soldiers so that each archer had a makeshift torchbearer next to them, ready to light their weapon.

'Wait for my mark,' Silrith instructed once each archer was ready to fire, trying to ignore the intense heat being emitted by the close concentration of torches, though it was not yet time to light the arrows, though each had been dipped in oil.

'Halt!' came the audible command from an officer down below. The enemy archers stopped and began arming their bows.

'Now!' Silrith bellowed and the air was full of the sound of firing bows as a barrage of shafts rained down on the ram and across at the foremost towers. Their wooden targets were peppered with arrows as they advanced. Silrith hoped they had got enough oil on to them.

'Launch fire arrows!' Silrith commanded and each archer on the walls now lit their next shaft and fired them at the approaching towers and the ram in an almost beautiful barrage of flame.

In response, the enemy archers loosed their shafts up at the defenders and the infantry behind them screamed their war cries, as a single note on a bugle ordered them forward defiantly into the hail of death.

'Shoot at the siege engines! Shoot at the siege engines!' Silrith called, willing them to catch alight, urging her troops not to get distracted by the ladders coming at them, though they also had to be stopped. Looking down at the oncoming infantry as they charged forward from the flanks, racing clear of the still stationary divisiomen, streaming around the towers, she could see that it was now the Defroni warriors that led the charge and who were first on to the ladders as they arced up towards the walls. As a warrior started to climb the nearest ladder, Silrith picked up a fire pot, lit it and hurled it over the edge, hitting the man square on the head and engulfing him and all around him in a ball of fire.

Seeing this, others followed suit and all below turned to a burning hell; men and women screaming as their flesh burned while they were pushed ever forward by the masses behind. Still, some began to make it on to the ladders and up the walls, towards the ramparts and the defenders' burning ammunition was running low.

Through it all, the archers still concentrated their fire on the siege engines, but eventually, the ram and foremost towers came into the range of a fire pot throw and the searing hail of flame intensified. Now the nearest siege tower was burning in places but still it advanced; looming large no more than thirty meters away, with two more behind as they began to splay out either side of it. Suddenly an especially large fire pot hurtled out in a graceful arc from somewhere on the ramparts, bursting into flame as it struck the already burning siege tower. That was all it took. The explosion engulfed the tower's head in flame to audible screams from those inside. A cheer erupted from the troops on the ramparts all around and Silrith found herself cheering too, but she knew there would be more.

The second siege tower had been close behind the first and had to pull sharply to Silrith's left to get around it, exposing its vulnerable broadside.

'Keep firing!' Silrith bellowed, though the barrage on the second tower had already intensified. She took up a fire pot as the tower attempted to turn again to face them and she hurled it with all her might. She could hardly have missed. The tower's size, the close range and its slow, clumsy movement as they tried to move around the obstacle presented by their immobilised comrades presented her with a massive target. The firepot exploded with awe-inspiring power and the tower rocked as it was struck by two more pots following in the wake of Silrith's. The soldiers inside screamed as the top half of the tower was consumed by searing flame.

There was a howl from the ramparts on the far side of the wall, on the other side of the Preddaburg Gate. Craning her neck, she saw that the first siege tower on that side, despite being on fire in some places, had reached the walls and she watched as its door was winched down. With the door in place, a torrent of enemy militia hurled themselves forward into a storm of flaming arrows and burning fire pots.

Despite the third siege tower on her own side of the walls still being out of range and shielded temporarily by the wreckages of the nearer two, Silrith had no time to watch as below them, the ram stopped in front of the portcullis and despite the fiery barrage, five or six divisiomen climbed out from underneath it and on to its roof, moving nimbly despite their heavy armour. Seeing them climb on to the ram with their shields raised, Silrith suddenly knew why no wet animal hide had been put on top of it. As the arrows and fire pots battered them, striking one of their number down and engulfing him in flame, the remaining divisiomen on the ram's roof hurried forward, throwing down their shields when they reached the portcullis. Each took its bars in their grip and in unison they heaved upward. The portcullis gave a horrible creaking noise, though the walls of the gate prevented Silrith from seeing how much it had moved. The bravery of those on top of the ram gave heart to those below and more began to lift the iron gate. The creaking noises got louder and louder. Surely the gate wasn't coming up? There was an enormously heavy lock in the gatehouse to stop just that.

'Shoot at the ram! Shoot at the ram!' Silrith ordered. The creaking noises were getting even louder and more intense. The enemy must be gaining some purchase on it. Silrith's heart sank as there was a loud cheer from all below. The portcullis ceased creaking. Surely it couldn't be up? Two more of the divisiomen on top of the ram were struck down under the rain of fire, but it was too late. The remaining three leapt off it and took up their positions with their comrades under the ram. With one slick heave, the ram lurched forward towards the wooden gates.

Then it happened. A spark. A small, arrow-born flame that took hold.

'It's alight! More fire! More fire!' Silrith bellowed. Another fire pot was ready. Silrith picked it up, hoping that what they had left would be enough before the attackers on the ladders, who were now at least half way up the walls, reached the top. It smashed down on the top of the ram, bursting into flame. Most of the siege engine's roof was now alight. The smoke must have been choking the soldiers underneath, but nevertheless, it reached the walls and there was an awful crash of metal on wood as the huge head slammed against the gates.

The Defroni warriors were almost at the top now and Silrith had to smash away a glancing blow with her shield as one thrust his spearhead over the edge of the ramparts and he hauled himself up the last rungs.

With a swift downward thrust, she split open the bare-chested warrior's pony-tailed head while he was still on the ladder and he flopped backwards and plummeted back to earth. In a moment another was coming at her; the attackers screaming their battle cries as they scrambled over the top of the ramparts to clash steel on steel with Silrith's troops.

The defenders were holding their assailants back, but then came the terrible moment when Silrith looked up to see that the third siege tower had got around the burning carcasses of the other two and was almost at the walls some meters to her right. With a terrible screech, the door began to winch down towards them. Yet Silrith could only look for a moment as she was forced to parry a blow from yet another screaming Defroni warrior.

Down on the ground, outside the walls, Jithrae advanced forward at a run amid the jostling crowd of advancing soldiers as more Defroni warriors climbed the ladders, swarming over the walls like a cloud of locusts. Despite the first of their allies having reached the top, arrows still fell, cutting down great swathes of men and women as they pushed forward, heedless of the two burning siege towers, desperate to get on to one of the four others or on to one of the ladders. The enemy seemed to have some other terrible weapon too and every so often a group of soldiers would be hit by something and they would disappear into a ball of flame to ear piercing screams.

Jithrae kept his round, white wooden shield held over his head, blocking much of his view, as the hail of arrows continued to fall. He was ruled by fear, but even as he tried to slow down he was being haplessly pushed into the embrace of death by the relentless wave of warriors hungry for blood and plunder. Despite carrying a ladder in the chaotic first attack he'd somehow avoided combat; escaping as the units broke. But now he was being buffeted ever forward in the thronging mass as all around him soldiers screamed and fell, while officers tried to keep some form of order and with its roof ablaze, the ram still rhythmically struck away at the gates.

In moments that incessant sound went from being in front of him to being somewhere on his right and before he knew it he'd been taken further by the momentum of the crowd and was on a ladder on the wall's left-hand side. Without having time to think, he tried to get a grip while still carrying his shield and spear and started to climb, but something sent him flying and he crashed to the ground with a force that jarred his whole body. There he lay, flat on his back, stunned and unable to move.

Inside the citadel's walled courtyard, Gasbron surveyed his troops. By Silrith's order, they had taken up position behind the Preddaburg Gate, where they listened to the repetitive bashing of the enemy ram.

'You hear that?' Gasbron barked. 'That is the sound of glory coming to us! The sound of lambs so desperate for the slaughter that they would break down our gates to reach our blades! So, we'd better not disappoint them, had we?'

The soldiers roared and beat their swords against their shields as he raised his own blade aloft. At the front, with their pristine armour and colourful shields that denoted their unit, were Rildayorda's elite troops, the men and women of Divisio One Bastalf. They had originally numbered five hundred and losses in the previous day's combat had been minimal. They stood at the heart of the battle line, in uniform ranks of twenty-five. They were flanked by groups of dismounted Hentani, including Chief Hojorak and Prince Kivojo, as well as Blavak, who translated Gasbron's words for those Hentani less versed in Bennvikan, causing a slight delay between the Bennvikan cheers and theirs. Behind them were a motley crew of militiamen, as well as some longbowmen waiting in reserve, taking the overall number to over a thousand troops crammed into the walled courtyard.

All they could do now was wait as battle raged on the walls and the ram carried on hammering. Gasbron took up position with his comrades, almost subconsciously readjusting to the weight of the rectangular shield, which was heavier than the oval one he'd become used to since his promotion to the cavalry. There was no room for horses here though and he overlapped his shield with the troops either side of him. The Hentani did the same with their circular shields, creating a wall of tribal and Bennvikan military might.

With one final blow, the metal head of the ram crashed through the oak gates, causing a loud cheer from outside.

'Wait for my signal! Let them think they're winning,' shouted Gasbron.

The buckled doors came apart as the roaring enemy militia charged in, but in their bloodlust, they had neglected to fully remove the ram. The obstacle slowed the advance of those behind and a group of only fifteen or twenty troops hurled themselves at the defenders. Gasbron almost laughed at their mistake.

'Front row only! Throw pilums!' he bellowed and a deadly volley followed Gasbron's own weapon into the air in an arc and struck the oncoming militia, felling each of them down with ease. The briefest isolation was all it had taken. Now though, the ram was removed and a torrent enemy militia and Defroni warriors burst through

'All units! Ready pilums!' Gasbron roared. He took the whistle that hung from his neck and put it in his mouth. He thrust his sword out from behind his shield and straight into the torso of an oncoming militiaman, then ripped it out and deftly tripped the man with his foot, before slashing his throat for good measure.

'Throw pilums!' he shouted.

A vast, dense wave of shafts flew over Gasbron's head from behind, but the enemy charged blindly onward into the storm of death, filling the air with their screams as the deadly weapons found their mark.

A woman of the enemy militia charged directly at Gasbron, screaming an animalistic cry. Their shields crashed together, but the woman's spear was too clumsy at such close quarters. With an almighty push, Gasbron made her lose her footing and just like the man before, she tripped backwards and Gasbron stabbed deep into his enemy's chest, before retracting the weapon ready for his next attacker. More enemies were piling in behind now, crashing into the shield wall. Gasbron ducked behind his shield and braced for impact as a loincloth-wearing Defroni warrior smashed into it. The man's momentum almost toppled Gasbron, but out of nowhere a blade came to his rescue and pierced deep into the warrior's neck. Gasbron regained his footing as the tribesman slumped down on to the other bodies at Gasbron's feet. He nodded his gratitude to the man next to him, Corpralis Candoc, whose sword it had been that saved him.

Gasbron gave a hard blow on his whistle and in a single movement every divisioman took a step backwards, while simultaneously the Hentani to their left and right intensified their attack, cutting down the militia with ease and advancing over their bodies. In the background, looking over the heads of the swarm of enemy soldiers, Gasbron saw that a unit of Jostan's divisiomen had formed up in the open gate and were advancing forward behind the peasant militia and warriors.

'Now!' came the shout of Silrith's voice from amid the fighting up above. Gasbron blew on his whistle twice this time and the reserve longbowmen at the back of the formation fired in unison, sending thousands of arrows high over the walls, just as in the previous battle.

Again Gasbron blew on his whistle and the divisiomen took another step back while standing firm as their shields took impact after impact. As the enemy hurled themselves at the battle line, Gasbron quickly got into his fighting rhythm. Whistle, step back, shield thrust, attack, whistle, step back, shield thrust, attack. After less than ten repetitions though, there was no more ground to give and as he fought, cutting down opponent after opponent, Gasbron couldn't see how far the Hentani had advanced on the flanks. But then - yes - that was it!

As he felled yet another assailant, he saw the faintest flash of a scimitar diagonally to his right and no Bennvikan, nor any Defroni tribesman carried a sword like that. A moment later, amid the carnage, he picked out more scything scimitars off to the left. The enemy started to panic as they realised they were being outflanked by the Hentani warriors. Gasbron's troops stood firm like an impenetrable rock, while the Hentani enveloped the enemy, like a serpent that had slithered out from behind them, pushing between the militia and Jostan's divisios. A bugle sounded in the distance, heralding the retreat. In the background, he saw the enemy divisios withdrawing barely minutes after they had entered that battle.

'Cowards!' Gasbron bellowed after them. 'You're a disgrace to the divisios.'

He looked at the divisiomen either side of him as he easily cut down an enemy peasant.

'Come on, you lot. Let's show these toy soldiers from Kriganheim what real divisiomen are made of!'

Gasbron's troops cheered and advanced forward as the enemy began to break. The Hentani warriors cut into the enemy on all sides, swinging their curved swords with a deadly grace. Within moments the tide of the fight had turned completely in the defenders' favour. Although a lucky few enemies had managed to escape through the gates, the defenders now completely surrounded the rest. Gasbron raised his sword to the heavens.

'Now let them join their comrades in death.'

Chapter 20

That battle ended the way all battles do. Bodies. A pile of bodies, surrounded by the cries of victory from the triumphant. Once they had surrounded the enemy, Gasbron's troops had pushed inward, constricting them further and further like a snake with its prey. With the enemy expelled from the walled courtyard and the battered gates pushed closed again, Gasbron's troops had then been called to the ramparts to help defend from a counterattack by the ladder climbers and those in the remaining siege towers. With the might of the extra divisiomen and Hentani warriors on the ramparts, the enemy had been unable to get a foothold, even once their own divisiomen had entered the fray. They'd soon lost their nerve and it hadn't been long before a second, full-scale retreat to the camp had been sounded. Now, with the siege towers torched and the ram withdrawn, came the calm after the storm and the citadel's walled courtyard reeked with the stench of death.

'Get the portcullis down and start work on those gates. They must be repaired and reinforced by nightfall,' ordered Gasbron as he picked his way over the corpses. As he trod on a hand he heard a groan. He looked down to see where it had come from and saw a middle-aged spearman with a large gash on his head, lying on the ground covered in blood.

'Please sir,' said the spearman, raising his head slightly, causing more blood to drip down his face and into his bushy beard.

Gasbron shook his head and raised his sword.

'No!' the man cried desperately. 'I have information about the king!'

Frustrated, Gasbron lowered the sword again. He knew Silrith would be angry if he passed up an opportunity to gain information.

'You there!' he barked at the nearest militiaman. 'Get this man's wound seen to so that he can be questioned.'

'Yes, Sir.'

'Gasbron,' called Silrith's voice. Gasbron looked over his shoulder to see her standing by the entrance to the gatehouse. He walked over to her, picking his way over the dead.

'Yes, my Queen?' he said as he reached her.

'Come and look at this,' she said. She opened the door to the gatehouse, walked in, strode past the spiralling, stone staircase that led up to the walls and opened the wooden door into the gate master's quarters. He followed her into the small, dark room, which had no windows and was lit by only a single brazier. He shut the door behind him, then raised his eyebrows at what he saw.

At the side of the room were some stone steps that led up to an antechamber in which the portcullis' pulley system was housed. It sounded like a soldier was up there turning the main winch as outside the portcullis creaked slowly downwards. Yet what had caught Gasbron's attention was the bloodied corpse lying at the foot of the steps. He was a relatively young soldier in a militiaman's uniform; presumably the gate master. The gaping wound in his neck was the obvious cause of death.

'So,' said Silrith who, like him, was looking down at the body. 'There has been an attempt on my life while I slept; someone tried to push me off the walls during the last battle and now this. If we weren't before, then we can now be certain that there is a second spy in our midst. The girl Vaezona wasn't working alone. Apart from the Gate Master, who has access to this room?'

'Just about everyone really,' said Gasbron with a sigh. 'It's not a job that is only done by certain soldiers. We all do our shift just as we do with guard duty anywhere else and the equipment is quite simple to use once someone's shown you.'

'Well,' said Silrith, putting her hands on her hips and beginning to pace around the room. 'Perhaps we'd better become clearer about the kind of men and women that make up the rank and file of our army. It is obvious that Jostan had devised his entire battle plan based on the knowledge that there was someone in the citadel who could undo the portcullis lock and work the pulley system so that they could simply lift it up from the outside.' She indicated the bloodied body.

'We may have dodged an arrow this time,' she went on. 'But we won't be able to forever.'

'No,' said Gasbron, looking at the corpse and then at Silrith. 'But, it is possible we may have found our man already. One of the prisoners we took today claimed to have information. I've given orders for him to be questioned the moment his wounds have been seen to.'

'Good,' said Silrith, looking at him sternly. 'With luck, it will have been him. But if not, I want everyone in the city to know there is a spy here, so that he or she may be exposed.'

THE CAPTAIN'S QUARTERS, THE IBBEZRON, THE ETERNAMIC OCEAN

Out on the Eternamic Ocean, Voyran sat in the plush soundings of the Captain's Quarters aboard the Ibbezron. He sat at his table looking at a map, lit by candles and by the moonlight that gleamed eerily through the ship's windows. They were well on course and were making good time. In fact, if their guide was to be believed, they would soon be entering Bennvikan waters.

Next to him sat Emostocran in his blue uniform and across from them sat the Bennvikan woman, Viktana. Like the two men, she also wore the blue uniform of the Rilanian Navy, looking every inch the Rilanian sailor, save for her physical appearance. After all, pale skin like hers was still almost unheard of in Rilana. Indeed, it was a symbol of weakness and low status. In many cases, even the country's lighter skinned inhabitants were darker than her. These people were generally the servants or slaves of the darker nobility; those who were descended directly from the founding citizens of Rilana.

Based on the Bennvikan's accounts of her homeland, it sounded like many races lived in Bennvika, with complexions ranging from the very darkest to the very lightest; though it seemed that social status was less affected by one's ethnic group than in Rilana, only their direct family heritage. Paradoxically, it seemed also that certain tribes, namely one known as the Hentani, lived under Bennvikan rule, yet keeping their traditions and cultural identity. This openness was very much like Rilana and its colonies, but it seemed that the Bennvikans were known to allow people to climb the social ladder to some extent and where the Rilanians were free to take, buy and sell slaves at their leisure, it appeared that the relative levelling of social status between the races in Bennvika had brought about an almost complete

282

abolition of slavery there. In many cases, servants were employed instead. The only slaves one could have were those taken as the spoils of war and the trade of these slaves was illegal. All this seemed most foreign to Voyran, but whilst he wouldn't have dreamed of fraternising with the primitive lower classes, he had always found the concept of slavery an unpalatable and decidedly uncomfortable subject, so it was gratifying at least to find that it wasn't rife everywhere. If only the rest of Rilana had shared that view.

Aside from their vastly differing levels of technology, it seemed that the biggest thing that set the cultures of Rilana and Bennvika apart was a difference in ideas and their stricter position against slavery wasn't the only one.

'I get the impression that religion is taken very seriously in Bennvika,' Voyran said.

'Yes,' said Viktana stiffly, as seemed to be her usual manner. 'The gods protect all who worship them. People of other cultures living in Bennvika are allowed to worship their own gods if they choose to, but that is additional to the worship of our gods, which is compulsory. Everyone in Bennvika pays homage to Vitrinnolf and Lomatteva, be it through upbringing or conversion.' She had been trying to convert Voyran for a while now. It wasn't going to work. In Rilana the gods were figureheads and nothing more, as it should be.

'You seem to see these gods in everything. They must command great loyalty,' he said.

'Wouldn't you show loyalty to someone who protects you?'

'It depends how effective they are at it.'

'The loyalty of the Bennvikan people to the gods is unbreakable,' Viktana said angrily.

'Unless the gods show weakness, it seems,' said Voyran. 'Didn't you say that these gods were once mortal? Who do you think they worshipped?'

'They showed our ancestors the folly of their ways in worshipping false gods. Those people saw the divinity of the true gods first hand. Before their conversion, famine stalked the land, but after, Bennvika was a land of plenty.'

'So in other words, holy Bennvikans can be not only bought, but can even be moved to convert in adversity. Potentially very useful. Your people fear your gods and yet despite what you say, it is clear to me that your loyalty to them has been fickle when tested. Very curious.'

'A god must protect their people in just the way that a ruler should,' Viktana conceded; a fiery but defeated anger in her eyes. She had the defiant look of one who knew she had been outmanoeuvred, but would not accept it. 'The loyalty between a god and a mortal must flow both ways.'

'Which is slightly different from what you said a moment ago with regards to the loyalty of a Bennvikan to their gods. I wonder though, could it simply be that when times are hard, your gods are testing you? It is a primitive idea, is it not, simply to blame others when things go wrong, especially if those you are blaming are gods? By my reckoning, the inability to take responsibility for one's own troubles limits progress.'

He looked over at Emostocran.

'It appears we have more to teach these people than we thought,' he laughed. Viktana bit her lip in fury but said nothing.

'Now,' said Voyran in a matter-of-fact tone. 'The country itself. The land. The terrain and the weather. What's it like?'

Viktana's eyes burned with fury, but she answered the question. She described a temperate and often wet climate, with a handful of burning hot days that were vastly outnumbered by those of summer drizzle. At least the winters didn't sound too bad though and the terrain sounded largely flat. The scattered hills and valleys it did feature sounded like they wouldn't present any problems. Apparently, the only mountainous areas were inhabited by the tribal peoples in the territory of the Defroni Kingdom, Bennvika's southwestern neighbour. The large forest she spoke of worried Voyran for a moment until she mentioned that it was in the kingdom's centre, so would not be an issue for some time yet.

After sending Viktana and Emostocran away, Voyran thought about the conversation further. He found his mind repeatedly wandering back to the complex relationship between the Bennvikans and religion.

Religion had never been seen as such an issue in Rilana. Not for many centuries anyway. People had their traditions and that was that. As in Bennvika, people in Rilana generally followed the national religion, but there were many others and these were tolerated peacefully so long as their practices didn't contravene any state laws. The difference was that the

Bennvikans seemed to believe that their fates were entirely in the hands of one god or another. Voyran wondered if that was what was holding back their technological and cultural development, in contrast to the flourishing of the sciences and the arts in the Rilanian world, where religion is more akin to tradition rather than a source of law and oppression. Religion was also never used as a form of politics in Rilana, whereas by the sound of things, the Bennvikan people were ripe for the manipulating, given the right religious rhetoric. Therein was the biggest difference between their cultures and it was one that Voyran planned to exploit.

THE PREDDABURG CITADEL, RILDAYORDA, BASTALF, BENNVIKA

That night, even the spirits seemed restless and not least in the dream world in which Ezrina found herself. She was well aware that this strange, dense forest of ferns and conifers was one that existed only in her own mind. However, she was intrigued, so she let the dream continue.

There was almost no sound, save for a gentle, whistling breeze and the swaying of the leaves. Even when she sensed another presence, she found herself strangely unworried by it as she felt its eyes on her.

'Come to me. Come to me,' whispered a voice in her ear. She started to move, following the twisting path between the trees.

'Come to me. That's it. Come to me,' the voice said again.

'Yes. Go to her,' said another, younger sounding, yet equally ghostly voice.

She carried on, but she stopped dead in her tracks when she rounded a bend to find an enormous brown bear blocking her path, only a handful of metres away. Backing away slowly, she instinctively felt for something she could use as a weapon, never taking her eyes off the sitting, panting beast as it surveyed her, but she found nothing.

'It's only a dream. It's only a dream,' she reminded herself.

The bear gave a long, low growl as it got up, slavering, and began to advance as she retreated.

'Ezrina, do not be afraid.'

'Jezna!'

Where had Jezna come from? Ezrina was stunned to see her lover in a brown dress, confidently walking out from the forest to stand between her and the bear. Suddenly she wished it wasn't a dream, except for the bear of course.

'Why do you fear him, Ezrina? Do you not recognise Ursartin? We have come to escort you to the goddess.'

Immediately Jezna and the bear turned and started walking down the path in the other direction.

'Jezna! You have to tell me. Do you live?'

No answer.

'Jezna! Answer me!'

Jezna turned.

'Come with us and all will be revealed.'

Obediently, Ezrina followed. Soon they reached a clearing. At one end, there was a particularly large tree. Jezna's ghostly image walked over to it and stood to one side, with Ursartin taking up position on the other, both facing Ezrina. As she watched, the tree began to change shape, morphing into a matriarchal, middle-aged woman sitting on a throne. She wore a golden crown, while her face was framed by long black hair and jewelled earrings. Her powerful looking body was clad in a long shawl the colour of ochre, while her belt, the rings on her fingers and the hoops around her bare, muscular arms were works of purest gold.

'Bertakaevey?' Ezrina was so stunned that the name almost stuck in her throat. 'Oh, glorious mother goddess,' she blurted out impulsively, dropping to her knees, bowing so that her forehead touched the grass.

'Arise, for it is you who shall be the glorious one,' Bertakaevey said in a powerful tone. 'You on whom your people will come to depend, or else perish; you who will be the bearer of my message.'

Obediently, Ezrina got to her feet, though in her fear, she still couldn't quite look Bertakaevey in the eye. She was overawed by everything she was seeing and hearing.

'Look at me, my dear. Show me your strength. The Bennvikans tell you that I am just a manifestation of their goddess Lomatteva. Know that this is not true. However, for your purpose, you must appear to believe this for a while longer, at least in the eyes of some. Find the one who knows both faiths and knows the truth. Be patient, my dear. Only strike when I give you the command. When I do, you will know it and the people will flock to you in search of deliverance from the terror that shall soon be raging upon them. You must protect them from that and lead them through the path that I will show you. Are you up to the task?'

Ezrina nodded.

'Yes, great one.' She didn't know why she said yes, except that the goddess' words filled her with a strange sense of power, even though the way that bear was eyeing her was distracting, to say the least.

'My lover, Jezna, does she live?'

Bertakaevey lifted her right hand and the image of Jezna moved over and knelt down at her side, resting her chin on Bertakaevey's knee, so that the goddess could run her fingers through her hair.

'She does, but doing right by your people will be the only way you can save her. When the time comes, people of all tribes will flock to your side, but only if you do as I say. Only then will you be able to save your dear Jezna.'

'I'll do anything. Anything! What must I do?'

Bertakaevey chuckled.

'Rise up, my dear, rise up.'

She was gone. Everything was gone. The woods. The Bear. Jezna. Looking around, Ezrina realised that she'd woken from the dream. She was in the room Gasbron had given her and Jezna a few days ago. She turned over and found Gasbron sleeping next to her. Then she remembered he'd wanted to speak to her after the battle, but one thing had quickly led to another.

She sat up in bed in the candlelit, windowless room, whose door was slightly ajar and wondered what time of day it was. She slipped her legs out from between the sheets and quickly put on her simple brown dress and her sandals, leaving Gasbron to carry on sleeping. She opened the door and walked out into one of the many alleyways of the inner ward; finding it to be just past dawn. She made for the gates out of the citadel into the city itself. The guards there knew her by now and she had no trouble passing through. It

287

was still quite early as she walked down the sloping path, but already some people were out, beginning their day, though the streets were as yet far from bustling. In the dim morning light she made her way south, certain of what she had to do next.

Her destination was the city temple, which officially doubled as a shrine to both Lomatteva and Bertakaevey and had been built by the Bennvikans as a peace offering to the Hentani, to help keep them pacified after their surrender. However, this revelation by Bertakaevey disproved the theory that the two goddesses were one and the same. She had to make others see this and make them hear Bertakaevey's message.

The Hentani had no stone buildings of any particular size, so the temple had been built in the Bennvikan style. It was rectangular, with steps leading up to many pillars, which were topped by a wide triangular fresco, which in its centre depicted a grand looking woman, seated on her throne.

'A wonder of Bennvikan architecture, is it not?'

Ezrina turned to see who had spoken and saw a middle-aged, greying, stubble-chinned man in light grey robes; a Hentani priest, easily identifiable from the Bennvikans, who mostly wore black. Yet his pale skin gave him a Bennvikan look. It was also devoid of the blue tattoos that most Hentani men adorned themselves with, though this was true of all Hentani priests. Equally, no Hentani priestess wore the red body paint that most Hentani women used. For the tribe's holy people, their unblemished skin was a symbol of their piety.

'It is,' she replied. 'Though it is what goes on inside those walls that counts.'

'Quite true, though the Bennvikans do like their grand stone gestures.'

'You speak of the Bennvikans as if they are another people, yet you are not Hentani.'

'And I see that you most certainly are, yet I have not seen you at prayers here before,' he said, gesturing at the red ochre patterns that Ezrina had now reapplied to her skin and surely noting her darker complexion, rounded face and slanted eyes. 'But you are right in your observation. It is no secret. I was born a Bennvikan, in Attatan, Hertasala. Now I live here, among the city's Hentani community, a different man, with a different name. They call me Jakiroc.'

'Ezrina. I came here from Quesoto.'

'You do not call it Lithrofed?' said Jakiroc, looking surprised and a little impressed.

'The Bennvikans may call it their city and force a new name on my home, but its Hentani heart beats as strongly as ever. Anyway, I came here with the army, though now it seems that I must pray to Bertakaevey for guidance.'

'A new arrival with concerns already. I presume that they are due to the city's current predicament?'

'Yes, among other things,' said Ezrina.

'It seems you have been here rather longer than I, if I understand your words correctly,' she added, changing the subject. 'Why did you defect?'

Jakiroc thought for a moment.

'Come,' he said, smiling wryly and taking her hand. 'I will show you the inside of the temple.' Ezrina was confused as to why he had been forthcoming with the information he'd given her up to this point but had baulked at the idea of going into why it had happened. Surely that too would be common knowledge if people knew what she already knew of him?

She followed him up the steps and past the tall pillars. As they walked further inside, they entered a wide corridor with a tall ceiling and with many doorways leading to what must have been a warren of interconnecting rooms. Wall-mounted braziers lit up colourful paintings, depicting stories from both the Bennvikan and Hentani faiths, though Ezrina guessed that if this place had been built to create a sense of political and religious unity between the Bennvikans and the Hentani, these depictions and stories had been carefully selected. Nobody would want the images from one faith to offend the members of the other and create what would be at the very least an unnecessary political headache.

Many visitors walked this way and that, talking in hushed tones, while the voices of chanting priests and worshippers echoed throughout the building.

'The main hall is at the end of this corridor, you can worship there,' Jakiroc said.

289

'No, I must worship in private.'

Jakiroc looked taken aback.

'Alright, here.'

He indicated a small room to their left. 'But you must be accompanied by a priest.'

'I have no quarrel with that. In fact, it is what I require. Will you do that for me?' Ezrina asked.

'Of course.'

They went in and Ezrina saw a room that was as highly decorated as the corridor outside, with the blue paint of the walls dominated by depictions of Bertakaevey and by more pictures showing episodes from Hentani mythology. Yet the room was still dominated by a long table at the end of it, on top of which stood a golden statuette of Bertakaevey, standing about a foot tall with her arms outstretched either side of her. Next to it was a wine cup. Jakiroc locked the door behind them and both knelt down before the statuette, bowing their heads.

'I have seen something,' Ezrina said quietly as they got back up. 'I bear a message that the temple must hear.'

'What have you seen?'

'Swear that you will not tell a soul without my permission.'

Jakiroc laughed.

'Oh, my child, what can-'

'Swear it! Swear it in the sight of Bertakaevey!' Ezrina pointed forcefully to the gleaming statuette.

'Alright,' he said calmly, holding up his palms with an awkward smile. 'I swear in the sight of Bertakaevey, blessed be her motherly guidance, that what you say to me now shall not be repeated, except with your permission. Now, I am unused to visitors expecting such subservience from me, so I must ask why.'

'I had a dream last night. A vision. A visitation!' Ezrina said.

'From who?'

'Bertakaevey! With Ursartin by her side.'

Ezrina deliberately left out the presence of Jezna.

'And what was said?'

'Ursartin led me to Bertakaevey's throne, where she told me that I must be the one to tell all that we have been misled by those who claim that the Bennvikan goddess Lomatteva is Bertakaevey by another name. She told me we must rise up with her blessing before our culture and livelihood withers away little by little.'

Jakiroc looked interested, if rather cautious.

'Your words do have a truthful sound to them, but the risk is great.'

'The risk? If we do not act then the Hentani are destroyed anyway. We have been conquered and the Defroni have long since turned to the side of the Bennvikans, convinced by their heretical preachings – and their gold of course. We must overthrow this oppression. We must make them see and hear our message and we must do the same for all Hentani living under Bennvikan rule. There is no risk. Not to us. Bertakaevey is on our side and will protect us.'

Jakiroc was silent. Ezrina understood. This was a man who knew both cultures like no other that she had met and when combined with the importance of this moment, she could see how there would be a battle going on in his mind.

'That's all very well,' he said eventually. 'But how do I know you're not just some mad peasant girl who claims that we should all listen to the voices in her head?'

'Because I can get you the Amulet of Hazgorata. I know where it is. The Dowager Queen no longer has it. It's here in Rildayorda.'

'How do you know this?' Jakiroc asked.

'Because Bertakaevey told me,' Ezrina lied. 'I'm telling you I can return it. If I do, then will you believe me? Conduct the ritual of divinity if you must. I guarantee I will come through it.' She didn't mention that she'd already had the Amulet and had it taken from her and deliberately didn't give a time scale, as she knew that if the city didn't fall, breaking in and reclaiming her prize would be very difficult, let alone holding on to it a second time. At least she knew the location though.

'Alright, but only if you come through the ritual as you so confidently promise to do,' Jakiroc said, with an expression and tone that made Ezrina wonder if he was holding something back.

291

'I assure you I will. After all, Bertakaevey herself predicted that I'd find you and I did it without even looking.'

'I'm sure she did. Follow me,' said Jakiroc, poker-faced.

He unlocked and opened the door and led her back into the main hallway, down to the far end and into an enormous room that was full of people praying. There must have been at least two hundred people there, all praying with heads bowed under the gaze of a massive gold leaf depiction of Bertakaevey that dominated the opposite wall, arms outstretched, just like the little statuette. The air was thick with incense and on a large dais at the front of the room stood many priests in their grey robes, save for the archpriest who led the worship, singing the psalms of Bertakaevey. He was in his seventies and was easily identifiable, dressed in blue and white, with his tall gold hat and long grey beard.

Jakiroc led Ezrina through the masses and found a position at the front and slightly to the side of the dais, where he could catch the archpriest's eye. Once he had finished his part of the service, the archpriest alighted the dais and approached Jakiroc.

'Jakiroc, who is this?' he asked, surveying Ezrina appreciatively.

'Askorit, I would like you to meet Ezrina. She says she has a message of great importance, but we must discuss it in private, not here. In fact, she has made a rather bold claim; one that requires the test of truth in the sight of the goddess herself.'

'Interesting,' Askorit said with an intrigued expression. 'Well, you'd better follow me then.'

Ezrina followed Askorit and Jakiroc to the back of the room. She saw some stairs leading down to a wooden door. She thought Askorit was about to lead them down there, but he walked past the staircase and carried on towards another door, also wooden, just to the staircase's left. He opened it and held it so that Ezrina and Jakiroc could enter.

Once through, Ezrina found herself in a room of dazzling brightness. It seemed the entire place was made of marble, especially the twenty-foot high statue of the goddess, who regally dominated the room from her throne in its centre. This image of Bertakaevey was much the same as one that the goddess had adopted in her dream, Ezrina mused silently. That was, at least, with the exception of the fact that this image showed her holding a

Bennvikan style sword in her left hand, with a large round shield in the other. Just to the statue's left was a six or seven-foot high statue of Ursartin the bear, sitting patiently at Bertakaevey's side, just as he had done in the dream.

The three of them stood at the edge of the room while two black-cloaked Bennvikan priests knelt before the statue, worshipping it as their false goddess Lomatteva. After a few moments, the Bennvikans got up, bowed to the statue and turned to leave without a word to their Hentani counterparts, though both gave them a sneering look, especially to Ezrina.

'Good, now that we are alone, let me explain a few things to you,' said Askorit pompously as he turned to face Ezrina. 'As you might have gathered through the presence of those two, this room is the Priest's Worship Chamber. Just like the rest of the temple, it is for Bennvikans and Hentani alike. Whatever the claim you wish to make is, you can make it here, in the sight of our goddess.'

'Thank you,' Ezrina said, bowing her head politely and moving to approach the statue.

'Ah,' Askorit exclaimed waving a finger in the air. 'Before you do anything, let me remind you that honesty is paramount here. Failure to adhere to this would be sacrilege of the worst kind. If you lie to our goddess, I will know. She may not tell me of her decision immediately, but before the sun has set twice more I shall know.'

'And the penalty for lying to our holy goddess is stoning, as I am sure you are aware,' Jakiroc put in sternly.

'Followed by an eternity spent burning in the underworld,' added Askorit with a sinister smile.

His attempt to intimidate Ezrina was amusing. She knew the authenticity of her dream.

'I thank you for the reminder, Archpriest,' said Ezrina, deliberately letting her amusement show with a smile of her own. 'But I assure you your warnings are not necessary.'

Askorit's stunned face was a picture. Evidently that threat scared most people. He clearly wasn't ready for the suggestion that it would fail to worry a young dancing girl like her.

She smiled to herself as she confidently strode towards the statue. She took a deep breath to compose her mind as she stopped in front of

Bertakaevey. Even though this was just a statue and one that, with the presence of the weapons, had been Bennvikanised at that, she felt the goddess' gaze on her just as strongly as she had in the dream. Yet it didn't fill her with fear, but courage and so her confidence held.

In the proper form, she got to her knees, bowed her head with her eyes closed and held out her hands with her palms raised.

'Holy mother,' she began. 'I declare five times to you, the blessed goddess Bertakaevey and all those present in your holy name, that I am the Daughter of Ashes and I will do your bidding only! I am the Daughter of Ashes and I will do your bidding only! I am the Daughter of Ashes and I will do your bidding only! I am the Daughter of Ashes and I will do your bidding only! I am the Daughter of Ashes and I will do your bidding only! Let me guide my people to freedom and glory, else strike me from this earth here and now. The Daughter of Ashes is risen and I am she. Holy Bertakaevey, on your own divine orders I will lead your loyalist offspring, the Hentani, from the ashes of our civilisation. I am the mother of many, mother of none, for I must be mother to our people, yet have borne no children. The Bennvikan Princess Silrith will surely die if the city falls and it must fall so that we may rise from the ashes and I, your chosen daughter, can lead the Hentani to freedom. In your divine presence, I make this pledge and give myself to you.'

Silence.

After a moment, Ezrina opened her eyes. She'd done it. She had declared to the one true goddess that she accepted her divine mission and with it, given herself hope that she would one day have the means to find Jezna.

She composed herself a second time, then got to her feet and turned to face Jakiroc and Askorit.

Jakiroc's face was unreadable, but Askorit's was one of shock and almost offence. He must have realised he was gaping though, as he closed his mouth and looked at the floor for a moment while Ezrina walked back over to them.

'Well that is quite a claim you have made,' Askorit blustered. 'But if it is true, then I will be damned if I am the one to denounce it.'

Ezrina sighed and gave him a hard look, straight in the eye. She knew that he was not using the phrase figuratively.

'Yet, I believe I do hear Bertakaevey's voice,' Askorit went on, his tone turning smug as if a thought had just come to him. 'She commands that a further test be conducted. Jakiroc tells me you claim you can find the Amulet of Hazgorata. Both the Daughter of Ashes and the Amulet are sacred. We lack the latter, but surely it can be found by the former. What would be holier than that?'

He shrugged sarcastically, while Jakiroc kept his face neutral. If only they knew that only days ago Ezrina had been in possession of the Amulet? Ezrina gave another very deliberate smile, causing Askorit's haughty expression to crease into one of frustration. He would believe. It was only a matter of time.

'As you wish. I will personally recover the Amulet,' said Ezrina confidently. 'How can I fail? After all, Bertakaevey is on our side.'

Chapter 21

That evening, standing in the walled courtyard, Silrith looked on at the patched-up gates. Her soldiers had worked through the night trying to strengthen it with any wood and steel they could find, but she knew that they were just delaying the inevitable. Jostan's army had not made an attack that day, apparently preferring to rest, but it surely wouldn't be long before hostilities were resumed.

'That gate won't withstand another frontal attack for long,' she said to Gasbron.

'Well, at least it makes our next move simple. A gamble isn't a gamble if you have no choice,' he replied.

That's easy for you to say. You're not the one that history will blame for so many deaths if this goes wrong, Silrith thought.

'Yes,' she said, affecting a positive tone. 'Now that we no longer have the chance to outlast them in a siege, our only option left is to attack.' They had briefly considered retreating to the city itself, but had come to the conclusion that they could never win back the citadel from there, fighting uphill as they would be and trying to orchestrate attacks from the city streets. In any case, it would be exactly what Jostan expected her to do and she didn't plan on doing that.

'In the meantime, what's the butcher's bill?' she asked.

A smile creased across Gasbron's dark features and it looked to Silrith like he appreciated her attempt to start using soldierly jargon.

'Not as bad as we might have anticipated at this point. Two hundred and fifty-seven dead at the last count over both attacks and four hundred and thirty-one injured, though some can still hold a weapon if it comes to it. Meanwhile, they've surely lost hundreds more. But that means nothing if they break through those gates again.'

Silrith nodded.

'Yes, and they won't fall for the same trick twice. They'll be prepared to be outflanked this time.'

'A frontal attack will be harder to defend now too,' sighed Gasbron.

'You think Jostan will send in his divisios first?'

296

'Yes. He's hardly used them so far. I believe that he may be saving them for the right moment,' Gasbron said.

'I share your concern. If I were him, that's what I would do,' Silrith replied, looking up at the sky. 'It's getting dark. It's not likely that Jostan will be able to assemble another attack before nightfall, which hopefully gives us until tomorrow to upset his plans. How many cavalry do we have?'

'Nearly three thousand, all told. Divisio One Bastalf is still nearly at full strength, so that's approaching five hundred to start, then there are Prince Shappa's knights, so that's another two hundred, then we have a thousand mounted Hentani Warriors and around a thousand of our spear militia were assessed as being competent enough to use a weapon on horseback,' Gasbron said. This had been part of the rigorous testing and training prior to the enemy's arrival.

'Do we have enough horses?'

Gasbron shook his head.

'No, not proper cavalry horses anyway. But fortunately, most of the militia are farmers and the like who own their own animals. They're big beasts that are more used to pulling ploughs but they'll have to do. We can put them at the back. Those who don't have one at all are few enough for Lord Yathrud's stables to supply them all. But the Hentani warriors have some decent mounts at least. '

'Good. I shall require you and your divisiomen to be my personal bodyguard. Find Prince Shappa and all other relevant officers and order them to congregate at the East Gate one hour from now. I shall inform Lord Yathrud,' Silrith said, turning to leave.

'Yes, my Queen. But first, there is one more thing that you should know.'

'What's that?' Silrith asked, stopping and turning back to him.

'It's your cousin, Bezekarl. He's still missing. I saw him come down from the wall to join the fight down here when we outflanked them, but I didn't see him after that.'

Silrith's heart sank and she was silent for a moment.

'Has anything of his been found?'

'No. No shield, no sword, no armour, nothing, not even a body. But that could be meaningless. It *is* possible that he's simply been taken prisoner, but I wouldn't want to give you false hope.'

Silrith let her eyes drop to the floor, biting her lip to hold back any hint of feeling as the fires of rage burned inside her at the thought of another one of her kin being taken by Jostan. Eventually, she thought it best simply to nod in acknowledgement.

'Thank you, Gasbron,' she added. Quickly she turned and walked away before she made a public slip of emotion. She knew she hadn't fooled Gasbron though. Everyone else maybe, but not him. She didn't know what it was, but something in the way that he'd looked at her told her that for that moment, he'd seen right into her soul. She was surprised to be comforted by the idea, but then she thought of Bezekarl again and felt the anger return.

She immediately swatted it away. Clarity of mind would be crucial tonight, if she was to stand any chance of avenging Bezekarl, or if he was alive, saving him.

The dripping of water on the damp walls. The scuffling of rats as they scampered by in the darkness. The moaning of fellow prisoners in other cells. With no chance of escape, down in the depths of Rildayorda's dungeons, after a day or so, or whatever it had been, Jithrae already knew he would never get used to these horrific surroundings and that was even before you considered the stench.

Yet there was still one noise that filled him with a colder dread than any other every time he heard it; the turning of the latch and the opening of the door at the far end of the dungeon. Every time it happened, he'd jump to the front of the cell and peer through the bars to see who was coming. Once it had turned out to be the man who brought around the bowls of food, or rather, he brought them in and flung them in the vague direction of the cells. Twice though, it had been the guards coming to carry some groaning half-starved prisoner to their death and both times this had looked like a mercy. He was convinced that it would be his turn soon. He had claimed to have knowledge of Jostan's plans, just to keep himself alive, but he had not thought of anything convincing in time. They had seen through his lies and when he had said he knew nothing of the alleged plot involving the opening of the portcullis in the last battle, they had grown frustrated and locked him away.

How could he possibly save Vaezona from here? He was just brooding on this terrible thought, thinking he'd feel a bit less scared next time the door opened, when exactly that happened and the wave of fright returned as strongly as ever, but this time with even more reason. As the latch was opened, he could hear voices shouting on the other side, as if there was some kind of struggle going on. The door was at the top of a few stone steps and when it eventually opened, Jithrae saw two guards manhandling a young woman at the top.

The prisoner was still trying to escape, even though her wrists and ankles were in chains, but her resistance lessened when one of them gave her a hard punch in the stomach.

'That should teach her a lesson,' said one guard as they dragged the groaning prisoner down the steps.

'How do you like your new room?' jeered the other as he opened the door of the neighbouring cell to Jithrae's and his friend threw the girl in. She was slender, with dark hair and for a wonderful moment Jithrae thought it might be Vaezona, but then she looked over at him and he saw only a stranger. Some of the prisoners in other cells started calling, begging for the guards to bring them their meal.

'Sit down. Shut up,' came the gruff answer.

One of the men slammed the girl's cell door closed and turned the lock. Jithrae's fear rose as the two guards then walked over to his own cell's door and one unlocked it. They opened the door and stepped in. Surely that could only mean one thing.

'You. You're coming with us.'

After gaining some level of backing from Jakiroc and the select group of other priests she had subsequently been introduced to, Ezrina knew what she had to do next - recover the Amulet of Hazgorata, and fast. Their support looked like it could waver easily. The tribal priests had been nervous of arousing the suspicions of their Bennvikan counterparts.

299

Fortunately, when Gasbron had taken it from her she had overheard him tell a guard where to take the Amulet, so she knew where it would be. Additionally, some equally valuable intelligence had recently been gained and this was outlined to her by Jakiroc in a secret meeting with the priests and priestesses in a room beneath the temple.

'Every day,' he had said, speaking directly to Ezrina. 'Separately, a priest or priestess each from both Bennvikan and Hentani denominations enters the city prison to bless the prayers of the prisoners. Failure to allow this risks offending the gods, but it also serves as an effective way of observing those in jail in the hope that they testify against others. People will say anything to a servant of the divine. The Bennvikans, of course, think that this favours them, as they demand that any clergyman who goes in must then speak with the guard captain, but of course, when they come back here, they speak to us as well. This was when I learned something very interesting.'

Ezrina and the others listened while he explained what he had discovered.

'If you can provide me with a priestess' dress and veil,' Ezrina had replied when Jakiroc had finished speaking. 'I'll go inside, bless the prisoners' prayers, then meet with the officer in his quarters. Maybe that way I can find a way of taking back the Amulet.'

Most had been happy with this suggestion, except for one who had protested that she was not a real priestess and for her to bless the prayers would be blasphemy. That was until Jakiroc had pointed out that if she was successful, then this would prove that Ezrina was chosen by Bertakaevey and what could be more holy than that?

All this was running through Ezrina's mind as she approached the entrance to the dungeons and prison guards' quarters against the backdrop of a lurid pink sunset, dressed as a Hentani priestess; much more colourful attire than was worn by the men.

She had dispensed with her red body paint and wore a flowing light green dress, which had a high neckline and reached down to her ankles; much less revealing than the short skirts she was used to. Only her arms were bare. On her head, she wore a thin, shimmering green skullcap, held in place with two tassels that were tied together under her chin. Four chains of tiny, shining emerald beads hung down in pairs over the centre of her forehead, reaching around her temples and attaching back to the skullcap just above her ears, perfectly framing her eyes. Long, beautiful tails of green fabric hung down from the skull cap and flowed down her back.

'I come to bless the prayers of the imprisoned and to speak with Captain Ankylodin, password – block,' she told the guard, as she walked off the city street and up the four stone steps towards the door to the conspicuous looking stone box of a building, which only had windows on a small section that sprouted off to the right.

The guard opened the large wooden door, but then seemed to notice that he hadn't seen her before.

'The dungeons are straight ahead and down the stairs, miss. One of the guards down there will show you where to go after that. Or if you want to speak to Captain Ankylodin first, that's the door to his office there to the right of the stairs.'

'Thank you, kind sir,' said Ezrina pleasantly. She wanted to see the prisoners first. Her meeting with Ankylodin and more importantly gaining entrance to his office had to come later, in case he was there and asked what the prisoners had been saying.

She walked into the prison's entrance and the guard shut the door behind her. By the light of the braziers on the walls, she could see the steps down to the underground floor below. She could hear voices coming from it. Slowly she moved down the cold stone steps. Once down, she found herself at the side of a much larger room, rectangular in shape, with six locked doors around the sides. Two guards loitered there. They were spear militia with red sashes, which were unique to prison guardsmen, worn over their brown leather jerkins. They stopped their conversation as they saw her.

'Hello there, miss. You speak Bennvikan? I've not seen you before. You new?' asked one.

'I am. Would you show me to the tribal prisoners?' Ezrina said.

'Of course, miss. But unfortunately, we've had to mix them in with the Bennvikans. Follow us. They're in here,' said the other. He walked over to a large wooden door and unlocked it.

Their manner seemed pleasant enough now, but nevertheless, Ezrina was sure she spotted them undressing her with their eyes. These Bennvikans. Why were tribal people just commodities to them? The Hentani would not be subject to Bennvikan oppression for much longer, she vowed, thinking of her early childhood memories of soldiers like these burning their villages, killing their men, raping their women and taking their children as slaves. Subconsciously her blood grew hot and her muscles tensed in contained rage at the memory. If they weren't so scared of the consequences surely no Hentani warrior would have come to fight for Silrith. Some said she was different; that she was a kind and just leader. But how could she be? She was a Bennvikan and anyway, had it not been her own father and grandfather who had wreaked such havoc on the Hentani in years past? All Bennvikans had to suffer for what had happened in those terrible times.

Ezrina snapped back to reality as she walked into the dungeons with the two guards. Feeling her blood cooling again, she took in the scene around her. She found herself at the top of another flight of stone steps and from here she had a good but rather distant view of the dungeons below and their wretched inhabitants.

'Your tribal prisoners are the ones at the far end,' said one of the guards. 'That lot there are Hentani and that big bastard at the back is Defroni. We keep him in a separate cell because of his lot being with the enemy and all.'

'Yes, I do realise that,' said Ezrina, holding back her annoyance. These Bennvikans might not be able to work out the physical differences between the tribes, but surely they could work out that she could. He'd talked about them as if they were different species and probably would have had no idea which of the tribes she was from under different circumstances. To them, they were all just barbarians, but to her even without the varying types of clothing to identify them, it was still clear as day who was from which. These guards had clearly just been told which tribes the prisoners were from because they thought the priests and priestesses wouldn't be sure without them telling them. She was certain that this sort of goodwill was all fake; all a façade so that the Bennvikans could use and abuse the tribes.

'We'll leave you to it then, miss,' said one of the guards as both turned to leave.

Ezrina made a point of not acknowledging them. Her surroundings were starting to make her feel uneasy. The door closed behind her. As she descended the steps to the cells, she could hear moaning. Some called and reached out to her, trying to touch her, while others simply rocked back and forth obliviously. She hoped with every fibre of her soul that Jezna wasn't at that very moment imprisoned in similar conditions in the enemy camp, though she knew that idea was hopeful at best.

One particularly crazed looking individual caught her eye and she instantly wished she hadn't looked.

'I smell you. I smell you,' he sneered, showering her in spittle as she walked on by.

The rest were less vocal and they watched her through glazed eyes, sitting in their own mess as if simply waiting for death.

Finally, she had passed all the Bennvikan prisoners' cells and reached those containing the tribesmen at the far end.

She couldn't wait to get out of there. She had feared that this part of the process may take a long time, but none of them had much to say and after completing the ritual of blessing their prayers, it wasn't long before she was hastily making her way back up the steps and out of the dungeon. She saw the guards again and despite their polite demeanour, she felt their predatory eyes on her a second time as she continued up the next flight of steps. Once at the top she turned left to stand outside Captain Ankylodin's office.

She knocked on the door.

No answer.

She knocked again.

Silence.

Her heart rose in spite of her tension. What a stroke of luck! He must be otherwise engaged. She turned the handle and slowly, tentatively, clicked the door open.

'Hello?' she said, tilting her head around the door. The room was empty. She breathed a sigh of relief and shut the door behind her. She had to be quick.

Compared to the dungeons she had just been in, the windowed room seemed strangely bright and airy. On the wall opposite was a head and shoulders portrait of King Lissoll, about a foot and half square, showing him in armour; his strong, almost sneering face framed by his silver hair and beard, with the scarlet and gold of a partially unfurled Bennvikan flag in the background. How fitting it was, that she was about to steal the Amulet of Hazgorata from right under the gaze of a man who had wreaked such havoc on her people.

Before her, below the painting, covered in a heap of documents, was a large wooden desk, with legs thick enough to house drawers. Maybe it was in there? Ezrina could see no other furniture in here, save for the chair.

She scampered silently around the back of the desk and, starting on the left, slowly, carefully pulled the first drawer open without a sound. Nothing. Not the Amulet anyway. Just more documents and writing tools. She tried the next drawer and the next. Still nothing. She moved to the drawers on the right-hand side. It had to be in here. She'd heard Gasbron say it and the other priestess had reported to Jakiroc that she'd seen the captain put a large pendant, just like the Amulet, in one of these very drawers. As she reached amongst a pile of papers in the final drawer, her heart leapt as she felt something round and metal. She pulled it out, but almost groaned with derision as she found that it was not the Amulet, simply a pendant that fell open in her hand, showing a tiny painting of a woman and a baby. She put it back, burying it as she had found it and shut the drawer. What was she going to do? She was so certain that it had been there, especially after hearing all the evidence. But this was not the holy relic she had come to find. Even so, she had to get out.

In seconds, she was through the door, walking quickly towards the entrance of the dungeons and into the street.

Finally, she felt safe to drop her speed to a normal walk and as she did, she had a sudden realisation. If the Bennvikans wanted to hide the Amulet from the Hentani, then where better than right under their noses? And if they wanted to do that, where better the somewhere that also retains a Bennvikan presence to look after it. Somewhere like the temple.

She was certain that was where it must be. The Bennvikan priests had to be hiding it from their Hentani counterparts. Tensions between the two sects had been greater than ever and she reeled at the idea that all the time the Bennvikan clergymen had been laughing at them and also at the idea that she had fallen for a red herring that Gasbron had clearly set up for her. He must have been suspicious. Well, they would all regret their actions very soon.

KRIGANHEIM, BENNVIKA

There was an art to lying, Capaea reflected, especially when it was for the greater good. In any case, being good at it certainly had its rewards, as was borne out by the grand house in which she was now a guest. Its owner, a wealthy nobleman, had gone out, leaving her to make herself at home. She pondered her situation as she explored the house's walled gardens, where only the faintest sounds of babbling voices reminded one that they were still in the city.

Only the nobleman himself knew her true identity. As far as the servants were concerned she was just a distant relation of their master. The truth was that the nobleman had orchestrated a mission that had seen her steal a letter from the palace, containing incriminating information about Lord Oprion Aethelgard while using the name of the fictional maid, Lyzina. She had robbed Lord Oprion, then distracted him while her fellow spy, Taevuka, assaulted Lady Haarksa, which in turn provided a distraction while both had made their escape. The plan had worked so well that it had seemed too good to be true – and it had been. That was why Taevuka had successfully escaped from Kriganheim and possibly even Bennvika entirely, while Capaea, still posing as the nobleman's guest, was stuck inside the city.

Yet Capaea was unworried by this. After all, it was situations like this that made her line of work so interesting and when it wasn't the intrigue and the subterfuge that got the blood pumping, it was the thrill of the chase. She had enjoyed meeting that young firebrand Zethun Maysith on the night before Taevuka had escaped the city. There had been such passion in him and yet she had simply played her part, affecting the appropriate character traits and led him on a verbal merry dance. She smirked as she imagined his face once he found out who she really was.

'There's some men here to see you, miss.' Capaea turned to find that a maid had entered the walled garden.

Men? They hadn't been expecting visitors, especially with their host absent.

305

'Who are they?' Capaea asked, though there was no time to answer, as from between the pillars of the grand house walked three Verusantian lance guardsmen in their full, black painted armour, though having dispensed with their helmets. These snarling-faced men and their comrades had sailed with King Jostan from across the sea and some, like these three, had been stationed in Kriganheim in his absence to make sure Lord Oprion did his bidding. They descended the steps and approached Capaea. The two at the back each carried a spear, while the foremost man, presumably their leader, had a sword and dagger in his belt. Surely the doorman would never have let these men in if he'd been here, but he'd gone to the Congressate to perform his guard duties there and would not be back for some time.

'Ah, so the master of the house has a guest. How surprising,' said the lead Guardsman in the harsh tones that the well-travelled Capaea knew to hail from the Verusantian south. He advanced on her with a smirk on his bearded face. 'Let me guess, you arrived here shortly after a visit to the palace? Now that would be a coincidence-arrh!'

With lightning speed Capaea had grabbed his dagger from his belt and buried it in his neck; the blood spurting all over her face. She kicked him to the ground; the servant's screams ringing in her ears.

The two other guards charged towards her. She grabbed the spear off one of them and pushed the spike downwards so that the man's momentum buried it deep into his dying comrade's groin. She ducked as the third man's spear thrust past her face. She stuck out a leg and sent him tumbling to the ground. She turned to the other spearman and saw the panic in his face as he tried to free his weapon from the leader's body. She ripped the sword out of the first man's belt and swung it around with all her might, cleaving the spearman's head from his shoulders, before darting over to the sprawling third man and burying the sword in his neck.

Capaea could feel the blood on her face and could see that her dress was covered in it. She ran to the centre of the garden, where there was a water fountain and splashed water over her face.

'Oh do be quiet!' she barked at the screaming maid. 'They came here to kill me. Now, fetch me a new dress. Quickly! I need to get out of here.'

By invitation of Hoban, Zethun was seeing the inside the Congressate Hall for the first time and a little earlier than originally planned. Looking around the bustling room, he noted that the other demokroi were all present too; their brown tunics sticking out from among the blue robes of the congressors. Naivard though was not present. A magistrate's clerk's status was too low to be in attendance here.

Zethun didn't like waiting. It gave him an unfamiliar feeling of tension. Furthermore, it gave him too much chance to overthink what he was about to do. After all, Lord Oprion Aethelgard would soon be arriving and the extra presence of the demokroi suggested that what he had to say was of some importance. Moreover, it was when they had been summoned to this meeting that Hoban had told Zethun quietly that one of his spies had made a discovery, though he did not divulge what it was as Oprion's messenger had insisted that they follow him to the Congressate Hall immediately. All Zethun knew was that Hoban had discreetly gone into his house to fetch something before they left. Even when they were in the Congressate Hall itself, when Zethun asked what had been discovered, Hoban had nervously declined to say anything direct, apparently for fear of someone overhearing and taking something out of context. All he had said was that they needed to speak with Oprion before he made his speech. Zethun wondered what it was that Hoban was being so secretive about. He thought of making small talk with the other politicians as they milled about, slowly migrating to their seats.

A stupid idea, he thought. They'd notice something was up. Finally, he felt a tap on his shoulder.

'He's coming,' said Hoban.

Zethun followed Hoban out of the large wooden double doors and closed them behind him. The gaudily-dressed Lord Oprion was striding towards them, followed by two Verusantian lance guardsmen.

'Lord Aethelgard,' said Hoban, with a bow of his head. 'I wonder if you would permit young Zethun and me to have a quiet word with you before you enter the hall?'

'If you must. But, I hope this is going to be a useful expenditure of my time, Congressor Salanath,' he said loudly, while still some distance away. 'I have barely moments.'

Hoban bowed his head and Zethun followed suit.

'Do not worry, my Lord, we will not keep you long,' said Hoban, as Oprion stopped before them.

'I wanted an audience with you because we have information. We believe that it is vital that it reaches your ears,' said Hoban.

'Of that I am sure. As it happens I too have interesting news, but I will leave that for my speech,' said Oprion. He turned to his two bodyguards. 'Guard the entrance of the building.'

He waited until the guards were out of earshot.

'Now that we are alone, you can tell me what matter can be so pressing as to delay me addressing the Congressate and doing the king's duty,' Oprion said, giving Zethun a suspicious look.

'We have made certain discoveries that call the new leadership of this kingdom into question,' Hoban said.

'Speak plainly, but be careful. That sounded a lot like treason,' said Oprion curtly.

'We have nothing to fear now,' Hoban said. 'As it is clear that under this new king a person need not have committed treason to be arrested for it. Our discoveries show us that right from the start, the noblest of ladies did suffer such a fate. Exiled for the most grievous of crimes and yet she committed none. I'm sure I need not tell you of whom I speak, my Lord.'

Zethun was confused. Where was Hoban going with this? Oprion looked momentarily lost for words as if he'd been caught off guard.

'A woman known very well to you,' Hoban pressed. Zethun could see why Hoban had been so nervous about revealing what he had intercepted. Whatever it was must have had some connection with Princess Silrith. Why had Hoban not told him what it was? Zethun hoped that it had only been a recent discovery and there had not been time.

'Yes, I am well aware of the woman in question,' said Oprion. 'Yet my position is precarious. As I said, I too have news. I have recently received some rather interesting letters from two of the most powerful men in the world. Naturally, they were for the king, but were read on his behalf by me.'

'Yet your pair now becomes a triumvirate,' said Hoban, pulling out a letter from within his sleeve. Its seal was broken and it seemed it had been strapped to his arm with a leather belt. He handed it to Oprion, who read it and something in his face lightened momentarily, then hardened again as he read on.

'You recognise the hand?' Hoban asked.

'I do not.'

'Oh I think you do, my Lord,' said Hoban.

'It's clearly a forgery,' said Oprion evasively, avoiding eye contact.

'Even allowing for the possibility that it might have been dictated,' said Hoban. 'You must at least recognise its voice. This was intercepted by one of my associates. You can imagine our surprise when we discovered that this secret letter was intended for your eyes.'

'There is nothing conspiratorial here. You can see, can you not, that this is a letter requesting assistance for Princess Silrith's rebellion? Assistance I have no intention of giving.'

Rumours of Princess Silrith's presence at a rebellion in the south had been rife recently, but nobody quite seemed to know how much was true.

'Even to your childhood friend?' asked Hoban.

'Even to her.'

'I saw how your expression changed when you saw evidence to suggest that she still lives,' said Zethun, trying to look like he knew about this before. 'You don't believe that she murdered her father, do you?'

'Don't you?' Oprion countered. 'Or what about you, Congressor Salanath? What do you really think?' Oprion advanced on Hoban, attempting to intimidate him.

'There are bigger things at play here than what I think,' Hoban said. 'And one of them is the answer to the question of why the princess clearly thinks that there is a chance you will help her.'

'And I will answer that question by burning this letter,' Oprion said coldly, tucking the letter into his tunic.

'I'm sure the king will understand,' said Hoban. 'I certainly hope he does. I only wanted to provide you with this information before you speak with the Congressate, my Lord. I just hope that nobody else made a copy before the letter reached me.'

'I support the king and no other,' Oprion said.

'The people do not support him, my Lord,' said Zethun. 'You know that.'

'Yes, but do not think that I have failed to realise that you have been directly involved in swinging public opinion against the king, Zethun. Yet, alas, there is nothing I can do to help you or Princess Silrith. I am a servant of the king,' Oprion said curtly.

'My public appearances have simply encouraged the people to express their anger at this new king's treatment of them,' Zethun said. 'I have reminded them that they do not have to live in a world where they are expected to lay down their lives for people who repay them by taking their lands. But even they know that this can never happen when even the man at the very top attained his status through trickery, greed, and deception. How can there be justice and honour under the rule of such a man?'

Zethun wasn't sure where he had found the bravery to utter such risk-laden words and a tense pause hung in the air for a moment.

'There is nothing I can do,' Oprion stated quietly.

'Is that an enforced position or a stance you have chosen to take?' Zethun asked.

'There is always something that people with your wealth and position can do,' said Hoban. 'Especially when their actions would be seen to be honourable ones.'

'The recent rioting should serve as proof that the people must be listened to,' Hoban went on. 'The discovery of any proof that Princess Silrith lives will only add to this. I am no royalist. That is well known these days, but better a benevolent monarch than a tyrant. She was kind to the people and that made her popular, which makes them resent their recent treatment by the king all the more. They are dangerous when united in one cause. Do you want them to see you as a weak leader who follows wherever the pendulum of power swings, forsaking even his dearest friends? Or would you prefer them to see you as a champion of honour and chivalry who stands for what is right and doesn't take his orders from a man who believes that his position of power is his given to him by his god? Is it really more likely that they'll support you when you serve a man that suppresses them or a woman who would liberate them?'

Taken aback by this verbal onslaught, Oprion visibly brooded on this for a moment. His face had gone a slight shade of pink and he was sweating a little. Clearly Zethun was right in his assessment and this man was not as strong as he was attempting to look.

'Alright,' Oprion said. He paused to think for a moment, then his face lightened as if he'd had an idea.

'Look, gentlemen,' he stated in a much calmer tone than previously. 'I can see that what we are discussing here is of great importance, but here and now is neither the time nor the place.'

Zethun opened his mouth to protest, but Oprion carried on anyway.

'Why don't you both dine with me at the palace later?' he said with a smile so large that it had to be fake. An awkward silence fell over them.

'Of course, my Lord,' said Hoban slowly. 'That would be most agreeable.'

'Of course,' added Zethun.

'Excellent,' said Oprion with a sickening turn of over-politeness. 'Now if you'll excuse me, gentlemen, I have a speech to make. Guards!'

Turning his body sideways he moved between Zethun and Hoban, who watched as he walked to the double doors. He waited as his bodyguards caught up and opened the doors for him, then turned round to face Hoban and Zethun. With his head, he indicted for them to go through ahead of him. The three of them entering together would look strange. Once inside the busy hall, again surrounded by impatient noise, Zethun and Hoban took their seats as they waited for Oprion to follow.

'That letter wasn't really written by Princess Silrith was it?' Zethun asked.

'No, I had to make a gamble. I decided that if Silrith really is enough of a threat to King Jostan then she'll have realised that writing a letter to a wealthy ally is worth the risk of discovery. I dare say a letter like this exists if the rumours of her escape are true. I got Capaea to write that one though. It's amazing what information rich ladies will confide in their maids.'

'Gentlemen, I present to you his Grace, the noble Lord Oprion Aethelgard, Governor of the province of Hazgorata.'

Zethun and Hoban's conversation was interrupted by the declaration made by one of Oprion's bodyguards, both of whom had now entered the room. In perfect unison they produced their bugles and played a fanfare as Oprion entered, looking rather burdened now.

He cast an uncertain glance at the speaker. Zethun watched as the old man tapped his staff on the floor three times and said 'Lord Oprion Aethelgard will now address the Congressate.'

'My fellow congressors,' said Oprion, in a tone that completely lacked even the slightest hint of confidence or charisma, as all around him took their seats.

'I find myself with a decision to make,' he went on. 'But the important thing that we all must remember is that normally the king would be here to make the final decision on what we do now. As it is, we do not have that luxury. We must try to do what is best for Bennvika and in so doing we must try to make sure we avoid compromising the king's position.'

Oprion's body language was utterly rigid, with his movement limited to the occasional hand gesture; his feet rooted to the ground.

'There are two letters that I believe should be brought to the Congressate's attention,' he went on. 'Both were intended for the king, but as I said, in his absence, we must step in. The first is from the King of Medrodor. Our friend King Spurvan has written to confirm his approval of our king's proposed marriage to the Dowager Queen Accutina. He says that he is pleased that the alliance with Bennvika will continue and that he looks forward to attending the wedding ceremony in due course.' He paused briefly as a murmur rippled through the crowded group of ageing politicians.

'What is of concern,' Oprion said in a raised voice after a moment. 'Is the content of the second letter. It would appear that the Verusantian Emperor, Graggasteidus, has cast his evil gaze over this kingdom. In his letter, he asks why our king hasn't formally recognised him as his liege lord.' There was an audible intake of breath from all around.

'It also appears,' said Oprion, raising his voice to be heard above the dissenting clamour. 'That the king has a spy in his midst, as the letter goes on to demand an explanation of why he has chosen a marriage alliance with Medrodor.'

'This is exactly what the king assured us wouldn't happen!' called out one congressor, painfully getting to his feet. His outburst didn't seem to fit with his image, with his withered skin and vulture-like features. 'Do you say he didn't plan this all along? Or if he didn't, how can we trust that he is in control of our nation's fate?'

'How dare you question our king's ability to rule,' Oprion blustered. 'I believe that it is the emperor who is making demands to which he is not entitled. Bennvika must not bow down to his demands. The alliance with Medrodor will remain intact.'

'What if the emperor attempts to force his will upon us?' called out another congressor.

'Then any course of action will be for the king to decide on.' It was a weak answer.

'How can we hope to defend ourselves if the king has the army in the south?' came another dissenting voice.

'Any drastic course of action will be for the king to decide on,' Oprion said again as the exasperated crowd began to quieten. 'The question is, do we deem the threat serious enough for us to recall him in order for him to deal with this?' Oprion said. A few continued to jeer at him. He'd lost his audience. Zethun looked on quietly amongst all the raised voices. This was almost painful to watch.

'It may be that the king returns sooner than planned.' Evidently, Oprion was trying a different tack.

'His original target may have been the Hentani,' he went on. 'But through the existence of a third letter, I can confirm that the rumours are true. Princess Silrith did escape her captors and is at large in the south, where the king has besieged her at Rildayorda.'

Hoban had not mentioned the location, but Rildayorda was the name that had kept coming up on the rumour mill.

'So the king lied to us about his true intentions?' Congressor Dongrath called out.

'No,' Oprion responded firmly. 'There was a change of scenario.'

Many congressors audibly scoffed at this.

'Now,' Oprion continued. 'We can only presume that the siege is progressing well, as the king has not asked for extra troops. However, it is possible that he may. If this comes to pass, we cannot send more. I propose that we advise him of the emperor's letter, so that he may adapt his strategy in case of invasion.'

'Does he plan to continue the campaign against the Hentani after Rildayorda is taken?' another congressor asked. 'How are we to defend the city with just a few thousand troops against the Verusantian legions if the emperor comes?'

'I do not doubt that if that happens the king will already have returned to Kriganheim with the army,' Oprion said.

'A tired and weary army,' called out another congressor. 'And what happens if the emperor seizes the king's Verusantian territories? He will have no access to his own riches. He'll exhaust the funds in the royal treasury and then he'll want your money, my Lord Aethelgard.'

'Then I will have the power to ensure that he uses it wisely,' Oprion replied, visibly sweating.

'I don't expect that he'd wait for you to give it to him, my Lord,' said Hoban, standing. 'I rather think it would be an order, on pain of death. Being a Kazabrus, our king is so wealthy that he's never had to manage an economy before, but that's what he'll have to do if he were to lose access to his Verusantian province. In short, if Bruskannia is taken from him by the emperor, it will only be a matter of time before the king's campaigns and extravagancies bankrupt Bennvika.'

'We'll be ruined,' another congressor moaned.

'More importantly, we'll be ripe for invasion,' said Hoban. 'Just as my esteemed colleague Congressor Tavigradd already alluded to. What is your response to this scenario, my Lord?'

Hoban sat down again. Oprion's face was crimson and he was sweating profusely, Zethun noticed, despite the distance.

'Even in the unlikely scenario of that happening,' Oprion replied. 'I have every confidence that with our northern army, supported by our allies, the Medrodorians, would be a more than sufficient force to repel the Verusantians. Even if they were to attack now we could keep them at bay long enough for the king to return with the main army. Furthermore, I am sure that if we were to suffer such an attack, the Etrovansians too would feel threatened enough for them to come to our aid. We need not panic.'

This man is both a coward and a naïve fool, yet assurance of his cooperation is still needed, thought Zethun. Hoban had done his part by publicly putting him under pressure, adding to that which was already upon him. Now it was time to win his favour through assistance.

314

Zethun stood. Some congressors looked angered by the sight. There was an unwritten rule that even on the occasions when they were invited into the Congressate Hall, the demokrois should be seen and not heard unless they were publicly instructed to do otherwise by the Speaker. However, Zethun was in no mood to heed that rule.

'Noble congressors,' Zethun said. 'Is it not the case that we are putting my Lord Aethelgard in an impossible position? Any quarrels you have about money will soon pale into insignificance. We have little time, so we must use it wisely. The emperor hasn't yet made any direct threats, but that does not mean that his forces are not yet ready to strike. I propose that we alert the king to the situation with all haste, but we assure him that the matter is in hand. Meanwhile, we raise a temporary army from the remaining local population and for those who are worried about the cost, we can limit this by having all the professional soldiers here in the city on hand to train the recruits. That will include the king's Verusantian lance guardsmen, just to assuage any worries he may have about this.'

So long as they felt protected, the common people wouldn't care who won at Rildayorda. Once the fearful rumours of the Verusantians spread, they'd support anyone who marched the remains of their army north to claim Kriganheim and protect it from invasion. If Jostan won, then that would be the expected result and if Silrith won, then if she had any sense then she'd cast herself in the role of liberator rather that oppressor and in the uncertainty and the upheaval, the hope of a republic lived on. Either way, the arming of more of the local population would give them a greater chance of fighting for their own destiny. As Zethun had expected, there were many grumbles from the congressors, but none openly voiced an opinion against him. It seemed they were more scared of the Verusantian Emperor than they were of the king.

'Does this meet with your approval, my Lord?' said Zethun.

Oprion looked slightly abashed. He was probably annoyed that his thunder had been stolen.

'Yes, yes it does,' he said eventually.

All turned to look at the speaker, who was seated some way behind Oprion. The withered old man hit his staff against the tiled floor three times before saying, 'The notion has been proposed, now let it be judged. All those in favour say aye.'

'Aye!'

'All those against say nay.' A few voices answered, but in negligible numbers.

'The ayes have it.'

A cheer filled the room, yet what Zethun noticed most of all was the hate-filled look with which Oprion now fixed him. The man's emotions seemed all over the place. Surely he wasn't stable enough for such a powerful position? After all, Zethun had just given him support and he had clearly taken it as an affront. This was a very vain and stupid man indeed.

Zethun was just about to tell Hoban about this as they left the Congressate Hall and headed towards the steps that led down into the street when something stopped him. He had noticed the rather slight form of a young woman buying food at the market that filled the crowded city forum. She was wearing a faded blue and white dress. But he knew her face, even though he'd only caught a momentary glimpse of it before she turned away again.

'Hoban,' Zethun said. 'Isn't that Capaea?'

'Capaea?' A passing Oprion interrupted before Hoban could reply. 'That's Lyzina. The queen's maid. Guards, arrest that woman!'

The girl heard the order and instantly turned and ran, dropping her basket of purchases. The Verusantian guards ran after her and four more soldiers of the Bennvikan divisios appeared from either side of the building and gave chase.

'That girl knows something about the murder of King Lissoll. I'm sure of it,' Oprion said.

'What are you going to do with her?' Hoban asked.

'Arrest her and question her, of course,' said Oprion. 'What does it look like I'm doing? My soldiers have been searching for her ever since she robbed me.'

'Robbed you of what?' asked Hoban.

'Oh, just some money,' said Oprion unconvincingly. 'But it was quite a lot. It was the very day I arrived at the palace too. It was almost like she knew something of the murder and wanted to get out and buy her way on to a ship to a foreign land before I realised her involvement.'

'Well as far as I can see, your troops haven't caught her yet,' Hoban chuckled. 'But once they do, I suggest you allow young Zethun here to have an audience with her.'

'And why should I do that?' said Oprion.

'I guarantee his approach will get her to speak faster than any of your torturers,' Hoban said. 'Wouldn't that make a fine impression on the king when he returns to find that where once there was a threat posed by a missing person who may carry dangerous information, there is now none.'

Zethun turned to look at the two men.

'That certainly wouldn't do me any harm,' Oprion said thoughtfully, surveying Zethun. 'But tell me, what would be so different?'

'It's simple,' said Zethun. 'I know what the common people want. Therefore I know how to make them feel that doing something for me is worth their while. I guarantee that I can get her to divulge any information she hides, so long as her life is not forfeit. We could exile her or something instead.'

'I cannot promise that. If she implicates Princess Silrith, then that goes in favour of the king and she will be free to go, but if she implicates the king or anyone else, she will hang, understand?'

Zethun's heart sank.

'Yes, my Lord.'

'Ah, you see. They have her,' said Oprion, pointing to where, through the crowd, Lyzina could be seen struggling to break free from the grip of two of Oprion's men.

'You,' Oprion called to the nearest guard. 'Have her brought to the dungeons beneath the king's palace. We shall question her there.'

Chapter 22

Zethun was surprised by Oprion's jovial manner by the time the three of them arrived at the palace. Others might have actually believed it to be genuine, despite their earlier conversation about the letter. Zethun wasn't fooled though. Oprion was trying just that bit too hard.

'We shall see to the prisoner soon,' he had said on their arrival. 'But first I insist that we dine together. I must introduce you to my family.'

He was the perfect host, making sure Zethun and Hoban always had their plates and cups full, while generally conducting himself as if the palace was his own. Over lunch they met his Medrodorian wife, Lady Haarksa, who was a haughty woman, wearing a demure white gown. She looked like she was approaching forty, making her at least ten years older than her husband. The left side of her face was marked by two large bruises, which she had clearly tried to cover with make-up. Zethun wondered what had caused those.

Also present were Oprion and Haarksa's four daughters, who ranged in age from infancy to around eight. There was also a blonde girl in her teens there, named Jorikssa, who was Haarksa's daughter from her previous marriage. Zethun noticed a distinct lack of affection between her and Oprion when she was introduced and even the chemistry between the girl and her mother was rather lacking.

Hoban engaged in the situation much more than Zethun, who felt that exchanging pleasantries over lunch was a rather bizarre activity to be engaging in right before questioning a prisoner.

'Oprion and I have been married nine years now,' said Haarksa, in the harsh, guttural tones of her highly accented Bennvikan.

She's definitely from the northeast of Medrodor, thought Zethun. It was unmistakable.

'My first husband died in a hunting accident,' she went on. 'Fortunately for me, when I came to Bennvika with Jorikssa, Oprion was looking for a wife.'

'Good timing for me, I'd say,' said Oprion, but his mock affection towards her wasn't fooling anyone. 'Anyway, my father was always in debt,'

318

he continued. 'Everyone knew it. That's what I inherited. But in finding my dear Haarksa I not only saved the family estate but made it what it is today – the richest and grandest in the country.'

Zethun didn't believe that simply gaining money through a dowry was much to show off about and he was hating sitting and socialising with these people who talked about poverty but had no idea what the word really meant, unlike much of the population. All he could think about was that Oprion clearly didn't have the strength that Jostan did and that for the sake of the people, if nothing could be done to make him turn against the king, then something must be done to destabilise his position before Jostan returned. Once some concessions had been made, in theory, it would be easier to gain more. But how could they get that first one? He thought back to the anger he felt after his proposal regarding the harvest was rejected by Jostan. He hoped that Capaea, or Lyzina, or whatever her real name was, might know something that would be of use; some leverage with which to force the crown to loosen its stranglehold on power. Certainly, Oprion had been very keen to have her arrested. But why? The idea that it was because she stole some money and may possibly have information on the murder of King Lissoll didn't seem enough. Oprion had seemed too excited by the capture of a lowly maid for it to be just that. Zethun's thoughts were interrupted as a Verusantian guard entered the room and spoke to Oprion.

'Thank you, Captain,' he said, before turning to Zethun and Hoban. 'The prisoner is ready to be questioned. Shall we proceed?'

'Of course,' said Hoban. 'It was an honour to meet you, Lady Haarksa,' he added.

'And you too Congressor Salanath and young Zethun. I hope we can become better acquainted in the future,' she replied. Zethun was momentarily annoyed at her patronising tone, but then he noticed a nervousness come over Hoban's face as he walked away from her. This puzzled him, but he didn't think anyone else had noticed.

They followed Oprion and the guard to the ground floor of the palace and then down some more steps into the palace dungeon.

'Normally prisoners are of course kept away from the palace,' Oprion was saying. 'But if it is a palace servant that has committed a crime, I'm told the usual procedure is to conduct the questioning here. We have a similar

319

room beneath my own home. A decent torturer can be so expensive. You don't want to fork out all that money only to have some wretched prisoner bleat at the first sight of a hot poker. No, always best to start here doing the questioning yourself and avoid that sort of expense.'

Zethun hated Oprion's callous attitude. Clearly, this man prioritised his money above all things. As they approached the bottom of the stone staircase that led deep underground, he saw four large metal doors, one of which had a guard outside, dressed like a militiaman but wearing a red sash.

'Unlock the door,' Oprion told the second guard.

'Yes, my Lord.'

'You two go in first,' Oprion told Zethun and Hoban. 'My presence may affect what she says. Go in there and see what you can get her to reveal. Tell her that I mean her no harm and send a guard up to fetch me if you deem it necessary.'

He ushered them through the door, along with the sash-wearing guard, shutting it behind them. Zethun found himself in a small, windowless room with three cells at the far side. Two of them were empty, but in the middle one was Capaea, or Lyzina, or whoever she was. The young woman had a black eye and was covered in purple bruises. Her hair was a mess and her clothes were reddened with blood and had been ripped as if she'd been assaulted sexually as well as violently. Yet her stare was still full of strength and anger.

'There's no need to torture me further,' she said firmly. 'As you see, I have already suffered unnecessarily at the hands of your brutes.'

Zethun wondered how long her strength would hold.

'Why did you run if you are so prepared to give away information?' Zethun asked.

'Because I would have preferred to reach safety of course,' Capaea spat. 'Yet given that you now hold me prisoner, there is no point me withholding anything. I'm not stupid.'

Zethun couldn't fault her logic. Her only hope now was to give all the information she could and hope that it resulted in her release. Otherwise, her chances were slim.

'We have been tasked with questioning you, but I assure you it is not us who hold you prisoner,' Zethun said. He expected a reply, but Capaea's only response was to look from one man to the other with a searching, distrustful gaze.

'How did you recognise Lord Oprion?' Zethun asked. 'It would appear that when we last met, you lied about your identity and lied again when you said that the maid belonging to Queen Accutina named Lyzina had been missing since the night Princess Silrith was arrested. What do you say to that now?'

Capaea gave a cold chuckle.

'Well, to be honest, most of the information I gave you that day was false. You might say that I was attempting to hide in plain sight.'

'So when did you really escape?' Zethun asked.

'Shortly after Lord Oprion arrived in Kriganheim,' she said. 'I am as good as dead already, so I might as well tell you everything. After all, who doesn't love a martyr? When I told you my name is Capaea, I was telling the truth. But there never was a lady's maid called Lyzina belonging to the Dowager Queen, though Lord Oprion couldn't have known that. Lyzina never existed. I simply needed to be her for a few minutes after stealing the letter in order to get him to find out about the theft. You see, if he begins to fret about who has it, then he will inadvertently begin to make himself look guilty of the things insinuated by the letter's contents, giving more weight to the evidence we have. This, in turn, makes it easier to disgrace him and dispose of him and if people find the strength to depose a lord by manipulating the king into removing him, then maybe they can make further gains and possibly even remove the king altogether. You see, this is all for the good of the people. That is what you claim to fight for, is it not? How strange it is that you stand here questioning me when we fight for the same cause. I know of your words with Lord Rintta at his feast. It is plain to see that Lord Oprion Aethelgard is the same threat to the rights of the common people as he is. They're all the same.'

Zethun was struggling to find fault with her argument.

'So you are a spy fighting for the people?' he asked, giving himself time for thought.

'Of course and my sponsor fights for the same cause. He tasked me with the mission and arranged everything for Taevuka and myself. He even sent his henchmen to find us and get us away from the palace, didn't you Congressor Salanath?'

'What?' Zethun asked, confused, turning on Hoban.

'Now Zethun, I was going to tell you as soon as Capaea and Taevuka were out of the country,' Hoban said with a worried look on his face. 'When Princess Silrith was arrested, I visited her in her cell before she was taken away. I knew that she had to be restored to the throne before Jostan could start killing any Bennvikans who would not submit to his god. We both knew that the next time Jostan left Kriganheim for any long period, then as Governor of Hazgorata, it was highly possible that Lord Oprion would be made regent in his absence. With that in mind, the princess told me of a love letter sent by Oprion to her, which she had kept in her bedchamber. If I could gain access to that, I could destabilize Oprion's grip on power while the king is away by insinuating that the king can't trust him. The very idea would weaken them both. From there we could have gained control of the city and launched a full-scale rebellion against the crown. The original plan had been to first steal the letter and then make sure he learned of the theft at a time of our choosing. Unfortunately, Lord Oprion arrived a little sooner than anticipated and when the letter was stolen, he was already here in Kriganheim. We tried to spin things to our advantage, as Capaea described and that was when he sent-'

'-Yes, I am aware that he sent the city into lockdown. I was there with you at the time. What I want to know is why you did all this behind my back,' said Zethun.

Hoban sighed. At least he looked like he felt some level of guilt. Yet Zethun made a mental note not to trust him so easily in future.

'I felt that the fewer the number of people who knew about it the better. We managed to smuggle Taevuka out of the city by lowering her over the edge of the walls with a rope,' said Hoban. 'I have no idea what happened to her after that. The plan was for Capaea to escape the same way, but she was spotted and only had time to evade the guards by running back into the city. After that, there were more guards placed on the walls and escape wasn't possible, so she had to remain in my house until such time as the lockdown is lifted.'

'I see. So are your loyalties with Princess Silrith, or with the common people?' Zethun asked angrily.

'Both. She is as much of a philanthropist as I.'

'Then I still don't understand why you kept this from me. Did Naivard know about this too?'

'He did not,' said Hoban.

'What exactly would you have told me if we hadn't been where we are now? The whole story, or just part of it?' asked Zethun.

'All of it of course.'

'And what about when we questioned Capaea the first time, with Taevuka, when you knew them to be your spies? I suppose every bit of information they gave us was a red herring wasn't it? Like she just said.'

He pointed to Capaea, who had come right up to the bars and was holding them, with her face pressed between two of them, grinning coldly as the two men argued. Clearly she was beginning to take some perverse enjoyment out of the situation.

'Look,' said Hoban. 'I have used Capaea for many missions in the past and I met with her shortly after Princess Silrith's arrest. I did what I did for the greater good. I know you feel betrayed but-'

'-Betrayed doesn't even cover it. How could you keep this from me this whole time?'

Hoban didn't answer but simply shook his head apologetically as if he couldn't find the words.

Zethun gave Hoban a last cold stare before turning back to face Capaea, who now feigned an innocent expression.

'So, Capaea, tell me of this love letter that you stole that Lord Oprion might find so incriminating?' Zethun sighed, breaking the silence. The edges of Capaea's lips curled into a smile of stone.

'Princess Silrith received it only weeks before her arrest it seems. Apparently, he was prepared to leave his wife for her; remove his wife even, then claim her fortune and marry Silrith, but it seems his feelings were not reciprocated.'

'When Capaea brought the letter to me, its seal was broken,' said Hoban. 'Which proves that she must have read it. Anyway, I know that she did. She told me personally. She'd already seen Lord Oprion when I visited her in her cell. She evidently anticipated that he would need to be blackmailed if there was to be any chance of stopping him giving his whole-hearted support to the king.'

'And you think he made his intentions clear at an earlier date and was persisting via a love letter after an initial rejection?' asked Zethun.

'Yes,' Capaea replied.

'So if his wife found out, a divorce would cost him his fortune and his estate. He might have even been found guilty of plotting to have Lady Haarksa murdered,' added Hoban.

'And now, for him, the stakes are even higher,' Zethun said with a sigh, though making sure to keep a curt tone. 'If the king found out about this letter, our friend Lord Oprion would very likely be seen as having allegiances with Princess Silrith. Something King Jostan will see as treason. It is obvious, therefore, why it might be fear of execution that causes Lord Oprion to be so desperate to recover the letter and destroy it.'

'And ever since I took it, he has been desperate to find it. I suppose it was only a matter of time before his troops reached the congressor's house,' said Capaea. 'That's why I was in the forum. I needed to get word to you.'

'Why didn't you just wait until I arrived home?' Hoban asked.

'I couldn't stay,' said Capaea. 'When Lord Oprion's soldiers came the first time and didn't find me, I thought it unlikely they'd disturb a congressor's house twice. But they must have had a tip-off. When they came the second time I had no chance to hide. I had to kill them. Then I had to find you and tell you before they were missed.'

Hoban nodded.

'So where is the letter now? The real one. Do you still have it?' asked Zethun. Before either of them could answer, the door swung open and crashed against the wall as Oprion swept in.

'Move over,' he said. 'I've changed my mind. I shall lead the questioning of the traitor.'

'My Lord, why-' Hoban said, but he was hushed by Oprion's dismissive wave. Zethun was stunned by Oprion's erratic behaviour. If Hoban and Capaea's plan was to make him look guilty of treachery through his sheer paranoia, it was working.

'Congressor Salanath,' said Oprion. 'You almost convinced me to put this, an issue that not only concerns my entire estate, but is also a matter of national security, in the care of you two men. Almost. But then I thought, *what would the king think if something was missed; some important piece of information that you neglected to tell me, maybe?* Maybe that would suit you? I'd rather not find out what the king would have to say about that. He could ruin me, or worse and all because of you. No, I will lead this myself and I will tolerate no objections.'

Zethun was shocked by this outburst, let alone Oprion's change of heart. This man was so changeable and seemed to care about nothing except for himself. Oprion asked one of the guards what had been said so far. The man told him everything, though the timing of the interruption suggested to Zethun that he'd been outside the door all the time, wanting to test their loyalty. It seemed there would be no hiding of any information; no cards Zethun could hold back against the nobleman.

Oprion looked surprisingly pleased with himself.

'A letter? I knew it. I knew you weren't to be trusted,' he said, pointing at Hoban. 'The letter, of course, is a forgery. You, Hoban Salanath, thought you could make a play for power, didn't you? You thought you could pay a maid to plant a letter allegedly sent by me to the traitor, Princess Silrith, so that when it was found I would be punished and you would be rewarded. Maybe you would even gain my estate and wealth? Even though all the while it was you who had the letter written. But your compassion got the better of you. When the plan started to go against you, your lack of ruthlessness prevented you from seeing it through. Your sense of guilt moved you to take this spy into your home. Why else would you protect her?'

'Because some of us have a sense of common decency, my Lord, and do not think only of their money. You know the letter is genuine and the thought of the king seeing it fills you with fear,' Hoban said, affecting a look of strength, unconvincing as it was.

'Liar. My concern was over the alleged theft of the Amulet of Hazgorata,' Oprion went on, unabated. 'I'm sure the Dowager Queen has it but people will get in such a panic about these things. Some people are never happy unless they can spook the common folk with talk of poor omens.'

'Then given that you seem so confident that this letter is a forgery,' interjected Capaea. 'How do you explain your erratic behaviour right now? Why are you so paranoid? We know the Amulet is not missing. Our other spy in the palace saw the Dowager Queen take it with her, while planning to claim that it was found in Hentani territory and knowing its alleged recovery would make the king look like a hero, just as the Hentani have feared for years.'

'Silence, prisoner,' Oprion snarled. 'The king's plans are not for me to question. As for the letter, regardless of who wrote it...'

He paused for effect.

'You're holding it in order to control me aren't you?' he said. 'That's your next move, isn't it? That's your slanderous plan to force me to help Princess Silrith back to the throne or to destroy me if I refuse. Your suggestion that you are fighting for the rights of the common people is all just a façade. Well, it seems you've missed your chance to act on your plans.'

'This is absurd,' scoffed Hoban. 'Zethun, you must be able to see that the people's rights were central to our actions. Reinstating the princess as queen just seemed more likely to succeed than attempting to abolish the monarchy. Surely you understand that?'

But Zethun didn't know what to think. Hoban had already been dishonest with him about his knowledge of Capaea's true identity and lies often did breed more lies. But then, had Hoban been justified in being economical with the truth? Was it all for the greater good?

'Well, Congressor Salanath,' said Oprion. 'I would say I have grounds to have both you and the prisoner executed. You have conspired to manipulate the king into ordering my execution, accusing me of such despicable treachery as this. And there's more. It may interest you to know that not a single one of your esteemed colleagues in the Congressate could vouch for your whereabouts on the day I entered Kriganheim. I realise we met on the following day, but the day itself? Who knows? Well, I have a theory. A surprisingly fleet-footed old man stopped me that day and in rather noble tones expressed his political views in a so-called *peaceful protest*. His ideas were rather similar to yours and he attempted to turn the local plebeians into a lynch mob set on my demise. Now, I believe it fits that a man who might try to get me executed by the king may also try to have me killed by the mob? Can you deny the accusation, Congressor?'

Zethun looked directly at Hoban, stunned at what he was hearing. He believed passionately in doing whatever it took to fight for the rights of the people, but why would Hoban make direct attempts to have an individual killed without telling Zethun, whatever the potential benefits for the population? But then, clearly, Hoban had another agenda. Had he been using Zethun all this time? Could it be true that Hoban only wanted further advancement for himself and that he would have got rid of Zethun the moment he no longer needed him? He didn't know what to think. All he knew was that right now Hoban did not look him in the eye, but simply pointed his fiery gaze at Oprion. It was an expression Zethun had never seen on the old congressor's face.

'I'd say that's confession enough. Wouldn't you agree Zethun?' Oprion said. 'He can't deny it. His pride prevents him from doing so. It seems there is more to your friend Congressor Salanath than meets the eye.'

Zethun said nothing. The unexpected revelations by and about Hoban had thrown him completely off track. Was it only what Hoban had admitted that was real, or was he still being economical with the truth?

'You call us traitors,' spat Capaea. 'Yet not only are you a traitor for serving the usurper King Jostan, but you are twice a traitor because you refuse to undo what you have already done. Yet you could easily do so by listening to us and doing what is best for Bennvika.'

'What are you suggesting? I hope it isn't what I think it is,' said Oprion.

'It was King Jostan and Dowager Queen Accutina who murdered King Lissoll,' she said. 'If you will not revolt against him, we will revolt against you and in time, against him also. Be it by our hands or his, you will die if you resist us.'

'Fierce words from someone inside a prison cell,' Oprion chuckled.

'You know she speaks the truth, my Lord,' thundered Hoban. Zethun's anger was quickly dissipating now, seeing a conviction in Hoban and Capaea's faces that he had rarely seen in anyone else. He wanted to add his argument to theirs and stand up to Oprion, but that would only get him arrested too. There had to be another way.

'The rumours of the disappearance of the Amulet of Hazgorata surfaced around the time of King Lissoll's murder,' Hoban continued. 'Open your mind, my Lord. What if it was the king's purpose to plant the rumour and then deny it until the right time? Maybe he meant for us to believe that it was missing, when actually he knew where it was all along? My Lord, while Capaea was only posing as Lyzina for a matter of minutes, I had another spy whose whereabouts I now know not, posing as a low-ranking maid for weeks. She heard the chatter of the staff. It was most interesting.'

Oprion paled, looking intimidated for the first time.

Is it possible that he might still capitulate? thought Zethun, feeling very much like an onlooker.

'Yes,' Capaea chimed in. 'She told us the rumour was that King Jostan had pretended to be a lover to Silrith's maid, Afayna, the one they executed. He even lay with her to gain her trust. The rumour was that he gave her the Amulet of Hazgorata, which he had been given by Queen Accutina. Our source said Afayna had been carrying it on the night of King Lissoll's death, but she wouldn't say who had given it to her. All the maids said she blushed when they asked if it was given to her by Jostan Kazabrus though. Apparently, she opened the Amulet's lid and put what she said was some weird Verusantian flavouring on the food. Complements of the Kazabrus family, she said. Now, that suggests to me that neither she nor the other maids knew that it was poison. How else would it have got on the food? If that was the poison, then it rules out Princess Silrith as a suspect, as we have no evidence to suggest that she knew that Afayna was in possession of the Amulet. Additionally, it's hardly likely that Afayna would have the reason, means or opportunity to put the poison in there off her own accord. It had to already be there in the Amulet when it was given to her. It has to be the new king that had it put in there, with the Dowager Queen's help. They murdered King Lissoll.'

Oprion glared at Capaea silently. Zethun hoped upon hope that he was giving the theory due consideration.

'You lying, treacherous little whore,' Oprion snarled. 'You think you can incriminate the king, convince me of his guilt and Princess Silrith's innocence and then use that letter to blackmail me into standing against him? Traitor.'

'My Lord,' said Zethun. 'A girl has already been executed for the crime of murdering the king. We have no need to threaten this girl with the same.'

'Oh I disagree greatly,' said Oprion. 'The ideas being spouted by this girl and her master could destabilise the entire kingdom. I say we stop the rebellion right now before it even starts by executing them both, on charges of attempting to bring down the nobility and ultimately, the king himself.'

'You may struggle to make the king see it that way once he knows of your former association with Princess Silrith, my Lord,' Hoban pointed out.

'Oh yes,' said Oprion. 'I forgot to mention. I now have the letter. My guards found it when they raided your house, Congressor Salanath. It appears you no longer have a bargaining tool.'

'Liar. Prove it. I don't believe you,' said Hoban.

'Oh and also, I killed your guards,' said Capaea, putting up her hand as if she were at school. 'The ones that came to Congressor Salanath's house.'

This girl almost looked excited to be martyred for her cause.

'There you are. The letter is still out there. Try burning it now,' Hoban said.

'All in good time,' Oprion conceded, visibly forcing a smile. Then his face lit up as if an idea just hit him. 'You will see it again on the day of your execution.'

'Coward,' said Hoban. 'That, of course, gives you time to write a forgery that is lacking in any incriminating evidence.'

Oprion laughed.

'Congressor, I believe you should be more worried about the letter I will write to the king, telling him of my discoveries. After that, he will see that I am loyal only to him and so your rebellion will never happen, the death of you and your accomplice will be in vain and if Zethun here wants any sort of career after this, he will do well never to mention this letter again. Guard, I tire of this old man. Lock him away.'

The guard marched forward from the door. Zethun smarted at the insinuation that his career was of more importance to him than what really mattered, but he said nothing.

'I will go,' said Hoban in a commanding tone, stopping the guard in his tracks as he made to accost him. 'I am a martyr for my cause and I shall make my sacrifice without complaint. I shall do my duty for the people.'

Hoban turned and approached the cell next to Capaea's. The unoiled metal creaked loudly as he opened the door. He entered the cell and watched with a grim look on his face as the guard locked the door behind him.

'Such vain nobility,' Oprion laughed. 'You should learn from this, Zethun. This is how a man will be forgotten by history. You will also testify to his crimes at the execution if you know what is good for you.'

Zethun didn't say anything, but simply held Oprion's gaze.

'Bennvika will rise and throw off its so-called nobles,' Capaea shouted.

'Liberty for all,' declared Hoban. 'Liberty for all.'

'Shut up,' said Oprion.

'Liberty for all,' Hoban called again.

'You, follow me,' Oprion told Zethun.

The heavy metal door slammed behind them and the guard locked it. They could still clearly hear Hoban and Capaea shouting their enraged protests from the other side, but their position seemed hopeless now.

Why hadn't Hoban told Zethun what he was doing? Zethun was still stunned that Hoban had kept it from him. It troubled Zethun greatly to think that Hoban had been simply using him to destabilise first Oprion and then King Jostan, in the hope of creating a void so that he could place Silrith back on the throne and claim all the glory for doing so. But then, in a moment, everything fell into place and he knew exactly what he had to do. He had no idea if it had been Hoban's plan all along. Probably not, he decided. Certainly, Zethun would have dismissed it as madness if Hoban had suggested it. But now it was the only option left.

'Oh, Zethun?' Oprion said lightly. 'I forgot to say. I'm sure you may be wondering why you haven't heard from your friend Naivard for a couple of days. He's been...otherwise engaged. You must come and see him.'

With Hoban and Capaea's rhythmic shouting still echoing in the background, Zethun followed Oprion to the neighbouring room, still in the palace dungeons. The guard opened the metal door and Oprion walked inside.

'I had my suspicions about you, but he killed himself before I could get any proof out of him,' said Oprion with a hint of frustration. Zethun felt his heart turn to lead as he saw that the man to whom Oprion was referring definitely was Naivard. His body was sprawled on the floor with his head against the wall, eyes vacant and with the remnants of froth still coating his mouth as it lolled open.

'I thought you'd recognise him,' said Oprion. 'Yet he refused to testify against you. Nevertheless, it appears that your friend Congressor Salanath has used you as a tool in his treachery.'

'What was he arrested for? He's done nothing wrong,' Zethun said slowly.

'Well, his decision to kill himself suggests involvement, doesn't it?' said Oprion as they stood over Naivard's body. 'After all, protecting a traitor is as bad as committing the treachery itself. One of my guards claimed to see two men assisting a pair of girls to escape from the city by helping them climb down the walls, using a rope. One girl escaped, but the second girl and the men ran off when they realised they were seen. The guard recognised one of them as being this man when he was brought in for questioning as a result of his association with your congressor friend. That was evidence enough to arrest him and the girl and now their guilt is proven. We didn't get as far as asking who the second man is, but I'm sure we can find a way to get the noble congressor to tell us. With this man though, I was more interested in knowing what your involvement was. So, knowing that Naivard was one of Congressor Salanath's close confidants, you understand why I had to question him. He didn't give any helpful answers, but I knew he was hiding something, you see.' He gave an inane grin and raised a finger. Zethun assumed this second man must have been Braldor and he realised he hadn't seen the big henchman since their arrival at the Congressate Hall earlier that day. He made a mental note to seek him out later.

'I decided I had to be more heavy-handed. I had him arrested to be questioned under torture,' Oprion went on. 'But clearly he'd smuggled in some form of poison and you see the result.'

Zethun had to concede that, amid the shock at Naivard's fate, he was impressed and inspired by the man's bravery and foresight; his anticipation of his arrest and his determination not to break under torture.

'This was disappointing,' said Oprion. 'As I cannot now arrest you without further evidence. The Congressate won't allow it. But I promise you I will have you watched from every corner and if I have even the slightest evidence that you were involved in this I will have your head. Do we understand each other?'

'Explicitly,' said Zethun, creasing his face into a curt smile.

RILDAYORDA, BASTALF, BENNVIKA

That night, Ezrina, Jakiroc, Askorit and the other Hentani priests and priestesses crept across the temple towards Bennvikan clergymen's sleeping chambers. Ezrina again wore her emerald green robes, as did the three other priestesses, while the seven priests wore their grey attire of office. The group numbered thirteen in all and Ezrina had told each one of them of her new suspicions.

'Pick up a torch,' she told one of the priests, pointing to one of the braziers as they walked through the enormous, dimly lit square room that was the temple's main hall.

'Of course,' he said.

He lifted one of the torches out of its stand and, following the light, they descended the flight of stairs at the end of the main hall and stood outside the wooden door to the Bennvikan priests' chambers.

'Wait outside while the rest of us go in. Only come in when I call for you,' Ezrina told the priest with the torch. A priestess opened the door, making a creak that seemed incredibly loud amid the silence, at least to Ezrina's ears. She held her breath for a moment, but the only sound she heard from inside was the soft breathing of the sleeping priests. She stepped forward into the darkness of the chamber, motioning for the others to follow her, save for the man with the torch. How ironic it was, that the sleeping Bennvikans looked so peaceful. Quietly they moved to the side of a priest's bed. He was an old, bearded man wearing a simple white nightshirt and was covered by a thin, dark sheet. Ezrina decided this simple approach was supposed to be some statement of penitence to their false gods.

Another irony, she thought, given the arrogance with which they normally conducted themselves.

She made a quiet prayer, then put her hand over the man's mouth. He woke, but she reached into her robes and sliced his throat open with a knife before he could cry out. One by one, this was done to each priest and Ezrina began to enjoy bathing her hands in Bennvikan blood, savouring the moment of her people's revenge as she continued her holy work. Finally, every Bennvikan in the room was a corpse, save for one.

'Wake him,' she said, as they gathered around the final bed; that of a young, almost clean-shaven priest. The others looked at her, but their faces were hard to read in the darkness. The man was shaken awake and he cried out in fear as he saw them all gathered around him, then looked about the place and laid eyes on the blood-soaked floors and the open necks of his fellow priests. Ezrina pushed to the front and grabbed the man by his shoulders.

'Where is the Amulet of Hazgorata?' she asked. The man said nothing, clearly too frightened to form words.

'Come on, do not delay us. Tell me what I want to know and you might not join your colleagues.'

The man frantically jerked his head in all directions as he took in the bloody scene around him, whimpering.

'Where is it?' Ezrina asked slowly. The trembling priest tried to grit his chattering teeth, shut his eyes in an attempt to hide his fear as he wept and pointed to the ceiling.

'Bring the torch in here,' Ezrina called.

The torch was brought inside, lighting up the centre of the room. Ezrina gave a cold grin as she saw a deep alcove directly above them. Standing on a ledge, blindly watching over all below were two wooden statues; one of Vitrinnolf and the other of Lomatteva, both dressed for battle and raising their swords aloft. Draped around the two of them was the chain of the Amulet of Hazgorata, with the medallion itself nestling between the figures.

'Thanks be to Bertakaevey,' Ezrina said.

'You three,' she said to the two youngest Hentani priests and most junior of the priestesses, all looking barely out of childhood but with their eyes filled with a religious flare as fanatical as any. 'Go into the street and fetch stones. As many as you can. Be quick now. We must destroy those heretical idols that yet withhold the Amulet from us,' Ezrina commanded. In moments they were out of the room, clearly eager to make an impression on their new leader. Ezrina turned back to the terrified young Bennvikan priest.

'Your usefulness has been exhausted,' she said without emotion. The other priests held him down while she leant over him and covered his mouth with her hand. She looked into his eyes as she took the knife and slit his throat, enjoying the sight of his life leaving him as his blood spattered in all directions, covering her face and staining her robes as well as those of everyone around her. She wiped the blood nonchalantly from her skin, just as she had done with the roomful of priests she had killed that night and thought no more about it. Minutes later the young priestess and the two priests were back with their arms full of stones. They dropped them to the ground before their colleagues. One of them picked up a stone and made to throw it at the statues, but a bark from Jakiroc stopped him in his tracks.

'Only she who is divinely chosen may cast the first stone,' he told the younger man.

Abashed, the priest bowed and handed the stone to Ezrina. She took it and with only the slightest hesitation hurled it at the statue of Lomatteva. It struck the wooden carving fully in the face, smashing off shards so that her features were unrecognisable.

'Praise be to Bertakaevey! The false goddess is defaced and shown for the heretical idol she is!' Ezrina declared. She bent to pick up another, now joined enthusiastically by the baying group of clergymen and the Bennvikan deities were soon battered and broken under a hail of stones. Remarkably the Amulet was untouched. It was if Bertakaevey was guiding their stones away from it and on to these idols of the false gods. Picking up the largest stone she could find, Ezrina launched her projectile at the base of the weakened statue of Lomatteva. With a crack the legs gave way and the wooden structure was pitched forward, sending it crashing to the ground.

Soon the statue of Vitrinnolf was down too and as it fell Ezrina reached out a hand and plucked the Amulet from the air by its chain. The crowd lurched forward, eager to crush the statues to dust. Only Jakiroc had noticed that Ezrina now held the Amulet in her hand.

'Silence,' he called, causing the clamour to turn to a deathly stillness. All watched as Ezrina held the Amulet above her head by its chain.

'...for the Daughter of Ashes,' Jakiroc declared.

'For those ashes that made Bertakaevey's holy body are reborn to bring life to me, her holy daughter. The Daughter of Ashes is risen,' said Ezrina as she placed the Amulet around her neck. She had won it back for a second time. For the sake of her people, as long as she lived, she would never be parted from it again.

Chapter 23

The spy was impressed with Jostan's command tent. It was hard not to admit how visibly the foreigner had gone up in the world since they had last met during the diplomatic visit to Bennvika that Jostan had made over three years previously. Though he had been in Jostan's service ever since then, this was the first time they'd met in the time after that most profitable autumn.

The tent's front was open. Jostan was in the centre, looking at what must have been some sort of map or diagram on a table, or perhaps a strength report for his remaining forces after the debacle that their previous attacks had turned into. He was accompanied by Feddilyn, the black-armoured royal bodyguard who was apparently named Gormaris and a chief invicturion, whose name the spy didn't know. Clearly he had been quick to replace Aetrun. Jostan looked up from the document as the spy was searched by two further guards, one Verusantian, along with a divisioman.

'Three years of loyalty from afar and still I get searched. Maybe I should have made all those sea voyages myself and handed you my letters personally, your Majesty? Perhaps then your guards might recognise their own master's most loyal servant?'

Feddilyn looked most surprised to see him, but said nothing. Jostan's face was one of naked fury, but he contained it.

'Lord Rintta, Gormaris, Rhosgyth, leave us, if you please?' he said in a flat tone. It was not a question. He said nothing further until the others had gone; never taking his eyes off the spy, who returned his gaze, while simultaneously craning his ears to see if he could pick up anything said supposedly out of earshot that could prove useful. He was rewarded, as he heard Feddilyn speak the words 'Vinnitar, come with me. I must speak with you.' So, that was the new chief invicturion's name then, Vinnitar Rhosgyth.

'What are you doing here? Why are you not in the citadel?' Jostan demanded.

'Such a response after all this time?' the spy chuckled. 'Don't forget, we're family. You don't know what it's like in there, having to be so quiet so that people forget I'm even in their presence, making them think I'm an incompetent fool so that they don't see me as a threat; and all so that I can report back to you, cousin.'

'Don't ever call me that,' Jostan raged, but the spy was unmoved. 'We appear on the same family tree only because your mother married below her station. Even if we were close blood relatives it would not entitle you to disobey my orders. You were instructed to stay inside the citadel. There has been an attempt on my life and my wife-to-be has been murdered with King Lissoll's unborn son dispatched to the afterlife with her.'

'Yes. Don't think I hadn't noticed your strained movements, however much you try to cover them. Do not forget that this place is full of people who would take advantage of such weakness, so my assistance to you is not to be scorned.'

'I need you now and you will be rewarded appropriately if you succeed, but only as a demonstration to my supporters that their new king is a generous one, nothing more,' Jostan seethed. A cold silence fell, as the two men eyed each other in subtle challenge. It was Jostan who broke it.

'My orders will not be undermined,' he said with quiet certainty.

'I had no choice,' the spy replied, with a calmness that now coated every word. 'That peasant girl you sent me went and got herself caught. I had to come here before my cover was blown and also so that I could draw your attention to the most effective way in which I may serve you now.'

'I decide how you serve me,' Jostan said. He bashed the table with his fist but clearly instantly regretted it, attempting to cover a wince while reaching behind him to where the pain had clearly come from. This was not lost on the spy of course.

'It appears they really did leave their mark. With a steel tent peg of all things, it would seem, if one believes the rumours in the citadel. They are in confident mood. Hardly surprising, since another interesting development that is on every defender's lips is that their spies have taken Amulet of Hazgorata. Apparently, it now sits in the Great Temple.'

'Then why haven't you taken it back?'

'I never received orders to do so. You'll be able to take it back when the city falls,' said the spy calmly.

'And what if it doesn't now fall? The Dowager Queen's death is a sadness and will be respected in the proper ways, but the Amulet has great power, even if it is only the power to inspire. We cannot allow that to work in the enemy's favour.'

'True, but I really thought you might be more concerned about Accutina's death and the attack on your own royal person, let alone the compromising nature of the attack's circumstances.'

'You insolent bastard. You think you are as silver-tongued as me but instead you are just beyond the pale.'

The spy laughed.

'In fact it must be the case that I am more silver-tongued than you, for you never manage to best me in that regard. Gods, I'm so busy in there being so quiet and unassuming that I'm completely out of practice, yet I'm still better at it than you. I wonder why that would be the case?'

'I make the orders. Not you!' Jostan shouted.

'No, but you need me and I'm sure that's why you have so far resisted the temptation to have me executed. I know how dearly you'd love it, but you know you'll be the worse off for it too. Now, I have a plan by which you can take the city at the moment of your choosing; all developed and planned based on the information that I personally have gained for you. I presume you have other spies in the citadel. But none of them have provided you with a breakthrough, have they? My proposition is that I can now be of better use to you from outside the castle walls.'

Jostan laughed ruefully.

'You coward,' he said.

'They know me. They trust me,' said the spy. 'If I could just play the act of political prisoner and make a heartfelt appeal to them from in front of the citadel's gates. I'll tell them of the folly of their venture and of the futility of their current position, then tell them of your mercy. Give me that chance and it will cause a mutiny and they will be forced to surrender.'

'Oh, you'd like that wouldn't you?' Jostan said. 'Well, if this wasn't coming from a man who's just disobeyed my orders then I might be prepared to listen. Insubordination or open rebellion, neither shall be tolerated lightly, so I've got a better plan. One that's of rather more risk to you, but all the same for me.'

He walked over to the tent's entrance and addressed one of his guards.

'Find Invicturion Rhosgyth and bring him back here.'

He re-entered the tent and faced the spy again with a smirk.

'With Rhosgyth by your side, I'm sure you won't stray from the path again. Falter a second time and he will see to it that the problem is swiftly eradicated,' he said, clearly enjoying his own words. The spy glared at him with steely eyes.

'What would you have me do, your Majesty?' he said in a tone laced with irony.

The time was approaching slowly. Silrith could feel the strange sense of anticipation growing. It didn't engulf her like a wave, but instead, it steadily built, as if it were a great wall being constructed piece by piece, hiding her fear so far from view that she almost no longer felt it. Almost. She kept her mind focused on the job in hand and all she wanted to do now was sit on her horse and be with her soldiers.

Already in full battle gear, she was intensely restless. Yet there was nothing more to be done until shortly before the attack and after finding herself pacing in frustration, she had remembered that there was somebody she needed to visit. Someone whom she regretted having barely seen since her arrival in Rildayorda. Entering the small but highly decorated room, with its intricate red, white and green patterns on the walls, she dismissed the maids and was greeted by the most excited little face she'd seen in days.

'Silfiff!' Yathugarra exclaimed. Silrith laughed as her two-year-old cousin leapt out of her little bed and charged towards her.

'Hello Garra,' Silrith said happily, using the shorted version of the golden-haired child's name.

She crouched down and gathered her up in her arms, holding her close and giving her a little kiss on the head. This was only the second time she'd had a chance to see her since her own arrival and even now, she knew the visit could only be fleeting. But for Silrith, looking into Yathugarra's innocent face was an extra reminder of what she was fighting for now, the safety of her family and her people.

She decided that after the coming battle, if Bezekarl really was dead, she would name Garra as her heir. She had wanted to do this already, in case she was struck down by an enemy blade, but to do so in the middle of a siege would make Garra far too much of a target for Jostan's spies and assassins. Nevertheless, it had to be done eventually. After all, even winning back the throne would be worthless if the country was thrown back into a blood-soaked struggle for power after her death. Moreover, while Silrith knew that her heir needed to be of her blood, she was certain she would not be capable of producing one herself. The problem was, she couldn't ask any doctors about this, for fear of her secret escaping.

Soon after her return from her ill-fated trip to Verusantium as a young girl, she had contracted a fever. It had been short but violent and she had almost succumbed to it, but the prayers of her family and the work of her physician had seen her well again in short enough time for the illness to remain a secret. The reason for this secrecy was that the physician had told her father that the fever was of the same kind that had famously struck Princess Azakrina more than two centuries earlier. Like Silrith, she had survived, but according to the story, for the rest of her life, she had been barren, despite having given birth to a daughter only a year before contracting the illness. Nobody except Silrith, her parents, her brother and the physician ever knew of Silrith's fever and the physician had been sworn to secrecy under pain of death.

Many times in her life Silrith had wanted to tell someone, as the secret felt like a lead weight inside her womb, but she knew she couldn't. She had to be strong and accept the path that the gods had chosen for her. She owed her people that much. Yet it angered Silrith more than anything that a defect in her own body had the potential to decide the fates of so many others. However, there was nothing to be done about it and she forced the thought from her mind, refocusing on the coming battle and on her plan. She stayed a while and played with the little girl until the toddler began to yawn.

'Garra, I need you to be a big, brave girl for me tonight. You're going on an adventure.'

With perfect innocence, Garra carried on playing, having pulled out one of her dolls from somewhere. Given that she was only two years old, Silrith wasn't sure how much Garra was understanding but at least saying the words helped her to believe that Garra would be alright.

'You're going on a boat tonight, Garra, and when the ship sets sail, you'll be on your way to explore a place called Etrovansia. Would you like that?'

Garra just giggled. Silrith stayed a few more minutes, savouring the time, but all too soon she knew she had to leave; to shut away her maternal instincts and become the warrior that Garra and everyone else within these city walls depended upon. Before she did, Silrith kissed her little cousin goodbye as the girl continued to play. As she walked towards the door, she called back one of the maids, telling her she was to take Garra outside. Out there she would find Yathrud's Master-of-Horse waiting with a cart, in which they would find dirty clothes and coats to help them blend in. Then the cart would take them, with luck, out of the city and on to a ship named the *Bastinian the Great*. It was fitting that a ship named after her own illustrious grandfather would be the bearer of such precious cargo.

She had instructed the master-of-horse to smuggle the child and the maid on board, then find the captain, a woman known loosely to Silrith, and tell her of Silrith's order for them to set sail for Etrovansia at the earliest opportunity. Of course, she had also told the Master-of-Horse to take enough money to bribe any guards if necessary. She hoped to the gods that if she could continue inflicting further losses on the enemy, then at some point Jostan's troops would be forced to withdraw from the port and would be called to support their comrades and that the shipping could get underway again so that Garra could be protected from all of this. Shappa had told her that if Garra was taken to Nangosa City, the staff living on his old family estate would take her in and care for her there. But for now Rildayorda's port was in enemy hands and it was believed that the crews of the various ships were now quarantined on the floating prisons that their vessels had become. Yet surely even Jostan knew that he would need these very ships and their crews so that trade could eventually get back to normal, so maybe a poorly dressed man, woman and child would get through.

From that point, it wasn't long before Silrith, under escort and now mounted, rode through the streets. Her entire cavalry force, around three thousand in all, had been ordered to congregate by the East Gate, ready to move out and get into position for the attack. Despite their occupation of the port, it seemed that Jostan's patrols of the forest were few at best. It was possible that his troops were nervous of ambush, especially at night.

As she neared the East Gate, she felt her gut muscles slowly tighten. The most crucial moment of the entire siege would soon be upon them. Instantly she chided herself for such a thought, telling herself that what she was feeling really was anticipation and not nerves.

Finally, she reached the gate. Apparently, its proximity to the forest meant that it was rarely used compared with the others. It was a strongly built, highly utilitarian structure; an image of pure functionality that was not in keeping with beauty of the city's other areas.

All around her, the narrow streets were filled with her soldiers, carrying their various banners. Most carried Yathrud's three golden dragons, surrounded by a deep scarlet. Despite carrying this emblem on their shields, however, Silrith had ordered that Gasbron's cavalry should also carry her own banner of emerald, with its white stallion, as she would ride with them personally. Then there were Shappa's knights, who carried a golden banner with the image of a black hound, crouching, ready to pounce. This was the flag of Shappa's Etrovansian duchy, Nangosa, and the design was also emblazoned across the knights' shields. The Hentani, meanwhile, had no banners at all.

More than half of the cavalry force that had grouped here were militiamen and Hentani warriors. Between them, the mounted divisiomen and Shappa's cavalry numbered around seven hundred. Their innate sense of professionalism saw them keep a soldierly silence, awaiting orders and the others followed their example.

Silrith hadn't had a close look at Shappa's knights until now and she noticed that they were equipped quite differently to the divisiomen and even from Shappa himself, fond as he was of plated armour, albeit of a very modern, sculpted kind. His troops, by contrast, relied heavily on chain mail and wore pointed helmets, which were open-faced except for a nasal guard and they carried large, diamond-shaped shields.

In stark contrast to both of these elite units and the battle-hardened Hentani warriors, Silrith's Bennvikan militia lancers had looked every inch the hastily thrown together force that they were. It had been known since before the siege that they may need to fight on horseback at some point, so they had received some training, but all were untested in a real battle. On her way through the streets to the gate, the tension had been written across all of their faces, but nonetheless they each bowed their heads, some calling 'My Queen!' as she had ridden by. At one point she had recognised Dazyan of the Southtown, the young soldier she had met on the walls of Preddaburg before giving her first speech. Without even thinking, she had winked at him; a respectful smile coming in return. Friendly gestures cost nothing and yet could be priceless.

The mood had been rather different when she had trotted passed some of the Hentani warriors only minutes later. In place of nervous motivation was calm confidence. They had seemed in a relaxed mood as they laughed and joked with each other under their breath in their harsh, gruff tongue.

Still silently reviewing these thoughts, Silrith drew her horse alongside Gasbron's. He'd been waiting with his comrades and now saluted sharply.

'Is everything ready?' Silrith asked, placing her horned, silver and gold ridged helmet on her head as Shappa trotted over, carrying a sugarloaf helm under his sword arm.

'Yes, my Queen,' said Gasbron. 'Our scouts say they have found a point in the forest from which we can make a cohesive attack.'

'Then we must move quickly before Jostan's troops realise what's going on. We have to hope that the enemy is the only threat,' Shappa added.

This isn't a time to be worrying about forest spirits, Silrith thought. She hoped her troops didn't share Shappa's unhelpful concerns.

'Then may the gods bless our mission,' said Silrith.

Nothing more needed to be said. All present understood that forest terrain was hardly ideal for a cavalry charge. Riders would be knocked from their saddles by low branches, horses would be sent crashing to the ground by the multitude of tree roots and all before they even reached the enemy. Yet a surprise attack was now their only chance of victory and in any case, light as their numbers were, a cavalry force this size should be enough to ensure that a good proportion of them still got through, so Silrith had decided that the risk was acceptable. Most importantly of all, it was the last thing Jostan would expect.

343

'Open that gate!' she ordered. Slowly the large oak doors were heaved open.

'Move out!' Gasbron called and the column began to rumble out of the city, into the wild surroundings of the forest.

Ezrina was impressed by her own authority as she stood at the top of the steps that led up to the temple's entrance. Joined by the full complement of her priests and priestesses, she surveyed her surroundings. For her newfound ecclesiastical followers, her retrieval of the Amulet of Hazgorata had proven beyond all doubt that she was blessed by Bertakaevey and, among the bodies of the Bennvikan clergymen, each of the Hentani holy leaders who had joined her for their divine mission had fallen to their knees. It was then that she had ordered them to go among their people, telling them that at the full rising of the moon that night they were to congregate outside the temple.

At first only a few had come. For some reason the eastern side of the city was full of horsemen that night, both Bennvikan and Hentani alike. Cursing, Ezrina presumed that on seeing so many armed riders, many civilians had been scared into staying in their houses. Then it happened. As the moon approached its zenith, more and more doors started to open here and there.

Like the earliest trickles of a stream, first a few, then many more Hentani families tentatively exited their homes. Soon great swathes of people were walking up the streets to join those who had been brave enough to go there first. Meanwhile, the Bennvikan families slept in their beds. Only members of the city's various tribal districts had been told to go. The sudden swell of the crowd from a handful of souls to near a thousand, possibly more, in just a few minutes was awe-inspiring and they looked up at Ezrina and the crowd of holy leaders expectantly. Consciously Ezrina took in a deep breath and began.

'Gather round, fellow children of Bertakaevey. I have words that you all must hear.'

Up on the ramparts of Rildayorda's West Gate, a young militiaman stood guard, shivering in the night's cold, or at the very least, he told himself that it was the cold and nothing else. Manning the gate was a heavy responsibility and he had to show the other troops that he was just as capable as they were. Like Captain Huthron had told him, fear keeps a person vigilant. The strap of his kettle hat still dug into his chin, as each one he had ever worn seemed to and up here with the extra breeze the metal rings of his chain mail felt cold against his skin, though at least the leather jerkin he wore over it provided some level of insulation.

Behind him, he could hear a rising babble from within the city, but outside, the night was almost still, though not quite. Opposite him lay the right flank of King Jostan's camp, lit by torches and a handful of campfires. In the flickering light, he could see soldiers moving about here and there, though they were probably just guards like himself, at least for the most part. The depression on that side of the city was fairly steep, so the enemy had been forced to pitch their tents some distance away. He kept reminding himself that he was out of arrow range, but he couldn't quite rid his mind of the fear that some lucky shot might take him in the night. He gripped his spear tightly as if that would be of some defence against such a weapon.

'Pssst!'

'Who's there?' the militiaman demanded, turning around and pointing his spear at where the noise seemed to have come from. He relaxed as he heard a familiar laugh from down on the ground, inside the city walls.

'Gods be praised, Calgred! Someone's on edge tonight,' said the voice.

It was Uthyann, Calgred's portly young neighbour and a member of the same unit. Calgred rolled his eyes and turned back to watching the enemy camp.

'Very funny.'

'Well, can I come up or what?' said Uthyann.

'Why are you asking?' Calgred laughed, trying to sound at ease.

'Is the captain there?'

'No, just come up.'

Calgred heard the creak of a door followed by footsteps as his friend climbed the spiral staircase of the gate's enormous towers. The wooden door

345

leading from the gate on to the ramparts opened and, letting it close behind him, Uthyann, with his orange hair and grinning freckly face, walked towards Calgred. He was holding out a bottle in one hand while clutching his spear in the other.

'Scrounged us a bottle of rum didn't I? Thought you might wanna share it.'

'Uthyann, where did you get this?' said Calgred, feeling slightly uncomfortable.

'That'd be telling. Want some company and a nice swig?' Uthyann said, holding out the bottle. Calgred looked at it. Common soldiers like themselves rarely and in many cases never, got to taste the finest wines, but even he knew that this was the polar opposite of that. Yet being cut off from trade meant that Rildayorda's supplies of any even semi-desirable alcohol had been exhausted long ago. Calgred almost surprised himself as the bottle of Padorak started to look strangely appealing. At least its fiery taste would warm his insides a bit.

Calgred didn't know what made him do it. Peer pressure? Fear? Or maybe something else. All he knew was that even though a voice in his head was screaming for him not to do it, he reached out and took the bottle. He raised it to his lips, but then at the last moment stopped and handed it back to his friend.

'No, I don't want it. I can never seem to get used to that stuff,' said Calgred.

'Well, you might have to if this siege carries on. Seems the taverns are all out of everything else. Sure you don't want some?'

'No, thank you. We need to stay alert, in case that captain comes for an inspection if nothing else. You shouldn't be carrying it.'

'Can't a guy even have a bit to take the edge off? I'm not gonna drink loads am I?'

Calgred shook his head and turned back to look out over the walls. He didn't have the advantage of rank, so he couldn't order Uthyann to get rid of it. He just hoped there'd be no trouble.

Chapter 24

'You may feel confused,' Ezrina said as she addressed the crowd of ragged onlookers. 'Lost, even. Have the children of Bertakaevey been so tamed by the Bennvikans that all their sense of pride is gone; buried beneath layer upon layer of subservience? I hope not. I certainly don't believe it to be so. In you, I see things that you yourselves may have long forgotten. My mother, holy Bertakaevey herself, will awake the sleeping lions within your hearts.'

She smiled as the crowd audibly drew in breath on hearing those words.

'Blasphemy,' she heard one man say. He must have thought she hadn't spotted him.

'Blasphemy?' Ezrina said. 'It is not blasphemy to spread the word of Bertakaevey. Blessed are those who protect their flock. You are all aware of the Amulet of Hazgorata, the last link between us and the promised land that the Bennvikan followers of Vitrinnolf and Lomatteva displaced us from the very first time they attacked us all those centuries ago. Our ancestors were children of the north, yet we languish here in the south and even here we are prisoners. But I tell you now that your imprisonment is over. You all know also that as long as the Amulet of Hazgorata is carried by a member of the Hentani, then we all have a future. We have lived at the mercy of the Bennvikans for all the time that the Amulet has been withheld from us. We have been controlled and manipulated by them. Even now our warriors – *our* warriors – march to fight for a Bennvikan. Yet as we all know, a divine prophecy predicted an end to this oppression. Therefore is it not a divine act that has seen the Amulet's recovery? My people, I proclaim to you now, that Bertakaevey has spoken.'

She flung her arms out as the crowd cheered in agreement. But then she slowly drew her hands inward, for the first time drawing the crowd's attention to the chain that hung around her neck. Her emerald robes hid most of it, but she reached in and the crowd gasped as she revealed the jewel for all to see.

347

'Yes, you see before you now the Amulet of Hazgorata, held by the girl who recovered it,' Ezrina declared. 'The time has come to throw aside Bennvikan rule. Only then can we control our own future and decide our own fate. Bertakaevey herself decreed that I would discover the Amulet and in bearing it, I now bear the destiny of us all.'

She paused to let her words sink in as the crowd cheered. It was wonderful to see such desperate people full of hope. It gave Ezrina a full-blooded belief that, with Bertakaevey's help, she would find Jezna again. Everything she held dear hung on this.

'It's true. The prophecy has come true,' called a man's voice from somewhere within the crowd.

'She has chosen me! I am formed of Bertakaevey's holy ashes,' Ezrina declared with a passion fuelled by her aching hunger to save Jezna; the crowd now hanging on her every word. 'The signal has been given by our Mother in Heaven. My mother. Your mother. Now she sends me to save her children and lead them from the flames of oppression. I declare to you now, that by divine order, the Daughter of Ashes is risen.'

'Can you hear that?' said Calgred. 'Sounds like shouting. Seems to be coming from the city centre.'

He watched as Uthyann turned and listened. Usually, it was fairly quiet up on the walls at night; often too quiet. Sometimes you could hear the odd noise from inside the city, but this was different. This sounded like a whole group of people, yet the voices, while clearly numerous, were only faint.

'Yeh, I hear it. Can't see anything though,' Uthyann said. 'Seems to be coming from the other side of the arena.' He strained his neck as if that'd help him see any more easily over the top of the hulking cylinder that was the gladiatorial stadium lying not more than a few hundred yards from their position. According to the better-travelled soldiers Calgred had met, this wooden structure was nothing compared to the huge stone stadiums in Kriganheim. This was barely the height of the city walls, but its presence, combined with the large numbers of houses, still meant that part of their view across to the far side of the city was blocked.

348

'Could be. I'll bet it's further away than that though,' Calgred said.

'Maybe the tribal lot have some festival going on at the temple?'

'Possible, I guess. Funny time to be doing it though, don't you think? I can't imagine they've got much of a feast.'

'I bet those bastards have loads of food and have been hiding it from us.'

'They're not all like that, Uthyann.'

Calgred was going to continue, but a shout made him stop.

'Open the gate! I demand that you open the gate!'

'Stop! Who goes there!' Calgred shouted instinctively, as he saw what looked like a silhouetted young man on a white horse slowing to a canter as he approached the gate.

'I am Bezekarl Alyredd. Son of your noble lord! You will open the gate immediately!' shouted the man, gesticulating violently with his sword drawn. He was clearly out of breath and was desperately looking over his shoulder, though no pursuers were visible.

Nevertheless, Calgred and Uthyann rushed down the steps to the bottom of the wall. There they were joined by two more guards from the ramparts on the other side of the gatehouse.

'Quickly! Help us open it!' Calgred told them. Though still enormous, this was the smallest of the city's entrances and featured only a portcullis, and with an exposed pulley system on either side instead of having a larger one housed in an antechamber above. Between the four of them, they could lift it. They heaved on the pulleys and slowly the steel frame creaked upwards.

'Come on! Hurry up you bastards! They're coming!' Bezekarl called from outside.

Calgred couldn't hear hoof beats, maybe that was just because of the heavy groaning of the portcullis. The four of them heaved again and again, inching the metal frame a little higher each time. Finally, the portcullis was in place and Bezekarl kicked his mount forward, but then he stopped once he was through the gate.

'My Lord, what-' Calgred's voice was cut short as Bezekarl's blade slashed into his neck. In horror, he tried to cover the wound with his hands but he fell to the ground, coughing and spluttering on his own blood, feeling the life drain from him as his three comrades were felled.

In the forest to the east of the city, the night was a deathly stillness. With Gasbron at her side, Silrith led the column of cavalry in complete silence. He may have been born to Gilbayan immigrant parents in Ganust, as he had recently told her, but as a Rildayordan resident of some years, for Silrith, Gasbron was as much a guide as a soldier. She was glad to have a man of such quality that she could trust. Nevertheless, she strained her ears for the slightest rustle, or the snap of a twig and scanned the area wide-eyed looking for movement, or maybe even the flicker of a distant flame.

The trees and the pitch darkness gave a pressing claustrophobic effect, especially as Silrith still wasn't used to her ridged helmet, with its long nasal guard and its face-enclosing cheek plates.

Soon they reached the edge of a small clearing.

'This is the place,' Gasbron whispered, confirming what Silrith already knew. She looked at him, nodded and put her hand up to call a halt. She listened again, looking into the clearing, which was lit just enough by the moonlight. When she was satisfied that they weren't being watched, she motioned for them to move forward again and turned her mount to face north in the direction of Jostan's army. They were too deep into the forest to be able to see it from there, however.

She briefly looked around and caught Gasbron's eye as the riders got into position behind them, though there was nothing more to be said. Both left the other to their private thoughts until the moment was right.

Thankfully it hadn't rained in some time, so the ground was hard, but there was no getting away from the fact that horses would be tripped by roots and riders would be ripped from their mounts by low branches. Still, there was no way around that either. It seemed to Silrith that the plan was ambitious at best and mad at worst, even though she had thought of it personally, but she reminded herself that this would be the only way to attack Jostan's army without them being ready. This would be crucial, as the much-weakened Preddaburg Gate almost certainly couldn't withstand another attack and the defenders would be hard pushed to repel the enemy again once they were inside. Yes, as risky as it was, this was their last chance of victory.

The three-thousand-strong force slowly reformed into a northward-facing column twenty steeds wide with the divisiomen at the front, then Shappa's knights, then the Hentani and finally the Bennvikan militia. She knew the formation wasn't ideal, but it would have to suffice. It was imperative that the experienced troops were at the front if they were to stand a chance of success. Yathrud would be at this very moment over at the Preddaburg Gate with the infantry. He had his orders and she knew he'd obey them to the letter.

Finally, Silrith sensed the level of movement behind her lessen, as the last riders got into formation. Consciously slowing her breathing and focusing her mind, she drew her sword, enjoying the rasping sound that was echoed behind her as her horsemen did the same. She raised the weapon in the air, motioned forwards and three thousand horses were kicked into a trot.

Bezekarl smiled with satisfaction at the sight of the four mutilated bodies around him. He turned his mount and trotted back to the gate to face his oncoming troops, who now cantered forward out of the darkness. The chief invicturion, Vinnitar Rhosgyth sat arrogantly astride his horse at the head of the column. These were the cavalry of Divisio One Kriganheim. Moving from the darkness into the light, they almost had a ghostly look as they appeared to materialise out of nothing, as they climbed out of the pitch black of the grassy slope and were lit up by the torches dotted around the gate, as ten horsemen became fifty and these were just the beginning. Bezekarl knew that as more riders approached fifty would become a hundred and a hundred would become a thousand.

'Loot all you find! It's yours!' Bezekarl ordered. 'Slaughter these traitors in their beds.'

The riders bellowed their war cries and kicked their mounts into a gallop. Bezekarl pulled to the side of the gate as his soldiers rushed past him into the city. As they went past, Bezekarl saw Vinnitar's standard-bearer pull out a war horn and blow one long note. There was a second war cry from far behind and, looking into the darkness outside after the last rider had passed, he saw the dark shapes of hundreds of militiamen, as well as some divisiomen and Defroni warriors charging out from within the densely packed tents of the camp. They charged forward and once they reached the light of the torches, Bezekarl could see that their shields were that strange, uniform white, just as those of the riders had been. Some of their banners showed the black and white trident of Lord Feddilyn Rintta, while others, of course, showed the sapphire and white eagle of King Jostan. He smiled with pleasure, urging them onward as they surged under the gate with the ferocity of a horde intent on victory and high on blood. Every one of them was hungry for plunder; eager to sack the city and engulf it in flame.

Chapter 25

There it was! The edge of the forest! Sensing the moment was right, Silrith kicked her cantering mount into a gallop. Within moments the ground thundered with the noise of three thousand sets of hooves. Keeping her body low, she looked ahead, seeing the light of Jostan's camp getting closer and closer. She saw the silhouette of a guard, but he turned and ran, raising the alarm instead of standing to fight.

'Stay in formation! Follow me!' Silrith called, hearing panicked cries and heavy crashes, telling the fate of some of her horses behind as the column surged forward.

They burst out of the forest and charged headlong into the camp. There were many soldiers there, but they'd had no time to form into any sort of order. Silrith slashed this way and that, sending anyone in her path straight to the afterlife. None could be allowed to stop her from reaching Jostan's tent.

Inside the Preddaburg Gate, seated astride his gelding in full armour, Yathrud heard the alert horns sounding all around the enemy camp outside. Silrith must have begun her attack. Now was the time to move. At his back, the remaining divisios were ready, crammed into the walled courtyard; each unit in a small square formation. Behind them, in columns that snaked all the way through the gates into the outer and inner wards, were the militia and the Hentani infantry. In all, they numbered around six thousand troops, with a further two thousand staying behind to defend.

Yathrud raised his sword high above his head.

'Open the gates!' he called. 'We advance!'

As the gates we hauled apart and the portcullis raised, he looked up at the walls and all the troops crowded on to them. He hoped those militia stationed there would be enough to hold the citadel if anything went wrong. In moments the gates were open and he could see the enemy. In the distance, thousands of Jostan's troops, now rallied into some kind of order, were rushing to the camp's eastern flank, towards sounds of metal on metal, the whinnying of horses and the screams of soldiers.

'Forward!' Yathrud bellowed and he kicked his horse into a trot.

'I am the Daughter of Ashes, Bertakaevey's holy ashes. For I was formed from the ashes of her once mortal body, guided by her immortal soul,' Ezrina declared. 'The prophecy is true. Follow me and freedom will be yours.'

The crowd erupted into an enormous cheer and Ezrina encouraged them, but their jubilation was short-lived. Through the noise came a terrible shout to the west of where they stood.

'Quiet!' Ezrina called and she listened. The crowd stopped celebrating and immediately heard the screams. They were all temporarily rooted to the ground as they listened, but in a moment hundreds of Bennvikan civilians, adult and child alike appeared out of the western streets, running headlong for the east of the city.

'They're through the gates!' they were shouting. 'Save yourselves from slaughter! Run for your lives!'

The crowd was sent into hysteria and before Ezrina knew what was happening they were stampeding towards the east gate. Anyone who tripped was trampled and crushed.

'Everyone head for the East Gate,' ordered Ezrina. 'Pray that my Holy Mother's fire protects us from any that *they* bring.'

'Jakiroc, get me a horse,' she said. 'Any horse! And a sword! Now!'

Charging through the camp, slaughtering soldiers left and right, carried onward by the rage of battle; this was what it was truly like to be a warrior. Enemy troops lunged at Silrith, trying to slash at her horse, or trying to pull her to the ground, but it seemed she was blessed by the gods this night. If she did not dispatch them by the sword, then either one of her horsemen did so, or the assailant was knocked to the ground by her stallion and trampled by those behind. Still she hurtled on, feeling that she could personally kill a thousand troops; troops that were here simply to ensure the destruction of her family and this city.

Now the enemy was doing little more than running and dying. With great satisfaction, Silrith realised that her soldiers had routed much of the east side of the camp. Yet there was still much fighting to be done and the sounds of battle all around still filled the air.

Then she heard it; Yathrud's war horn, somewhere towards the centre of the camp, opposite the Preddaburg Gate, confirming that the infantry, led by the remaining divisios, had engaged the enemy. She smiled and kicked her horse again, pulling it in the direction of the note, beginning the second stage of her plan.

Moments later, the fight could be seen. Her uncle was directing things from astride his war horse and had sent the divisiomen forward in a tight tortoiseshell. They formed the point at the front of a triangle of militia and Hentani warriors. The opposing warriors of the Defroni hurled themselves against Yathrud's force and their resistance seemed to rally some of the enemy militia, though nevertheless, their line was buckling in the middle under the pressure from the divisiomen at the spearhead of Yathrud's formation.

To Silrith's left, Gasbron's standard-bearer blew on a war horn and enemy faces looked up in dread as they saw the cavalry charging in to outflank them from their left. Many turned and ran just at the sight of them, while those that remained were quickly slaughtered as the torrent of horses smashed into their east wing.

As the enemy formation collapsed and broke in terror, Silrith called a halt and was echoed by a bellow from Gasbron. Amid the chaos, she had noted that those who had retreated west had routed like a wild rabble, while those that had retreated north had done so in a little more order, amid calls from some petty commander for them to fall back.

'My Lord Alyredd!' she called to Yathrud, using the formal term in front of her troops.

'Yes, my Queen?' he replied from his position.

'We follow those who retreated north,' she ordered. 'That's where Jostan's tent will be. I'll lead, then you follow us.'

She looked at the soldiers all around her.

'Who wants to kill the usurper who brought this war to us?'

Her answer was a clamour of battle cries and she kicked her mount again. She and her cavalry galloped past the infantry and they moved towards the place where Silrith hoped they'd find the one who had taken everything from her. As she rode, they caught up with more soldiers who had become isolated from their units in the confusion and they paid for it with their lives. The exhilaration of battle pulsed through Silrith's body like nothing she'd ever experienced before, yet she fought the feeling. Jostan's army was in disarray, but her victory so far had seemed just a little too easy.

As they reached the north of the camp, sighting the royal enclosure barely a few hundred yards away, she laid eyes on something that confirmed her suspicions.

'Halt!' she called. Gasbron repeated the order and it was relayed backwards, preventing the horses form piling into each other as they slowed. 'Keep out of bow range!'

Before them was the royal enclosure, though it more closely resembled a porcupine of soldiers. It looked large enough to be the camp of a small army on its own. There must have been room for ten thousand troops in there. The gate was blocked by many divisiomen with their large rectangular shields in a tortoiseshell formation. To Silrith's eye, from what little she could make out with her blocked view, it looked like many of the divisios were in the enclosure, with the remains of Jostan's army visible behind them in reserve. Either side of the gate was a low fence made up of wooden stakes that had been driven into the muddy ground, each of them bound together in groups with rope that overlapped into the other groups of stakes around them. Through square openings that had been cut into the wood, the fence bristled with spears.

Silrith wondered how long they'd been there, waiting. It seemed unlikely that many of those retreating soldiers she'd seen would have been in position in time. The idea that Jostan may yet win the battle stung worse than the attack of a thousand hornets. Silrith swatted the thought away. Now was the time to seize the moment with a clear mind. She turned to Gasbron and to Shappa who had ridden to the front of the column.

'The infantry will catch up soon, but there's no time to wait. In the meantime, we must launch skirmishing attacks, concentrating on the divisiomen blocking the gate and avoiding the spears at all costs.'

'Yes, my Queen,' Gasbron said.

She watched as he called to the riders waiting behind.

'All units to skirmish! Dead centre!'

Silrith raised her sword above her head, bellowing her war cry, which was echoed by three thousand voices at her back. She kicked her horse to attack. Seeing the solid enemy line at the gate, it seemed reluctant to advance, but as it cantered forward she hustled it into a gallop as her comrades followed and the enemy visibly braced to defend their position. At the bellowing of an order, the front two rows of the enemy divisiomen threw their pilums in a sudden volley. One zipped past Silrith's head so close that she gasped and there was a sharp cry as Gasbron's standard-bearer was gutted by the deadly missile, though she did not see where the others went. Onward she charged and just as they got close she heaved on the reins with one hand to pull the horse left, slicing her sword down on the enemy divisiomen. The tip of her long blade found a gap between the shields and she was almost pulled to the ground as it bit into somebody's flesh, but mercifully her momentum pulled it free. A glinting enemy blade sliced up at her, but as she turned it tore only into the material of her tunic, glancing off her chain mail and she galloped away as the riders behind attacked under a hail of pilums as the enemy divisiomen launched another volley.

The bulk of the damage to the enemy was done by pilums thrown by the divisio cavalry and subsequently the spears of the mounted militia, but only at great cost to the latter. They attacked the enemy divisio infantry head on, with many of their foes falling, impaled on their weapons, though the troops in reserve quickly moved to fill any gaps. Meanwhile, those enemy soldiers at the front who stayed standing raised their white shields, attacking from underneath them and slashing at the horse's legs as they tried to withdraw and regroup with the rest of Silrith's cavalry out of arrow range.

Suddenly Silrith caught sight of marching soldiers approaching them from behind. Yathrud's infantry were back with them.

'Infantry to the front, cavalry to the rear!' she called. Each rider moved to one side to allow the infantry through.

'What are your orders, my Queen?' Yathrud asked as he drew his mount alongside Silrith's after calling a halt.

'Uncle, you and I must lead the infantry forward to attack the enemy position. The cavalry are too vulnerable on their own.'

'Very good, my Queen. May I suggest that we both dismount? Two isolated horsemen would be easily felled.'

'Of course. We shall lead from the front. Gasbron, tell your divisiomen to dismount also. Take up position in front of the rest of the divisio infantry. Your troops must form the boar's snout that will lead the assault on the gate. The remaining infantry will protect our archers but must remain close to the divisiomen so as to capitalise when you break through the enemy line. As for the fences, if we can get in their faces their spears will be useless at close quarters, even with a fence to protect them.'

'Yes, my Queen,' Gasbron said and he started issuing orders to his soldiers.

Silrith turned to Shappa.

'Prince Shappa, I'll leave you in command of the remainder of the cavalry. Lead them around the edge of the royal enclosure and make sure the enemy see you do so. With luck, they may divert some of their soldiers away from here. If you find another way into the enclosure, use it. We may need you to outflank them. They'll be at a disadvantage if they're worried about what's coming up behind them.'

'As you wish, my Lady,' Shappa bowed. He sent a soldier to relay orders for the Hentani and militia to follow him before raising his sword and calling 'Knights! On me!' and the ground thundered as many hooves galloped past.

Once they had gone, Silrith slithered off her horse. She checked the strap on her helmet and flexed her hands on the grip of her shield and the pommel of her sword. Then she joined Yathrud just to the side of the first Bastalf divisio, with a group of Hentani infantry on their left. Silrith felt that it was fitting that it would be Yathrud, the man without whom her rebellion would have never taken place, who would fight directly at her side. Then she looked into the face of the Hentani man who would fight at her other shoulder and despite the fact that he was a stranger to her with potentially no common tongue, she felt a connection of a different kind with him too.

'Lock shields!' she called and shield walls formed either side of her divisiomen, who had formed their tortoiseshell. Silrith hoped that they would stand up to the challenge of Jostan's more numerous divisiomen blocking the gate.

'Advance!' she bellowed with all the strength she could muster. The whole line lurched forward, with Gasbron's infantry at its head and Silrith and Yathrud on the left wing. Many of her troops started rhythmically beating their swords against their shields and Silrith did the same. It was like a combined heartbeat for every soldier in the line, pushing them forward.

From somewhere behind the enemy line there was a shout. Almost in slow motion, a hail of dark, thin shafts flew up into the air.

'Under shields!' Silrith cried, instinctively crouching and curling as much of her body under hers as she could. She'd never felt her own mortality quite as much as this as the arrows fell and began to thud against her shield. She knew that her life was for that moment entirely in the hands of the gods.

Here and there she heard cries of pain as her troops were hit, but mercifully these were minimal. The hail stopped and, fighting the urge to turn and run, Silrith leapt to her feet, raising her sword and bellowing out a war cry that was immediately taken up by all those with her.

She saw with pleasure that Gasbron's troops had carried on advancing under the cover of their shields in spite of the enemy attack. She hurled herself forward to bring her part of the line back level; Yathrud staying right at her side. The divisiomen's flanks had to be protected in case of ambush. Some of her own archers fired arrows back at the enemy, though they were fired at a run and their level of success could not be known. She tried to keep her head down as she ran, knowing that she had to get either underneath or in between the spear tips.

With perfect timing, she slipped between two spears that were protruding from a square gap in the fence, just as she heard the divisio lines clash together. She hurled herself at the fence, rejoicing in the look of horror in the nearest spearman's face as she crashed into it and buried her sword in his flesh.

Silrith found herself in a claustrophobic frenzy of violence. The fence now provided less protection than a shield wall for those inside, as the stakes began to creak and crack under the force of the attack as the soldiers on either side thrust their weapons at each other through the gaps, while others began to climb over the top of it.

Losing herself and succumbing to instinct, Silrith hacked and stabbed at the enemy men and women, though with less success now as the vulnerable spearmen withdrew and many swordsmen pushed their way to the front of the line. She kicked and pushed at the fence as she fought, desperate for it to fall.

'All together! Push!' she ordered and every soldier in her force hid behind their shield and used their combined strength as a battering ram. The soldiers on the other side shouted in horror and pushed back as they realised what Silrith's troops were trying to do, but the moment it took them to see it was enough. The creaking got louder and the attackers' momentum stronger and finally the stakes began to fall out of position. Soon the gaps were enough for Silrith's troops to break through and under the increased pressure, there was an almighty crash as the fence collapsed completely.

Silrith roared as she and her followers surged onward.

'Forward! Outflank their divisiomen,' she commanded, hoping that the troops to the right of Gasbron's soldiers had broken through as well. The ploy had worked. Jostan had thrown all his divisio units forward in a line against Gasbron's own divisiomen. Silrith climbed over the fallen stakes; her bloodlust-filled soldiers pouring over them in her wake or pushing through gaps between any that still stood. They had to get through the enemy militia and reach Jostan's divisiomen before they could reform to defend their flanks, while still facing Gasbron's troops.

But any move now would be hard to coordinate. The two bellowing forces smashed together once again and Silrith's shield crashed against that of a roaring Defroni warrior with a thick beard. He bellowed his war cry and his sword came down close to Silrith's head, but at the last moment, she was able to parry the heavy blow. She pushed forward and hooked her foot around his, causing him to stumble backwards into the warriors behind as they pushed to get to the front. The distraction was fatal, as he lowered his guard just for a moment and Silrith buried the point of her blade in his neck. He made a burbling sound, but it was cut off as Silrith ripped her sword back out again and he dropped to the ground.

She stepped forward on to his body so that even as her next opponent came at her, it was she that had gained ground, punching forward into the line of enemy militia. She despatched the next man with ease, but this time the blade caught as she tried to wrench it out of his torso and all she could do was throw up her shield hand as another militiaman swung his sword down at her.

With a loud clonk, the blow was deflected and she tried again to pull out her sword, which still stuck, but from behind her a long spear was thrust forward into the man's chest and he looked at his new attacker in shock as the head of the weapon burst out of his back.

There was no time for Silrith to thank the soldier who had saved her life. She pulled her sword free of the corpse's ribs with a snap of bone, pushing the skewered man's body from in front of her, off the spear tip as she advanced, deftly smiting down the next warrior who blocked her path.

Then she saw him, Jostan, behind his army's lines, astride his horse. He was wearing the long, flowing bright white robes of a non-combatant with a ceremonial golden cuirass and no helmet. Yet he was accompanied by a group of mounted guards in black armour and was gesticulating and shouting some unintelligible words at his troops.

'Shout all you like, Jostan,' Silrith bellowed. 'Death comes for you now.'

He didn't seem to have seen or heard her, as Silrith locked her sights on to him through the haze of battle. In her mind, the hunter became the hunted. She would be the lioness to see off this pack of wolves.

She barely looked at the troops she felled as she hacked and slashed, hardly even thinking about what she was doing. It was like the goddess Lomatteva herself had taken control of her body, pushing her forward and slaying everyone in her path in a mad, crazed dance of death.

She was through! She charged directly at Jostan, looking him straight in the eye as he bellowed for his royal bodyguard to protect him from the sudden danger. It was clear that for an instant Jostan had been the only one to see Silrith, leaving him exposed, but just as Silrith's way seemed clear, one of the horsemen, wearing the black armour of a Verusantian lance guardsman, blocked her path and knocked her to the ground; his sword glancing off her helmet as he thundered by.

She scrabbled in the mud as she tried to stand up again, expecting to see more of her soldiers arriving in support of her, but it seemed that any more who had come through the gap in the line had been killed, though the reformed enemy formation was on the verge of collapse.

She charged forward and attacked again, but now the remainder of Jostan's bodyguard had reformed in a tight group around him, leaving the first horseman to deal with Silrith and the chance to kill Jostan was surely gone.

The horseman rounded on her again, but she buried her sword into the neck of his horse and the man crashed to the ground, his leg stuck underneath it. He desperately tried to pull it out, but Silrith raised her sword above her head and brought it down with all her strength, decapitating the rider. There was a cheer behind her and she turned to look. The enemy line had broken. Some of her soldiers now charged to assault the flank of Jostan's divisiomen, who still defended the gate, while others pursued the militia in Silrith's direction.

Reinvigorated, she ran past the dead horse and rider, again charging at Jostan's party, who had turned and were now in full retreat. So focused was she on getting to Jostan, that she only vaguely heard the distant shout of 'My Queen!'

She was hardly aware of it initially; just a hard thump against her left side that knocked her off balance. She tried to regain her footing and carry on, but then there was an explosion of pain as her muscles and flesh tore against the arrow that had embedded itself in her shoulder, causing her to cry out.

Almost stripped of conscious thought, she instinctively tried to wrench the arrow free of her flesh, but suddenly she was grabbed from behind and pulled away.

'No! Leave it in there!'

She looked up through hazy eyes. Dark features. A strong build. Was that Gasbron's face? She hoped it was. Had the enemy divisios been broken by Gasbron's troops? Could the battle still be won? Her vision was blurring and her head was swimming until swimming felt like flooding and she was engulfed by a strange sense of drowning within her own body.

'Forward! Attack!' she tried to shout, but her movements were limp and her words weak.

Gasbron looked at her.

'My Queen, you must live!'

'No, I must fight on!' she said with all her strength.

'You must live! You! Quickly! Help me take her from the field!

She was being carried by more than one man now, or so she thought.

'See! The rebel queen falls! The rebel queen falls and your city burns!' Jostan's voice carried over the carnage; piercing Silrith's soul so deeply it felt like being hit with a second arrow. She tried to turn her head to see for herself. She couldn't see past those carrying her, but even amid her hazed senses, the expressions of dread on the faces of so many of her soldiers confirmed the awful truth; while dozens of them were cut down as they looked over their shoulders. Through it all, she heard Yathrud's voice.

'Rally to me! Rally to me!'

And then all was gone.

Chapter 26

Rocking. Gentle rocking against the sound of waves and the creaking of wood. Tentatively Silrith opened her eyes, squinting as they adjusted to the light. She was lying down on a bed of some kind, surrounded by blurry faces.

'She's alive,' someone said.

'The gods be praised! My Lady?' said another voice.

As her vision began to clear, she saw that the closest face was that of Shappa, just to her right. To her left was Gasbron. Both wore full armour, except for their helmets and were streaked with blood and dirt.

'My Lady, try not to move,' Shappa said.

But it was too late, Silrith had already tried to do so and felt a searing pain in her left shoulder.

'You were hit by an arrow,' he said. 'We have stemmed the blood flow but you are very weak and must rest.'

'Where? How?' was all Silrith was able to say.

'Well I'm no physician,' said Gasbron. 'But you were in the hands of the gods when we got you here. Now though, we've patched you up and if you let yourself rest, the wound will heal and you'll live to fight again.'

He was direct and to the point as always, but Silrith felt strangely calmed by his formal public demeanour, despite the pain she was in.

'We'll land in Etrovansia one day hence,' said Shappa. 'You'll be able to recover there.'

Etrovansia? They were on a ship? Suddenly she was wide awake and aware of everything. Trying to ignore the pain, she looked around and took in her surroundings. They were in a hastily constructed tent, but the sound of wind against the canvas, the splashing of water against oars and calling of voices from outside gave away that it was true; they were out to sea.

Aside from Shappa and Gasbron, all the five or six other faces were those of soldiers and servants that she recognised by sight but not by name. She inwardly scolded herself for the truth of that. Then a horrible thought struck her, piercing as deeply as the arrow had done.

'Where is my uncle?'

Her fear rose as a look of sorrow appeared on the faces of all present. It was Gasbron who spoke first.

'My Queen, Lord Yathrud did not make it back to the ship, not this one at least. After seeing you fall and witnessing the city burning, our army broke. Your uncle stood firm, calling for our soldiers to keep fighting, but I lost sight of him in the chaos. We fear that he may be dead or taken prisoner.'

Silrith tried to find the words for an answer, but this was all too much to take in at this moment and nothing came. Not for the first time, she fought to hold back any sign of emotion from such public view, but she felt sure that the tears that welled up in her eyes were visible. Yathrud had given his life for her and yet here she was, still alive and sailing away.

'We must return and soon,' she said with certainty as her thoughts began to de-cloud. 'My uncle must be avenged, in the way that he came to avenge me. It may be too late to save him, but not to save his memory.'

'Of course, my Lady,' Shappa said. 'But you are still weak and you must-'

'-I will recover,' Silrith said, fighting not to show the pain of it despite her feelings of weakness. 'And when I do, we will raise a new army to add to any who remain loyal to us and we will return to Bennvika. Now, leave me to rest.'

All turned to leave.

'Gasbron,' Silrith said, just as he, almost the last of them bar Shappa, ducked his head to leave the tent.

'Your Grace?' he asked, turning around.

'Stay a while. I would speak with you more about what happened at Rildayorda.'

Shappa gave her a look of surprise, but she just stared back at him until he left, as Gasbron came to stand beside her bed, which she realised now was just a physician's table with a pillow and a few sheets of linen thrown over it. She looked at Gasbron. His face wore a gentle expression, yet it was impossible to read his thoughts on the exchange he had just witnessed between herself and Shappa. He was frustratingly good at hiding them.

'When you were hit by the arrow,' Gasbron said once they were alone. 'We attempted to move you away from the action to increase your chances of survival. Lord Yathrud assumed command of our troops in the heat of battle, rallying them while we tried to get you to safety. Things started to unravel when one of our soldiers saw that you were wounded and cried out, obviously assuming that you were dead. By doing that he caused a load more to turn and look for themselves and all of a sudden one of them says there are flames coming from the city and there were. The whole city was ablaze. Then Jostan starts shouting his mouth off and everyone's looking. Looking at you. Looking at the fire.'

Silrith listened intently as Gasbron continued.

'I've never seen anything like it. In that moment it was like they'd all forgotten about the enemy around them and some of them were punished for it. Just like that, our soldiers broke; all of them, running towards the city. Despite everything, we managed to get you out of there. I found a horse for us both and I tried to regain some sort of order, but it was no good.'

'And controlling a horse despite having me slumped in front of you amid such chaos must have been very difficult and at great risk to yourself, Gasbron. To say that I am grateful that you have once again saved my life doesn't even begin to describe my thankfulness,' said Silrith.

'I thank you for your gratitude, Silrith,' he said. It pleased her to hear him remembering to call her by name in private. 'But it was my duty and any good soldier would have done the same. Anyway, I tried to restore some order, but anything like that had gone out of the window, especially once we got near the city. Most of the soldiers seemed to be fleeing around the sides of it. I guess they didn't want to get penned into Preddaburg and have no way out. I rode down the east side, still trying to get them back, but there was no chance really. It was obvious that somehow the enemy had got inside and were causing havoc. There were civilians everywhere too; hordes of them coming out of the East Gate. Most seemed to be heading deeper into the forest, but a few were heading south, which gave me an idea.'

Silrith could see where he was going with this, but let him continue.

'The only chance we had was to escape by sea. I thought that it was a good bet that our sailors were still on the ships. As we knew, a few of Jostan's troops had simply commandeered them. I thought if we could overwhelm the guards we may be able to get some of the ships out to sea before the enemy could stop us. I remembered talking to one of the prince's knights weeks ago.

He said it doesn't take much to get these Etrovansian vessels moving, something to do with the shallow hull. They can carry a lot of people too. So I managed to rally some of the troops and others followed their lead. It worked. We lost a lot of troops in retaking the ships, including the Hentani princes, and it seems and some vessels were put to the torch. But I guess most of their soldiers were more interested in plundering the city than chasing us, so a few of our ships still got away, even a couple of our big Bennvikan ones. So here we are.'

Silrith thought of the terrible things people are capable of in such circumstances and shuddered as a horrible realisation came to her.

'And what of my cousin, young Yathugarra?' she asked.

'I know that she and her escort left the city safely, but whether or not they are on one of the other ships, I can't be sure. We will only know that when we land in Etrovansia.'

Silrith nodded solemnly, trying to force her worries about Yathugarra to the back of her mind.

'You did well,' she said. 'Your quick thinking during the battle might just have saved the entire campaign. Thanks to you, we live. But of course, that is only so that we can fight again. We will take back Bennvika. For the sake of our people, we must.' She steeled herself as she said this, trying hard not to show the emotions she felt. She had a second chance and she vowed she would see it through. But if she was to regain her throne now, to avenge her father and now to avenge her uncle, she would desperately need people like Gasbron around to advise her.

'Gasbron,' Silrith said.

'Yes, my Queen?'

She hesitated and inwardly cursed herself. On impulse, she had almost said that she loved him. She didn't know why. She hardly knew him really. But she felt secure when he was around. It gave her hope and in any case, having someone save your life, especially more than once, builds a strong connection, binding you to them. Was it debt? Or gratitude? Or even loyalty? Or was it more? She thought the latter, but couldn't form the words.

'Thank you,' she said eventually. 'I thank the gods for your support and loyalty. It will be needed more than ever from now on.'

'You will always have my loyalty, Silrith,' said Gasbron, with a grave expression.

'We will still win this war, Gasbron. I assure you. I can see now that the prophecy on the Amulet of Hazgorata is more than just that. It is an instruction for what we must do now. Mother of many, Mother of none, a Queen will fall and a Warrior will come. I must be a mother to my people, even though I have no child of my own. I fell in battle and I must be reborn from that setback as more than just a queen. I must be a warrior.'

Gasbron's worried expression gave way to a wry smile.

'Well, we can only hope that's true.'

'Yes,' said Silrith with a sigh. 'Once we make landfall and as soon as I have fully recovered, tell the army what I have said, and tell them that my recovery is proof of the gods' blessing.' A flame of excitement flickered inside her, but she refrained from letting it show.

'It would be an honour.'

'Thank you. Now, would you fetch Prince Shappa back for me, please? I have just thought of something else that I would speak to him about.'

'Of course, my Queen,' he said, his formal tone returning and after a slight pause, he bowed and left.

A moment later Shappa lifted the tent flap and re-entered.

'You wanted to see me again?' he said; a look of confusion dominating his features. For the first time, she noticed that there was rather less sparkle in those blue eyes than there had been only days ago. His flowing locks were now ragged and dirty and his bouncing joviality had been replaced by the drooping shoulders of a defeated man. Yet he looked at her expectantly, as if he still took some hope from her, as she took hope from Gasbron.

'I have a proposal for you and your agreement would be of great assistance to me, bringing my eternal gratitude,' she said.

'I'm all ears. What would you have me do?'

Silrith winced again at the pain in her shoulder but proceeded anyway. 'We both know that we are not going to be welcomed with open arms when we arrive in Etrovansia. Not by your family anyway. After all, you have been banished from the kingdom and I think it is likely that as soon as

Jostan finds out where I am, he will put pressure on your father to find me and return me to Bennvika. We must be strong if we are to see off such a threat. More than that, we must demonstrate our intent to our remaining followers by making a solid statement of unity.'

Shappa raised his eyebrows. Silrith smiled appreciatively.

'I think you know what I am about to suggest,' she said. 'We must unite our houses and create a new dynasty. It is that or our destruction.'

'I am flattered by your proposal, my Lady, and of course I accept,' he said.

Silrith's first reaction was internal frustration at Shappa's persisting reluctance to call her by her name even in private. She wasn't bothered if Gasbron forgot occasionally, as she could see where his habit came from, but with Shappa, somehow it didn't fit with the rest of his personality.   Then another thought struck her.

'You have reservations?' she asked.

'No, but if we are to pursue this course of action, our next move must be carefully planned,' he said. 'As you said, once we arrive in Etrovansia, my father and brother will see our arrival as a threat. They could be bought, but we have little to bargain with, so it is vital that we have enough soldiers to defend ourselves if need be. How do you propose we do that?'

Silrith thought for a moment.

'When we were introduced by my uncle, you boasted of your popularity in Nangosa. Surely you can utilise that to recruit soldiers from the local population if we dock there? After we've gained control of Etrovansia and you have the throne, we can return to Bennvika to take back my kingdom as well.'

Again Shappa looked reluctant.

'Shappa, is there something you're not telling me? Something that may make it harder for you to convince people to fight for us? This doesn't fit with the man who got over two hundred knights and their families to move across the sea with him. So why the lack of confidence now? If we are to survive and my family are to be avenged we must have no secrets from each other, only trust.'

She was getting angry now. Shappa sighed.

'My Lady, I assure you there is nothing to cause you concern. Nangosa is my duchy and the troops will be of the finest quality. I am confident they will serve us well.'

Silrith eyed him suspiciously.

'And I'm sure you will lead my army well,' he added.

Silrith resisted the temptation to rise to the curt statement.

'Good,' she said eventually. 'Now leave me. I must rest.'

RILDAYORDA, BASTALF, BENNVIKA

Rildayorda had been reduced to smouldering ruins. The walls still stood of course, as did the remains of most of the city's smoking buildings, but now they had a ghostly feel. Sooner or later, any refugees who had gone into hiding or had escaped would return to take over the place; wretched souls clinging on to life.

They should have allowed themselves to be killed and retain some small amount of honour, thought Vinnitar as he surveyed the walls of the dead city, standing outside his tent. He'd have happily stayed to seek them out and kill them himself, but now he had new orders from Jostan. The bulk of the army may have been preparing to leave, but his mission wasn't over. He ducked back inside his large, personal tent. He sat down at his expensive wooden desk, on which sat a single burning candle, brought in by a servant a moment earlier. He opened the desk drawer and took out a quill, a pot of ink and a roll of parchment and began writing a letter.

To the most Imperial Emperor Graggasteidus, divine son of Estarron, Lord of the Verusantian Empire, first among Senators and all men, King of Kryatovia, Hingaria, Hetchitovinia, Aevania and Veuunessland, Conqueror of the Jotaeans, the Lopari, the Yotivii and the Asdannii, King above all others, I humbly write to you now with the most grievous news and with confirmation of what your Imperial Highness already suspected. It is clear to me now that despite his initial promises that he would rule Bennvika only as your vassal, Lord Jostan Kazabrus has no intention of doing any such thing. On the contrary, he sees no authority above himself here, other than mighty

Estarron. His ambition will only grow now that he has defeated the rebel army that stood against him here at Rildayorda.

I also believe that he may have become suspicious of my presence, as he has ordered me west with just a single cavalry unit to lead his remaining Defroni warriors on one last mission before escorting them back to their hovels. Hentani mercenaries fought at the side of Princess Silrith and I must pursue and catch any who are making for their homes and burn their villages in retribution. He has ordered me not to return until the entire Hentani tribe is back firmly under the rule of the Bennvikan crown. I cannot know whether this is out of trust that I will complete the mission, or out of distrust and an attempt to see me killed.

But all is not lost. From what I have seen I can tell you for certain that Bennvika is ripe for invasion. Jostan has defeated Silrith and for now, still holds power, but he haplessly allowed her to escape on a boat and there will be people here who still support her. The unrest continues and now is the perfect moment for your Imperial Highness to take what is yours for the glory of the Empire and crush Bennvika for all eternity.

Carefully he stamped his secret seal on the letter so that the emperor alone would know who had sent it. Containing his sense of urgency he tucked it inside his tunic and made his way down to the port.

The port may have been recaptured along with a handful of ships, which would allow any remaining trade vessels to leave within days before the area was finally abandoned for good, but frankly, it was an embarrassment for the Bennvikan crown that the enemy had escaped at all. This was good. At the beginning of the siege, Jostan had listened to Vinnitar's assurances that a small unit of professional soldiers would be enough to maintain control of the port and all the vessels in it. Now it was clear to everyone that Jostan's orders had left the area woefully undermanned when the port and its ships were stormed by a desperately retreating opponent. By all accounts, the guards had put up some level of resistance, but as soon as the ships' crews, still loyal to the enemy, had risen against them from behind they stood little chance and there hadn't been much that Jostan's troops could do but watch aghast as their prey sailed out to sea. This would drastically reduce their confidence in Jostan. Any feelings of unrest against the king would be most welcome and would smooth the way for the emperor, should he lose patience with the insolent Jostan and choose to intervene in his rule.

Vinnitar smiled. It would be easy now. All that remained was for him to pay a messenger to board any one of the remaining trade ships that was bound for Verusantium and get his message to his master.

Chapter 27

CELRUN, HERTASALA, BENNVIKA

Some days later, Jostan's army was camped outside Celrun, the provincial capital of Hertasala. He had marched into the city earlier that day, joined at the front of the column by the ageing Lord Lektik Haganwold, as the jubilant crowds flocked to welcome their troops home, apparently unaware of the significance of the white shields the soldiers carried.

Once the celebrations had finished, Jostan had given orders allowing all the soldiers of Hertasala to leave the army and head to their homes, on the condition that they told everyone they saw that it was the divine and mighty Estarron who had come to their aid and delivered them to victory, when Vitrinnolf and Lomatteva had turned their backs on them. The use of the word of the common soldiers to expose Bennvika's weak and fickle gods for what they were and drawing them to the light of the one, true lord of all mortals, would make it easier to convert the whole population when the time came. It would also make it easier to mark any unrepentant heretics as early as possible.

He had written a letter to the Verusantian Emperor, telling him of this and requesting priests of Estarron be sent to Bennvika, as well as extra troops to help force the conversion of the people. This letter was in reply to the more threatening one that had been sent on to him by the Congressate. Jostan had been at pains to make clear his apologetic feelings to the emperor, writing passionately about how all on Estarron's earth were simply mortal people and that Jostan's intentions were only to please their divine lord and in so doing, to honour his god's most illustrious son, the emperor. That sort of sycophancy should be enough to get what he wanted from the old man, Jostan decided.

The only thing that troubled him was that, despite the fact that Bezekarl had said that the Amulet of Hazgorata was hidden in Rildayorda's main temple, it had not been found there. Probably it had been looted by some opportunist. It was a small matter though and he certainly wasn't going to weaken his reputation by telling Bezekarl or anyone else that he had failed to recover it. Image was everything. Anyway, he had only wanted the old relic in order to inspire his soldiers in their first battle in the name of Estarron. Now the divine victory provided for them by the one true god would be their guiding light and if it was ever found, the Amulet was no more than an idol to be smashed and destroyed.

In any case, he was now the undisputed master of Bennvika. He was both a conquering hero fresh from a great victory and a chosen mouthpiece of Estarron, come to bring the lord's holy word to his subjects. Now he sat in his command tent, discussing this with Feddilyn over a chalice of wine.

'It will be an honour when I return to Saviktastad and tell the people of your victory, your Majesty. It shall give me much joy,' gushed Feddilyn.

'We are glad of that,' said Jostan. 'But do not forget who your true lord is now. The lord of us all. Do not forget the divine blessing that has brought us this victory. Just as we have brought you to Estarron, you must help guide others in the same direction. It shall not take long, especially when they hear that poor Accutina, their own queen, was murdered by the enemy while fighting simply to rid this nation of blasphemy. They need not know the real details. We must use her fate to our advantage. They must know that their queen died a martyr for the righteous and is reborn in the heavens, just as Estarron himself dies for our sins every night, but is reborn with the coming of the day to watch over us all and protect us from our enemies. I tell you, Lord Feddilyn, all must hear of the fate of our vanquished enemy. Nobody in Bennvika can deny the power of the one true god. Princess Silrith must be made an example of. We must use her to show the entire kingdom what happens when you stand against us because to stand against us is to stand against Estarron himself.'

'But your Majesty, we don't have Princess Silrith,' said Feddilyn with a confused expression.

'Or do we?' smiled Jostan. 'How many people really know what she looks like?'

Feddilyn's eyebrows rose as he caught on to what Jostan was telling him.

'Your Majesty,' said the divisioman who had been guarding the tent. 'There is a messenger for you.

'Bring him in.'

The messenger entered, bowed, walked over to Jostan, handed him a letter, bowed a second time, then backed away before turning to leave. Jostan looked at the letter.

'Strange,' he said. 'It bears the seal of Congressor Hoban Salanath.'

'There must be urgent news from the Congressate. Though I can't imagine what, considering any member of any importance is here with the army,' Feddilyn said as Jostan broke the seal and began to read. His anger flared as he read the intercepted letter.

'Guards! Bring that messenger back!' he demanded.

A few moments later the confused looking young man in his militiaman's brown tunic was standing before him.

'How did you come by this?' Jostan asked the messenger.

'I was stationed at a messenger post near Kriganheim, Sire,' the man said nervously. 'It seems that Lord Oprion sent the city into lockdown on his arrival. I heard there was rioting, but some girl got out and made it to our messenger post. She looked like she'd run all the way. She told me her master had urgent news to be taken straight to you, Sire.'

But Jostan was barely listening.

'Alright, now get out,' said Jostan. He couldn't take his eyes off the letter and he paced around the tent reading it over and over as the man nervously bowed and left.

'Traitor,' he said.

'Lord Rintta, I think you should hear this. Our friend Lord Oprion begins by saying *To my sweet and goodly friend Silrith*.' He used a mocking tone as he read Oprion's words. '*The summer that you and I spent together was the happiest of all my life and it pained me so deeply to see you leave, especially in such saddening circumstances. Yet my soul will not rest. I love you with every heartbeat. I know my marriage prevents us from being together, but when the time is right I will be free from the marital union that circumstances obligated me to agree to. Without my wife to keep us apart, one day we can be together again; happy again. I desire nothing more than for us to be married. My heart burns for your reply.*'

'Sickening, isn't it?' said Jostan. 'This is the way in which the man we left in charge of the north as our regent addresses a known traitor. It seems

375

that our campaign continues. See that your troops are ready to march by morning.'

'Of course, your Majesty.'

'It appears that all this time Lord Oprion has been acting as Princess Silrith's ally. Send a messenger to Lord Haganwold. Tell him to have his troops on standby if called upon. And send a messenger to Ganust. Lord Tanskeld must be told the same. This further rebellion must be crushed before it does too much damage.'

'Attack Kriganheim?' said Feddilyn, finally catching on to Jostan's meaning. There will be mutiny, your Majesty. As soon as the army crosses the River Lavaklan without disbanding the militia there will be many among them who will know-'

'-Silence,' Jostan raged. Feddilyn bowed his head, almost cowering.

'Do you think we are unaware that it will be seen as an act of war if we lead the army across the Lavaklan and march on Kriganheim? Do you think we haven't thought of that? We know the law. But we also know that we march in the name of the one true god. He will see us to righteousness. When we get to Kriganheim, any one of Estarron's children who wishes to leave the city walls, renounce their faith of falsehoods and join us in our crusade against evil will be allowed to do so. But once the black flag has been raised, there will no quarter given. We will slash as many necks as we need to in the name of Estarron. Now, Lord Rintta, we say again, send your messengers. We march on Kriganheim.'

RILDAYORDA, BASTALF, BENNVIKA

In the days after the fires had disappeared and the besieging horde had left, to walk the streets of Rildayorda had been almost like taking a stroll through the underworld itself. Every day since the Hentani survivors had returned to the ruined city, Ezrina thought back to what she had seen there. Amid the rubble and the acrid smoke was the overpoweringly pungent smell of death. Jostan's soldiers had left a cruel legacy. Surely they weren't mortals at all, but demons of a most bloodthirsty and evil god.

376

Yet Ezrina had felt little sorrow for the dead as she had picked her way through the bodies. Many of them were Bennvikan after all, and this was little different from what they had done to Hentani settlements in the past. Most of the tribesmen had been able to escape due to them having been outside the temple at the time of the attack. Many of the Bennvikan population, on the other hand, had been asleep in their beds, giving them no chance of survival.

Nevertheless, the bloodbath had reminded Ezrina of the ruthlessness of the enemy she had to protect her people from. She prayed that Bertakaevey would give her the strength to achieve such a destiny. People had been slaughtered in the most despicable ways. The burned corpses of men, women and children had been spitted on spikes all about the place. Even the bodies of babies had been found amongst the dead on the outside of the city, presumably having been hurled from the city walls. What could move even the cruellest of people to do such a thing?

Yet out of the pits of despair, hope bloomed.

It's funny how, even when surrounded by death, life clings on, she thought. Every survivor turned to look at Ezrina as she passed, walking through the ruined streets in her priestess' regalia. Some gazed at her as if they were simply waiting for death. But there was a rage in the eyes of many. The fire of hate she felt in her heart was spreading amongst her people. Their whole world had fallen into the abyss of destruction, but the very idea of revenge was a bringer of hope. Revenge on those who had taken everything from them.

In truth, Ezrina's evacuation of the city's tribal population was more of a mad, panicked exodus of those who were lucky enough to escape the enemy's fire and swords, but it had saved many lives. While the Bennvikan population were being slaughtered in their homes, Ezrina's people had burst through the East Gate and made for the forest. In the confusion caused by the chaotic retreat of Silrith's army, some had turned and run for the ships, but the goddess had been with Ezrina that night and many had moved deeper into the eastern forest where they had hoped Jostan's troops either wouldn't dare to follow, or wouldn't bother, hungry for city plunder.

In the hours after the soldiers withdrew, people had slowly begun to filter back into the city, each headed for the rubble that had once been their home. As well as her Hentani followers, there were a handful of Bennvikan survivors, who were tolerated by the tribesmen. Now they all looked to Ezrina for guidance. The tribesmen did so because of Ezrina's revelations to them on the night of the attack, saying that their survival was down to her and the Bennvikans did so because there was no other source of hope left for them now.

Ezrina was keen to ensure that this led to the tribesman having the higher status in this new society, but the Bennvikans would be able to live peacefully as second class citizens so long as they recognised that their country had turned on them. More importantly, they must also renounce their religion and instead convert to the worship of Bertakaevey, or face the consequences.

'You won't be in this position forever, you know,' said Jakiroc, interrupting her thoughts as they walked. 'Look at them. You give them hope enough for them to try to rebuild their lives, but what when King Jostan realises the city is inhabited again and comes back? Right now we wouldn't stand a chance. We need to do something fast if we are to be strong enough to survive should such an attack come.'

'You worry too much, Jakiroc,' Ezrina said. 'I am aware of that issue, but hope is everything. For as long as they are able to hear Bertakaevey speak through me, we have a chance.'

Not only that but also for as long as nobody knows the truth about Jezna and me, she thought.

As they walked, more and more people followed behind them and slowly a large crowd built up. The key to creating order was to establish routine and this was already very much a part of that. Within hours of their resettling of the city, she had decreed that on every third day, every man, woman and child who had resettled in the city should follow her out of the Port Gate and into the fields to the south, where a large mound in the earth created a natural stage and where the mighty sapphire ocean presented an awe-inspiring backdrop. There, she would stand before them in her emerald robes and they would listen to her talk. Sometimes it was about what they would have to do to live, sometimes it was about how one day soon they would have their revenge on Jostan, but always she spoke of how they were Bertakaevey's chosen people.

Standing on her grassy platform, she looked at her audience. Their numbers seemed to be growing every day as more people dared to return home and there looked to be over a thousand of them now.

'Barely a month ago, King Jostan's army was here, camped outside this very city, intent on our destruction and he will continue to attack our kin. But he is making a mistake. He thinks that no souls still reside here and in his arrogance he allows our numbers to swell. The blessed goddess Bertakaevey has guided you to me; guided you to your salvation.'

Ezrina knew that this was all good talk for now, but it took all her faith to trust that Bertakaevey would sustain them when their reserves of food ran out. After the siege, much of the ground was in no state to be farmed, so they would soon exhaust their resources, despite the rationing that was being meticulously monitored by the priests and priestesses.

'We may be hungry and therefore weak in body,' she said. 'But we are strong in will and that is why the goddess favours us. She tests us now and if we endure that test, she will provide the means for us to grow strong in body again, to retake this land from the Bennvikans and to convert the non-believers. Trust in Bertakaevey's divine providence. She will provide for us. Am I not her daughter? Did we not rise from the ashes of her holy fire? Now ash surrounds us all, but you must have faith. We are the goddess' chosen people and our destiny is to rise and rise and rise!'

The crowd cheered, energising Ezrina further.

'In the past, too often the livelihoods of our people have suffered because of the Bennvikans. We have lived under their boot and too many times they have been allowed to attack us and burn our lands. Chief Hojorak and Prince Kivojo clearly thought that making allies of some Bennvikan factions would bring a change in fortunes, even if it meant becoming a Bennvikan lapdog like the Defroni. Yet now they are sent to the afterlife and our lands are burning once again. Let that be a lesson to us. Our people will only prosper if we stand up by ourselves and fight for our own future; the future of all who still worship Bertakaevey, not that of any king, queen, prince, lord or chief.'

'Furthermore, Princess Silrith was a falsehood-worshipping heretic, as were all those who fought for her, in the eyes of the goddess. I know that all of you here who did that have long since repented, but there are many

379

elsewhere who will still fight for her if she yet lives. Let it be known that she is as much an enemy to us as King Jostan. All those who do not believe solely in the divine Bertakaevey are enemies to the goddess; even those who falsely claim that the Bennvikan demon they call Lomatteva is Bertakaevey in another form, or the Defroni, who insult Bertakaevey by accepting other fictitious deities alongside her. They simply want to pull her followers away from the true light. I must warn you all that this will only get worse for us once King Jostan starts to convert his people to the worship of his god, a fiendish monster with serpents for hair, crushing fists and an insatiable hunger for blood.'

A bit of embellishment added to an already threatening truth never hurt in swinging public opinion.

'I have seen with my own eyes that he plans to do this. If we are to survive, then the followers of all gods other than Bertakaevey must be destroyed or converted.'

The crowd cheered wildly.

'High Priestess!' called a voice, cutting through the noise and using Ezrina's newly acquired title, which had been officially and permanently bestowed on her by Jakiroc after Archpriest Askorit had been found slain.

Ezrina turned in surprise at the interruption and saw a young man in tattered clothes running from the direction of the abandoned port. He looked like a fisherman, judging by his image.

'Do not go near her,' Jakiroc commanded, blocking the man's way as he tried to mount the stage from behind.

'It's alright, Jakiroc, I wish to hear what he has to say,' Ezrina intervened in a kindly tone. She reached out to the man and lightly beckoned him forward.

'What is it?' she asked him.

'A great ship, High Priestess. I was out fishing in my boat when I saw it. It was far out to sea, but it's heading this way.'

'And why are you telling me this?'

'Because it's unlike any ship I have ever seen. It's huge, with many sails and it's coming from the south.'

Ezrina was suddenly most interested.

'It's coming from the south?'

'Yes, High Priestess.'

She looked at Jakiroc.

'Well that's no Bennvikan vessel if it's coming from the south, or of any other origin, I am familiar with. We must go to the port. If they dock here we can find out who they are, what they are doing here and if there's anything we can gain from their presence.'

'Yes, High Priestess,' Jakiroc bowed, all formality now, in stark contrast to his earlier manner.

The crowd looked confused by this turn of events, most of them having heard only bits of the exchange if anything at all.

'Tell the other priests and priestesses to ensure that the ship's approach doesn't panic the people,' Ezrina added, still speaking to Jakiroc, though still looking at the crowd.

'We will go to the port,' she declared to her followers. She found herself overcome with anticipation as they walked down towards the port, as were the crowd by the sound of their babbling. Would this development be their saviour or their destruction? There was no way of telling. Yet it was definitely not fear that she felt and she took that as a sign from Bertakaevey that it was not something that would threaten them.

She found herself struggling not to break into a run, such was her impatience to see who or what the goddess had sent them. Finally, she reached the abandoned port and made her way along the length of the main wooden pier. She stopped just before its end and remembered the crowd again as the wooden planks creaked and vibrated with their hurried, heavy steps until they too came to a nervous halt.

Out to sea, she saw a ship. It was like nothing she had ever laid eyes on. It was still far away, but clearly heading towards them, just as the fisherman had said. It was a tall vessel, with a huge, bulky hull and three main masts with enormous sails, as well as many smaller ones that were dotted all over it and reached as far forward as the ship's pointed prow.

She had no doubt in her mind as to the vessel's significance. On that ship would be the warrior from the prophecy. The Hentani's freedom would be won back and most of all, Jezna would be saved from King Jostan's demons. Feeling a level of certainty that she could only describe as the goddess' divine blessing, Ezrina turned to face the crowd.

'You see,' she announced, pointing to the ship. 'The prophecy is true. My mother, the mother of earthly fire, mother of the world, has decreed that I, Daughter of her Ashes, must be a mother to you all. Yet I have no earthy child of my own blood. So I must become a mother of many, while still a mother of none. A queen has fallen and now our warrior has come and though the Bennvikans tried to deny it, the prophecy has proven holy and true in its entirety; for it even predicted the fate of our great city and its rebirth, for now as the divine Bertakaevey said, amid the burning of our homes by the Bennvikan king, our warrior has come in a rain of fire and from the ashes of destruction, a daughter shall rise. I shall rise.'

KRIGANHEIM, BENNVIKA

In the teeming streets of Kriganheim, throngs of people had turned out to see the death of two who had risked all to fight for them. Of course, many had no idea that fighting for the rights of the common people was what they were really going to be put to death for, regardless of any connection with Princess Silrith. Zethun hoped that some, at least, might recognise Hoban's face, or at least his name. But then, during all his secret dealings with his various contacts, Hoban had kept his identity concealed from all but his closest allies. Zethun had thought he was one of those close allies and maybe he was, but he still felt that he had been played for a fool. Yet, he could see now that it had, for certain, been for the greater good.

Seated astride his horse, he looked over the heads of the babbling crowd at the scaffold and the pair of nooses. Next to them stood the executioner, in his black, hooded mask.

A blaring fanfare caught the whole crowd's attention and there was much jeering as Lord Oprion Aethelgard rode into view surrounded by his Verusantian lance guardsmen, some mounted, with others on foot, though he seemed unintimidated by the crowd's aggression.

Zethun's horse spluttered. He had never enjoyed riding, yet now he was astride an enormous grey gelding. He had bought the animal from a livestock trader who had apparently become stranded in the city when Lord

Oprion had sent it into lockdown. Zethun had been forced to pay way over the odds to buy the animal, but at least the muscular beast was in prime condition.

He hoped that by riding such a large steed, yet using only the cheapest and most basic saddle and reins while wearing a brown tunic and breeches meant that he looked imposing without appearing overtly rich. Yes, strong but humble was what he needed.

Keeping to the back of the crowd, he scanned the scaffold for any sign of Hoban and Capaea, but still he could only see guards and the executioner. The general babbling of the crowd turned to jeers from those at the front. Zethun's heart sank at the dishevelled, undignified look of Hoban as he was led on to the scaffold, now wearing only the dirty white robes of one who is about to be put to death. The days spent in the confines of a cell had clearly not been good to him. Capaea looked much the same by now and neither gave any resistance as the guards marched them towards the gallows. Zethun hoped that the fact that they were prepared to die for their cause wasn't lost on the crowd. He noticed that the jeering was largely coming from those at the front. Had Oprion been forced to employ paid jeerers in an attempt to further sully the name of his opponents? Zethun wouldn't have put it past him. The executioner walked to the front of the scaffold to address the onlookers.

'Behold the faces of traitors,' he declared; his traditional black mask giving him the look of a demon from the underworld. He strode over to where a pair of nooses dangled in front of Hoban and Capaea. Even from the other side of the crowd, Zethun could see the glee on Oprion's face as he watched.

'Stop,' Zethun commanded, causing the executioner to hesitate and look over his shoulder at the crowd. Many other heads turned to lay eyes on Zethun.

'What is this?' Oprion shouted in palpable consternation.

'Good people of Kriganheim,' Zethun said, ignoring the question. 'Do you not see what is happening here? These two people have risked all to fight for your rights and yet you believe the words of those who think themselves your betters and simply look on as these two heroes are put to death?'

There was murmur amongst the crowd, though whether it was through fear or anger Zethun couldn't be certain.

'Traitor,' Oprion bellowed.

'On the contrary, my Lord Aethelgard. I do believe that a traitor is a person who betrays their own people, whereas I am actively fighting to protect the welfare of mine. Good citizens, I implore you, you must understand that once in a lifetime a person realises the sheer unacceptability of their position and that of their comrades. Even rarer though is the chance for them to stand up and fight and to tell their suppressors that they will live at their whims no more. But I tell you, that time has come.'

'This is treachery of the highest order,' Oprion jeered, though his voice faltered and Zethun sensed fear in him.

'I know that I am not from an un-moneyed background, as you are,' Zethun said to the crowd, ignoring Oprion. 'But I do ask the most important questions of all. Why is it that the working people of this nation are not given the full ownership of what they produce? Why instead, is so large a sum of it claimed by people who have done nothing to deserve such a right, save claiming to be the lords of the people who produced it? In the recent past, these people have taken more of your crops from you than ever before. They are happy for you to watch your families starve. They have forced many of you from your homes. Yet you are still expected to fight and die for these nobles and this king in times of war. Right now, the soldiers of this kingdom that marched away to fight for the king are in the south, not fighting the Hentani as the king told them they would be, but suppressing a rebellion led by Princess Silrith.'

There was an audible intake of breath at the mention of that name. Clearly these people were all aware of the speculation surrounding the events in Bastalf.

'Yes, I tell you that it would appear that the rumours are true and Princess Silrith is very much alive. There is a letter to prove it and the reason that his lordship here wishes to see these two good people dead is that they discovered another letter that proves that Lord Oprion Aethelgard was in love with her. How can the people trust a man who pledges his loyalty to one candidate for the throne, while being known to be in love with the other? How can we know what he will do when the king returns with the army? Will

384

he order you to open the gates, or to stand and fight? The people cannot be used as pawns in this way. The people have a right to know what is going on and have their say and they must fight for this right. Right now, Bennvikans slaughter other Bennvikans to decide who rules us, while King Jostan and Princess Silrith each convince their own soldiers that it is the other and not they who killed King Lissoll. Either way, we risk spending further years under the boot of a tyrant.'

There were cries of indignation from the crowd.

'Tyranny in Bennvika has gone on for generations and must stop now. I propose that instead of welcoming back the victor of this war, we stand up for ourselves. If we are strong, then the troops in any opposing army will see their folly in fighting for a leader who believes themselves their lord by right and will join us in our revolution.'

Another cheer.

'There is only one way forward for the people of this nation and that is for it to become a republic, starting with this very city,' Zethun declared, punching his fist in the air. The crowd cheered again as an army of fists were violently raised in unison.

'That's enough!' bellowed Oprion. 'Arrest that man!'

Two of Oprion's bodyguards kicked their mounts forward into a trot towards Zethun, but their way was blocked by the angry crowd, who held firm despite the soldiers ordering them out of their way. As the crowd continued to block their path, Zethun spotted one of the soldiers look over his shoulder towards Oprion; his face unreadable under his Verusantian helmet but his body language distinctly uncertain.

'Let them through,' Oprion commanded. 'This man will be arrested! Any who defend him will be branded traitors. Listen to me! I am giving you a chance to save yourselves!'

'See how our noble lord and his soldiers fear our unity,' Zethun said amid the chaos of the fight. 'They try to intimidate us and suppress us, but when we stand together against them it strikes fear deep into their hearts. Our oppressors would tell us that would be impossible. They would tell us that we need them in order for there to be any law or organisation in our society. But if we pull together and if every man and woman works for what they get, we can prove them all wrong. Now, behold. Here is the stooge of the man who would take from you all your liberty. I beseech you, seize the day, starting with him.'

He pointed at Oprion and his entourage and the crowd erupted with an angry roar, hurling themselves at the guards.

'Execute them! Execute them! Arrest the traitors!' Oprion commanded. Zethun saw the executioner hurriedly forcing the nooses around Hoban and Capaea's necks, clearly desperate to dash any attempt to save them. With every fibre of his being Zethun willed his newfound followers onward. The guards had drawn their swords and members of the crowd were cut down as they fought their way forward, but the flood of desperate people would surely soon burst its banks.

'The city is its people and the people will rule. Here and now, I declare the independence of the Republic of Kriganheim,' Zethun proclaimed amid the clamouring rabble, which erupted into a new roar. Zethun saw a guard slip and fall at the front of the line. The inspired crowd forced their way into the gap, crushing him, heedless of the swords of the other guards. The enemy line buckled but somehow still held against the disorganised mob, with some of the peasants pushing forward, trying to reach Hoban and Capaea, while others seemed hell-bent on reaching Oprion.

Oprion looked on aghast. This couldn't be happening. All control had been lost. Finally, the line of guards on foot protecting him collapsed and the wretched peasants burst through. Oprion watched in horror as his soldiers were overrun. Now there was nothing between the crowd and him, save for his mounted bodyguard.

'Retreat! Retreat!' he commanded. He turned and kicked his horse into a gallop, with the Verusantians following suit. He looked over his shoulder and saw that the crowd had given chase, picking up stones and hurling them. His horse reared in panic, throwing him from its back as a projectile struck its skull and he felt his arm crack as he hit the ground.

Dazed, he attempted to lift himself up, but a large peasant threw himself at him and the last thing Oprion knew was a hail of blows amidst the clamour of a jeering crowd, before his soul left his battered and broken body for the afterlife.

Seeing their master fall, those few soldiers protecting the scaffold turned and ran, as did the executioner himself. Some of the common people chased after their retreating prey, but most poured toward the scaffold as the first men and women reached it, taking the weight of Hoban and Capaea's bodies while others untied the nooses. Even from the back of the crowd, Zethun could see Hoban and Capaea gasping for breath as their lives were restored to them. He kicked his horse into a trot. The crowd, now beginning to calm into a stunned silence, opened up before him.

He dismounted and walked on to the stage, very aware of dozens of expectant eyes watching him. By now Hoban and Capaea seemed able to stand, albeit uneasily. He approached them and ushered them to the back of the scaffold, away from where the majority of the crowd could hear.

'All is forgiven and what is done is done,' he said to them quietly. 'Now I must tell them what we need them to hear.'

Both looked confused.

'Come, we must address our people,' said Zethun, turning to lead them back to the front of the scaffold.

'We have thrown off the shackles of tyranny,' Zethun bellowed, punching his fist in the air. The crowd roared.

'We have ushered in a new era for our city, for today, our city becomes a nation and that nation is a nation of freedom.' The crowd exulted into a chant, as they too punched their fists into the air.

'Kri-gan-heim, Kri-gan-heim, Kri-gan-heim.'

'We shall pull down all memory of all kings and queens. We will have an elected Congressate and we shall fly our flags and banners of freedom from every turret, every gate and every rooftop, so that all will know that here is the capital of the free world. Our gods were never mortal kings and queens as our more recent rulers would have us believe to their own benefit. They were always gods, who chose to come down to earth in human form and create Bennvika all those centuries ago. It was then that this event was prophesied, for almighty Lomatteva, whose blessing we all have, is a mother to all Bennvikans and therefore the mother of many. Capaea, here, the common girl who infiltrated the nobility to make this illustrious event

387

happen, is yet to assume motherhood and is therefore perhaps the foremost mother of none in the land. You all know the rest of the prophecy and yes, a queen has fallen, as will our king. All that is left is the warrior. I shall be that warrior. We must all be warriors. Warriors of liberty. And so I say to you now, Mother of many, Mother of none, a Queen will fall and a Warrior will come.'

THE END

Also by P.J. Berman

Silrith Series

King of the Republic – Due 2019

War of Mercy – Due 2021

Printed in Poland
by Amazon Fulfillment
Poland Sp. z o.o., Wrocław

54105797R00230